INNOCENT DESIRE

Wordlessly, he reached out and pulled her toward him, and she looked up and smiled. His face seemed as if it were carved of stone, but his eyes were bright and alive. His hands ran through her flowing blonde hair as his lips feverishly sought hers. For one instant, Althea thought to resist, but the urgency of his lips, and the sweetness of his tongue teasing hers drove everything but desire from her mind. She could sense the passion he held in check, and this knowledge made her dizzy with a feeling she could not understand or control.

Then, as suddenly as he had taken her into his arms, he stopped. Gently, he pushed her away so that he could look into her eyes. For an instant which seemed like an eternity, he studied her. Althea saw different emotions war in his face, and she knew that he was trying to decide on something. She no longer feared him, and a slight smile came to her lips.

And as if that smile were the answer that he was seeking, he again drew her into his arms and his kiss was so intense that it left her almost faint . . .

A PASSIONATE FLOWER

BETSY McCARTY

AVON
PUBLISHERS OF BARD, CAMELOT, DISCUS AND FLARE BOOKS

A PASSIONATE FLOWER is an original publication of Avon
Books. This work has never before appeared in book form.

AVON BOOKS
A division of
The Hearst Corporation
1790 Broadway
New York, New York 10019

First Avon Printing, November, 1983

AVON TRADEMARK REG. U. S. PAT. OFF. AND IN
OTHER COUNTRIES, MARCA REGISTRADA, HECHO EN
U.S.A.

Printed in the U. S. A.

WFH 10 9 8 7 6 5 4 3 2 1

A PASSIONATE FLOWER

PROLOGUE

GRYDWYN CASTLE, WALES, 1333

The cell was cold and damp beyond reason for such a warm
May evening, and the smell reminded the young priest of
death and decay. No taper lit the tiny space, and the priest
was grateful, for he could hear the scurrying of rats and
was glad he did not have to look upon them. Only a faint
light from the setting sun came through the tiny window,
revealing the trickle of sewage that overflowed from the
courtyard into the tiny opening. His sandals and the hem
of his cassock were soaked in filth. Inwardly, he shuddered, wishing that he were back in his tiny cottage next
to the manor church. But before he could sink into self-
pity, he railed at himself. He was here to perform God's
work, and earthly comforts could wait.

He peered into the shadows and made out the figure of
the woman who sat at the other end of the moldy cot. She
sat with her head bent, fingering her rosary, and sobbing
so quietly that it sounded like the sighing of the wind. Her
long gray tunic was hooded, and she blended into the shadows so well that the priest was reminded of an apparition,
rather than a woman. Earlier, when there had been more
light, the priest had noticed the luxuriant blonde hair
escaping from under the hood, and he thought about it
now. She was truly beautiful, he thought sadly, already
using the past tense. What a tragedy. Sometimes he could
not fathom the plan of God or the cruelty of his fellow man.

Then, with the discipline of his training, he turned back

to his rosary. She had confessed. Soon she would die. Then she would be in God's hands, and God was merciful. Perhaps He would forgive her for her terrible crime.

His prayers were interrupted by the sound of footsteps outside the cell. He felt, rather than saw, the woman stiffen as she, too, heard the sound. A bolt was lifted and slowly the door creaked open. A serving woman entered, carrying a taper in one hand and leading a girl of about three years. The child's blonde hair and blue eyes made her exceptionally pretty, but now her face was red with crying and confusion. The woman on the cot jumped up, throwing back her hood, revealing a once beautiful face now ravaged with grief and fear. She grabbed the child from her nurse, who was also silently weeping.

Clutching the little girl to her breast, she paced across the cell, her tears mingling with those of the child. The priest cleared his throat, his eyes misting over. He tried to concentrate on his prayers, but he could not hide from the agony he was witnessing. His hands shook and he looked at the open door, longing to flee the tragedy in this room. It was not only his duty, but the grim-faced guard who carried a sword, that prevented him from fleeing.

His eyes reluctantly turned back to the woman and child. The woman was now kneeling on the floor, oblivious to the filth. Clasping the child tightly, she babbled words of love and terror that only served to increase the heart-rending wailing of the little girl. How pitiful, thought the priest, shifting in his seat. He was young and had never administered last rites to a condemned person before. Why hadn't he become a monk instead? he thought bitterly. To be cut off from the terrible realities of life would have suited him better.

Suddenly the woman stopped her crying and threw back her head, gasping for air. The priest was reminded of a deer in its last death throes. After a moment she turned, looking for the serving woman, who stood in the corner, tears rolling down her cheeks.

"Edwina," she said in a hoarse voice. "Take care of her."

The serving woman nodded, too moved to speak.

The cell door opened again. The guard who entered looked ill. "It's time," he said, his harsh voice breaking.

The woman in gray stared at him. Looking at her wide green eyes, the priest could see that fear had started to drive sanity from her mind. The serving woman reached out and grabbed the child by the hand, but the girl clung to the now silent, shrouded woman. Finally the child had to be dragged away, kicking and shrieking, and the priest heard her cries fade away in the distance. He turned to look at the woman, expecting to see great grief, but her eyes were blank and unseeing.

The guard began to move impatiently, and finally jerked his thumb at the priest. "You better get her up, father. She won't be leaving by herself." The priest felt his heart quiver. This was the part he dreaded most. He, who could not bear to see a lamb slaughtered, would have to watch her die. Slowly he rose, and gingerly touched her shoulder. She remained still. Then he took her hand and pulled, expecting resistance. Surprisingly, there was none. She rose quietly and looked at him with those large green eyes. She was somewhere else.

They led her out of the cell and down the long dark passageway that ran through the bowels of the castle. The priest gave his most fervent prayer of the day. "Please God," he whispered out loud, "may her mind be mercifully gone when she is taken to her death."

The guard murmured, "Amen." He had no taste for this job. He was a warrior of men, not an executioner of women.

As they rounded the corner of the passageway, they could see the entrance to the courtyard ahead. The priest's steps faltered, but the woman walked ahead calmly, never hesitating, her long gray tunic, which so resembled a shroud, rippling around her slight body. She seemed unaware that ahead lay the stake, awaiting her burning.

CHAPTER ONE

THE FOREST OF MYWELYN, WALES, 1347

The old woman stirred the fire in the hearth with her long, crooked stick, peering into the flames as if searching for an answer. Although the fire was feeble, it filled the small hut with a pall of smoke. Laying down the stick, she reached into a small bag tied with a string around her waist and withdrew a brown herbal substance. Rubbing the concoction between her hands, she finally tossed it into the fire. Immediately, the flames whipped up in colors of green and orange.

The woman stared into the fire. The dancing light gave her face a sinister cast, and her eyes became glazed. Waving her hands slowly in front of her face, she began to chant in a low and surprisingly melodious voice. The chant was made up of seemingly meaningless sounds, but the woman uttered each carefully. As the flames rose and fell, she kneeled in front of the fire swaying from side to side, her black hair, streaked with white, cascading down her shoulders to her waist. Her face was thin and pale. Even her lips, moving in the chant, were almost white. Only beautiful high cheekbones and lustrous black eyes remained of the beauty she had once possessed.

Abruptly, she stopped her chant, dropping her hands to her sides, her head hanging down. "It's no use. I see nothing," she muttered.

"Magara, no." The voice came from a dark corner of the

4

hut. The light, feminine voice was filled with anxiety.

Magara rose slowly from the hearth. The eerie priestess of a few moments ago was gone. The tall, thin woman dressed in a black shift now seemed a commanding but human figure. Although her clothes were those of a peasant, she carried herself with a regal quality. "Enough, Althea, I am weary."

"Magara, how will I know what to do? How will I protect myself if I do not know what danger lies unexpectedly ahead?"

Magara looked intently at the girl in the corner. As always, her heart constricted with a strange combination of joy and sorrow whenever she looked closely at Althea. My God, how she resembles Rosemund. Her young body, just starting to flower into soft curves, gave promise of a sensuality still only latent in the seventeen-year-old girl. She would not be tall, but in another year her body would be a woman's, and a very desirable one. Her face, already beautiful, was not made less captivating by the dust on her cheeks. Her high cheekbones were like Magara's, but her mouth, unlike the pale lips of the older woman, was full and red. Long, golden hair fell to her waist in waves. Only her dark blue eyes were different. Rosemund had had green eyes. She could have been the reincarnation of Rosemund, Magara thought, except that Althea had already been three years old when her mother had died.

Magara brushed her hand across her eyes as if to wipe away the memory. Whenever Magara thought of her sister, she felt cold with fear and sorrow. Rosemund had died fourteen years ago, but it could have been last night to Magara. She forced herself to return to the present.

"Althea, perhaps you are distressing yourself unduly." Magara's voice and words belied her simple garb. This was no peasant hag brewing the spells of the common fortune-teller. Magara had been nobly born, and although her fortune was now that of the common serf, her words and tone would have made her an equal at Caernarfon, the greatest castle in Wales. She seated herself at the plain wooden table and regarded Althea quietly.

"I am not upset without cause, Magara," Althea replied. Sensing her aunt's concentration, the girl sat back quietly, trying to keep still. Since the day when she was nine and Magara had found her in the orchard of the castle crying her heart out, this hut, hidden in the forest of Mywelyn, had been her refuge. Magara had always helped her, had been her friend and her confidante.

Althea looked at her aunt, affection erasing some of the worry in her blue eyes. To others, Magara was a sinister figure, mentioned only in whispers. If her father, Sir Richard of Grydwyn, knew that she was here, he would have her whipped. And if her stepmother, the Lady Maura, knew, it would be worse. A beating and no food for two days. Althea shuddered, then tossed her head defiantly. The risk was worth it. Magara may have raised fears in the hearts of others, but to Althea she was a source of love and comfort. Only she and Althea's nurse had shown her kindness in her young lifetime.

Magara looked from the dying fire to her niece. "Althea, when I discovered you in the orchard many years ago, I felt the greatest happiness that I would be able to keep watch over you, my sister's child. Since her death . . ." Magara stopped.

Althea looked down at her hands. She knew why her aunt had stopped. Both always felt horror overcome them whenever they had to remember Rosemund's fate. For Magara it was a vivid memory. For Althea it was an awful tale to be told by the cruel and thoughtless people who inhabited her father's castle. ". . . Since her death," Magara went on, "I know you have been at the mercy of your father. And when he married Lady Maura, things became much worse. You look too much like your mother to let Lady Maura sleep in peace."

"I hate them both, Magara. They both dislike me so." Althea unconsciously clenched her hands into fists. Despite her pale complexion and delicate build, she had fire inside her. Magara, watching Althea's response, nodded to herself. The girl would need all the courage she could muster. Life for all women was hard, but for the weak it could be a nightmare. How could she begin to explain to this innocent, unworldly child that her face was a constant reminder to her father of the woman he had loved to distraction and whose love had turned him into the ogre he now was. Love and hate were so very close, but to a child not yet exposed to the complications of sexual love, this was too difficult a concept to explain.

With the impatience of youth, Althea interrupted her aunt's train of thought. "They are intent on marrying me off to the Count du Vendome. They have moved me from the common room and I now sleep in a chamber of my own. They are making clothes for me to wear like I have never known. Silk and velvet." For an instant, her pleasure in the clothes broke through in a smile, but it quickly disappeared when the reason for their existence returned to her mind. "Magara, Lady Maura told me that if I raise a fuss, she will sell me to the Jews."

Magara frowned. It was an idle threat, for there were no Jews near this castle in northern Wales. But Maura was a hard, shrewd woman. She knew that as long as Althea lived close to Sir Richard, Rosemund would remain alive in his mind. A marriage would be perfect. All would laud their compassionate concern for the disgraced Althea, since many had felt that Althea should have died when Rosemund had. But Althea's dark blue eyes, so much like Sir Richard's, had saved her life. Now he and Lady Maura would be praised for their kindness in seeing Althea married.

Ha, kindness! Magara thought bitterly. Raising the girl with the servants, dressing her in rags, teaching her little except proper speech, and beating her at every provocation!

"The count may not be a bad husband," Magara now said soothingly. "It is not a bad fate, Althea." She quelled the doubts she felt. Marriage could be a disaster for a woman. A hell on earth. A wife had no rights to protect her from her husband. He could beat her at his whim, or even kill her. If things got too bad, and the wife came from a powerful clan, then perhaps her kin would back her up. But Althea would have no kinsmen to help her against a cruel husband. She, Magara, could never cross the Channel to France. She could never leave the protection of this forest, this hut. When Rosemund died, Magara, who was a widow and had lived with her sister, was forced to flee to the woods. She had been taken in by an old man, so ancient that she never guessed his age. He had been a priest of the Druids, the Old Ones, and he had taught her his skills before he died.

The villagers, overcoming their fear when life became too hard for them, visited her at night for potions to ward off the evil eye, arouse love in a disinterested partner, cure boils. The list was long, for Magara was known for her success in the old ways. She was allowed to live, tolerated if not accepted. But only here. She could never leave.

"You must go, Althea. The sun will set soon and you will be missed."

"No, Magara, no!" Althea lost her self-control and threw herself sobbing at her aunt's feet. "Please. They say he is cruel! They say he is marrying me only because he owes my father a debt that cannot be repaid."

With surprising strength for one so thin, Magara reached down and dragged her up. Harshly, she shook her. "Listen! Listen, Althea! It is your fate. You cannot change it. Accept him and make the best of your life. You will soon be a beautiful woman. That will be your weapon." Or your downfall, she thought, looking sadly at the girl.

Althea stared woodenly at the floor. Magara had always helped her, but now she had failed. The magic fire, always giving some hint to the future, had told nothing. Ahead was a fat, slothful husband with a reputation for cruelty.

"Althea, listen to me." Magara lifted the girl's chin so

she had to look at her. "My powers are small. I can cure an ailment of the skin, or give a girl a potion that will make her beloved stare at her with longing. But I cannot save you from this marriage that your father has planned. It has turned out better than I had hoped. Your mother's disgrace ended in her death. My refusal to testify against her led to my banishment in these woods. Her shame has tainted your reputation although you are totally innocent. Few men would marry you. Unless you marry the count, you will spend your days as a servant in the castle. Or worse, if the Lady Maura makes good her threat. This marriage is better for you."

Althea looked at her aunt, then slowly put her arms around her. "I love you, Magara. I will do as you ask."

Her voice was so young and sad. Magara wiped back the hair that had fallen across her pretty face. "Go now, child, or the night will catch you in the woods."

Althea nodded, and opened the flap at the door. "Goodbye. I will see you again soon."

Magara watched her as she walked across the clearing toward the woods. "God help her," prayed Magara. "God help her and save her from her mother's fate."

Althea had much to overcome. Rosemund's crime had been picked up by the troubadours and had gone into legend. During the last fourteen years, many a lord and lady had sat by the fire and heard sung the tale of Rosemund the Fair, who had blinded her husband's mind with witchcraft so she could lay with another man.

Magara's hut was in a tiny clearing created years ago when lightning felled several great oaks that had stood there. Since the night of the storm, the villagers regarded the place with a superstitious awe and avoided it whenever possible. So it was a perfect spot for Magara, for she could look out and see anyone who approached from the deep woods surrounding the clearing. She used the land to grow herbs and weeds for her magic, and Althea loved to linger with her aunt and examine the different plants. But today she hurried across the clearing. She had been so intent on her problems, she had not noticed that twilight was only a half hour away, and she was a good two miles from the castle. The woods would darken quickly, and it was not safe to travel at night through the forest, for it was easy to lose one's way. Much worse, if she came late to the castle and it was noticed, she would receive a beating for having dared to visit Magara.

She strode along rapidly, trying to avoid the branches and plants half-blocking the little-used path. A larger person would have had to move more slowly or risk being entangled in the growth, but Althea was small. Her height was that of a twelve-year-old page and she was thin from lack of proper food. A quick appraisal would label her scrawny, but a closer look would indicate fine bones and a thinness that would slowly grow curved and soft if properly fed. Even now she possessed a beauty that made more than one knight and squire who visited Grydwyn Castle stop and stare at her with speculation.

Althea strode along the familiar path, picking branches out of her way without thinking. Enough light still filtered down through the trees to the forest floor so that it was easy to see, and she drank in the wonderful scent of the forest in the spring. She stopped for one moment and picked some bluebells that were growing in a cluster and tucked them into the top of her bodice. They were the exact color of her tunic. She loved the forest, especially in the spring. She knew that dangerous animals and runaway serfs lurked in the shadows, but she still felt no fear. On days when she had more time, she would bring nuts and feed the squirrels, or she would find a quiet spot and look at all the wonderful things the forest sheltered. Magara had taught her to love the woods, and Althea often thought it was the best gift she had ever received.

She reached the huge double oak that was her midway point through the woods, and looked at the sky. In ten minutes she would be out of the forest and then it was another ten across the fields. She would be at the castle just as twilight began. Now, with her fear of being late lessened, Althea let her thoughts return to her other problem. Perhaps Magara was right and she should make the best of her marriage to Claude, Count du Vendome. Perhaps he was not the ogre she feared. She glanced around the woods and was filled with sadness. She loved the woods, and marrying Claude meant moving to France. She would never return to the forest of Mywelyn, or to Wales, for France was a lifetime away. She knew, for she had looked on the map her father owned. It was hung in the great hall in the castle and was very old. She had loved looking at it as a child, for it was decorated with fantastic things, such as dragons and serpents. A kindly knight had explained to her once that these were the inhabitants of the uncharted waters off Ireland and Wales. They devoured the reckless who ventured far from land.

Althea smiled to herself as she walked, for she had a secret. Several years ago, Magara had started to teach her to read and write. It was almost unheard of for a woman in Wales to read and write. In truth, her father could barely scrawl out his own name, and he sent for a priest whenever a written message arrived or needed to be sent. Althea had a good mind and was an excellent pupil. Magara had been a noted scholar before her sister's fall from grace, and she taught Althea to read and write in English, Welsh, and French besides tutoring her in the science of herbs and medicine. It amazed even Magara how fast the child had learned, for she could only practice her lessons at the cottage. A request for a quill, ink, and parchment would have aroused great suspicion at Grydwyn and would have brought about a beating.

Althea's pleasure at her secret disappeared as she once again thought of her aunt's advice. Although she rebelled against Magara's words, she knew that her aunt's counsel was sound. Her life was hard and full of misery now. Her position in the castle was like that of a serf, and she scrubbed and cleaned like the lowliest servant. Until the news of a marriage had been discussed, she had slept in the servants' room with five others, sharing her straw pallet and tattered blanket with her old nurse, Edwina. Her father hated the sight of her; her stepmother despised her. And all but Edwina reminded her that she was a lucky girl for not being totally abandoned by Sir Richard.

Althea's eyes filled with tears as she walked. Oh, she was lucky, all right, she thought bitterly. An outcast, the daughter of a condemned witch and adulteress. Often, her sleep was disturbed by nightmares in which she would be hiding under her bed, screaming, trying to blot out the light of the leaping flames. Edwina would awaken her and comfort her until the terror had passed, but the four other women in the room would look at her with fear and dislike.

"It's the witch coming to claim her own," she once heard one of them say. "The dead one wants her child, and will take her in her sleep." Edwina had heard the woman, too, a scrawny girl in her early twenties who had no teeth left and was usually scratching at the lice in her hair. The next day the girl had bruises on her face, and there was no more talk in the sleeping room, but Althea knew they still discussed her among themselves.

Perhaps she should marry Claude. Already life was getting better. They were trying to make the duckling into a swan so he would not reject her when he arrived. There were new clothes in a chest, and she now slept in her own chamber. Her stepmother, Lady Maura, kept ordering her to bow, so that she would do it gracefully when Claude arrived; and her tasks at the castle were eliminated so the calluses on her knees and the redness of her hands would disappear. But it had been made plain to her that this was in preparation for her wedding. If it did not go off as planned, she would once again go back to the life of a serf, or worse.

At least I will be rid of my father and stepmother and the beatings and hunger, she thought. I will be the wife of a nobleman. And he could not be worse than my father.

Althea was so caught up in her dismal thoughts that she did not see the bramble bush to her right. She was moving quickly, and when her shift caught in the thorns, it ripped the material from her ankle to her knee. Stopping in her tracks, Althea looked down at her dress in horror. Lady Maura would beat her for this. The shift was new, a simple, pale blue linen. She examined the rip. It could be mended. Perhaps, with luck, it would not show too badly.

Desperate to return to the castle in order to mend the rip, Althea raced down the path, her slim white legs now revealed as she ran. In a few moments she came out of the woods at the top of the hill and stopped to catch her breath. She gazed at the view, which encompassed what had been her whole world for as long as she had lived. The hill was covered with spring green grass and wild flowers, and sheep with their lambs grazed with contentment. The hill sloped down to a small clear stream that ran parallel with a dirt road. Both traveled together through the valley to the castle a quarter of a mile away. The road ended at the drawbridge, but the stream fed into the moat, which encircled the castle on three sides. The rear of the castle was on the edge of a cliff that jutted into the Irish Sea. Waves crashed on the rocks far below and capture from the sea was impossible. Strategically, Grydwyn Castle was in an excellent position, and the castle had never been taken in war. Built before the Norman Conquest of 1066, it had remained in the hands of the Welsh Grydwyn family until Althea's grandfather, Lord Llewelyn of Grydwyn, produced only two daughters, Rosemund and Magara. Sir Richard, a Norman, had married Rosemund and inherited the castle on her death. It was a small but strong fortress, with stone walls six feet thick and two lookout towers. The third tower housed the twenty men-at-arms Sir Richard retained; the fourth tower contained the living quarters of the family. At times Grydwyn Castle appeared grim and forbidding, especially in winter when the gales from the sea howled through the turrets and the waves crashed against the rocks at the foot of the cliff.

But today the view was breathtaking, and Althea, feeling a premonition that she would never see this again, paused. The sky was starting to turn gold and pink as the sun began to set, and the light painted the stone walls of the castle a soft hue. From the height of the hill she could see the sea, now the color of turquoise flecked with gold. The whole land had taken on a magical quality, as if it were one of the enchanted places that the bards told of in their songs, a place for love and romance.

Althea smiled at herself. She knew that her thoughts were romantic nonsense culled from the tales of the minstrels, but her little dream made her feel better. Home covered with a veil of fantasy was more acceptable than the fearful scolding she would receive if she were caught returning from Magara's with her dress torn.

Shaking her head at her own foolishness, for she knew there were no handsome knights in store for her, she began to descend the hill, then stopped abruptly. As she gazed at the road, she saw a low cloud rolling slowly toward the castle. She watched carefully, and soon realized it was not a cloud, but dust kicked up by horses. She strained to see. It must be quite a retinue. She calculated quickly. The cloud, growing larger every second, was about a quarter of a mile from the spot where she would descend. If she ran, she could cross the road and head for the castle before the horsemen could see her. Then she could cut through the meadow. The grass would slow her down, but if the horsemen looked ominous, she could hide in the high grass. Making up her mind, she dashed down the hill, keeping her eyes on the growing cloud. Her ripped gown gave her greater freedom of movement, and she moved rapidly, oblivious to the startled sheep that scampered out of her way. Only when she reached the bottom of the hill did she realize she had miscalculated. As she scampered across the dirt road, she heard the shouts of the men, and with a sinking feeling, knew that she had been seen. Plunging quickly into the high meadow grass, she ran for her life.

CHAPTER TWO

The high grass ripped at her dress and scratched her legs, but Althea felt nothing as she ran for the safety of the castle. The past few years had been relatively tranquil, but one never knew when a seemingly peaceful friend would turn foe, and attack. A knight's reason for existence was to fight. He trained for it throughout his youth and relished it as a man. The novelty of peace quickly wore thin, and soon became an irritation. If no great conflict loomed on the horizon, the urge to fight had to be assuaged by a skirmish of some sort. And it was spring, the time of year when the nobles, frustrated from the confinement of winter, would search for any pretext to leave their lairs and ride out. Since childhood, Althea had been warned that the approach of unidentified horsemen could mean danger, and the protection of the castle walls should be sought.

Her fear increased as she heard shouts behind her and realized she was being pursued. Glancing back, she saw that two horsemen had followed her into the high grass and were loping along toward her. She could hear them cheerfully calling to each other, as if they knew that she could not escape and were amusing themselves in their chase.

The castle loomed ahead of her, but she still had to cross the last part of the meadow. The ground now sloped slightly upward and it was slowing her down. She had determined that this could be no war party, for soldiers would never risk chasing a girl so close to their point of attack. But another fear now spurred her onward. Peasant girls were fair game for an amorous knight, and in her ripped blue shift, she looked of no higher stature than a sewing wench. A castle was not a place of privacy, and Althea knew that any peasant girl who had reached her flux was usually introduced to lovemaking by one of her father's retinue, or by her father himself. In fact, Sir Richard thought it was his right to take the pick of the maidens. The girl was rarely considered, and if she protested too strongly, the men would include a good beating along with the lovemaking.

These thoughts gave her new impetus, and she forged ahead, the rip in her shift increasing, her long blonde hair tangling. In the high grass, even as the castle grew closer, she knew she was lost. The two horsemen were gaining, and with a wave of horror she saw one pass her on the right, the other on the left. When in front of her, they reined in their horses and sat laughing.

Stopping dead in her tracks, Althea stared at them, gasping for breath. She knew she was caught. They would catch her no matter where she fled. They had enjoyed their sport, for one of them chuckled loudly. She could not see their faces, for their visors were down. For several seconds they regarded each other. Then one of the knights lifted his visor and laughed.

"By the Rood, Guerre, she's an uncommon pretty wench. She looks clean, too, although covered with sweat."

Althea bridled at his words. Years of abuse had made her appear passive, but her true nature contained a streak of temper, an inheritance from her father. Looking up at the knight's red, beefy face, she felt a surge of distaste. Of course, he didn't realize that she understood him, for he spoke in French, the language of the Norman nobility; a peasant would speak only Welsh.

"A beauty, I agree, Armand," the other knight said in a deep husky voice, "but still a child. Let her go back to her mother."

"Are you daft, Guerre?" laughed the knight called Armand as he lumbered out of the saddle. "She is at her peak.

Why, I would tumble her right here if his grace had not commanded that we bring her to him.''

Althea shrank back as Armand approached her.

"Come here, little one," he said, laughing at her. "What's your name?"

Althea, wild with fear and still breathless, did not reply. He grabbed her by the arm. Althea struggled to shake him off, but he pinned her with his arms, pressing her back against his stomach.

"Guerre, you speak English. Tell her I won't hurt her if she is good." Armand increased his hold on Althea as she continued to struggle.

"I must remind you, Armand, that we are in Wales, not England, and they have a language that is totally incomprehensible." Guerre's tone showed that he was getting annoyed at Armand's antics.

Suddenly, without warning, Armand threw Althea roughly to the ground. Sprawled on her back, she had no time to recover before Armand threw himself on top of her. His chain mail cut into her flesh, and Althea cried out in pain.

"Armand," the other knight said harshly, "control your rutting nature. The others wait for us."

Armand paused, pinning Althea to the ground. Looking up, he said with good humor, "Rest easy, Guerre. I'm only going to inspect her charms. I'll take this flower later." With a sudden movement, he plunged his hand into Althea's bodice, grasping one of her small breasts in his callused hand. With a cry of humiliation, Althea bit his other hand, biting down so hard that she drew blood. Armand, surprised and angered, pulled his hand free and slapped her face with such force that for one moment everything went black. Then she could feel Armand's hand under her skirt, caressing her thighs. Althea began to beat blindly at his chest with her fists.

So violently was she struggling that it took her a moment to realize that she was lashing at air, and that Armand was sprawled next to her, rather than on her.

Looking up, Althea saw that the other knight had dismounted and was standing next to her. He had lifted his visor and was watching her closely. Armand groaned, but Althea forgot him as she looked into the face of the knight called Guerre. Was it Lucifer himself? she wondered. It could be, with that dark, swarthy face and steady gaze, and the scar on the right side of his face that ran from his eye to his chin. Instead of disfiguring him, it added to the strength and arrogance of his features.

For one moment they stared at each other, black eyes burning into blue ones, until Armand staggered to his feet.

"Damn you, Guerre, you'll pay for this," he sputtered angrily.

"I did it for your own good, Armand. You had best find out who you handled before things go too far. The girl cried out in French, but you were too besotted to notice."

Armand looked disbelievingly at Althea. "What is your name, girl?" he asked, with a slight uncertainty in his voice. Althea stared at him, trembling. Would it be worse for her if they knew her identity or not? Deciding that she was already in serious trouble, she told the truth. "Althea, daughter of Sir Richard de Champs, the lord of yon castle."

Both men stared down at her, Armand with apprehension and Guerre with speculation. Her blonde hair was tangled and caught with twigs from the wood, and her blue shift, ripped far up her thigh, revealed shapely white legs. She was beautiful, but she certainly did not resemble the daughter of a nobleman. Yet her voice was clear and her French impeccable. Guerre's mouth twitched; whether with amusement at the situation or with irritation, Althea could not tell. Armand just stared at her with mounting horror on his face. "You've saved my life, Guerre," Armand whispered hoarsely. "By the Holy Grail, who would have imagined that this tattered wench—" He broke off suddenly, remembering that Althea understood every word.

"Think quickly, Armand, for Claude has grown impatient. Here they come now." Guerre pointed to the rest of the retinue, approaching through the meadow.

Althea jumped up, angrily brushing aside Armand's outstretched hand. Although she did not understand his fear, it made her braver, and her anger at his misuse of her grew. Silently, she glared at Armand as the horsemen rode toward them.

"What brings this delay, Sir Guerre?" a man called out irritably.

"A bit of a misunderstanding, Your Grace," Sir Guerre replied, glancing at Armand.

Althea noted the attempt at an explanation and was infuriated. She had thought that Sir Guerre had been defending her when he lifted Armand from her, but she had been wrong. He was only trying to save his friend, although from what, she did not know. For some reason this angered her even more.

"I do not see a misunderstanding, but rather a fair wench. I appreciate what occurred all too well." The man who was obviously the leader spoke with cynical amusement. Althea looked at him closely. Although he was seated in the saddle, she could see that he was a tall man, and quite fat. Even the chain mail armor he wore could not disguise the softness of his body. He wore no helmet, and his hair was brown and curly. Small eyes like two gray pebbles set above his plump cheeks held a look of cold amusement. He was close to her father's age, she determined, but his face seemed ravaged by indulgent living. As she appraised him, Althea realized he was regarding her leg, which was revealed by the torn shift. Flustered, she grabbed her skirt together.

The man laughed at her. "Ask her what her name is, Guerre."

"My lord, she understands French." Sir Guerre looked at Althea thoughtfully, as if trying to frame his words to everyone's best possible advantage. "Sir Claude, I would like to present the Lady Althea, Sir Richard's honorable daughter. The misunderstanding is that we did not recognize her identity. She was dressed thus to gather flowers in the meadow."

All looked at Guerre. If he felt any anxiety at his deception—and the notable lack of flowers—he certainly did not show it. Tall and powerful, he was the perfect picture of a strong man amused at the whimsical antics of a young girl who had broken a rule and gotten into a bit of trouble. His manner was so forceful that one was tempted to believe him. Althea looked at him with gratitude and perplexity. Why had he lied? To save his friend, perhaps. With a start she realized that Sir Claude was staring at her with a mixture of amazement, anger, and disbelief.

"By the Rood," he said angrily, "Sir Richard is certainly lax in his control of you, my lady. Why, I hope it is not damaged goods I'm getting."

Althea looked at him with growing alarm. Who was this man? "I do not understand, my lord."

"I grant you don't, my Lady Althea. Even someone as careless as you appear to be would probably present yourself to your future husband with more decorum." Althea looked at him dumbly. After a moment, she was aware that everyone was waiting for her to acknowledge his identity, but fear and disgust made her speechless. This fat, middle-aged man could not possibly be her future husband. He resembled a painting of Nero watching the Christians being fed to the lions that she had seen in Lady Maura's Book of Hours. Ruefully, she thought she now knew how the Christians felt.

As the silence became painful, she heard Sir Guerre speak again. "Sir Claude, the Lady Althea is but a child, and has had quite a scare. I am sure she is in a state of pleasant shock."

Althea heard his voice although her mind did not really comprehend his words. But long training in keeping her composure with Lady Maura and Sir Richard began to assert itself. With as much dignity as she could muster, she attempted a curtsy, although the rip in her gown made it difficult to do it with modesty. Raising her eyes, she spoke in a composed voice that amazed even herself. "My lord, please forgive my rudeness. I am truly overwhelmed by your presence." This, she thought, was not a lie.

Sir Claude was still extremely annoyed with Althea, but he was moved by her beauty, tarnished though it might have been at the moment. Feeling generous, he decided to play the part Sir Guerre had established as appropriate. Sitting a little taller, he smiled down with a patronizing look. "My lady, you are obviously undisciplined, but I will accept youth as your excuse and will train you in more appropriate manners. I notice, also, that you seem to have a problem finding flowers," he added sarcastically.

Althea's brain was recovering, and her quick mind noted that while Sir Claude might be physically distasteful, he was not stupid. She also realized that she would need an excuse for her father. She glanced at Armand, who was staring at her with the face of a condemned man. "My lord, I left too late in the day to venture far, and this field lacks the flowers I sought to decorate my chamber."

Sir Claude had also noted Armand's look of apprehension and said suspiciously, "If either of my two knights behaved unchivalrously, they will pay dearly."

Not quite sure why she did so, Althea decided to protect Armand. Perhaps it was because she understood fear so well. "No, my lord. I did not know who they were, so I became frightened and started to run. When they tried to detain me, I'm afraid I became hysterical and they had to restrain me."

Claude looked at her keenly. There was no way of knowing if she was lying, and it would be inconvenient to start trouble now. Besides, he was hungry, and he wanted to get to the castle.

"Good. Sir Armand, please give the Lady Althea your horse."

As Armand helped swing her into the saddle, he gave

her a look of gratitude, which she ignored. As she turned her horse to follow Sir Claude, she saw Sir Guerre staring at her. She could not decipher his look, but she thought it held amusement.

CHAPTER THREE

Lady Maura was angrier than she had been in many a year. As Edwina carefully brushed the tangles from Althea's hair, she paced back and forth, momentarily discontinuing her tirade for lack of breath. The silence was appreciated by Edwina and Althea, who had both endured over an hour of Lady Maura's wrath. Now the quiet in the small chamber was broken only by the swish of Lady Maura's green woolen gown as it dragged on the stone floor.

At thirty, Althea's stepmother retained much of the beauty of her youth. Tall and regal, she prided herself on her graceful carriage and shapely figure. Her brown hair had no gray in it, and her dark eyes could still shine when pleased. This occurred rarely, however, and years of disappointment and bitterness had etched fine webs around her mouth, which was usually pursed in anger. Now was such a time. How could that stupid girl have managed to leave the castle unseen!

She glared at Althea. If it weren't for the fact that the girl would be wed tomorrow, she would take a whip to her herself. The stupid wench had almost jeopardized her marriage with Claude, Count du Vendome, and all of Lady Maura's plans would have been for naught. Furious, she began to pace again, pausing for a moment at the casement that looked out into the courtyard of the castle. Torches lit the courtyard, painting the servants and soldiers who bustled back and forth with a strange reddish glow. Involuntarily, she shuddered. It was in the courtyard that her predecessor had met her terrible death, and

though Maura had always felt an intense dislike for Rosemund, in the ten years that she had lived at Grydwyn Castle, she had never succeeded in overcoming her revulsion
of the courtyard. It was too vivid a reminder of what befell
unfaithful wives.

Damn the past, she thought viciously. For ten years she
had been living with the spectre of Rosemund. Sir Richard
never spoke of his first wife, but Maura was astute enough
to know what weighed on his mind when he brooded by the
fire at night, drinking flagon after flagon of wine. At night
he would often groan in agony during his sleep, and Maura
knew he was haunted by the ghost of the wife he had
executed.

In the first year of her marriage, she had hoped to exorcise the memory of Rosemund by praying for a son who
would turn Richard's mind to happier thoughts. But year
after long year passed, and hope had turned to bitterness
and dissatisfaction as she remained barren. And her bitterness had been slowly aggravated by the constant presence of Althea. Rosemund had left a legacy that was hard
to ignore.

Lady Maura turned and stared at her stepdaughter. She
had to admit the girl was a beauty. Sitting quietly on a
small bench in front of the hearth, Althea was being transformed from a servant into a lady who could rival any of
the great beauties at the court of King Edward. As Edwina
began to carefully braid Althea's long blonde hair, Lady
Maura observed her appearance carefully. Angry as she
was at Althea for her disgraceful behavior this afternoon,
she still knew her own interests were best served by seeing
that the girl looked as ravishing as possible. If Claude was
having any second thoughts about this marriage, it would
be best to blot them out with as beautiful and dignified a
woman as possible.

Lady Maura tilted her head to one side and regarded the
clothes laid out on the bed. The blue velvet tunic was perfect. It would bring out the blue of Althea's eyes and was a
perfect foil for her long blonde hair. The garment had been

sewn carefully to emphasize Althea's round breasts, making them appear more voluptuous than they really were. The tunic came to Althea's knees, but was slit on each side far up each thigh. Under the tunic she would wear a white linen underskirt trimmed with blue and gold thread. Yes, she thought, satisfied, she'll turn every man's head. Although it would help if she would smile. The expression on Althea's face was blank, almost as if she were in a trance.

Lady Maura thought once again of Althea's mother. She knew that Rosemund's love affair had been real, for both she and her lover, John de Viller, had freely admitted their guilt. But she had long doubted the charge of witchcraft. She would have loved to believe it, but she was basically too honest with herself. Ten years as the wife of Sir Richard had taught her how deeply her husband's thirst for revenge could run. Sometimes she thought he was tainted with a touch of madness. When he lost control of his temper he could be a violent man, extreme even in a land that regarded violence as normal. Once he had hurled his favorite dog, a collie, off the tower ramparts when the dog had disobeyed. Maura had discovered later that Sir Richard had intimated the same fate to the priests who had stood in judgment of Rosemund if they should find her innocent. Lady Maura's innate sense of survival kept her from voicing dangerous opinions out loud, but she secretly attributed her husband's nightmares and unwarranted display of temper to a guilty conscience.

Maura knew Althea was terrified of the marriage that would take place tomorrow, and revolted by the appearance of her bridegroom. A bit of Lady Maura's heart softened toward Althea. It was sixteen years ago that she had wed her first husband, Sir Francis of Wessex, and she remembered her despair as she, a fourteen-year-old lass, was prepared for her bedding to the fifty-four-year-old knight who had a granddaughter one year older than she. Lady Maura could still vividly recall the horror of her wedding night as the old man struggled on top of her for hours try-

ing to reach his climax, unaware in his own frustration of
the agony suffered by a young virgin girl.

With something close to compassion, she regarded Althea closely. Would Sir Claude be a kind husband to her,
considerate of her innocence and gentle with her fear? She
rather doubted it. Her shrewd eye had told her immediately that Claude was a man who enjoyed his pleasures
greedily, whether it be food, wine, or women. He had a
streak of cruelty in him, too. She frowned as she remembered the way he had shown his displeasure when he had
arrived. His cold, sarcastic comments to her and Sir Richard about Althea's appearance had been humiliating. He
had even intimated that he doubted her virginity, since
any girl so unchaperoned must have had ample opportunity to experience the coarser side of life. It had taken all
her tact to assure him that all was as it should be with Althea, and to flatter him into good humor.

Her husband had been even more difficult to control. In
the privacy of their chamber, Sir Richard had ranted and
raved in fury at Althea. Only Maura's argument that
bruises and broken bones would increase Claude's doubts
of her virginity had prevented him from beating the girl
senseless.

"I'll kill her myself if we find she is no virgin," cried Sir
Richard, beating his whip on the table. "I tell you she is a
whore like her mother."

Maura agreed that if that turned out to be true, he could
do what he willed, but they should let Claude take her to
bed and let him discover the truth. Until then, today's incident should be treated indulgently, as a lighthearted
prank by an impetuous and slightly fanciful girl. Finally,
he had calmed down, and Maura had hurriedly begun
preparations for the wedding the next day.

Ordinarily, wedding preparations would have taken
many weeks. At least fifty guests would have come; cattle
and sheep would have been slaughtered, and the forest
hunted for wild game. The castle would have been cleaned,
and entertainment planned for at least a week's festivi-

ties. It would have been a gay and busy time. But the
circumstances were different now. Claude wanted the wedding to take place tomorrow. So Maura had sent a rider to
invite their five nearest neighbors, and then set about preparing the best feast that could be summoned on such
short notice.

Now, as she sat in Althea's chamber, Lady Maura congratulated herself on her ability to arrange everything to
her best advantage. It had taken over a year of scheming
and subtle persuasion, but it had all worked out well. That
is, if Althea played her part. Perhaps a little flattery was
in order. "You'll be a lovely bride for your eager bridegroom," Lady Maura said in a pleasant tone.

Althea looked coolly at her stepmother. She was still
smarting over the tirade of anger that had been leveled
against her, and rebellion against her fate was smoldering
within her. "I do not think he is too eager, my lady. After
all, he was blackmailed into marrying me."

Lady Maura willed her voice to be soothing. "Not blackmailed, Althea. To arrange a marriage such as this is common. All will benefit."

Yes, all would benefit except herself, Althea thought bitterly. Without answering, she thought of the complicated
feudal system that dominated their lives. Sir Richard's
family, which had originally come to England with Wil-
liam the Conqueror in 1066, still held land in Normandy.
Thus, Sir Richard owed allegiance to King Edward of England and King Philip of France. Claude du Vendome was
Sir Richard's vassal in Normandy, and he owed allegiance
to both Richard and the King of France. This could be a difficult situation in peace, and almost impossible in time of
war. When hostilities broke out between France and England, Claude, knowing that it was safer to side with
Philip, had quickly aligned himself with France, although
Richard, his direct overlord, had pledged himself to Edward. Distance and expense had made it impossible for
Richard to dislodge Claude from his fief; he probably
would have succeeded in his treachery if he hadn't been

such a miserly vassal to King Philip. He had ignored the king's request for money and men, and had remained at his castle when others went off to war. Disgusted, King Philip wanted revenge. He decided to woo Richard to his side, and offered to evict Claude if Richard would remain neutral in the hostilities between France and England.

Althea glanced at her stepmother. That was where Lady Maura's scheming had come into play. Subtly, she had convinced Sir Richard that evicting Claude would be costly and time-consuming. Wouldn't it be better to wed him to Althea? He had just been widowed for the second time and had no heirs. If Althea produced one, it would be Sir Richard's grandchild, doubly increasing the security of the land in Normandy.

Sir Claude had had no choice. He faced either the immediate armies of the French king or the eventual armies of the English. Unlike most noblemen, he detested the discomforts of war and feared the danger of combat. He knew that marriage to Althea was a small price to pay for safety.

Althea knew it also, and she felt like a trapped animal being used as the bait for a greater kill. Everyone would be successful except her. She would have been even more disturbed at her fate if she had known that in Normandy, another woman sat by a fire, brooding in anger over this marriage and cursing the people who had brought it about.

Thirty minutes had passed in silence, and Althea was now almost ready for the banquet. With relief, she saw Lady Maura nod with approval. "Perhaps this afternoon's folly will be forgotten when you appear thus," Lady Maura said, circling Althea and checking every detail of her attire.

Some of Althea's natural spark was starting to return, and the pleasure of being dressed in fine clothes for the first time in her life could not be subdued. She smiled tentatively at Lady Maura.

Maura looked back at her, stunned. She knew Althea was lovely; but when she smiled, as she did now, she was absolutely dazzling. Her teeth were white and perfect, and her lips were naturally pink and seductive. Her smile lit up her eyes so that they seemed like two pools of blue fire flecked with gold. It was a magic transformation, Lady Maura thought. Seconds before, Althea had been a pretty girl. Now, she was a beautiful temptress.

Althea was puzzled by the expression on Maura's face. She turned slowly and looked at her reflection in the polished silver mirror that Edwina held for her, not really comprehending at first that what she saw was her reflection. It could not be possible. That creature in the mirror was lovely and proud. It could not be her.

Edwina smiled happily, pleased by Althea's bewilderment. The faithful woman had cared for the girl all her life, and she now felt vindicated. Her poor little duckling had turned into the proverbial swan.

"My lady, she's truly lovely, isn't she?" she asked Maura, smiling happily.

Lady Maura did not answer. With terrifying insight, she realized the true effect Rosemund must have had on people, especially on Sir Richard, and she was consumed with bitterness and defeat. How could she have ever hoped to erase such a dazzling ghost from her husband's memory? She knew now that not even Althea's removal from Grydwyn Castle would accomplish that. Rosemund's image would haunt him until the day death mercifully released him. Overcome with jealousy, Lady Maura could not control the spite in her voice. "I hope Althea remembers that obedience and a sweet disposition will please her husband more than her good looks."

Althea's pleasure evaporated with Maura's words. Frowning, she looked down at the floor. Lady Maura smiled with pleasure at her dejection and continued in a silky voice, "I hope that Sir Claude meets with your approval, Althea."

Althea felt a combination of anger and despair rise in her. Recklessly, she said, "He is too old and too fat to be appealing, my lady. And his disposition strikes me as cruel. If I had my choice, I would prefer another."

"Prefer! Prefer!" shrieked Lady Maura, her bitterness transformed into rage. "You, the worthless daughter of a whore, prefer! You should be down on your knees in gratitude that a nobleman would take you!"

Lady Maura paced quickly back and forth like an outraged panther. "By the Rood, it was all your father and I could do to arrange for Sir Claude to take you away! You disgusting whore! How dare you even utter the word 'prefer'!"

Althea, pale with shock at the unexpected outburst, looked at her speechlessly. Before she could retort, Lady Maura went to the door and swung it open. "Remember this, girl," she said, her eyes dark with fury. "You had better please Sir Claude, for once you leave here, you will never return. And lest you are tempted to dally with someone you *prefer,* remember the fate of your mother."

She slammed the door behind her then, and Althea stood there, staring at it. The brief pleasure she had felt was gone, and she was now fired with rage and humiliation. Damn them, she thought furiously. Damn you, Father; and damn you, Maura. Edwina put her arms around Althea and tried to hold her, but Althea pushed her away.

"Damn them, Edwina," she cried hoarsely, pacing around the room. "I'll never marry Sir Claude. I'll enter the convent at Chester before I wed that pig!"

Edwina let her pace back and forth. She knew, better than anyone else, that underneath the passive image the girl had been forced to adopt to survive there was a passionate and fiery personality. Best to let her get it out of her system.

"Edwina, I can't stand it! I won't! In all the years that I've had on this earth, only you and Magara have shown me love and kindness. Now to spend the rest of my life with that disgusting lout is more than I can bear!"

"My lady," murmured Edwina soothingly, "the convent

is not for one so lovely and young as you. It is a calling, not a place to escape."

"You lie, Edwina," Althea spat out bitterly. "You know that convent walls hold more women forced there by fate than by faith! Besides, beauty never did one any good! Look at my mother! A whore who died a witch's death! Damn her too!"

"Stop it," Edwina hissed so coldly and angrily that Althea halted. "You stop it, now! Your mother, God grant her peace, was no whore. I grew up with her, her friend and her servant. She was driven to her lover's arms by your father's cruelty. He loved her madly, but he was mean and suspicious, and when he would take offense at something she did, he would beat her."

Edwina paused, her breath heaving with emotion. She was facing Althea, but her eyes were far away. "Many a night I would nurse her wounds while she wept in despair. Once he broke her arm, and another time she was unconscious for two days. We thought we had lost her then. That vile monster had the nerve to sit by her bed and weep. When Sir John came here to serve Sir Richard, it was like a breath of life to her dying heart. She fought her love for him for months, but in the end, she gave in to its warmth. They were sinners, I grant you that, but let God be their judge!"

Althea looked at Edwina, who was trembling with emotion. Then she threw herself on the bed, sobbing with despair and shame. Edwina rushed to her and clasped her in her arms. Tears streaming down her face, the faithful old woman held the young girl closely, murmuring words of comfort. "There, there, my lamb. Forgive me, I didn't mean to yell at you. I only wanted you to understand."

"Oh, Edwina," choked Althea through her sobs, "I feel so guilty. I was just angry and upset and hurt."

"I know, I know," soothed the old woman.

"Oh, how I wish she were alive. She would never have let my father marry me to Sir Claude."

"Perhaps."

"No, I know she wouldn't. I just can't bear the thought of him."

"It won't be so bad. You are lovely. He will treat you well. Be clever and you will have a good life."

"You sound like Magara."

"She is a wise woman, Althea. You are young and do not yet know the ways of survival. Learn to cover your feelings and things will go well for you. Your mother never learned that lesson, but you must."

Althea sat up dejectedly. She knew Edwina and Magara were right, but it seemed so hopeless.

"Let me wash your face, my pet. You musn't be late for the banquet." Edwina went over to the table and poured water from an earthen jug into a bowl. She dipped a cloth into the water and wrung it out. Then she poured some wine from another jug into a goblet. She handed Althea the goblet. "Take a little wine. It will relax you and make your cheeks glow. You are too pale now."

Althea sipped it obediently while Edwina dabbed at her eyes with the cold compress.

Satisfied that Althea was better, Edwina clucked happily, "My dear, you are lovely again. No more tears now. Hurry along. I'll walk down with you."

Althea rose as one in a trance. She knew there was no escape, and now her pride was starting to take command. She might be crying inside, but no one save Edwina would know. She would be dignified and regal. She straightened her skirt and lifted her chin. No one would laugh at her.

Althea wanted to delay the future for one moment longer. She stood quietly in the shadows of the stone gallery that overlooked the main hall, and looked down at the scene below her.

The main hall was bustling with activity. A huge fire roared in the great stone fireplace, and a blaze of torches burned in iron sconces on the walls. Although a pall of smoke was already forming, Althea could still make out the large tapestry that was against the far wall. Her great-grandmother had made it, and she had captured the beauty of the Welsh seacoast with her fine needlework.

Four wooden tables had been brought from the barracks to accommodate Claude's men-at-arms, and most of them were already seated, drinking ale and laughing uproariously at their own jests. Servants were moving around setting out wine and ale, and kicking the great hunting dogs who lived in the main hall out of their way. Occasionally, one of the huge curs would object, setting off a round of barking and cursing that added to the general confusion.

Althea's gaze went from the lower end of the hall up toward the tables in front of the dais. Here, the few retainers of rank who belonged to Sir Richard would be seated, along with the knights of Claude's party. Some men were already sitting down, boisterously talking to their friends and slapping each other on the back like good-natured bears. These men had ridden long and hard since crossing the Channel, and they were ready to celebrate.

Althea saw several of the servant girls in the clutches of two eager knights. One was actually trying to fondle a girl's breasts, and the poor girl, burdened by a heavy tray she dared not drop, was squirming with embarrassment. It was rare that this type of behavior started before dinner, although many a feast had ended with knights carrying off their terrified choices for a night of fun. Althea realized that these men were pretty well gone with wine and ale, so her father must be sparing nothing for Sir Claude.

On the dais, Lady Maura was seated next to Sir Claude. They were talking animatedly, and he seemed to be in high spirits. Althea regarded Claude, and decided that his elegant tunic of red velvet did nothing to hide the grossness of his body. His face was red with wine, and she could see from here how he sweated profusely, his face gleaming with perspiration. Her father was seated one chair away from him. It was planned that she sit between Sir Richard and Claude.

Suddenly, she was aware that she was being observed. One person in the crowded, noisy room had seen her. Her heart skipped a beat as she looked down into the face of Sir Guerre, who was standing behind Claude. Unable to draw her eyes away, she regarded his tall, lean body, now clothed in an elegant tunic of dark blue velvet embroidered with gold thread. Even under this garment she could see the muscles of his arms, and her heart again missed a beat. His legs were encased in dark brown leggings of soft leather that showed that his thighs were as muscular and solid as his arms. Althea felt him studying her as carefully as she was regarding him, and a slow warmth enveloped her, making her ache with a pain she had never felt before. Her nipples grew hard and pushed urgently out from the cloth of her gown, and she felt her face flush with excitement. Her eyes met his, and for one eternal second she forgot everything and everyone as she looked down at Sir Guerre.

He broke the trance by moving suddenly, and Edwina pinched her arm. "Girl, watch yourself!" she hissed with fear.

Looking down, Althea saw that all eyes were slowly turning up to her, and a quick glance at Sir Richard showed her that he was annoyed. Grabbing Althea's arm, Edwina pulled her along, whispering urgently, "They think you were looking at Sir Claude. Play the lie well."

Althea came to the staircase, hesitated for one moment, and then began to descend the stone steps. She walked slowly, for she was desperately trying to retain her composure. Never in her life had she experienced the feeling that she had had a moment ago. She tried to focus her eyes on Claude, but they strayed back to Sir Guerre. She saw that he had seated himself on Sir Richard's left. The bored expression on his face surprised, then angered her. Althea looked back at Claude, who was smiling with delight as she approached the dais. She heard the murmurs of approval from the men, and she realized that she must look good. Lady Maura was smiling at her, but her eyes were cold. Sir Richard was regarding her with an expression she could not read. His face was almost blank, as if he were numb with shock at her appearance. With startling intuition, she realized that he was seeing Rosemund's ghost in her.

Claude rose and came toward her. At that moment Althea smiled at Sir Richard. His expression openly registered shock, and she felt a sense of triumph within, as if she had avenged her mother in some way.

Everyone stood motionless. Althea turned her eyes toward Claude, forcing herself to smile. She could feel her father's eyes boring into her face, but she ignored him. Claude was looking at her breasts, lust glowing in his eyes. Involuntarily she shuddered, and to cover it, Althea looked down at the floor, hoping Claude would think she was shaking from maidenly modesty. He reached for her hand, surreptitiously squeezing it so hard she winced. She glanced up at him and saw that he was still smiling, but now it was a mocking smile. She looked into his small, red eyes and knew that he had noticed her revulsion, and she would pay for it. Fear filled her soul, but so did pride. She would play this game through, she thought angrily. No one would know her fear.

"My lord, you are crushing my hand," she said sweetly. "I fear you do not know your own strength."

"I beg your pardon, Lady Althea, but the enticing look in your eyes quite unnerved me. A woman's desire often makes me forget myself." Althea heard the taunt in his voice and knew it was a warning.

He helped her to her seat, and the others, who had been standing, now sat down. Out of the corner of her eye, Althea glanced at Sir Guerre. He had overheard her conversation with Claude, and she could see him staring down at his goblet, a grim look on his face. As if feeling her gaze, he glanced up, and their eyes locked. Sensing the others were watching her, Althea turned away and reached for her goblet.

"My lady seems quite taken with Sir Guerre," Claude remarked.

"Not taken, my lord," she answered coolly. "I was just

curious about the men in your retinue, since I will soon be
part of your household." No one but Althea knew how
much it cost her to say those last words.

"Of course, my dear," Claude said, his tone indicating
that he did not believe her for an instant. "I will be glad to
tell you about all my men, but since you seem particularly
interested in one, I will tell you about him first. He is Sir
Guerre du Reims, my brother-in-law. Or should I say my
late wife's brother. Alycia was very fond of him."

A servant laden with food came up behind them, and he
paused to help himself from the platter of meat. Althea
looked at his plate with disgust as he piled it high with
rabbit, wild pig, and pheasant. He took four times more
than the ordinary man might. Turning toward her father to cover the look of revulsion on her face, she noted
that Sir Richard was also looking at Claude's plate with
consternation. She smiled to herself, thinking of her father's miserly ways. He would be glad to see this wedding
over and the guests gone. Taking only a small piece of
pheasant, for she thought she would gag if she had to eat,
Althea turned back to Claude, hoping that he would tell
her more of Sir Guerre. Choosing her words carefully so as
not to arouse his suspicion, she said, "It must have been a
terrible blow to you to lose Lady Alycia. I have heard that
she was quite a beauty."

Claude grunted. "Yes, but if she had lived, we would not
be here now." With this callous reply, he continued to
gnaw at a piece of meat, and Althea realized that when
food was in front of Claude, nothing else could hold his attention. She watched with a sinking feeling as he devoured
his meat, stuffing it into his mouth so that the grease drib-
bled down his chin. He looked like a pig at a trough. So this
was to be her fate, she thought in despair. To spend her life
with this obese, callous man, to share his bed: her heart
thumped in horror at the thought. Althea looked around at
the guests, now all merry with wine and good food. None
realized her torment, or if they did, they did not care. Indeed, all thought her fortunate to have found a husband at

all. Even Edwina and Magara had told her to accept her fate and be happy that Sir Claude would wed her. But she could not make herself feel grateful or happy. She felt like a trapped animal unable to escape its fate. Had Rosemund felt like this when she had married Sir Richard? Or did the anguish come when love had died? Althea looked at her goblet of wine sadly. She would never know.

Suddenly her reverie was broken by the feel of a hand on her thigh. Glancing down, she saw that Claude was fondling her, his fat, greasy fingers soiling the blue velvet as he probed her flesh through the material of the tunic. Sick with revulsion, she sat motionless, pretending that this wasn't happening, hoping that he would stop.

But Claude had eaten his fill, and now, content with the fine food and half-drunk with wine, he felt amorous. Sensing that Althea was repulsed by him only aroused him more. He would show her who was master, he thought wickedly. He let go of her thigh and took hold of her hand, squeezing it with passion. "Althea, I think you will satisfy me well," he whispered into her ear.

His breath smelled of the heavy meats he had eaten, and Althea could not hold back the shudder that passed through her body. "Please, Claude, this is not the place for lovemaking," she said, praying that he would not touch her again. But her prayer went unanswered as she realized with growing horror that he was moving her hand over to his thigh. Before she knew what had happened, he had placed her hand over his private parts. She struggled for release, but he held her hand tightly, and she could now feel him growing hard under his tunic. Frantically, she looked around the room, realizing that no one could see since they were hidden by the table and its banquet cloth. Even her father to her left and Lady Maura to the right were unaware of her humiliation. She struggled again, trying to be inconspicuous, but Claude laughed at her efforts, pressing her hand more firmly down on himself. It seemed to her that her squirming seemed to increase his desire, for he was now red and panting.

"Please stop," she begged in a desperate whisper.

He laughed hoarsely. "I wish our wedding night were now, my dear, instead of tomorrow, for I have a great ache in my loins that must be satisfied."

She turned to him furiously, her fear fired into anger. "I dread the thought of bedding you, my lord, for my tastes do not run to pork," she hissed recklessly. Emboldened by the look of shock on his face, she suddenly pinched his member sharply. He released her hand with a cry of pain, and all eyes turned to them with surprise. Suddenly, the enormity of what she had said and done hit Althea, and she went white with fear. Claude pushed back his seat and was regarding her with fury.

"What ails you, Sir Claude?" Sir Richard asked with concern.

"The wedding is off!" cried Claude, standing up.

Consternation broke out in the great hall as Claude's men, now well oiled with wine, reached for their swords, and Sir Richard's returned the challenge. No one really knew what was going on, but all were ready for a fight, and any excuse was good for a bout. As bedlam broke out in the hall, Althea saw that only Sir Guerre stood silently, hand on his sword, alert but assessing the situation. Suddenly, Sir Richard pounded the table with an ale tankard, and the battle-eager knights stopped for an instant to see what was happening.

"Sit down, all of you. Let us discover what is wrong before we fight." His voice was commanding, and Althea realized that in spite of all his faults, Sir Richard was a leader of men, for they all stopped, though none sat down. As they shuffled their feet and murmured insults at each other, they kept their eyes on the dais to see what would ensue between their leaders.

Sir Richard now turned to Claude. "Explain, sir, why this sudden change of heart. I thought you were well pleased by your bride."

Claude looked at Althea craftily, vengeance on his swinish face. "I would be, Sir Richard, if I thought my bride were a virgin, rather than a hussy."

Althea's face went pale with fright and anger. She saw all eyes turn toward her, and she guessed what Claude would say next.

"Explain yourself," demanded Sir Richard with angry exasperation.

"Gladly." Claude was the picture of an injured man. "I made this marriage contract in good faith, even though the lady's mother was notorious. I assumed that you had taken care to shield Althea from her baser instincts. My suspicions were aroused this afternoon by her unseemly freedom, but I took you at your word that the girl was innocent. Now this confirms my earlier fears!"

"What confirms it?"

Claude hesitated, as if embarrassed to go on, but then, as if overcome by righteous indignation, he continued. "She is a bold lass, and her actions at this table were not those of a virgin filled with modesty, but rather a wench who has experienced many men."

"He's lying!" Althea cried, standing up. Her father gripped her arm in a painful hold that took her breath away.

Claude turned toward her, looking her in the eye. "Deny that you grabbed my manhood under the table and begged me to take you tonight, like the strumpet that you are!" Althea was stunned to hear him utter those lies. She regarded him speechlessly. Only as she felt Sir Richard's anger rising to a murderous pitch did she come to her senses. "He's lying," she insisted. "He held my hand and forced me to fondle him."

"Whore," hissed Sir Richard. "Just like your mother." He began to shake her violently, but suddenly Sir Guerre grabbed him. Everyone was stunned by this breach of etiquette. No one interfered when a husband chastised an errant wife, or a father his daughter.

"Leave her be," Sir Guerre said coldly, his hand on his

sword. Sir Richard's color rose; he released Althea's arm and reached for his sword.

"You dare to interfere in her just punishment! Why, I'll teach you to defend this strumpet!" He began to draw his sword, and Sir Guerre stepped back, preparing to fight.

Lady Maura quickly rushed between them. "Stop, stop!" she pleaded. "I have a plan." Her husband looked at her menacingly, enraged by her interference, but she held her ground. Turning to Sir Claude, she smiled at him. She knew that he was lying, for Althea had been revolted by him. But all was not lost. She would kill two birds with one stone. Satisfy him, and get rid of Althea. "My lord," she said placatingly, "if you have doubts about Althea's honor, then they must be appeased before you wed her. Take her to bed tonight and discover for yourself if she is a virgin." She saw the look of pure terror on Althea's face, and the cold anger on Sir Guerre's. His murderous expression left her speechless for an instant, but she recovered herself and turned to her husband. "We lose nothing, my lord. If indeed she is not a virgin, her honor will not be lost, and you can deal with her tomorrow as you see fit. But if, as we believe, Althea is a virgin, tomorrow she and Sir Claude will wed. This has been done before when the bride's honor has been in doubt."

Althea saw the look of delight and triumph on Sir Claude's face. She felt as if she were going to faint, and put out a hand to steady herself, but Sir Claude grabbed her hand and smiled wickedly into her stricken face.

"I agree to your terms. It seems fair enough to me."

"Agreed," said Sir Richard. His expression was still thunderous, but he was regarding his wife with something close to admiration.

"Good," said Lady Maura, as if all were settled. She took Althea's arm and began to guide her toward the staircase. Calling over her shoulder, she said cheerfully, "Give us time to prepare her, my lords. Enjoy another glass of wine!" The mood was festive now and lusty. The men began calling out obscene remarks to each other, and the serving girls knew that the real trouble would soon begin. The hall was filled with laughter, and one squire picked up a lute and began to sing a lusty song about a bride and groom that left little to the imagination. Althea heard all this as she walked down the gallery, but it seemed as if it were a thousand miles off. She felt Lady Maura's fingers pressing painfully into her arm, but that was a distant pain, too. The only thing she really saw was the horrible image of what would soon befall her.

CHAPTER FOUR

Althea stood at the window of her small chamber and stared out into the night. There was a storm brewing over the Irish Sea; she could smell it in the wind. The clouds that would bring the rain had not yet been driven over the sky, and she could see the moon. It hung over the castle like a giant lantern, adding its light to the torches that burned in the courtyard below. Althea watched as the servants and soldiers of Sir Richard danced and drank, creating their own merriment with lewd songs and jests.

A sudden gust of wind made the banners at the bridge flare out, and Althea's eye caught the crest on Sir Claude's standard. It was a wild boar in the attack position, with a bloody sword in its mouth. She had noticed it this afternoon, but it had not truly caught her attention in the confusion. Now it seemed like an omen to her, a reminder of what would take place tonight. Soon the nightmare would begin. No, not the nightmare, but the terrible reality. One could wake from a nightmare, but she would wake from this night to a fate far worse than her dreams could conjure.

Sadly, Althea turned from the window and went to the small table that stood by the hearth. She poured herself a goblet of wine, not noticing the fire burning cheerfully on the hearth or the candles that had been placed around the room to create a soft, alluring light. Her chamber had never been so warm or inviting. If she had noticed, she would have been bitterly amused, for the extra log in the hearth, the candles, the incense, and the fine fur cover on the bed were all placed there by Lady Maura for the bridal night to come.

But Althea could think only of the scene in her chamber after she had been led from the great hall in disgrace. "I'm innocent. It was he, not I, who acted like a wanton," she had cried in desperation to her stepmother.

"Of course, you're innocent," the older woman had agreed. "But you and I are the only two that know that. Except for Sir Claude, of course. The others, including your father, all think you a strumpet. This is the only way we can prove your innocence."

"But I don't want to marry that pig," Althea pleaded desperately. "Not only is his body revolting, but so is his mind and spirit. He's coarse and vulgar and a liar as well."

"Not the least bit like Sir Guerre," added Lady Maura quietly as she calmly took a nightdress out of the wooden chest that was placed at the foot of Althea's bed.

"Not in the least," cried Althea heatedly, before she realized that she had been trapped. Embarrassed, she sat on the bed and regarded her stepmother uncertainly.

"Did you think I didn't notice?" Lady Maura asked with a cold smile. "You're very lucky that Sir Claude was well gone with wine, as were the others. But take care. Your future husband is very shrewd, and tonight you may have given yourself away."

"I did nothing but look at an attractive man," protested Althea.

"Ah, but such a look. It is very dangerous to be so open in one's desires." As she talked, Lady Maura had been arranging the necessary things for the night to come: the nightdress of pale gold silk, the perfume for the bath, a comb, and some gold hair ribbons. She had been calm, pleased that she had won this battle. When the bridal sheet was displayed, with its stain of virgin blood, Sir Claude would have to marry Althea.

"I won't go through with this," Althea said defiantly. "Nothing can make me marry that man."

"Althea, must I remind you that your father's temper is

vile," Lady Maura said, "and can be murderous when confronted with a wanton woman. If you refuse to cooperate, all will think you guilty of whoring, especially your father. I can promise you that if he doesn't kill you outright, the punishment you will receive will make you wish that he had run you through with his sword."

Althea knew with a desperate sense of hopelessness that her stepmother was right. Sir Richard would be more than ready to believe her guilt, for in his mind, she was the product of a wanton whore, tainted from her birth.

Althea was not ready to die. Lady Maura had won, but Althea silently vowed that she would not show how bitterly she felt the defeat. Unconsciously, she put on the mask of pride that she had worn at the beginning of the banquet. She would pretend, she decided; no one would know of her anguish.

Now, as she stood in the chamber, she recalled the flutter of activity as the servants had bustled around the room following Lady Maura's commands. As Althea had sat in her warm bath scented with rose water, her body carefully scrubbed by Edwina, Lady Maura had directed the laying of fresh rushes on the floor, the lighting of the fire, the layout of the candles, and the scenting of the room with incense. In less than an hour, the small stone chamber looked tempting and warm; even sweetmeats and wine had been placed near the bed in case the lovers found themselves hungry. After the room had been arranged to her satisfaction, Maura had left to confer with her husband.

Returning quickly, she had entered the chamber just as Althea was donning her pale gold robe. "Your father, Althea, has wisely decided that this will be treated as your wedding night. All our guests will be here for the bedding ceremony. Then Sir Claude will have no excuse to claim that the sheet was changed or anything else was amiss."

Althea's heart had sunk in despair. Of course it was common to have all present at the bedding, but it was still an embarrassment for many women. For one second she saw Guerre's face before her and her face flushed at the thought. Hesitantly, she asked, "Will all of the guests watch the coupling?"

"No," said Lady Maura, sounding disappointed. "All will watch the bedding, but we will leave when that is done. Your father and Sir Claude will each post one guard at the door, until Sir Claude cries for all to enter. They will then get the rest of us to see the bridal sheet."

"My father is kind," Althea lied, but she was grateful for at least some privacy.

"It wasn't your father," snapped Lady Maura. "It was Sir Claude. I assume that with his size it must take a while to accomplish that which a trimmer man could do in minutes, and he wished no aspersions cast on his lovemaking."

Now, sipping on the sweet wine, Althea forced herself to remain calm. At least she looked beautiful, she thought. "Like a golden princess," Edwina had whispered in her ear. They would be here soon, and Sir Guerre with them. Why did she keep thinking of him? she thought angrily. He had given her no indication that he liked her. Even when he had come to her rescue he had been aloof and cold. But she could not stop herself from wondering what he thought of her. Did he think her wanton? Why shouldn't he, she thought with bitterness. Lady Maura was right. All had believed Sir Claude. Wouldn't his own brother-in-law? But he had stopped Sir Richard. Had it been an act of chivalry? Or something more? As she puzzled on this, she heard sounds in the gallery and realized with a sinking heart that the boisterous guests and Sir Claude were approaching.

Feeling faint, she steadied herself by gripping the table with both hands. The door flew open and the merry guests, by now very drunk, poured into the room. All were laughing and joking, and some of the comments were crude even for a crowd of drunken knights. The few women in the group, wives of Sir Richard's vassals, were also tipsy and laughed at the men's jokes. A bedding was always great entertainment, although it was cloaked in social necessity.

It proved that the marriage had been consummated, a vital fact if the marriage was to be legal in the eyes of the Church. Everyone was fairly lenient about the bedding, however, and the rules were flexible. This was not the first time it had taken place before Mother Church had conferred the vows on the participants' heads.

The small chamber quickly filled, and Althea, numb with embarrassment, saw Claude enter, wearing a scarlet silk robe, smiling with anticipation. Behind him stood Sir Guerre, his face expressionless. Althea's eyes briefly met his, but she could read nothing in his face. She turned toward Claude, forcing herself to appear calm. He held a goblet of wine in his hand and he raised his arms for silence. With good humor he turned toward Sir Richard.

"After the bedding," he said, "Sir Guerre and Sir John will remain outside the chamber until I call for witnesses. Agreed?"

"Agreed," Sir Richard said loudly. "And if she is a virgin, as she proclaims, you will wed her on the morrow. If not, she is mine to do with as I please." At the grimness of his words, more than one person in the room remembered Rosemund and inwardly shuddered. Althea paled, but kept her composure. She would never let him see fear from her.

"Good," Sir Claude said, raising his goblet again. "Let the bedding begin."

Lady Maura led Althea forward. "Here she is, my lord," she said ceremoniously. Althea, pale but beautiful, stopped before Sir Claude, defiantly meeting his eye. Her long blonde hair, several shades darker than the pale gold gown, fell loosely down her back, and her blue eyes glittered brightly through a mist of tears.

"She's a beautiful one, Sir Claude," cried out one of his retainers, "but do not keep us, or yourself, in suspense any longer. Reveal to us her charms!"

"If I were not as eager as you, I would hold you in suspense; but I, too, am impatient." Sir Claude turned toward Lady Maura. "Begin."

Lady Maura stepped forward and reached for the sash of
Althea's gown. With a tug, the gown separated, revealing
the tempting picture of small round breasts and a silken
stomach leading down to curling gold. Althea braced herself as Lady Maura reached behind her to remove the robe
entirely. In a second, she stood naked, and the crowd of
onlookers gasped at her beauty. Claude stood silent. Even
he, as lustful of women as he was of wine and food, was not
prepared for this vision that stood delectably in front of
him. Althea's face was impassive. Only a faint blush on
her cheeks revealed the turmoil that raged inside her. She
forced her blue eyes to meet Claude's, but his glance
was now traveling slowly down her body, taking in the
long blonde hair falling to her waist in a mass of gold, and
the creamy unblemished skin. Althea stepped back just
as his hand reached out for her breast. Claude's desire
amused the onlookers, who had been silent, the men filled
with their own desire and the women with jealousy. Now
they burst out laughing, and one man yelled out, "Patience, my lord."

All were laughing as Maura led Althea to the bed, where
she quickly got under the fur cover, filled with relief to
hide herself. As she drew the cover over her, she sensed
Guerre's eyes on her. They were glowing like coals, and his
face was taut with tension, but Althea could not tell if it
was desire or anger that he was trying to suppress. He
stared at her for one long moment, then abruptly turned
and left the chamber.

Claude then started to disrobe. Disgust filled her as
he removed the silken garment, for his body was worse
than she had imagined. His skin was pasty white, and the
few black hairs on his chest ran down to his stomach,
which was so large that he could not see his feet when he
looked down. His member, although aroused, was small,
and looked ridiculous on that huge body, as did his legs,
which were surprisingly thin and hairy. Hair everywhere
but on his chest, thought Althea with growing nausea.
Sensing that he was not an appealing sight, Claude did not

linger for the surveillance of the crowd, but made quickly for the bed. Feeling his lumbering body crawl in beside her, Althea felt the worst despair that she had ever experienced.

The crowd moved toward the door, calling out good wishes, encouragement, or lewd comments. Turning to the couple on the bed, Sir Richard said, "Sir Guerre and Sir John will be at the door. Call when you are ready," and then he and Lady Maura left, and the couple were finally alone.

Claude threw off the fur cover, exposing his gross body. Althea was so startled that she sat up, tensely clutching her hands together. Claude propped himself up on one elbow, his stomach so large that it rolled over and covered his private parts entirely.

"You are very nervous, my dear," he drawled. "Could you perhaps actually be the virgin that you profess to be?" His fat, bejeweled hand reached out and caressed her thigh, sickening Althea with his touch. Then she noticed the signet ring he wore. It had the picture of a wild boar on it.

Hoping to distract him, she asked about the jewel that so resembled the man next to her. "My lord, that is an interesting ring," she remarked, trying to keep her voice light.

He glanced down at his hand, which never stopped stroking her thigh. "It's the family crest. The wild boar is a dangerous and cunning creature, and it defeats most of its foes. It was on my standard as we rode here today. I'm surprised that you didn't notice it before. Or were you too preoccupied with Sir Guerre?" With these words he suddenly pinched her thigh so hard that she cried out with pain.

"Your imagination runs away with your reason, Sir Claude," she said hotly. "And as for being a virgin, you know that you lied today. You're a liar, and a bully, and I share this bed by no choice of my own."

"Ah ha! At last there is some color in your cheeks. I enjoy my women passionate, like Mathilde." With a laugh he reached for his wine goblet.

"Who is Mathilde?" Althea asked, curiosity getting the better of her. Lady Maura had told her that Sir Claude's first wife had been Eleanor of Lemoin, and he had said that his second wife was Alycia, Sir Guerre's sister.

"My mistress, of course," he said calmly, watching Althea's face carefully. He would teach this proud virgin some humility, he decided. He had been planning to save Mathilde as a surprise when they returned to Normandy, but stung by the obvious disgust that she felt for him, he felt that telling Althea on their first night together would be a sweet revenge.

His words had the desired effect, for Althea was staring at him speechlessly. She knew that men had mistresses, but few were so callous as to discuss them with their wives. This man was more decadent than she had imagined.

Enjoying her obvious shock, he continued. "Mathilde and I have been lovers since the time of Alycia's illness, and she is invaluable to me. In fact, she is preparing my castle at Vendome for us and will be there to greet us upon our return."

My God, thought Althea, had Alycia known about Mathilde? Looking at Sir Claude's smirk, she decided that no doubt she had. He was not the type to spare the feelings of an ailing wife. Fired with anger, Althea threw back the tresses that had covered her breasts, not realizing the wonderful effect her anger was having on Sir Claude's virility. "And what does the— Is she a lady?" At his nod, she continued, "What does the Lady Mathilde think of your new marriage, my dear lord?" Her voice was filled with acid.

"She has become accustomed to the idea," he told her with a chuckle, reaching for her breast.

"Well, I haven't!" Althea cried, trying to struggle with his groping. "I won't be humiliated any more by you, and this marriage is off even if it means my death." She began to tussle with him, but he was far stronger than she. He pinned her down with one arm and began to fondle her breasts, his face close to hers.

"Struggle a little if you want, my dear, but this night you'll be mine." Reaching down, he placed his fat lips on hers and tried to force her mouth open. His lips were still greasy from the meat he had devoured, and Althea almost gagged from the fetid smell of his breath. Filled with panic, she used the only weapon she had, biting him on his lower lip until she drew blood. Claude jerked his head back, stunned, then furious, but he did not release his hold on her body.

"Bitch," he said savagely, and with his free hand, he slapped Althea across the face. She let out a scream from the pain, and then lay still, only half-conscious from the blow. Unable to move, she felt Claude's fingers probing between her legs, and with all the strength she could muster, she kept her thighs together. After a moment, though, he managed to pry her legs apart and pushed one of his legs between hers. As he thrust himself over her, Althea felt his fat stomach press onto hers, and his eyes, wild with wine and lust, gleamed at her like the eyes of a wild animal that has subdued its quarry. With horror, she felt his hand roughly moving between her legs, and then something was prodding against her virgin flesh. As he panted above her, Althea thought that death would be merciful now. Closing her eyes, she prayed for it, and for an instant she thought her prayers had been answered: Claude was no longer on top of her. Opening her eyes with a start, she realized that he was next to her, a sword thrust close to his throat, and she looked up, unbelievingly, at Sir Guerre.

"You'll die for this, Guerre," Claude whispered hoarsely, his fat body trembling with fear and shock and the efforts of his former exertions.

"Perhaps, but I couldn't leave her to the same fate as Alycia." Guerre's voice was low and tense. He looked at Althea, unsmiling. "Get dressed for travel. We leave immediately."

Althea did not question him for a second. She leaped

from the bed, but the blow she had received made her head reel for an instant. Guerre grabbed her with one hand, steadying her. "Did he beat you?" he demanded angrily.

"One blow," she said, leaning against him. His body was security and she did not want to let go.

"I should kill you, Claude, but I'll spare your life for Alycia. She begged me to spare you, and even from the grave, I'll honor her wishes, no matter how misguided."

"Why are you doing this?" asked Claude quietly, now that the fear of death was gone. His tone was soft, but Althea could see the cold glitter of his eyes.

"You know why." For one moment the two men stared at each other silently. Althea realized that there was more to her rescue than her own safety, but she didn't dare ask questions. They were like two animals, each silently wishing for the other's destruction, but each unable to do what he wanted. The tension was so great that Althea heard her heart thumping wildly. She looked at Guerre. . . . He turned and urged her to hurry. Suddenly, she realized that her clothes had been removed from the chamber, and all that remained was her golden nightdress.

"Then put it on, and hurry," Guerre commanded when she told him. Turning toward Sir Claude, he lifted the sword, and ordered him to get up. When Althea had dressed, he motioned her over to the bed, and she saw that he held rope in his other hand. "Tie his arms to the headboard, and make sure the knots are tight. Don't try to grab her, Claude, or I'll run you through." It was difficult to tie him, but Claude lay still, for he knew that it was hopeless to struggle. He would get his revenge, he vowed, but it could wait.

"I think he's well tied," Althea said at last, "but won't he cry out?"

"Sir John will be unconscious for a while yet, but we'll gag him so he can give the others no notice."

As Althea approached with a cloth, Sir Claude smiled at them. "May I say one word before you silence me?" At Sir Guerre's nod, he continued. "First of all, we'll meet again, and the time will be sweet for me. Secondly, lest you value your prize too well, Guerre, take a look at the sheet."

Puzzled, Althea and Guerre looked at the sheet. Seeing their incomprehension, Claude laughed. "What innocence. The sheet, you dolts! There is no blood. She is no virgin!"

Althea stared with dismay and puzzlement at the sheet. She knew that she had been a virgin, yet the highly treasured blood that would proclaim her innocence was not there. Looking at Guerre, she saw his face grow dark with some emotion that she could not read. Was it anger? "I was a virgin, I swear it, Guerre."

He looked at her, and for one moment she thought she saw hurt in his eyes, but it quickly died. "It matters none to me," he said coldly. "Gag him." After she stuffed cloth in Claude's mouth, Guerre grabbed her arm and pushed her toward the door. Glancing back at Sir Claude, he smiled mirthlessly. "You look as if you were a trussed chicken rather than a wild boar," he said. Althea smiled until she saw Claude's eyes. They were the eyes of the wild boar, cornered but dangerous, gleaming back at her. She stood rooted to the spot, unable to tear her eyes away, until Guerre finally put his arm around her and they left the chamber, walking swiftly down the deserted corridor.

Wind and rain whipped at them mercilessly as they fled through the night. Guerre bore the brunt of the storm, for Althea, riding behind, had buried her face in his back. The storm had started minutes after they had mounted Guerre's horse and raced across the drawbridge. The guard, anticipating late arrivals for the wedding tomorrow, had left the bridge down. He recognized Sir Guerre, and thought that Althea, covered with a cloak, was some serf that he fancied. "Enjoy yourself, my lord," he called out merrily, "but it will rain soon, so do not tarry at your pleasure."

Guerre had called out an equally merry "Thanks for the advice, but I need it not. I'm more than eager for this lass."

Now, as they rode through the rain, she began to think back on their escape, and on Sir Guerre's reason for aid. He certainly did not love her. In fact, she thought at times that he despised her. He had half dragged her down the corridor from her chamber, although she had been more than eager to escape. Sir John was nowhere in sight, and Althea had longed to ask what had happened to him, but Guerre had motioned her to be silent. They could hear the revelers in the great hall, and Althea's heart was in her throat as she tried to figure out how they would escape, when suddenly Guerre opened the door of the last chamber before the gallery. Althea felt numb with shock, for this had been her mother's room, and it had always been kept locked. She had not been inside it since Rosemund's death. Now they entered easily, and Althea tried to see around the room, her curiosity momentarily stilling her fear. "How did we get in here?" she asked.

"Quiet, you little fool," Guerre said harshly. She could see he was trying to find something against the wall in the dark. Suddenly, the stone seemed to part, and Althea, her eyes growing accustomed to the dark, realized that he had sprung a hidden door. Grabbing a cloak that lay on the floor, he grabbed her hand and pulled her into a secret passageway. Then he quickly pushed the door back into place, and they were immersed in total darkness.

"We must walk a little ways down this passage to stairs that go down to the dungeon," he said softly. "I will go slowly ahead, and you hold on to my hand. Careful."

"How did you know of this tunnel?" she asked as they torturously made their way in the darkness.

"Edwina. I spoke to her after I left your chamber. She had a key, and she unlocked the door for us. She left the cloak for you too." Althea concentrated on following Guerre, but her eyes filled with tears as she thought of Edwina's loyalty. How she would miss the faithful woman who had been like a mother to her.

"Here," said Guerre sharply, "We're at the stairs. Be very careful."

Slowly, they made their way down the black staircase. Althea heard something flutter over her head and gave a little shriek.

"What is it?" said Guerre, tightening his grip on her arm.

"A bat, I think," she said fearfully, grabbing his tunic.

"By the Rood, you stupid wench," Guerre hissed. "Careful or you will push us both down these accursed stairs."

His voice was filled with disgust, and Althea felt both silly and sad. It was ridiculous that she should be frightened by a bat when a much worse danger could meet them at any moment. Had Claude been discovered yet? she wondered. They had been gone for about twenty minutes, but she doubted that anyone would think a half hour to be a long time to consummate a marriage. She shuddered inwardly. Thank God she had escaped Claude's clutches. Even here in the dark staircase she could see his leering, fat face, and her stomach gave a lurch of disgust.

Her thoughts were interrupted by Guerre's sudden stop. "I see some light ahead. We must be nearing the dungeons. Do you know if your father is keeping anyone in there?"

She thought a moment. "Not that I know of, and I'm sure that I would have heard if he had imprisoned one of the serfs."

"Good. Then there will be no guards. But just in case you're wrong, don't utter a sound till I speak to you."

They proceeded down the stairs and Althea saw that the light did get brighter. Finally, they reached the bottom and paused to listen for a guard. Hearing nothing, they moved slowly down the corridor. Althea's heart felt as if it would burst with fright. She had dreaded the dungeon for as long as she could remember, and it was only the desperation of their situation that had enabled her to conquer her fear and enter. As they moved down the long passageway, she looked at the cells and thought of all the misery this place had seen. Which one, she thought with mounting horror, had been her mother's cell? Mercifully, they did not pass the room used to torture prisoners, but Althea knew where it was and what it held inside. Once, when she had run off to see Magara, she had been caught, and Sir Richard had dragged her down to the torture chamber. With malicious cruelty, he had explained in detail the purpose of all of the equipment: the rack, the thumbscrew, the whips, and the branding irons. When she had been almost faint with terror, he had laughed and told her that she would see some of his equipment put to use on her if she were ever caught at Magara's again. It had taken her many months to overcome her fear and visit her aunt again.

Sick with anxiety, she wondered what her father would do if he caught her this time. Would she meet the fate of her mother, even more horrible than the dreaded torture chamber? Would she die in agony at the stake? These thoughts almost paralyzed her. She barely realized that Guerre was pushing open a door. Seeing no one in sight, he pulled her outside. She breathed the fresh air as if it were the gift of life, gulping it in gasps. Guerre peered into her face, shocked at how pale she was.

"Are you all right?" he demanded. "You almost collapsed in the dungeon, and now you look like death."

"That place brings back terrible memories for me, but now I'm fine." He studied her keenly for a moment to see if she spoke the truth; satisfied, he pulled her cloak over her to cover her face, and led her quietly to a horse that was tied to a post. Swinging her lightly into the saddle, he led the horse around the corner.

"The guard will think you're a servant. I spoke to him earlier and primed him to believe that I sought a wench for the evening."

Althea nodded, and he swung himself into the saddle. Trotting through the courtyard, Althea kept her face hidden so that no one would recognize her. She prayed that no one realized yet that she had escaped. They rode through the gate and passed the guard, and after they were some distance from the castle, Guerre urged the horse to a gallop. The storm broke moments later, and now they fled through the bleak and howling night with the rain pelting their bodies. Were they yet pursued, or did the guests think that Sir Claude had difficulty in matters of lovemaking? If their suspicions were not yet aroused, they soon would be. What then? Would they pursue them tonight or wait until morning? All these questions nagged at Althea as they rode recklessly into the storm. The night seemed created by the devil. They were riding across a bleak and lonely countryside that was eerie on a clear night. With the wind and rain, Althea felt that they crossed some cursed land and would soon be caught in its sinister grasp. Only Guerre seemed real. She could feel his muscles, hard and strong, through his tunic; and pressing her body next to his, she could feel the warmth of him. It gave her comfort to know he was close, but she wondered again why he had saved her. Why had he taken such a risk? And even if they escaped, would they ever be safe from Sir Claude? Would they always be hunted, always living in fear? Finally exhaustion overcame her and her mind went blank, except for one thought. Hang on to Guerre and escape. She said it to herself over and over again, like a chant against exhaustion. She became numb to the rain, to the wind, to the movement of the horse. Reality became Guerre's body, and the words she said over and over in her head to keep herself from slipping off the horse into oblivion.

They had been riding for over two hours when she realized that Guerre had slowed the horse to a trot. They had entered a grove of trees, and the branches sheltered them somewhat from the storm. Althea lifted her head wearily and looked around. Guerre dismounted and led the horse through the woods. He seemed to be searching for something, and Althea was puzzled. Finally he stopped and tied the horse to a tree. "We are here," he said matter-of-factly.

"I can see that we are somewhere, but I didn't think this was our destination." Althea's voice was sharper than she had intended, but her nerves were taut from fear and exhaustion.

Guerre looked up at her coldly. "You should be grateful, my lady, that we reached any destination at all, other than the end of a sword."

Althea's face flushed, for she knew that the reprimand was warranted. Before she could apologize, however, he swung her down from the saddle and set her none too gently on the ground. Then with a curt "Follow me," he strode between the trees. With her wet clothes weighing her down, Althea had to struggle to keep up with him, but at last he stopped before a clearing. Actually, it was not a true clearing, Althea saw.

The treetops were so thick and so close together that they formed a roof of sorts, shielding them from the rain. It was as if Guerre knew it existed, Althea thought.

"I had planned to come here," he said as if reading her mind. "I discovered this place on our way to your father's castle. I was hunting and I literally ran into this spot. Sit down, while I make us a fire."

Althea sank to the ground and watched him silently as he worked. She saw that wood and kindling had been carefully left here. It was then that she realized with shock that Guerre had planned to abduct her before he ever laid eyes on her. Her heart thudded in her chest. What had she gotten herself into? she wondered desperately. But then the image of Claude passed across her eyes and she felt calmer. Whatever lay ahead had to be better than life with Claude.

CHAPTER FIVE

Guerre quickly put together the twigs and logs that were needed for a fire. His eyes had adjusted to the meager light in the clearing. The rain had stopped, and the moon had come out. It was a mixed blessing, he thought sardonically. Now they could see where they were going, but their pursuers could also travel more quickly. As he worked, he quietly studied Althea. She was sitting on the ground, her arms around her knees, which were pulled up to her chest. The hood of her cloak covered her head, and she had wrapped the wet garment around herself in a futile attempt to ward off the dampness of the night. The girl looked wretched.

At last he had his revenge on his brother-in-law, he thought. A smile creased his face, but it was filled with bitterness. If only they had known, his father and he, what sort of man Claude truly was, they would never have urged Alycia to take the Count du Vendome for a husband. It had seemed like such a good match, since Alycia, who was beautiful and noble, had only a small dowry. By the law of primogeniture, Guerre's father, Sir John du Reims, second son of the Duke du Marton, had inherited only the title of count, and a small but strategically important castle. Sir John's brother, the present duke, had graciously offered a small dowry to Alycia, and Claude, a widower, taken with her beauty, had asked for her hand in marriage. Sir John and Guerre had been pleased, for Alycia had talked of entering a convent. Remembering back, Guerre felt overcome with remorse. They had practically forced her to marry Claude, and the poor girl, motherless since the age of six, had tearfully left her father and brother and gone to the Castle du Vendôme. Guerre and his father congratulated each other on having taken care of the girl's best interests, and had then immersed themselves in the affairs of their estate. Claude and Alycia lived about fifty miles away, too great a distance for a quick trip. They postponed visiting her for quite some time—a mistake that Guerre would always regret.

The fire caught, and he added twigs to it. He glanced at Althea and saw that she had fallen asleep. With more tenderness than he thought he was capable of feeling, he gently picked her up and placed her near the fire. She murmured in her sleep but failed to wake, totally overcome with exhaustion from her ordeal. He sat back down and warmed his hands by the fire. He would not sleep this night. Their pursuers would now be on their trail, and he and Althea could rest here only shortly before resuming their flight.

As he sat by the fire, he looked at Althea and frowned. Damn, he thought angrily to himself, he had never expected her to be so beautiful. He had never anticipated the feelings that this girl would stir in him, a combination of lust, desire, tenderness, and anger. And she was a whore to add to it all. Claude's comment about the unbloodied sheet had affected him more painfully than he ever thought something could. Better to stay clear of her, he decided. But at least he had gotten his revenge, and had still kept his vow to his sister.

Guerre stared into the fire, his black eyes penetrating the flames as if he were trying to conjure up answers in the glowing embers. His mind's eye saw nothing but the past. He saw his father slowly start to tire, and then become ill. The old knight had made light of his sickness, but Guerre saw the old man's pain and by January, when the storms of winter chilled the castle, he knew his father would not live to see the spring. It was at that time that the message had come from Alycia that she was with child and would deliver in June. Her message, delivered by one of Claude's

servants, was brief, but she asked that her father and
brother visit her as soon as possible at Castle du Vendome.
Guerre was puzzled at her request that they visit in January, for he knew that Alycia was aware that only necessary travel was attempted in the dead of winter. Turning
his attention to his dying father, he put Alycia's strange
request down to a pregnant woman's whim. Another
tragic mistake, he mused to himself.

The old knight passed away in March, his end consumed
by pain. Guerre then had decided to visit Alycia and tell
her about their father. Alycia had met him in the courtyard at Vendome, and he was instantly distressed at her
appearance. Although her belly was large with child, the
rest of her was thin to the point of gauntness. Her hands
were like little bird claws, and her collar bones jutted
out above her chest. The once plump and merry face was
now gaunt. Could pregnancy do this to a woman? he had
asked himself. Alycia had thrown her arms around him,
crying with joy. But as she buried her face in his strong
arms, she whispered, "I will explain all later. Do not ask
questions in front of Claude." He had pushed her away to
look into her eyes, but before he could utter a word, a
booming voice from behind hailed him.

"Greetings, brother. We had no idea you would visit us,"
welcomed Sir Claude. His manner was hearty, but Guerre
sensed a feeling of irritation beneath his welcome.

"Greetings to you, Claude," Guerre had said, putting
his arm around Alycia protectively. He looked at her
smiling but thin face and wondered if he should tell her
about their father. He didn't know if she could stand the
shock, but she would have to know eventually.

"Alycia, I fear my visit brings bad tidings to you." He
hesitated for an instant and she looked at him sadly.

"It's father, isn't it?" she whispered.

"Yes."

Both were so moved with emotion that they could not
speak. Guerre held her close as tears silently moved down
her cheeks.

Finally, Claude, who seemed at a loss for words, patted her shoulder. Did Guerre imagine it, or did Alycia cringe slightly at Claude's touch? He looked at his brother-in-law and saw that the sorrowful expression did not look quite genuine. He also noted that Claude had put on even more weight since the wedding, and that his face was quite mottled from wine. Something was wrong at Vendome, but remembering Alycia's warning, he asked no questions.

"That is why we did not come to see you in January, Alycia. Father was too ill to travel." As he spoke, he felt Alycia stiffen, and saw an expression of anger flit across Claude's face, almost instantly replaced by an oily smile.

"I didn't realize that you invited your brother and father to visit us in January, Alycia." Claude's words were silky, but Guerre sensed the anger behind them.

"I didn't." Alycia's lie took Guerre aback, and he hoped that his surprise didn't show on his face. "I sent a message to them telling about the coming baby." Her fingers squeezed Guerre's arm, and he picked up the tale.

"We were overjoyed at the news and would have liked to come," he said easily. But he couldn't resist adding, "I would hope that our visit wouldn't have been unpleasant to you?"

"Of course not. I merely was surprised that Alycia would have forgotten to mention such an important invitation." Claude rubbed his hands together cheerfully. "Let us go to my chamber, for it is silly to stand in this chill wind when we can enjoy a flagon of wine with our talk."

Claude's cheerful manner showed that he had quite forgotten his father-in-law's death, and Guerre began to feel an intense dislike for his brother-in-law. He vowed to speak privately with Alycia, but Claude stayed with them until it was time to dine.

As they entered the great hall of Vendome, Guerre was surprised to see a woman sitting at the head table. Alycia's cheeks reddened at the sight of her, but she quickly took her place at the table. Guerre sat next to his sister, and then came Claude, with the woman on his right.

Seeing Guerre's questioning expression, Claude said, "Let me introduce you to Lady Mathilde. Her late husband was one of my vassals, and she is seeking temporary shelter with me. Poor widow."

Guerre acknowledged Mathilde's greeting, but noted that the beautiful, raven-haired woman did not fit the description of a poor widow. Her clothes did not indicate mourning, but rather seduction. The tight bodice of her red tunic clung to her breasts, outlining her nipples clearly, and she wore a heavy scent, like musk, that kindled the senses. If her eyes had not been so cold, and her smile so sweet, he would have been interested, but her expression made him wary. He had had enough experience with women to recognize a predator.

The atmosphere at dinner was strained for everyone except Claude, who ate heartily and consumed a great deal of wine. He had talked cheerfully, ignoring the sadness and tension on Alycia's face, the ironic smile on Mathilde's, and the brooding look on Guerre's. Finally, Alycia excused herself, claiming indisposition due to the news of her father's death. Mathilde left shortly after, reminding Guerre of a cat slinking away.

Alone with Claude, Guerre decided to get some answers. "My sister looks ill. This pregnancy does not go well," he stated bluntly.

Claude looked into his wine glass. Assuming a look of sorrow, he said, "I fear not. She is far too frail to be a good brood mare."

Guerre stiffened at Claude's callous words, but he forced himself to be calm. "She is young, and this is her first child. Have you been taking necessary care of her?"

"What a question. Of course." Claude's look of outrage seemed genuine. Nevertheless Guerre did not believe it.

"I meant no disrespect. I am her brother, and it is natural for me to be concerned about her welfare."

Claude took up the game. "Of course. But I think I should tell you that your sister does herself little good. Perhaps it is the delusions of pregnancy, but she has taken on some jealous ideas that have no foundation."

With a sickening flash of intuition, Guerre suddenly knew what was coming, but he held his anger in check and waited for Claude to continue. His brother-in-law seemed to be framing his words carefully. Finally, half smiling, he looked up, and Guerre realized that Claude didn't care if he believed the lie he was about to tell.

"I'm afraid that your sister has taken it into her head to be jealous of poor Mathilde. She actually thinks that I have taken her to bed."

At this pronouncement, the two men stared at each other. Guerre thought how wonderful it would be to kill Claude there and then, but as he sat motionless, trying to control his rage, he forced himself to think. Would Alycia thank him for killing her husband and the father of her coming child? Many men kept mistresses, although few as crudely as Claude. Would she hate him for harming Claude? Before he acted, he should find out. Also, stupidly, he had come with only his squire, leaving his experienced men-at-arms at home. He could not hope to escape and take Alycia. He had to bide his time.

"I truly hope that she's just consumed with the maladies of pregnancy, Claude. For your sake." The threat behind Guerre's words was clear.

"Of course that's what it is, and I hope your remark was not intended as a threat."

"Only if it is true, and you have wronged my sister."

Claude had given him a penetrating look, and Guerre felt he could read his brother-in-law's mind. Sir John had fathered Guerre ten years before Alycia, so Guerre was no callow youth. He was an experienced knight with a reputation for being a ruthless but fair fighter. Few had beaten him at the sword or in a tournament. Claude did not want Guerre du Reims for an enemy if it was not necessary. Better not to antagonize him until he found out if Guerre believed his story. Time would prove what course of action he should take. Until then, it would be far smarter to be diplomatic.

Their conversation was interrupted by the approach of a woman servant, who half ran into the great hall. "My lord," she cried, "the Lady Alycia's time has come!"

Both Claude and Guerre rose. "But she is not due till June! Three months early!" cried Claude.

The woman nodded. "But the shock of her father's death may have brought it on early. And she is so frail, and has gone through so much." The woman's voice was accusing.

"Get back to her, woman, and keep us informed if anything changes." The meddling bitch, he thought angrily. He turned to Guerre. "I am going to my chamber to wait. You might want to do the same."

Guerre only nodded, his mind on the woman's words.

Claude left the hall, but Guerre sat at the table and waited. He and his father had made a terrible mistake in not learning more about the Count du Vendome. As he mulled this over, the fire died in the hearth, and as the evening deepened into the night, he finally drifted into sleep.

Suddenly, a hand shook him awake, and before he could utter a sound, the woman who had come before indicated silence with a finger to her lips. "Come with me. She wants to see you."

Following the woman, Guerre experienced a feeling of terrible dread. As they entered the passage that led to Alycia's chamber, the woman spoke. "I must tell you the truth. She is dying, but she wants to speak with you before we call Sir Claude."

"She can't be dying," whispered Guerre hoarsely, as if his words could dispel the truth.

The woman looked at him sadly. "'Tis true. She delivered a stillborn boy an hour past, but she bleeds so badly that there is no hope. She knows, so be brave."

She pushed Guerre into the brightly lit chamber, and Guerre saw the priest praying at the foot of the bed. Guerre looked with horror at his sister. She was the color of wax, as if all her blood had spilled out of her. But the pitiful little mouth smiled, and Guerre's heart broke.

"Come here," she whispered. He knelt by her side, and tears filled his eyes. "Guerre, I am dying. Yes, it is true. Listen. I know that you have guessed about Mathilde. You are not stupid."

"I will kill him for this," he vowed in a choked voice.

"No. That is what I do not want. I want no stain of murder on your hands, my brother. Let me go to my rest knowing that. So we can meet in heaven some day. Promise me, please."

Guerre looked at Alycia. She was fading before his eyes. Everything in him wanted to reach out and destroy Claude, and his fury and grief were so great that he couldn't speak. It was Alycia's gentle fingers squeezing his hand with the last of her strength that made him grant her dying wish.

"I promise," he said, and with those words she closed her eyes for the last time.

"I promise not to kill him," he repeated to himself. "But I will make him pay for this. I will avenge you, Alycia. I will follow him, and visit him, and know him, until I find where to strike. But I won't kill him. On that you have my word."

Guerre drew his eyes from the fire and looked over at Althea's sleeping figure. Here was his revenge. He had taken Claude's intended wife and humiliated the Count du Vendome. All would hear of the man who had lost his bride on the nuptial bed, and Claude would be the laughingstock of France and England. But as Guerre watched Althea sleeping like a child, he knew it had been more than revenge that had motivated him. When he had dragged Claude off Althea's soft body, rage had flamed through him—rage that Claude had dared to touch this girl. But they said she was a whore, and the daughter of a whore, and he knew that she must be avoided at all costs. Desire mingled with disgust, and he grew restless.

He put out the fire with dirt, carefully destroying any trace of their presence. It was unlikely that Claude's men would find this spot, but he wanted no trace of their trail to be found. Althea still slept the deep sleep of exhaustion, and she did not stir as Guerre moved around her. He forced himself not to look at her as he worked, afraid of his reaction. But finally he could put off the inevitable no longer. They had to break camp. He reached down and shook her shoulder roughly, trying to ignore the blonde tendrils of hair that escaped from under the hood of her cloak. She was so deep in sleep that he could not wake her, and the feel of her body under the cloak suddenly aroused him. Furious with himself, he grasped her roughly, shaking her till her blue eyes snapped open in shock and fear.

He stared at her intensely for one brief moment, and then let go of her. "Get up. It is time to go," he said coldly.

CHAPTER SIX

When they left the secret clearing, Althea was again filled
with the fear of capture. As Guerre urged his great war
horse, Le Fer, to a canter, she could almost feel their pursuers at their backs. But as they rode along and nothing
unusual occurred, she began to relax a bit. The sun broke
through the morning mist, and Althea looked around with
curiosity. In her whole life, she had never been farther
than five miles from her father's castle. Now here was an
entirely new world. At first their path traveled along a
crest overlooking the Irish Sea, and Althea looked at the
turquoise water with longing. Then they started inland,
and the unexplored forest held her attention. Magara's lessons on nature now came back to her, and she looked eagerly at different plants and trees. With surprise, her
sharp eyes spotted the yellow flowers of the mistletoe, and
tied to the plant the red ribbon that let followers of the Old
Religion know that a priest or priestess lived nearby. She
had opened her mouth to exclaim to Guerre when she suddenly thought better of it. He was not from these parts and
would be suspicious of the Old Faith. In fact, Holy Mother
Church had declared that followers of the Old Faith were
heretics, perhaps even witches, and should be stamped out
with good Christian zeal. It had taken Magara's gentle
teaching to allow Althea to see that love and worship of nature were not in conflict with the love of Christ and all the
saints.

So Althea did not comment on the mistletoe and kept all
other observations of the forest to herself. In fact, Althea
was not inclined to speak to Guerre. Her first attempts at

conversation had led to curt, cold answers, and Guerre had made it plain that he did not want to talk to her. At first she had felt hurt, but after a while her pride began to change the hurt to anger. Who was this man to treat her so contemptuously? Granted, he had saved her from Claude's grasp. But why? And why did he now treat her with such scorn?

As she mulled over these questions, she also felt the strange stirring of another emotion. She had to put her arms around Guerre as she rode behind him, and since they were traveling at good speed, she had to hold on tightly to escape falling. Guerre had removed the chain mail vest that he had worn last night, and beneath the soft wool tunic that he wore, she could feel the warmth of his body and the strength of his muscles as he guided the horse. She could not help but compare his strong, masculine body to the softness of Claude's, and she was surprised at how pleasant it was to hold on to Guerre.

In all her life, Althea had never been kissed or hugged by a man. Her father's touch was a slap of his hand, or a beating that left her bruised for days. As for the other men of the castle, they knew full well the fate that would befall them if they touched Sir Richard's daughter. Nonetheless, life in a castle was a life of little privacy, and the act of love was no secret to Althea. Holding Guerre so closely awakened feelings in her that she didn't know she had. But as she relished the closeness of his warmth and strength, she also began to despair. Guerre obviously didn't even like her. His coldness had made that plain to her, and if he had saved her from Claude, it was for reasons other than desire.

As they rode along, Althea noted that they followed the path of a river. She could barely make out the water through the thickness of the surrounding trees, but occasionally she could catch a glimpse of the sunlight on the river. By watching the movement of the sun, she knew that they were traveling west to east. She wanted to question Guerre on their destination, but she was too afraid of his brusque manner. She decided that it would be wise to irritate him as little as possible, so she kept silent.

After a while, they came to a bridge that spanned the river, and Guerre urged Le Fer across the rickety wooden planks. On the other side of the river, he stopped and turned in the saddle. Shading his eyes with his hand, he looked at the sun. "I think our best move would be to turn south," he said.

Althea was startled; she had assumed they would head into the heart of England. "We turn toward Cornwall, then?" she asked.

"Yes. They would not expect that of us. Cornwall is an unfriendly land, although beautiful along the coast. The men of Cornwall do not like outsiders any more than you temperamental Welsh. They would not expect us to seek succor there."

Seeing Althea frown, he laughed. "Don't look so worried, little one. I have kin in Cornwall, but Claude does not know that. Tonight we will sleep under the stars, but tomorrow we should reach Prwyntn Abbey, where we will rest in comfort for the night. In four days' time we should cross the border into Cornwall."

"But isn't Cornwall a great distance from Wales?" Althea asked, still puzzled by this choice.

At this moment, Althea looked so beautiful and earnest that Guerre found it difficult not to stare at her. He had not had a woman in a fortnight, and his eyes lingered with longing on her soft red lips. He felt desire rise in his loins, and he thought how easy it would be to take her here and now. For one instant he almost lost control as his glance dropped to Althea's curving breasts, but then his eyes returned to her face. Something there stopped him. Perhaps it was the look of innocence in her blue eyes, or the gentle but determined set of her lips. Somehow, he didn't want to take her quickly and brutally like some drab from the villages. His mind warred with his body, but the mood was broken when she called his name.

"What?" he asked, trying to remember what she had

asked. His face flushed with desire, and it was difficult for him to concentrate.

Puzzled, Althea repeated her question. "Is it not far to Cornwall?"

"Leave the traveling plans to me, Althea. I know where we must head." Guerre had not meant to answer her so sharply, but his frustration made him bark at her.

The hurt expression on her face disturbed him still more, making him long to take her in his arms and comfort her. He turned abruptly and kicked Le Fer into a canter. Althea gasped at the sudden start and involuntarily grabbed on to him tightly to keep from falling off the horse. Tears of hurt confusion filled her eyes as they rode along. What had she said to anger him so? As time passed, anger replaced her depression. Guerre was like all men. Just like her father. Cruel and moody, with a wicked temper that lashed out at innocent people, especially women. Well, she would act accordingly, she vowed. Guerre would see her only as a cool, reserved companion. She would never let him see that she felt anything else for him. She would squash those warm feelings that he aroused in her until they were only a memory.

If Guerre had turned around, he would have been tempted to laugh at the determined look on Althea's face, but he was intent on his own thoughts. In trying to avenge Alycia, he had embroiled himself in something deeper than he had intended. Althea was supposed to have been a pawn in the game of revenge against Claude. Now he realized that he had abducted her because he really wanted her. This was unexpected, and totally unwelcome. He had had many women in his life, but none had reached his mind and heart. His prowess as a lover had been well known, and he was a welcome guest in many a noblewoman's bedchamber, but he had never fallen in love or been distracted like this. For over an hour he had been lost in his own thoughts, harassed by an inner turmoil that seemed more dangerous to him than the real pursuer chasing them.

* * *

As the sun traveled across the sky and the shadows
lengthened, Althea began to feel hungry. She had not
eaten since the night before, and then she had been too
nervous to take more than a mouthful of some gruel
Guerre had prepared. He had stopped today only to drink
from a stream and to let the horse rest, and Althea was too
proud to say anything to him. As hunger and exhaustion
began to take their toll on her, she began to feel faint. Forcing herself to concentrate on something other than her
own discomfort, she looked at the surrounding country.
They had entered the mountainous region of Wales, although the trail they took kept them in the valleys.
She gazed at the rugged mountains, whose peaks were
shrouded with mist. They looked brooding and mysterious,
and she could see why so many legends had been told
about these forbidding but magical peaks. On many
nights, wandering minstrels had entertained at the castle
with tales of the ancient people who had once inhabited
this land, and who had fled into the mountains when the
Christian church gained a foothold in Wales. Althea, hiding in the gallery to hear the minstrel, would listen raptly
as the bard would sing of these ancient people who were
her mother's ancestors.

Now, as the sky clouded over and the mist swirled above
them, Althea believed that the mountains of Wales could
contain anything, real or supernatural. Magara had once
told her that she should not fear the Old Religion, for it
held much good. The healing arts that Magara practiced
came from these ancient people who had now become a legend to their own descendants. Althea was a practicing
Christian, but she saw no conflict with the Church of Rome
and Magara's worship and love of nature. In fact, to her
they seemed to go hand in hand. Nonetheless, she had
never felt the power of the Old Faith as she did now, when
she looked around at the citadels of the ancients.

A light cold rain began to fall, adding to Althea's misery. She was chilled to the bone, and hungry, and the hope-

lessness of her future began to weigh her down. She felt faint again, and her grip on Guerre began to slacken. As if sensing a change in her, Guerre slowed Le Fer and turned in the saddle to look at her. Exhaustion was etched on her face, and he was appalled to see how white she had become. Used to long days in the saddle and the hardships of military campaigns, he had schooled himself to withstand hunger and fatigue, and had forgotten that a slip of a girl would be suffering far more than he. Quickly, he dismounted, and pushed Althea forward in the saddle. Then he remounted behind her and started the horse into a slow trot. "Lean back against me, Althea," he said with a gentleness that surprised her. "It'll be easier for you to ride this way."

Althea leaned back, and the feeling of faintness turned to one of peace and drowsiness. Just as she started to drift into sleep, he spoke. "Up ahead is an inn. We dare not stay for the night, but we'll eat and rest for an hour."

"Thank God. I'm famished," she answered, not seeing Guerre's smile at her sudden revival. He was relieved at her appetite; if she was hungry, she probably was not ill.

It was almost dusk when they arrived at the Inn of the Caernwelwyn. Althea could barely make out the bright red letters on the signpost that hung near the gate. They entered the small courtyard, Le Fer gingerly stepping around the chickens that filled the yard. No one was in sight. They dismounted, and the delicious aroma of stew reached them. Althea sniffed the air hungrily.

Guerre told her to wait outside while he took the horse to the barn. As she huddled in the shelter of a huge old oak, attempting to avoid the drizzling rain, two men came out from the side door of the inn. They didn't notice her presence in the gathering night. She watched them carefully, thinking that she had never seen two such disgusting-looking men in her life. One was short, about her height, and very skinny, with a large nose and pointed chin. He looked exactly like a rat, and his tattered clothes, which were too large, hung on him so that he resembled a boy dressed in a man's clothes. The other was huge, both in height and weight, with black matted hair and a droopy mustache, and Althea could see from where she stood that his face was covered with sores. The two men were talking softly, something about having been thrown out of the inn for not being able to pay the bill. They were arguing about what kind of revenge they would use to get back at the innkeeper. The tall one wanted to go inside and wreak havoc on the place, but the rat was urging caution, saying there would be other ways to get even. Suddenly, as if sensing her presence, the rat whirled around and spotted Althea by the tree.

"What have we here, Ruthin?" he asked the fat man, although it was obvious that he did not expect an answer. He sidled up to Althea, with Ruthin following behind him. It was obvious to Althea that Rat, as she had mentally named him, was the smarter of the two.

"Why, Ruthin, 'tis a pretty wench that we have here," continued the small man, coming closer to Althea. She stepped back in repulsion; when he smiled, he showed his yellow teeth, and the stench of his breath nauseated her. "Me name is Johnny the Mouse, and this here is my friend, Ruthin," the man said, jerking his thumb at the giant.

Althea almost smiled at the accuracy of Johnny's name, although *mouse* did not convey the evil aura the man gave off. She said nothing, praying that Guerre would return soon.

Sensing her distress, Johnny poked a dirty finger in her face, and she jumped back. "We have a nervous filly here, Ruthin," he said with a chuckle. "But spirited in the hay, I wager you."

Ruthin nodded happily, his huge grin revealing that he owned only two teeth, which looked like yellow fangs. He put out a large paw and tried to stroke Althea's breast, but she was too quick for him. She leaped between the two men and darted for the inn, but Johnny the Mouse grabbed her by the waist, almost knocking her over. She was amazed at the strength of the little man, and fear made her reckless.

Reaching up, she scratched his face, drawing blood. With a cry, he held on tighter and went for her other arm. With one sure swift movement, he pushed her down on her knees, and then on her back.

"Now that you're not on your feet, missy, perhaps you will be more friendly," Johnny cackled. He thrust his face closer to hers, and the putrid stench of his breath made her stomach reel. "Now, for a start, your name," he hissed.

When Althea did not answer, he slapped her across the face. She remembered that Guerre had said they should use false names, so she blurted out, "Mary," the first name that came to her mind.

"Well, Mary, no one marks the face of Johnny the Mouse and gets away with it." He turned toward Ruthin, who was drooling with excitement. "Now, Ruthin, what punishment should we meet out to this reckless minx? A whipping perhaps?" Ruthin's face reflected his disappointment. "Well, if that doesn't suit you, let me think." He leaned back, pretending to consider, but Althea could see the leer on his face. "Ah ha, I've got it," he said. "We'll teach the lass a little respect, and combine business with pleasure." As if to give meaning to his words, he began to move his hips suggestively, and his hand reached for Althea's breasts.

Suddenly, before he could touch her, he was kicked off Althea and sent sprawling on the ground. As Althea leaped to her feet, she saw Guerre standing there, his face black with rage and his sword drawn. "Prepare to die, you dirty dog," Guerre said with cold deadliness. As he raised his sword to strike, Ruthin lunged forward, and Guerre stepped back. In that instant, Johnny scurried into the woods and disappeared. Only Ruthin was left, and one could see by his confused expression that he had only the mind of a child. Guerre hesitated, undecided about whether to kill Ruthin or release him. The big man stood looking helplessly for his friend.

After a few moments of consideration, Guerre sheathed

his sword. "Listen, you fool, your partner has deserted you."

"He's my friend," the man said with sullen stubbornness.

"Well, he's a bad one, and you would do well to find another for company," said Guerre.

"Can I go?" the man asked. Shifting from one foot to another, and watching the forest carefully, he seemed undecided whether to flee or stay.

"Go," said Guerre menacingly, "but if I see your friend again, it will be the death of him, and probably you, too."

At this the man lumbered into the woods, and Althea began to tremble. "The small man was so vile," she whispered, close to tears.

Guerre put his arm around her. "Don't worry, Althea. They won't bother us again. They thought you were alone, and so were bold."

"Like rats," Althea said with disgust.

"Yes, but they'll keep their distance now. They feed on the unprotected, and you have me for safety."

At the unexpected gentleness of his voice, Althea glanced up at him in surprise. He looked down at her, a smile hovering on his lips, his rugged face seeming younger and softer in the failing twilight. He gave a little chuckle and cupped her chin with his hand. "I never saw a lady who attracted so much misfortune. I can't leave you for a second without something happening. I can see that being your champion is going to be a full-time job."

"Since you took on the task with no request from me, my lord, I don't think you should complain," Althea said tartly.

"Unfair, but well put," Guerre said with a laugh. "I could argue the point that you didn't want to remain with Claude, but I'm famished."

"Me, too," Althea said, laughing.

The strain between them was eased, and they entered the inn with anticipation. The friendly innkeeper, a huge burly man, welcomed them warmly, and his wife made a spot in front of the fire for them to eat and warm themselves. Guerre introduced Althea as his wife, and told them about the incident in the courtyard.

"I would have killed them both if I had seen," the man said angrily. "They are a bad lot, they. Tried to drink here without paying, and harassed my wife. No good, those two! People in these parts stay away from Johnny the Mouse and Ruthin."

"Well, I think I scared them from returning here for a while," said Guerre, pouring himself some wine.

"I hope you're right, my lord," the innkeeper said uneasily. "Those two are sneaky bastards whose work would not be done in the light of day."

"Are they robbers?" Guerre asked.

"Worse. 'Tis said they have been known to rob the dead."

Althea looked at the innkeeper in horror. To think that those monsters had touched her!

"Don't fear, Althea. Men like that are cowards who would never face a foe that could fight back. That's why they prey on the dead."

"But it's so disgusting. And they touched me." Fatigue, hunger, and fear combined to bring tears to her eyes.

"Ah, come now. Don't dwell on it."

He could see that Althea was at the end of her rope, and he knew he must calm her down. "Come, let me move your chair closer to the fire. And shame on me for not pouring you some wine. I have lived too long in my lonely keep and have lost my courtly ways." He laughed at his exaggerated good manners, and soon had Althea smiling, too.

The innkeeper's wife returned with two large bowls of the best-tasting stew that Althea had ever had. Along with it, the woman served fresh bread, still warm from the oven, and large chunks of homemade cheese. It was an excellent meal, and Althea and Guerre ate well. Guerre then told Althea about his life in France, and about his escapades in battle, although he was careful not to mention Alycia. He knew that soon he would have to explain that story to Althea, but he wanted to wait until he felt sure she would understand. Althea, in turn, told him a little about Magara and her life in Grydwyn Castle.

"Your father is a hard man, Althea," said Guerre grimly as she discussed her life. She had not meant to tell him so much, but the good food, plus several glasses of wine, had made her relax, and she talked more freely than usual.

"Yes. I know it is my duty to love him, but I cannot. I can see why my mother was unfaithful to him." She stared so sadly into her wine, looking so innocent and troubled, that Guerre experienced an overwhelming desire to caress and comfort her. His pleasant reverie was suddenly broken by shouts of alarm, as the innkeeper's wife ran into the room.

"Fire! Fire!" she screamed, her face distorted with fear.

"Where?" demanded the innkeeper and Guerre simultaneously.

"The barn!"

The men flew out the door, and Althea, thinking quickly, grabbed up a pitcher of water. The other woman, gaining control of herself, grabbed a blanket, and the two ran outside. The barn was burning on one side. Guerre and the innkeeper took the blanket and water.

"Get more water and another blanket," yelled Guerre as he and the innkeeper hurried to the barn. The women raced furiously into the inn and were soon back, but Althea realized with horror that only the innkeeper was fighting the fire, and that Guerre had taken the blanket and had entered the barn. Sick with fear, she ran to the entrance where smoke was billowing out, screaming for Guerre.

Just as she was about to go in after him, he appeared leading his stallion, whose head was covered with the blanket. Althea grabbed him by the arm, tears of relief falling down her face, but he shook her off. "Take Le Fer, and I will go back for the other horse." Before she could protest, he had raced back inside.

Althea led the great war horse to a tree, where she tied him up, her eyes glued all the time to the barn. The innkeeper and his wife were both furiously beating the fire with blankets, and she forced herself to run over and help, although the entrance was not visible from the blazing side of the barn. As she fought the flames, she realized that most of the fire was not the barn burning, but some hay next to it. In seconds they were joined by Guerre, and in her relief, Althea beat at the fire with even more strength. In a few minutes the flames were quenched, and the exhausted people stood back staring at the mess.

The innkeeper wearily looked at Guerre. "There's no question about it. The fire was set deliberately."

Guerre nodded in agreement, a grim look on his face. "You think it was them?" he asked, although it was more of a statement than a question.

"This would be typical work for those two vermin," the innkeeper said.

With a shudder, Althea realized that they were talking about Johnny the Mouse and Ruthin. "At least the fire didn't cause too much damage," she said quietly.

"And the horses are safe. Let's go have some wine," said the innkeeper. They followed him back to the inn, and all sat down in front of the fire, silently thinking.

Finally, Guerre broke the heavy silence. "Do you think they'll return?"

"I doubt it. They probably feel repaid and will be fleeing to a safer place. This isn't their country. They come from Festiniog and seem to wander through every several months or so. I think it will be a long time, if ever, before we see them again."

Guerre looked with concern at the innkeeper. "We had only planned to dine with you, but if you would like us to stay the night, we shall."

"No need, but thank you," the man said. "My three sons, all strapping lads, will be back shortly. They went to Wyndow Village for a wedding, and they'll soon return."

"Well, then, I think we better be on our way," said Guerre, rising. "Thank you for your kindness."

"Thank *you*," said the innkeeper, warmly grasping

Guerre's hand. Soon, Guerre and Althea had again mounted Le Fer, who seemed undisturbed by the fire, and after being thanked by the innkeeper and his wife for the tenth time, they set off down the road into the darkness.

CHAPTER SEVEN

When they could no longer see the friendly lights of the inn, Guerre turned slightly in the saddle. "I suppose you want to know why I chose to leave?" he said with a hint of amusement in his voice. Although she could not see his face in the dark, Althea was reassured by the tone of his voice. Before she could answer, he continued. "We must remember that we are being pursued, and though I think Claude and his men are going east, rather than south, I don't want to take any chances. Men can so easily storm an inn, so I think we're safer in the open."

In the present excitement, Althea had almost forgotten Claude, and now her worries on that issue surfaced. "I hope they don't find us," she said with a shudder. "It'll surely mean the end of me."

Guerre laughed. "And for me, too, little one. So we had best be careful and take our chances with those two bastards. Although I think that this time they are gone for good."

Guerre spurred his horse into a slow canter, and they rode down the path. It was a beautiful evening, although quite chilly. Althea held on to Guerre for warmth as they rode. The moon was near full, and the night was clear, so they could see the land easily. The road had left the wood, and they were now traveling across a flat meadow filled with spring flowers, whose scent filled the night air with a sweet fragrance. Althea felt exhilarated by the wind blowing through her hair and the sway of the horse beneath her. Never had she felt more alive than she did at this moment, holding on to Guerre as they rode through the night. Suddenly, from sheer joy, she laughed out loud, and Guerre, as if sensing her mood, called out a wordless cry to the horse. The stallion broke into a gallop, and they raced through the land.

They rode with abandon for several minutes until Guerre abruptly pulled on the reins. "Why did you stop? It was breathtaking," she asked, frowning.

"Over there. Look."

Althea followed his hand as he pointed to the west. Something huge loomed in the darkness, but she couldn't identify it. "Do you know what it is?" she asked.

"No, but we will soon find out." He turned Le Fer in the direction of the dark shape. They rode slowly, and the moon, which had gone under a cloud, suddenly reappeared; the darkness in the distance took shape.

Althea gasped at the large, mysterious stones that stood silhouetted against the night sky. They were not a regular rock formation, but, rather, three large stones standing on end, as if placed there by a giant. The moon, which was behind the stones, cast a shadow, and the design of the stones and shadow was almost a perfect triangle. So mysterious was the sight that they stopped and stared as if seeing something not of this world.

"It's like a place in England that I've passed through," Guerre said quietly. "They called it Stonehenge. This is much smaller, but it's the work of the same men, I'd wager."

"I've never heard of Stonehenge," Althea whispered.

"It's in the southwest of England, on a vast plain. It's like this, but much larger." He dismounted and helped Althea off. Leading the horse, they walked slowly toward the stones, each of which was the height of ten men.

"How did they get here?" Althea asked, puzzled.

"No one knows for sure. Legend says that an ancient people brought them here from far away so that their priests, called Druids, could perform their pagan services. They're very old, and shrouded in mystery. The people in England stay away from Stonehenge, for legend also says that human sacrifices were part of the ceremony, and the serfs fear the ghosts of the sacrificed."

Althea looked at the stones with awe, but she felt nothing sinister about the place. Instead, she sensed that something magical existed here. Thoughts of Magara and the legends of the bards crossed her mind, and she felt as if she were coming home to a place in time that was part of her. She turned toward Guerre, and she realized that he was watching her intently, his face a brooding mask in the moonlit night.

Wordlessly, he reached out and pulled her toward him, and she looked up and smiled. His face seemed as if it were carved of the same stone that towered over them; only his eyes were bright and alive. He pulled her into his arms, and his hands ran through her flowing blonde hair while his lips feverishly sought hers. For one instant, Althea thought to resist, but the urgency of his lips, and the sweetness of his tongue teasing hers, drove all thoughts except desire from her mind. His lips now sought the hollow of her throat, and instinctively, Althea arched her head back. Although he held her gently, she could sense his passion, and this knowledge made her dizzy with a feeling she could not understand or control.

Then, as suddenly as he had taken her into his arms, he stopped. He held her away from him so that he could look into her eyes. For one instant that seemed like an eternity, he studied her, and Althea saw different emotions war in his face. At this moment, she no longer feared him, and a slight smile came to her lips. As if that smile were the answer he had been seeking, Guerre again drew her into his arms and kissed her deeply.

Releasing her, he spread his cloak on the ground and drew her down so that she lay on her back. Althea looked up at the night sky filled with stars and at the towering stones that rose beside them, and she felt as if everything were beyond her control. Something even older than these stones was ruling her now, making her body ache with desire. Yet mingling with her passion was a fear of the unknown, and even of Guerre. She had never felt this way in her life, and the emotions that were searing her soul frightened her.

Sensing her confusion, Guerre cupped her chin and turned her face to his. "You shiver, little one. Is it the cold or my passion that makes you shake like a kitten?"

"Both," Althea answered honestly. "I don't understand what I am feeling."

Slowly he lowered his lips to hers, and then gently kissed her neck. "I can at least help you with the cold, Althea. Let my body warm yours till you become so hot you will welcome the night chill."

His voice was husky with desire, and Althea felt the passion that he had kept in check start to unleash. This both aroused and frightened her, and she turned slightly away from him. "Please!" she whispered.

He heard her, but he did not know whether it was a plea for restraint or an invitation of desire. Perhaps he knew instinctively that it was both, for when his lips once again found hers, she offered only slight resistance before opening to him. His lips moved to her throat, and his tongue gently tickled the hollow where her pulse throbbed. Not thinking, just feeling, Althea strained her body upward, and gently, his hand pulled down her bodice and released her breasts to his touch. He stroked them softly, still sensing that she was frightened, and he forced his lips to move slowly as they traced a path from her throat to her nipples. He heard her cry out when his lips took her nipple into his mouth, but he would not let go of her, and his tongue teased her until she moaned with passion.

Then he pulled up the skirt of her tunic, and in a moment she felt his hand caressing her thighs. With his other hand, he pushed the skirt above her waist, and Althea was suddenly overcome with fear. She tried to push him away, but he took both of her hands in one of his. "Don't, little one. You can't stop me now." Althea continued to struggle, but then he began to stroke her gently, persuasively, and her struggle turned to the delicious stirrings of pleasure.

He pushed her legs apart, and his fingers sought the hot, moist spot inside her. His fingers stroked her over and over, and she felt as if her need would become unbearable.

When she felt that her whole body was consumed with fire, he suddenly stopped and quickly stood up. "I don't think you're cold any longer, are you, little one?"

"Please." This time he heard only the cry of passion in her voice.

Quickly he pulled off his tunic, and she saw the dark, curling hair on his chest. The moon was bright, so the night hid nothing from her eyes. Fascinated, she watched him as he undressed. Guerre was a warrior whose body was shaped and hardened by the demands of war. In combat he had few equals, and his sinewy body was his most valuable weapon. He could fight for hours without tiring, his muscular arms controlling his great war horse and also wielding the heavy sword and axe that were the weapons of every knight. In tournament or joust, he could outthrust almost any man when he charged with his sharpened lance. It was this power and strength that Althea saw now. His arm muscles and wide shoulders gleamed in the moonlight, and she could see that his stomach was hard and flat. As he pulled off his breeches, his long, hard, muscular legs were exposed, and Althea noticed several long scars on his thighs. And then he removed the tight undergarment that covered his manhood, and Althea gave a small gasp of wonder. For a moment that seemed suspended in time, he stood above her, his long legs slightly apart, his manhood straining upward with desire.

Then he slowly knelt beside her and reached for her hand. She tried to pull away, but he whispered, "Don't be afraid," and placed her hand on him. She held it, frightened for an instant, but then she began to move her hand, caressing him gently. He groaned with pleasure, and seeing this encouraged Althea to stroke him harder. After several moments he stopped her and helped remove her gown. In seconds she, too, was naked, and he leaned over her body, his lips kissing her breasts with an urgency that excited and enflamed her. As his tongue sucked on her nipples, his knee slowly pushed her legs apart. She cried out in fear as she felt him place his manhood between her legs, but as his shaft began to tease her, she clutched him tightly, not quite understanding why her body was pushing toward what she feared.

"I can wait no longer, my love," he whispered huskily in her ear, and with a cry, he thrust into her. The pain tore through her, and she screamed. He pulled back, puzzled at her cry.

"What is it, Althea? Don't you like it?" he asked anxiously.

"I did until it hurt," she admitted.

Dumbfounded, Guerre stared down at her. He had not thought her a virgin, but now he realized that Claude had not finished what he had started last night. With a cry of joy, he sat back and laughed.

Althea tried to sit up, furious with his laughter, but he held her down. "Why are you laughing at me?" she demanded.

"I am not laughing at you," he said with a chuckle, "but at Claude and myself. Don't fear, little one. Now that I know that you are a virgin, I will be gentle."

Still outraged, Althea fought to get away, but he pressed her closely to him and began to kiss her neck.

"Let me go!" she cried, trying to claw at his face.

"Never," he whispered with an intensity that made her stop. "You are mine, Althea, now and forever. You will love what I do to you tonight, and our lovemaking will claim you for my own." Holding her down with one hand, he pushed her legs apart with his knees and began to stroke her with his hand while his lips sought hers. At first she fought him, but his strength and passion overcame her, and she moaned with pleasure.

"This will hurt, but I will make it as painless as possible," he said. "Bear it for me, Althea, and soon you will love it." He moved slowly into her, and she bit his shoulder in pain, but her body arched upward to meet his, and slowly, so slowly, he pressed into her, each thrust growing more and more insistent. As his arms tightened around her, and his body pounded into hers, she once again was overcome with the immense strength and passion contained in Guerre. And as his desire was fired to greater heights, so was hers. The pain was now gone, and as she felt Guerre lose control and begin to ride her with unleashed hunger, her own body responded. Waves of pleasure washed over her, and she became wild with the blazing need he had aroused in her. Finally, she reached the pinnacle of ecstasy, and as her passion spilled over to every nerve of her body, Guerre clasped her tightly to him and cried out his moment of supreme pleasure.

As they lay looking at the stars and relaxing in the afterglow of love, Althea became lost in contemplation. Puzzled at her silence, Guerre leaned over and kissed her nose. "What are you thinking about, little one?" he asked.

Althea smiled at him and sighed contentedly. "I was just thinking, Guerre, that now I am a woman, for I know all about the act of love."

He smiled at her satisfied little face and chuckled wickedly. "There is a lot more to the act of love than that, Althea, but never fear. I'll be only too glad to show you the rest."

"Like what?"

Kissing her tenderly, he said, "Never mind. You'll find out. But I promise you, it will be as nice as this."

While Guerre slept, one arm thrown across her chest protectively, Althea thought again about what had happened earlier. Never had she imagined that making love could mean such ecstasy, or that loving a man could bring such peace and contentment. Two days ago she had been a lonely child, abused and despised. Fear had been her constant companion, and the future a time to be dreaded. Now she was a woman, beloved and loving, and the future was going to be wonderful.

They would marry in France and live there, she imag-

ined. Of course there were many obstacles to overcome.
Claude, naturally, would be a big problem. He had threatened them when they had fled the castle, and she knew
that he was a cunning and dangerous man. But they would
solve that problem when they came to it. Tonight was not a
night for worry.

Althea looked at Guerre and smiled. He looked so peaceful when he slept, and so much younger. His dark hair
curled around his forehead, and his lashes were much longer than they appeared when he was looking at her. Perhaps it was because his dark eyes were so piercing when
they stared at her that she didn't notice anything else. She
had met many knights before Guerre, but none had been
his equal, she decided. Then a thought crossed her mind
that made her frown. He must have had many women before her. Jealousy overwhelmed her, and she felt like
scratching the face of any predecessor who had had him.
She was surprised, for she had never felt jealousy before.
She mused for a moment on this, and then realized that
she had never had anything to be jealous about before now.
Well, she would be philosophical and take the good with
the bad. Anyway, Guerre loved her, and there would never
be any other woman for him now that he had found her.

Having settled the problem to her own satisfaction, Althea watched the shadows that the stones cast on the
ground. Suddenly, she was aware that one of the shadows
moved. Puzzled, she thought that perhaps her eyes were
playing tricks on her, but it made her nervous. She hesitated to wake Guerre. Why wake him for naught, since all
appeared calm. He was exhausted, not having slept since
two days past.

Her fear increased as the moon suddenly went behind a
cloud, and the night became darker than before. She
strained to listen for a sound but heard nothing. Finally,
she convinced herself it was nothing and tried to relax. Sleep was just starting to come to her when she heard
a sound. Before she could cry out, something was thrown
over her head, and she fought desperately to throw off the

blanket that covered her. As she screamed and fought, she felt Guerre rise, and then slump again to the ground. The heavy thud of a blow told her that Guerre had been injured.

Suddenly, she was dragged to her feet, and the blanket that had covered her fell away. To her horror, she looked into the face of Johnny the Mouse. She turned to Guerre, only to see him unmoving, either unconscious or dead, blood oozing from an ugly gash on his head. Above him stood Ruthin, smiling and holding a club. With a cry, Althea tried to run to him, but Johnny held onto her arm. Althea fought with the desperation of the damned, but the little man was wiry and he finally knocked her to the ground. Before she could get up, he jumped on top of her.

Pinning her to the ground, he screamed at Ruthin, "The rope, you ox!" Althea still fought them, but Ruthin held her down as if she were a kitten, and Johnny quickly tied her arms behind her back. After she was secured, he yanked her to her feet.

"Well, my little wildcat, we meet again," he said with a viciousness that made her shudder.

"Let me tend to Guerre, please!" she begged. "He may die if I don't help him!"

"That would be a great pity, wouldn't it, minx?" Johnny taunted. Ruthin gave a snort of anger, but Althea felt that the huge giant did not really understand. He just copied Johnny's emotions.

"Please," cried Althea, straining at the rope. "We'll pay you anything you ask if you'll just leave us alone."

"Not as much as the Count du Vendome will pay, I warrant," said Johnny, smiling evilly. He was amused at Althea's stunned look. "We know who you are, miss, although we didn't put two and two together until after we parted company at the inn. Such an unfortunate farewell." He sighed mockingly.

Ruthin shuffled uneasily. "Let us be gone," he said, peering around. "This place gives me the fright, Johnny."

"All right, but make sure his grace is done for good."

"He's right dead," said Ruthin, nervously looking around the stones. "I'm going."

"He'd better be dead," Johnny warned. "Well, come, girl."

"No!" Althea screamed, fighting and straining against Johnny.

"Ruthin, help me with the wench," he yelled to the retreating giant.

Ruthin hesitated, as if debating this idea, and then reluctantly turned back. The huge man picked her up like a sack of wheat and threw her over his shoulder. As they walked away from the stones, Althea wept for Guerre, lying dead on the ground where they had spent their passion.

CHAPTER EIGHT

Althea slumped forward in the saddle, despair and exhaustion reducing her to a state of numbness that nothing could shake. The rope around her neck chafed her skin, but she barely felt the rawness of her flesh. Only when Johnny pulled at the rope to be cruel did the flashing pain make her respond with a moan, and she would involuntarily raise her eyes to the little monster who rode ahead of her. They were a strange caravan, and the few people they passed stared openly at them. Ruthin, who was in the lead, would occasionally burst into song, usually of a lewd and ugly nature. Johnny, riding behind Ruthin, would join in the tune, although his voice was nasal and toneless. If the song was lively, he would jerk the rope in time to the music, increasing Althea's agony. She was forced to ride a miserable mule that refused to keep up with the horses, so Johnny would yank on the rope when he wanted her to kick the beast to a faster pace. They had started off with Le Fer, Guerre's great war horse, but the stallion was uncontrollable by all but his master, and he had almost trampled Johnny to death. The horse had escaped, and Althea had been forced to ride with Johnny until they had purchased a mule.

They had been traveling east now for four days. Wearily, Althea's mind went back again for the hundredth time to the attack on her and Guerre, and to Johnny's explanation for it. The reason had chilled her blood. Hers was not to be a quick end, like Guerre's, but a dreadful fate. Johnny and Ruthin were taking her to Claude.

Claude and her father had decided on a plan for her cap-

ture. Claude would head toward England, the route that
was considered the probable one she and Guerre would
have taken. Richard would head for the south of Wales,
since he was more familiar with that territory. Johnny and
Ruthin had been traveling near the route Richard followed, and had been questioned by Richard himself. No,
they had said, they had not seen a girl or a man who fit
that description. They were sincerely disappointed, for
Richard was offering a huge reward for Althea's capture.
Later, when they had met Althea at the inn, they had not
been aware that she was the missing girl until Guerre had
appeared. Back in the forest, they had realized that both
fit the descriptions given to them. They had set the barn on
fire in the hope that Althea would remain inside the inn
while the others fought the flames. They had been surprised that a noblewoman would dirty her hands like that.
Since they were unable to abduct her at the inn, they followed her and Guerre through the night until they saw
their chance at the stones.

Althea prayed that Johnny and Ruthin would not be
able to find Richard, but late in the second day they came
across a scout from Richard's entourage, and in an hour
Althea was standing in front of her father. So completely
did she believe that he would kill her on the spot, that she
had said all her prayers to God as she rode the last few
miles to Richard's camp. She faced her father with composure, for death would be welcome to her now that Guerre
was dead.

"You have disgraced my house in such a manner that
only death would be sufficient punishment for you." His
words were measured and slow. Several of the older men-
at-arms who listened to Richard shuddered inwardly and
remembered back to a similar scene played fourteen years
prior. "You're as wicked as your whore of a mother was.
Lust grows in you like a poison that only the flames can destroy."

With a scream, Althea threw herself at Richard's feet.

"Father, father, kill me if you will, but I beg of you, please don't make me share my mother's fate!"

Frantically, she looked up at Richard's cold face and noticed that his eyes were glazed. He was looking at her but seeing another woman, and the vision was destroying his mind. Richard had lived with guilt and hate as his companions for years, and they had eaten away at his sanity since the day he had executed his wife. Now it was her ghost that came back to haunt him, and with a moan, he stared blankly at the people around him. He had retreated to another time, another hell.

Nervously, his men stared at him, and finally one left the tent. In a few moments he returned, and Althea looked up into the angry face of Lady Maura, who ignored Althea and took her husband by the arm. After removing Richard to her tent, she returned to the waiting group.

"My husband is not well," she said to his men. "From now until he recovers, you will take your orders from me." As they started to mumble, she added, "And your pay. My husband has been getting more ill with the passing of each month, and I have prepared myself for this time. You will find me a just mistress."

The men again shuffled their feet, but they stopped talking when one of the nobles who were vassal to Richard spoke. "What Lady Maura says is true. Sir Richard is afflicted with the malady of the mind, and until he recovers, we are bound by our oath of fealty to Lady Maura." Since he was the strongest of Richard's vassals, the others finally gave their consent.

Althea had been kneeling on the floor throughout this unexpected scene. Finally, she mustered the courage to speak. "Please, Lady Maura, may I have a word with you?"

Maura nodded.

"I know that I am to be executed for running away, but please be merciful and spare me the stake."

Maura looked at Althea with puzzlement. "The stake?"

"My father said I was to die at the stake, as my mother did."

Maura burst out laughing. "It was the madness talking. Your punishment was arranged back at the castle. It appears that your bridegroom still wants you, although for the life of me, I know not why. It was arranged that if we found you, we would send you to France, where he will do with you what he will."

Althea was speechless. She feared Claude almost as much as the stake. She had never dreamed that he would still want her. It must be that he planned a terrible revenge.

"I have arranged for your two captors to take you to France," Lady Maura went on. "I have given them coin for expenses, but their reward will come from Claude."

"When do we go?" asked Althea, praying for a respite.

"Immediately."

Althea's recollection of her last conversation with Maura was interrupted now by a painful tug at her neck. "Wanted to see if you were awake, my lady," Johnny said with a malicious laugh. "I don't want you to fall off your pretty mule and hurt yourself. No reward for us if harm befalls you."

Althea glared at him. The disgusting swine! But what he said was true, and it had been a blessing in disguise. Maura had warned that she must arrive in France in good condition. Claude would not want any damaged goods. So Johnny and Ruthin had to restrain themselves from injuring her in any way other than what was absolutely necessary. Also, she discovered that her two captors had not followed her and Guerre directly to the stones, but had lost their trail for a short time. This delay had prevented them from discovering Althea was no longer a virgin. Therefore, they did not dare rape her. What if the count were to inspect her first, and then kill them for deflowering his bride? This forced restraint made them nasty, however, and the painful rope was only one way they had devised to taunt Althea. At times she could not decide what was worse, the terrible present, or the terrifying future.

She had much time to consider this question, for their travel was slow. The weather turned rainy, and they spent the days traveling through mud so deep it threatened to drown the horses. The cold, damp wind whipped at them, and Althea began to grow feverish. It didn't seem to bother Johnny and Ruthin, though, and they refused to take shelter. In fact, her complaints seemed to spur them on to longer days in the saddle.

It did not take long for both her mind and body to grow totally numb. Her mind barely registered the rocky trail that had led them out of the mountains of northern Wales. And her body did not feel the wind and rain that slashed at them for two solid days as they crossed the marches into England.

It was not kindness or concern that made them take shelter at the small convent. It was greed. It was fear of losing the girl, and thereby losing the reward. She had become delirious that fourth morning, and her body was consumed with fever. Johnny saw the gold disappearing with her death, and he swore to fight. They had passed the small convent only an hour before, so he threw Althea over his saddle and turned the group around. The nuns made a warm pallet for Althea in the barn, and one of the nursing sisters made bitter brews for her to drink and warm poultices for her chest.

During the night, the fever broke, and although Althea was terribly weak, Johnny decided to move from the convent. He sensed, like the animal he was, that the nuns did not like him and Ruthin, and they might try to detain Althea. He wrapped Althea in several blankets and placed her in front of Ruthin so that she would not fall off the horse. He led Althea's mule, and he carried a dead chicken that he stole from the convent. They traveled only until Johnny felt safe, and then he made camp, covering Althea with the blankets and making a soup from the stolen fowl.

He forced the girl to drink the broth, and then pushed her close to the campfire. In the morning, he could tell that she was much better, and he breathed a sigh of relief. For the next few days he was more considerate of Althea and made their traveling day shorter. But as her health returned, his concern lessened, and he soon forgot how easily he could lose his prize. He and Ruthin again began to bait and torment her, and Althea drew on all her courage to survive this ordeal.

They passed through tiny hamlets so isolated that strangers were a rarity, and the whole village would come out of their hovels to gawk at the procession. Seeing Althea with a rope around her neck, covered with mud from head to toe, the villagers took her for a felon of some sort and often threw mud and stones at her while calling out lewd taunts. Johnny encouraged them, laughing with glee at being her jailor, while Ruthin guffawed and waved to the peasants.

At night they would take shelter in filthy inns. There were cleaner spots, but Johnny said the clientele in those places was not to his taste, and he felt more at home in the rat-infested taverns and inns. Althea soon surmised that it was primarily greed that kept them in these filthy sties, for Johnny was the worst kind of miser, carefully guarding his hoard of money.

There was another reason that they stayed in these pest-holes, and this made Althea's nights a time of dread. The lowest of prostitutes frequented these places, and Ruthin and Johnny always took two for the night. Since Althea was forced to stay in the same lice-infested chamber with them, she had to witness their disgusting acts. A few of the whores had protested an audience, but all had come around when Johnny would reluctantly part with an extra coin. Althea would turn her head to the wall and try to blot out the revolting grunts and cries that filled the fetid room. Once they had forced her to watch, but her look of sheer panic had upset the two whores, and Johnny finally gave her a good slap and told her to turn her face to the wall. How impossible, she thought, with tears streaming down her face, that this perverted mating could be the same act of love she and Guerre had enjoyed. Each night she would cower on her filthy, flea-infested mattress, trying to blot out the sounds, and tears would course down her face until sleep took her into merciful oblivion.

Youth and courage finally roused Althea from her lethargy. She was too young to die from grief, and her natural spirit was beginning to kindle a spark of defiance at her fate. As each day passed, the sadness that had engulfed her receded, replaced by an urge to defeat her adversaries. She did not know how she would do it, but she would survive and avenge Guerre's death.

With a new curiosity she surveyed the countryside. The empty, wild spaces of Wales were long behind them, and as they headed for Dover, the area became more populated. They met many more travelers on the highway and at the inns, and Althea found she could forget her two jailors in her contemplation of the fascinating characters who shared the road to Dover. There were merchants, their mules loaded down with goods, who tried to sell the trio all manner of things; and pilgrims bound for the holy spots of their choice. Some of these pilgrims scourged themselves with whips as they walked along, and Althea saw with horror that their naked feet bled into the dusty road as they walked. What terrible crimes were they trying to expiate? she wondered. And then there were the pitiful beggars. Used to the self-sufficiency of her father's castle, Althea had never been exposed to the homeless, hopeless poor of England. She watched, sickened, as men with stumps for arms and legs, their bodies covered with sores, crawled into the road to beg for alms. Rage consumed her when Johnny and Ruthin almost trampled one such soul who could not crawl out of the road quickly enough.

Occasionally, a nobleman and his entourage would pass. Wales was far away from the world of fashion, and Althea noted with great interest the garb of the aristocracy. The

men wore, not fighting armor and furs, but silk and velvet.
Their multicolored tunics were embroidered with elabo-
rate designs and had sleeves so long that they often
reached to the wearer's knees. Their women were also
decked out in splendor, with gowns of the most vivid hues.
They wore headdresses that had multicolored veils attached to the top. These veils blew in the wind as they
rode, and made a colorful sight. Both men and women wore
long, pointed leather shoes that seemed faintly ridiculous
to Althea.

Nonetheless, her interest in her own looks came back
abruptly, and at the next inn, she demanded a bath. Surprisingly, Johnny agreed. Althea washed and dried her
hair, luxuriating in the feeling of cleanliness. The innkeeper's wife also provided Althea with a new gown, a
plain blue linen garment that had belonged to the woman's daughter, now dead three months from the lung disease. Althea thanked the woman for her generosity and
put on the gown with relief. The red linen tunic that she
had been given at her father's camp was ripped and
stained beyond repair. Nevertheless, she carefully washed
it and let it dry by the fire. She didn't want to have only
one garment with her.

Johnny and Ruthin taunted her the entire next day
about her bath. Evidently, neither one had ever taken one
in his life, considering it to be a terrible health hazard.
They relied strictly on rain or a fall in a creek to get clean.
And that, thought Althea ruefully, explained the terrible
stench that surrounded them.

They had been traveling close to a fortnight when at last
they reached the sea. Dover was a bustling little town,
with ships from all over Europe docked in the harbor. Althea hoped that Johnny would have difficulty in finding a
ship bound for France, but luck was against her. He
quickly found passage on the *Marietta*, bound for Calais
the next morning. They spent the rest of the day walking
the streets of Dover, looking at the fascinating stalls of

goods that came from all corners of the world. Althea gazed longingly at a bolt of white silk embroidered with pale yellow flowers. She would have chosen that cloth for a wedding gown if Guerre were still alive.

The following morning they set sail for France. Althea was delighted to find that she was a good sailor. The sea was rough, but she was exhilarated by the adventure, and the captain of the ship, John Roffe, captured by her beauty and enthusiasm, spent as much time as he could explaining different things about the ship to her. Ruthin and Johnny were both seasick and could barely lift their heads, but they were not worried about Althea escaping, so they let her roam the ship at will.

It was only twenty-two miles from Dover to Calais, and the winds were with them. As Althea sat on the deck and watched the approach of the coast of France, her mood began to darken. Here, in France, she would meet her fate, and the prospects were not good.

"It's a pretty sight, isn't it?" John Roffe had moved next to Althea, and his words broke into her sad musings.

"Oh, yes," she said with a wistful smile at the approaching harbor. "I was thinking how free a sailor's life must be. You're only bound by the wind and the ability of your craft."

"Well, we have a few more restraints," laughed the captain. "But once it's in your blood, nothing can take a man from the sea." He then began to point out the various ships in the harbor, telling her interesting facts about each one.

"Why does that one ship fly a black flag when all the rest are colored?" she asked.

The captain turned quickly to where Althea pointed, and stared intently at the ship that was off to the right of the rest in the harbor. Althea was surprised to see how grave his expression had become.

"My God," he finally whispered. "It's arrived."

The captain continued to stare at the black-flagged ship, and Althea's curiosity grew. After a few moments she ventured to ask if the ship belonged to pirates.

"Would that it did, my child," the captain said sadly. "A pirate ship would be a thousand times more welcome than what that poor, ill-fated vessel carries. The name of the ship is the *Montreanna*, bound from Venice, and she wears the black flag because she carries the plague." The captain shook his head. "You have never heard of a plague like this, child. They call it the Black Death, for its victims turn black and grotesque before death mercifully spares them more agony."

"Why did they let the ship dock?" she asked with a tremor in her voice.

"Probably didn't know that the pestilence was on board. Someone must have died after they disembarked, and now the ship is quarantined. God help the poor souls on her."

"Do they know what causes this plague?"

"No. Some say it is the curse of God on man for all the wickedness in the world, but I don't believe that."

"Did it start in Italy?"

"No, in Asia. But ships first brought it to Italy. It has started to spread north, but I didn't think it had reached this far."

"Is there something we can do to protect ourselves?"

"We can pray," the captain replied solemnly. Then, "Perhaps it isn't too bad. Maybe only the ship is contaminated. I better go now and help in our docking. Be sure that I will dock far from the *Montreanna.*" He turned and left, but Althea stayed and watched the black flag waving above the stricken ship. It reminded her of a vulture circling its prey.

Ruthin and Johnny joined her on deck as the ship was docking. "I'll get our stuff and we'll be off," Johnny said after the docking.

"Don't rush," Althea said nonchalantly. "We can't leave until the inspectors come on board."

"What inspectors?" Johnny asked, grabbing Althea by the arm and yanking her toward him.

Althea grimaced with pain, but her voice was calm. "The inspectors who will check for the plague."

Johnny's grip on her arm slackened. "What plague?" He had seen his own mother, the village harlot, die of the plague when he was eight, and fear of illness had always stayed with him.

Althea pointed to the *Montreanna.* "Yon ship carries the Black Death, the captain said. We're to stay on board until we're cleared."

Johnny felt a cold sweat break out on his brow. "We leave immediately. Damn the captain."

"I doubt that we can," Althea said, relishing Johnny's fear. "See the soldiers who guard the gangplank?"

Johnny muttered a vile oath when he saw the soldiers, five in all, who stood at the end of the plank. Escape from the ship was impossible. Forcing himself to be calm, he gestured to Ruthin to sit, and then began to pace the deck. Ruthin promptly fell asleep, causing Johnny to curse his fearless, uncomprehending mind with all manner of acts, both natural and unnatural. In fact, Althea heard him curse everyone, from herself to the poor souls on the *Montreanna.* She realized that Johnny frightened easily, and made note of it. As for herself, she hoped they would not be allowed to land for quite some time. At the end of the gangplank waited not only the plague, but Claude and his revenge.

It was a good two hours before four men dressed in the garb of merchants boarded the ship. All four looked petrified with fear, and they kept glancing around as if they expected the plague to reach out with long, bony fingers and grab them. Then one of them, a tall, skinny man with a long, wispy beard, addressed the captain. "Do you carry any sick on this ship?"

"None that I know are sick," the captain answered honestly.

"That is not an encouraging answer," barked the tall, thin man.

"But a true one. I have ten crewmen and three passengers, and all seem to be in fine health. Also, we have come from England, and the plague has not reached there."

The four men seemed to brighten at the news. "Bring all on deck so that we can see for ourselves," said one of the other officials.

The captain whistled, and in seconds the entire crew had joined them on deck. The four men, who were obviously terrified of contamination and detested their enforced roles of inspectors, did not come too close. Instead, each person had to come forward and turn around. It was not a careful inspection, but they seemed satisfied. In moments they gave clearance for landing and rushed off the ship with relief.

As Johnny, Ruthin, and Althea prepared to disembark, the captain came forward. "I would recommend that you make haste in leaving Calais. I have been told that there are only five confirmed cases in the town, but the Black Death can spread quickly. You will be much safer away from the port."

They all nodded and bid the captain good luck. Althea turned back and waved at the kindly man who had befriended her, and then stepped off the gangplank onto French soil—to meet her fate.

CHAPTER NINE

They took the captain's advice and left Calais as soon as they purchased three horses. Althea knew that Johnny would have preferred to buy only two, but that would have slowed their progress, and he wanted to put the plague as far behind them as possible. Althea smiled wryly to herself, for the disease had done her some good—sparing her the disagreeable experience of riding behind Johnny or Ruthin. As they rode through the peaceful countryside of northern France, she thought with horror of the dreadful sight they had seen in Calais. While they had been purchasing their horses from an innkeeper who sold livestock on the side, one of the patrons, a tall, burly man, suddenly began to vomit. As the others stared at the poor man, who was still vomiting a disgusting black mess, he fell to the floor, groaning in agony. The innkeeper had rushed over and prodded the man with his foot, but he refused to touch him. Finally, the sick man's son had rushed inside. As he tried to lift the heavy man off the floor, the boy accidentally ripped the tunic his father wore, revealing ugly black pustules on the man's chest. With a scream of fury, the innkeeper then literally kicked the man out the door, while the poor son, who could not have been more than ten, tried to help his father. The last they had seen of them was the boy dragging his father down the narrow street.

This shocking incident had increased their haste, and Johnny had been so intent on leaving he even omitted tying Althea with the rope. They had galloped out of Calais as if the devil were at their heels, which perhaps he was. Nothing but evil could create such a horrible disease, thought Althea. They were now some ten miles inland and would soon stop for the night.

Althea prayed that Johnny would get lost in such unfamiliar territory, but the map Claude had left with Lady Maura was very clear. In fact, they were now traveling along the Vendome River, named for Claude's family. The area was pretty, with rolling hills and green meadows, and the spring wild flowers gave off a wonderful scent. It was just like the description that Guerre had given her when he had told her what their lives would be like. But although the land was how he had pictured it, the future she was envisaging was not the one they had been planning.

They finally rested for the night, and any chance of escape was made impossible by the ropes that Johnny once again tied around her. They rose with the dawn and started their journey. Althea's heart hammered in her chest as they drew closer to Claude's castle and the dreadful fate that she knew awaited her. She vowed to make the most of the last remaining hours of freedom. Hungrily, she sniffed the scent of the wild flowers and the fresh spring grass. Her ears sought the song of the birds and the gentle hum of the honeybees, and her face turned toward the warmth of the sun with eagerness. She watched the peasants at work in the fields, the cows grazing in the pastures, and the spring lambs dancing in the meadows, imprinting their images on her mind to remember when she could no longer ride out to see them. She was so intent on her careful study of the world that the hours passed quickly, and the sun reached its zenith and moved farther to the west before she realized that it was midafternoon and she was ravenous. They had not eaten since last night. Pride warred with hunger, for she did not want to speak to Johnny, but she desperately needed food. As she debated what to do, she glanced at the horizon, and her hunger died. Ahead, visible on a distant hill, were the turrets of Castle du Vendome.

They were still some two miles away from the castle, but

Althea could readily see that it was a large fortress, much larger than her father's keep in Wales. It was strategically positioned on a hill, overlooking the Vendome River. The castle was square, with four turrets, one on each corner. As they rode closer, Althea could see a small group of peasant huts on the outer side of the moat that surrounded the fortress. The drawbridge was lowered; evidently, Claude did not fear attack, she thought.

It took them about a half hour to reach the drawbridge of the castle. She had told herself she would remain calm, but as the walls of the castle threw a dark shadow over them, her hands began to shake with fear, and her heart thudded wildly in her chest. The trio made a strange picture as they approached, and she could tell that the guard on duty was suspicious. He laughed outright when Johnny pointed to Althea and said she was the count's betrothed. Great ladies did not arrive this way, but with a huge entourage of servants and retainers. He had a good mind to send them away, but there was something regal about the girl's carriage that made him wonder about her. He was a cautious man, and he decided it would be better to check with his superior before he drove them off the drawbridge. The guard was amazed when his captain quickly returned, granting the ragged trio entrance. And he was even more amazed when he saw the count himself walk out into the courtyard.

Althea thought that all could hear the beating of her heart, but she forced herself to keep her face impassive. Sitting on that wretched old mare, her blue cape in tatters from weeks of travel, her face grimy, she felt like sobbing; but years of terror and abuse at the hands of her father had taught her control. She looked haughtily down at Claude, not realizing that she was still beautiful, still arousing. It was her innocent ignorance of her own appeal, in fact, that made its effect even more intense. Besides conveying the promise of sensuous delight, the dignified carriage of her body commanded respect.

Looking up at her, Claude was pleased. He had almost

given up hope of finding her, but here she was, her spirit
still unbroken. The pleasure of breaking the bitch would
be all his. Smiling, he bowed mockingly. "Well, my lady,
we are delighted with your arrival." Althea stared down at
him silently, and her composure seemed to amuse him.
Still playing the part of the noble gentleman, he bowed
again. "I hope my humble surroundings will be adequate
for such a fine lady as yourself."

Althea was about to answer, but her eyes caught the figure of a woman coming down the stone steps that led to the
outer gallery. As she approached, Claude turned and
smiled at her, and Althea realized that this must be
Mathilde, his whore. Althea studied her closely. She was
above average in height, with a voluptuous figure. Even
from a distance, Althea could see her large breasts revealed clearly by the too-tight bodice of her tunic. She wore
her black hair loose, and it fell to her knees. As she
walked, her hair swished back and forth, and her gait reminded Althea of a cat stalking its prey. As she came
closer, Althea saw the red lips, the green eyes slanted
slightly upward, and the pale white skin. A very beautiful
woman, she thought, and a very dangerous one.

"So she has arrived," she said. Mathilde's voice was low
and husky, and Althea could hear the undercurrent of anger in it.

"Yes," Claude said with unhidden satisfaction. "May I
present to you the Lady Althea, daughter of Sir Richard of
Grydwyn Castle in Wales." The woman looked at Althea
stonily and did not acknowledge her.

Ignoring Mathilde, Claude turned back to Althea. "And
this is the Lady Mathilde, a recent widow who has taken
shelter under my roof."

Althea nodded coldly, her eyes traveling over the bright
purple silk gown that Mathilde wore—hardly a gown of
mourning. Her eyes revealed her thoughts, and Mathilde
flushed scarlet with fury. With the quickness of a panther,
she reached out and tried to drag Althea from the saddle.
Instinctively, Althea kicked out with her foot, and the

force of her kick almost sent Mathilde sprawling. The black-haired woman spat out an oath and sprang again, but this time Claude grabbed her and gave her a shake.

"Is that the way to greet our guest?" he chided. "You will make her feel unwelcome."

"She is unwelcome," hissed Mathilde, glaring at Althea. "I do not want her here."

"But I do, and I am master of this castle. You will do well to remember that, my lady." Claude's voice was light, but Althea heard the warning contained underneath, and so did Mathilde. Althea heard Johnny and Ruthin shuffling in their saddles, and she knew that they wanted their reward. As soon as Claude helped her dismount, Johnny spoke.

"Excuse me, Your Grace," he said in a sickeningly ingratiating tone, "but we were wondering about the reward."

"What reward?" Claude asked.

"The reward for bringing the wench—I mean, the lady—to you."

"I was unaware that I offered one."

Johnny, fearing the loss of his money, became reckless. "Lady Maura said that you would reward us well for bringing the girl to you. She swore it!"

Claude looked at the little man for a moment, then a sly smile spread on his face. "Well, the Lady Maura is a liar. I asked that she send Althea to me if she were found, but I never consented to pay for a reward. My God, the girl has cost me enough as it is." With a chuckle, he reached into the silk purse that he wore on the belt around his waist. "Here, this should suffice." With that, he threw two copper coins at Johnny and turned, taking Mathilde by the arm.

Disappointment overcame all caution, and Johnny began to scream vile oaths at Claude, who turned to his head guard. "Throw these two pigs out of the yard, and if they resist, kill them."

The seriousness of Claude's words penetrated Johnny's

mind, and he fell silent. Althea, Claude, and Mathilde started walking toward the gallery staircase, but Althea could not resist looking over the stone railing and grinning with satisfaction at Johnny's infuriated face.

CHAPTER TEN

Life might not be too bad after all, Althea mused, some time later in the shelter of her own chamber. From what Claude had told her, he still believed that his retention of his estate rested with keeping Althea, and she was careful not to enlighten him about Richard's true condition. And he seemed in no hurry to marry her, having made an off-hand remark that it needn't be rushed. Evidently, he planned to keep her here, unharmed but an honored prisoner of sorts, to safeguard his own interests.

Althea lay back on the bear rug that covered the bed and luxuriated in the feeling of warmth and cleanliness that was now hers. A hot bath and a clean gown had helped her spirits immensely. Contentedly, she surveyed the tower room that had been assigned to her, once again marveling at how luxurious French castles were compared to those in Wales. Two windows allowed light to enter the chamber, and beside each hung embroidered cloths that could be used to shut out the wind. One window overlooked the courtyard far below, and the other faced the countryside. Across the room from the bed was a fireplace, with a tapestry of the Madonna to the right of it. In front of the fireplace stood an intricately carved oak chair with a red velvet pillow for a seat. To the left of the chair was an oak table holding a silver vase filled with spring flowers, and a silver candle holder. Althea's bed was also made of carved oak, and had a goose-feather mattress and several overstuffed pillows. The room smelled sweet from the clean rushes that covered the floor.

She looked to her left and smiled as her eyes fell on the

only other piece of furniture in the room. A cedar chest stood next to the wall. The pretty little maid called Simonette had told Althea to help herself to its contents, and Althea had been amazed and delighted with what the chest contained. On top were three tunics of silk, one of rose, one of green, and one of blue. Below there were skirts of white linen, yellow silk, and scarlet satin. Althea had carefully lifted these out and found yet more things below the skirts. There was a silk gown of rose, and another in pale blue. There was also a gown of deep blue velvet embroidered with pale white silk, and below that, dozens of silk stockings and scarves, silk and velvet caps of every color, and several pairs of fine leather slippers.

As Althea had gone through the chest with fascination, Simonette had directed other servants in filling a wooden tub with hot water and laying out the essentials of a proper bath, such as perfume, scented rose soap, and several towels and combs. After her bath, Althea selected the gown of rose silk, a pair of silk stockings of the same color, and a pair of soft leather slippers, and Simonetta helped her dress. The gown was just a bit too small, and Althea realized that the clothes had been made for someone about two inches shorter than herself. Now, as she sat on the bed, she thought about the previous owner, and with insight, she realized that they must have belonged to Alycia, Guerre's sister. Instead of upsetting her, this made her feel closer to Guerre. Yes, perhaps things would not be as bad as she had at first imagined. Claude had Mathilde to warm his bed, and Althea suspected that would keep him occupied, with little time left for her. It was obvious that the dark beauty hated her and would tolerate her only if forced to do so.

Althea's thoughts were interrupted by the opening of the door. It was Claude. Althea noticed that he had changed into a light orange tunic that made him resemble a large melon.

He sat down on the oak chair near the fireplace and smiled at her. "Are you pleased with your chamber?"

"Yes, very," said Althea, trying to sound pleasant. No use in aggravating him.

"I was not satisfied with the escort your father provided you."

"Nor was I, sir, but I had little choice in the matter." Althea's voice was bitter.

Claude gave an amused laugh and rose from the chair. He came over to the bed and seated himself on the edge; Althea caught the full strength of his scent, a heavy sweet perfume covering the sour stench of perspiration. He reached out and ran his ringed fingers through her hair. Althea tried not to cringe, but her distaste was obvious. Instead of angering Claude, this seemed to amuse him. He looked at her like a cat who knew that he had the mouse cornered and that it could not escape.

"I see that you still are not eager for my touch, Althea," he said softly.

Althea noticed that some bread crumbs clung to his mustache, and that there was grease on his chin. He was a fat and ugly sight, but he looked far better than Johnny the Mouse. Trying to be diplomatic, she hesitated, then said, "I fear I want no man to touch me. I have decided to enter a convent and take the veil."

Claude looked at her with astonishment, and then burst into laughter. "My God, what a waste that would be. Well, Sir Guerre's prowess in bed must have been exaggerated if you find lovemaking so distasteful."

Althea had been almost as surprised as Claude when she uttered her wish to enter a convent and take holy orders, but now she was stung by Claude's derisive words, and she lied again. "I am a virgin, and no man has touched me."

"Bah," said Claude, amused. "Now you truly lie. The first night at your father's castle you were a virgin, I think. But after your escape with Guerre, I know for certain that you could not still retain your maidenhead. I am not a fool, Althea, and Guerre has a reputation with the ladies that few men could challenge."

Althea looked down at her hands. He seemed so positive that she had been seduced that lying seemed silly. But he made it sound dirty, as if she had been one of many women for Guerre, when she knew it had been an act of love. "You speak the truth, but it was no tawdry thing," she admitted in a low voice.

"Silly twit!" Claude's tone was scathing. "For you, perhaps, but for that womanizer, you were just one of many."

"That's a lie! If he had lived, we would have married. He told me so." Althea heard the tremor in her voice, and so did Claude.

"He had an excellent way with words. There are many court ladies who can attest to that. His smooth words achieved their intended end. You were a toy for him."

"No! I loved him, and he loved me. I will know no other man in this life!" Althea got off the bed and stared defiantly at Claude. "Besides, you have Mathilde to keep you company. You have no need of me."

Claude reached out and grasped her arm so painfully that she winced. "Now listen to me! I will have you tonight, and any other night that I want. You are my prisoner, and there's no escape from this castle. You may grieve for your silly love to yourself, but I want no reference to that bastard in my presence. If you anger me, Althea, I will let you rot in the dungeons of this castle till all have forgotten that you ever existed!"

So menacing was his tone that Althea was silent. She knew he meant every word he spoke, and her life depended on her compliance with his wishes. He released her arm. "The evening meal is in a few minutes. I expect you to attend. Afterwards, I will join you in your chamber, and perhaps then you will get a truer impression of the act of love." He left the room, and Althea stared down at the floor, tears of defeat rolling down her face.

* * *

Althea sat at the main table and tried to force some venison down her throat. She could barely swallow, so she sipped some wine and looked around the main hall. Castle du Vendome again impressed her with its grandness. The main hall was twice the size of her father's, and instead of bare, cold stone, the walls were hung with colorful tapestries depicting scenes from Greek mythology. The hall was crowded with retainers and servants, for Claude kept a retinue of forty knights and squires. At the main table sat Claude, Mathilde, and herself, and Althea could tell that they were the object of much discussion and joking by those who sat below the salt. Most of the knights had traveled to Wales with Claude, and she could tell by their expressions that they were highly amused at her capture.

Claude was in good spirits and indulged heavily in food and wine. The amount of food served for the meal shocked Althea. There was pheasant, swan, venison, lamb, and pastries stuffed with rabbit in gravy.

Like Althea, Mathilde ate sparingly. The woman's face was clouded with anger throughout the meal. Mathilde was furious that Althea had arrived safely, and now posed a threat to her influence with Claude. Mathilde knew that Claude frequently strayed from her bed with a serving wench, but that was far different from having him sleep with a beautiful noblewoman who was the daughter of his overlord. Mathilde looked at Althea with venom. She had been told that the girl despised Claude, but how long would it take before she succumbed to him?

Mathilde did not have long to wait, for as soon as the meal ended, Claude stood and offered Althea his arm. She rose without looking at him, and Mathilde burned in rage as the two walked out of the hall toward Althea's chamber. Then she retired to her own tower room and spent the night planning Althea's downfall.

As for Althea, the night was spent in despair and shame. When they reached her chamber, Claude sat on the bed, watching as Simonette helped Althea prepare for bed,

leaving her no time alone to compose herself and prepare
for the ordeal ahead. When Simonette began to unlace Althea's gown, Althea asked Claude if he would retire so
that she could undress privately, but he brusquely told her
to continue, and she tried not to think of his eyes on her
body as she took off her garments.

"No," he said hoarsely as she reached for the white silk
nightdress, and he curtly dismissed the servant, who
scurried from the chamber. Lazily, he held out his hand
and drew Althea toward him. She sat down on the bed and
looked at him coldly.

"Come, come, Althea," he said. "Your expression would
do credit to a nun. It does not spark my heart."

"A nun is what I desire to be. I have no wish to spark
your heart," Althea spat out angrily.

"Damn it, stop such talk," Claude said irritably. "I'll
have you if I wish, and I *do* wish."

With those words, he pushed her onto the bed and
achieved his purpose, but it was a cold and miserable
mating. Althea, feeling his weight on her, let him do
what he wanted, but she lay lifeless and unmoving below him. He tried to arouse her by licking her nipples
and fondling her between her legs, but Althea did not
respond to his touch. In frustration, he mounted her,
and for many minutes huffed and panted on top of her.
She felt him enter her, but his passion did not arouse
any in her, and she lay lifeless on the bed, praying that
he would soon finish. Finally, he gave a groan of pleasure and lay still on top of her, his weight crushing the
breath from her lungs.

Just as she thought he had fallen asleep, he whispered
in her ear, "You bitch. If Guerre had lived he would not
have kept a bitch as cold as you for long." With that, he
rolled off her and turned to sleep.

The oblivion of sleep, however, was denied to Althea. Besides the shame and humiliation of the past few hours, she
was also torn apart by Claude's words about Guerre's
other women. Was it true? She knew that he was a man ex-

perienced in the ways of love, but she had assumed that she had been something special to him. Now she doubted her own confidence. She had thought that it was love, but she knew so little. In agony, she tossed and turned until Claude, awakened by her restlessness, cuffed her on the head. She forced herself to lie still, but sleep did not come to her until an hour before dawn.

When Althea awoke the next morning, Claude was gone, and an old woman whom she had not seen yesterday was straightening the room. She sat up, suddenly famished, and saw with pleasure that the serving woman had brought her some bread and cheese.

"Good morning, my lady," the woman said. "You missed the matin service, but his lordship said I was not to awaken you."

"I did not sleep very well," said Althea.

The woman looked at her kindly, and with something akin to pity. Althea read the look and realized that everyone must know how unwillingly she was brought to France. Her cheeks flamed with embarrassment.

"I just returned to the castle late last night," the woman continued as she swept the floor. "I took leave to stay with my sister, who was ailing, but she has now recovered."

"Have you lived here all your life?" asked Althea. It was more of a statement than a question, for almost all servants were born, lived, and died in the same castle or nearby village.

"No, I come from Provence, to the south." Seeing Althea's look of interest, she went on. "I came with the Lady Eleanor, the count's first wife, when she married. When she died of the lung disease, the count asked me to stay on. I can cook the dishes of the south much better than these northerners, and so when the count wants a specialty, I'm asked to prepare it."

"I take it he must crave your good cooking often," Althea said with a mischievous grin. She had risen and put

on a white silk robe that the woman had placed at the foot
of the bed. Now she sat in front of the hearth, eating the
fresh bread and cheese.

"Not really. I have other duties. I spin and embroider."

"What's your name?"

"Rachel, my lady."

"Perhaps, then, Rachel, you might know whose clothes
these are." Althea pointed to the chest.

The woman hesitated slightly, and then answered.
"They belonged to the Lady Alycia, the count's second
wife. Poor soul."

"Did you know her well?" Althea asked, curious.

"I was her personal maid, my lady," the woman said
defensively. "She was a kind, good woman, and she did
not deserve her fate." Then, fearing that she had said
too much, she turned quickly and began to straighten
the bed.

"You mean the Lady Mathilde?" Althea said quietly.

"Yes. She's a vixen from hell, she is." Rachel turned toward Althea. "Some say she murdered her own husband,
and many who don't say it believe it. Bad blood there, I tell
you." She suddenly realized what she had said, and she
looked frightened. "Don't tell her what I said, my lady, or
it will be the end of me. Not that I fear death, but the way I
would go at her hands."

"I wouldn't say a word," Althea said with passion. "She
hates me, and I'm afraid would do me harm if she got the
chance."

"That she would, never fear. Her blood is bad. They say
her father lay with his own sister to beget Mathilde, and
then passed her off as his young wife's child. No one knew
for sure, for the wife never left the tower room. Mathilde's
father locked her in there soon after they were wed. Only
came out when they buried her."

"My God, how terrible. Why?" Althea felt a chill creep
up her spine.

Rachel lowered her voice and came close. "Witchcraft,

they say. Legend has it that he found her in the woods sticking knives in dolls and making spells, and decided to lock her up rather than turn her over to the Church."

"He loved her, then?" Althea felt sick.

"No. He wanted to use her power for his own ends. But it did him no good. They all sickened and died. First the sister, who was simple, drowned in the well; and then the three boy children, Mathilde's elder brothers, each wasted away and died. Their lands and castle were small to begin with, and as the serfs and retainers grew more nervous, they began to run away. By the time Mathilde was twelve, the family was very poor, and their keep in great disrepair."

"You were there?"

"Yes, with Lady Eleanor. We went with the priest because we heard that Mathilde's mother was dying. But when we arrived, there was only the girl and her father. They said they had buried the mother already. The priest blessed the ground and said his prayers, but something was not right. Rumor has it that she did not die, but escaped into the woods to practice her heinous crimes. Who knows?" The woman shrugged her shoulders.

"What happened to Mathilde and her father?" asked Althea with fascination.

"Soon after, Guy du Bonfont, a neighbor and lord of a small manor, asked for the girl's hand. He was four times her age, with grandchildren. But she married him, and shortly after that her father was found dead. He either jumped or fell from his own battlements. The castle is empty now. No one wants to live there."

"I can see why," said Althea with a shudder. "And Guy du Bonfont?"

"They were married for seven years, and then he fell sick and died."

"But he was an old man. He could have died from natural causes." Althea thought carefully. If he had been four times older than Mathilde when she was thirteen, then he had been fifty-two when they wed, and fifty-nine when he died. That was a great age for a man to reach. "Why do they whisper murder?"

"The Lady Mathilde was very unhappy living with him in his small little keep, and shortly before he died, she met the count. The whole countryside knew they were lovers, and the Countess Alycia was very frail. I think Mathilde gambled that Alycia would not survive the ordeal of birth, and decided to make herself free to marry the count."

"Did anyone ever prove that she murdered Sir Guy?"

"No, but the Lady Mathilde was trained by her mother. She is skilled in the ways of the devil. She was careful not to get caught."

"And then he brought her here to live, right under Alycia's eyes." Althea spoke her thoughts out loud, but Rachel knew what she meant.

"Yes, and it certainly killed her. Her grief and humiliation at their hands brought the baby on early. They both died. The sight nearly broke her brother's heart."

"He was here when she died?" asked Althea, puzzled.

"Oh, yes, and he was furious with the count for his treatment of his sister. He vowed revenge, he did. But the Lady Alycia made him promise on her deathbed that he wouldn't kill the count. He finally swore that he wouldn't, but I heard him say that he would revenge her in some other way." The woman sighed. "But he changed. He became very good friends with the count and practically lived here. I think he forgot all plans for vengeance. He even went to Wales to fetch you. . . ." The woman had been rambling on without thinking, and it wasn't until she saw Althea's stricken face that she realized what she had said.

"Oh, my lady, please forgive me. I meant you no hurt."

"I know. Please leave me now. I wish to be alone." After Rachel scampered away, still apologizing, Althea's anguish really took hold. So that was it! He had abducted her for revenge. He had found a way to strike at Claude through her. She felt sick with humiliation. She had just been his tool for hurting Claude. Suddenly everything became clear to her, and she ached with the pain of knowing. Everything was lost now, even her memories.

CHAPTER ELEVEN

Althea sat in her chamber, staring out the window that faced the meadow. It was a beautiful June day, and the sun was shining high in the sky. Spring had softly turned into summer, and wild flowers were coloring the green of the meadow with patches of red and blue. How she would love to be on a horse today, galloping through that meadow in freedom! Instead, here she sat, a prisoner of Claude's. Dismally, she looked down at the needlepoint in her lap and, with a sudden burst of anger, threw the cloth across the room.

She had been here almost a month now, and life had taken on a routine circumscribed by the three rules Claude told her she must never break. The first rule was that she could not go beyond the castle walls, although she could roam as she chose about the castle and courtyard. The second rule was that she could never miss a meal. Claude was firm on this, for he did not like to eat alone. He enjoyed the hostility between Althea and Mathilde, and was bored when the two women ate in silence. If this quiet lasted too long, he would usually bait one of them until anger overtook their control and the waspish comments would begin. Mathilde would rise to the bait more often than Althea, for her temper was more mercurial.

Althea wondered if Mathilde really loved Claude, or if she wanted to be the Countess du Vendome. It was hard to tell, but one thing was certain. Althea was a threat to her, and she would remove her if she could. Althea smiled ironically to herself, for she would like nothing

more than to give up her duties as mistress to Claude.
That was the third rule that she could not break. Whenever he wanted her, he could take her. Luckily, he preferred a passionate woman, and Althea's disinterest in
bed made his visits to her only occasional. Actually, he
did it more to punish her than to satisfy himself. Often,
after making love to her, he would leave and go to Mathilde. It was the not knowing that made Althea ill with
nerves. She never knew what night she would have to
endure his lovemaking, and he took pleasure in keeping
her guessing. Once he had made a great show of retiring
with Mathilde, but a half hour later, he came to Althea's chamber. This had upset Althea, and had enraged Mathilde, who had been a witch at the midday
meal the next day.

"You filthy little tramp," Mathilde had screamed, losing her control and menacingly waving the dagger that
she used to cut her food. She had looked like she was about
to kill Althea, but Claude had intervened, although in
great humor. He had placated Mathilde with an unfavor-
able description of Althea in bed, his voice audible to his
retainers sitting below the dais.

She had been so upset that she became physically ill
and had to run out of the great hall. She had barely
made it to the common latrines before vomiting her entire meal. Now, thinking back on that incident, Althea
frowned. She had been ill frequently during the last few
weeks, and she was beginning to worry about the cause.
She had to leave Mass yesterday when nausea overtook
her, and she had thrown up her breakfast several times
this week. She had attributed it to nerves, but now she
was uncertain.

With a start, she got up and began to pace the room.
When had she had her last flux? As she counted carefully,
she realized that it was the week before Claude and
Guerre had come to Grydwyn. That had been toward the
end of April, and now it was the end of June. She had

missed two fluxes. She could not be pregnant, could she? It was impossible! She was ill because she was so unhappy, and because she lived under such awful conditions. Fatigue and worry had stopped her flux. She was so lost in her own arguments that she did not hear the door of her chamber open, or Rachel enter.

"Is something wrong, my lady?" the old woman asked with concern.

"No. I'm just confused about something," she said in a flustered voice.

"Can I be of help?"

"I was just worried about my health. I've been rather nauseated lately," she admitted, hoping that Rachel would tell her it was her nerves.

"Have you had your flux lately, child?"

"Over two months ago." Althea's voice was dull.

Rachel hesitated, trying to find the right words. Long service with noblewomen had taught her that not all greeted pregnancy with joy. "Answer me honestly, Rachel," Althea said abruptly. "Do you think that I am to bear a child?"

Rachel looked at Althea and nodded. "It is too soon to be sure, but you have all the signs." A tense silence followed. Feeling awkward, Rachel picked up the discarded needlework and excused herself. Alone, Althea began to pace, her thoughts in a turmoil. If she were pregnant, whose child was it? She had no way of knowing, and neither man was acceptable to her now. She hated and despised Claude. He was a disgusting, corrupt man who enjoyed the torments of others. True, he had not harmed her, but he was cruel and lazy. She had no wish to bear his child.

And Guerre. She had spent every day since she realized his duplicity trying to forget his existence. It was difficult, but given time, she was sure she could harden her heart against him. How could he have told her that he loved her, when all she was to him was a tool of revenge? It made her ill with grief. She had vowed to forget him, and now she might be carrying his child!

She stared at the ceiling in a daze. Who would be worse? And then again, would she be able to tell? Would that, in fact, be the worst of all things? To look at the child and never know who its father was would be hell!

June turned to July, and Althea knew that she was definitely pregnant. In the first week of July, she decided to tell Claude. She was surprised by his excitement at the news. "Wonderful, wonderful. If it turns out to be a boy, we can perhaps plan to think of marriage," he said gleefully, rubbing his hands together.

"And if it's a girl?"

"Then it's another bastard brat for me, I think," said Claude, leering at her. "You don't think I would tie myself to you for a girl, do you? A son would be worth matrimony so that he could inherit this estate. Your father would never take up arms against his grandson's father."

Althea looked at him grimly. How little he knew Sir Richard—or his present condition. He still feared him and thought that Althea kept him secure in his position. Well, she hoped the child was a girl, for she had no wish to marry Claude.

"Of course, Althea, the child may not be mine at all but Guerre's."

So he had thought of that possibility, too, Althea realized. Seeing a possible way to escape, she smiled at him. "Yes, that's true. Perhaps now you would prefer that I retire to a convent? Certainly you would not want to have a child you could not definitely claim as your own?"

Claude gave her a cynical grin. "It makes no difference to me who fathered the brat as long as the child is considered mine. You were not listening before, Althea. The child makes my position secure. For that purpose, I need an heir."

"Your fatherly feelings overwhelm me, my lord," Althea hissed.

"I have never had any particular desire to be a father," Claude conceded. "But this is good news, and since you are so concerned about the health of the child, I will leave your cold bed for a while. Although if I desire, I will return." With that, he left.

Althea sat in her room, thinking how much she despised him. Her thoughts were interrupted by screams in the stairwell, and she realized that Mathilde was the one who was creating the commotion. Althea's door burst open, and the hysterical woman rushed in. Althea looked at Mathilde in shock. She knew that the news of her pregnancy would not be welcomed by the woman, but she had not expected this crazed creature. Mathilde's hair was disheveled, and her face was distorted by anger and tears.

"I'll kill you before you deliver that brat!" she screamed in fury. "Beware of me, for you'll not usurp my place here!"

Her words were cut short by a cuff to the head from Claude, who had rushed in with a guard. She fell sprawling to the floor, and Althea jumped up to help her. Like lightning, Mathilde reached out and scratched Althea's face, and as Althea jumped back in pain, Claude gave the woman a hearty kick.

"Pick her up and take her to her chamber," Claude ordered the guard.

Claude smiled meanly at Althea. "Remember, my lady, that I am much more fond of Mathilde than I am of you."

As he left, Althea took heed of his warning. If he would treat Mathilde like a dog, then what would he do to her?

The scene in Althea's chamber appeared to have subdued Mathilde for a while, and the next few weeks passed with relative tranquillity. The weather turned hot, and Althea spent a lot of time in her chamber, wearing nothing but her light silk robes to fight off the heat. She would look out of her tower window for hours, watching the peasants toiling in the sun, and wishing endlessly that she had the little freedom they possessed.

Then, in the last week in July, the peace ended. The castle was to host royal visitors. On Sunday, during the morning meal, a messenger had arrived, announcing the impending visit of Prince Philip du Bois, a cousin of the King of France, Philip VI. This was a great honor, and Claude had taken the unprecedented step of leaving his meal half-eaten to confer with his chamberlain about the comfort and amusement of his guests. The prince would be arriving on the morrow, his messenger had haughtily informed them, so there wasn't much time.

Althea and Mathilde sat at the table alone. Mathilde, who ordinarily would have loved such an opportunity to bait Althea, forgot her animosity in her excitement. "He's said to be very handsome, and a great admirer of beautiful women," she said happily.

"The messenger said that the prince and his retinue are traveling to Flanders," said Althea, repeating what they had been told.

Mathilde looked at Althea and shrugged knowingly. "Last March the Count du Boiselle visited with us for a fortnight. He told us all the news of court and the latest on the prince. He was betrothed to Princess Mary of Flanders last December."

"Ah, then he is spoken for," Althea said thoughtfully.

Mathilde gave her a disgusted look and laughed sarcastically. "You certainly didn't think you would catch the eye of a cousin of the king, did you? I said he loved beautiful women!"

"I meant no such thing," Althea protested heatedly. "I just thought that with a princess waiting, he would not linger here for a long time."

"Don't be a fool," said Mathilde, tossing her long black

hair in exasperation. "If there is a desirable woman somewhere, the prince would not hesitate to linger."

Her tone left no doubt about who she thought would
catch the eye of the prince, and Althea almost smiled at
the woman's vanity.

"The prince even had to leave court once for a while,"
Mathilde chatted on, eager to gossip. "He had an affair
with the Lady Bridgette, and she became pregnant. She
was lady-in-waiting to the queen, and it was a terrible
scandal. Her husband took her to their castle in the south,
and a week later she was dead."

"How terrible," said Althea, shaken.

"She was a fool. They say she took her own life, but I
think her husband killed her. They found her at the bottom of the staircase, her neck broken." Mathilde smiled,
her lips red and glittering.

Althea saw the smile and shuddered. "Does the prince
still grieve for her?"

"You are truly an idiot. Of course not! When she died, he
had already started a liaison with a Madame Harnalt, the
wife of a wealthy merchant. It was a brief affair, although
her husband was very happy about the honor of having the
prince be his wife's lover."

"The prince sounds rather cold-blooded," Althea remarked. "I feel sorry for his poor bride."

"Who cares for her?" shrugged Mathilde. "Perhaps he
can get Claude and me invited to court."

"Why can't you go now? Claude is a noble of the land. He
went to court with the Lady Eleanor."

Mathilde gave Althea a sharp look, but she saw that the
question was not meant to wound. She tossed her hair back
over her shoulder and rose. "There are several at court
who do not care for us and have made trouble." With that,
she left the hall.

Althea remained, enjoying the coolness. The prince certainly did not sound appealing. She pitied poor Mary of
Flanders, who would have to wed such a cold, heartless
man. Then a smile crossed her lips. She remembered some-

thing Rachel had told her about Mathilde and Claude. Evidently Mathilde's behavior, both during her marriage and after, had reached the court and had offended the queen. When Claude had given in to her demands to be taken to court, the word had come from Paris that they were not welcome. If Mathilde hoped to influence the prince in her favor, this should be a very interesting visit.

CHAPTER TWELVE

The next day Althea and Mathilde were ordered to stand on the battlements with Claude to await the arrival of Prince Philip. Claude had dressed in his best finery. His long, knee-length tunic of scarlet, with billowing sleeves and gold embroidery, seemed too bright for Althea's taste, but Mathilde had complimented him handsomely on his choice. He had also put on hose of gold silk, and wore leather shoes that tapered to a long point. His fingers were loaded down with jewels, and a heavy pendant of gold hung around his neck. Althea thought wryly that Prince Philip would be able to see Claude much faster than he would be able to see the Castle du Vendome.

Mathilde was even more excited than Claude, and had dressed with equal care. Althea had to admit the woman certainly was a beauty. She wore her favorite gown of emerald green silk. The gown's sleeves were heavily embroidered in red and gold thread and fell almost to the ground. The dress clung to her and clearly showed the lushness of her body. She had put on a green velvet cap with a long golden veil, although her hair still hung like a black satin curtain to her waist. Looking at her, Althea almost felt pity for one moment. Mathilde would have been a great court beauty if fate had dealt her a kinder hand at the beginning of her life. Now the highest match she could ever hope to attain would be Claude du Vendome, and although being his countess was nothing to sneer at, Althea felt that for someone as ambitious as Mathilde, it must be a bitter medicine to swallow.

Althea looked out on the valley below them and smiled.

It was a beautiful day. Up here on the battlements, she felt free and calm. She knew this was just an illusion, but she decided to savor the moment. With satisfaction she glanced down at the pale gold silk gown that had materialized with six others yesterday afternoon. Silver thread had been used to embroider the neckline and sleeves, and the gown caught the sunlight and shimmered like polished gold. It was a bit tight in the bodice, but it accented Althea's swelling breasts nicely. On her head she wore a white cap and veil, although, like Mathilde, she chose to wear her hair loose. Her golden locks fell almost to her knees, and Althea knew that she looked lovely by the way the men's eyes had followed her when she walked to the battlements. For some ridiculous reason, she was quite pleased with herself, although she couldn't figure out why. Perhaps it was the beautiful summer day, or maybe the excitement the prince's visit had created.

Althea's happy reverie was shattered when Mathilde cried out. "I think I see them," she said excitedly, pointing down the road that crossed the valley to the south.

Claude shaded his eyes and peered in the direction she pointed. "You're right." Turning toward Althea and Mathilde, he frowned slightly. "I don't need to tell you, I hope, that I expect you both to do everything you possibly can to make the prince's visit a pleasant one. Everything."

Mathilde smiled lewdly and nodded, but Althea felt herself grow cold. What did he mean by "everything"? At her frozen look, Claude gave an angry grunt, and his eyes glittered. Realizing that this would not be a good time to cause trouble, Althea also nodded. After giving her a long, hard stare, Claude turned back to the road. Althea gave thought to his words, however, and her excitement about greeting the prince was not as great as before Claude had spoken.

Slowly, the cavalcade made its way to the castle. The banners of the entourage soon became visible, and the mass of men started to take individual shapes. Althea swore that the retinue must have consisted of at least five hundred men, and Claude agreed with this figure gloomily as he tried to calculate the cost of hosting this huge party. Finally, the prince's party halted, and the trumpeter gave salute to Claude. Claude's own trumpeter returned the salute, and the cavalcade once again started forward.

"Which one is he?" Mathilde demanded.

"He's in the front row in the center, I think," said Claude. "It's hard to tell with his armor. We'll go down to the courtyard to greet them."

They descended quickly, and Althea watched curiously as the prince's party crossed the drawbridge and entered the great courtyard. It was immediately apparent to her which one of the many mounted men was Prince Philip du Bois, cousin of the king of France. He was surrounded by an aura of arrogant self-confidence that made him stand out quickly as the leader of this entourage. Claude immediately launched into a lengthy welcome speech, although before he was even halfway through, the prince impatiently removed his helmet.

Claude continued to speak, so Althea had ample opportunity to observe the prince. He certainly lived up to his legend, she thought. He was one of the most handsome men she had ever seen. Although his armor concealed his body, she could tell that he was tall and of medium frame. His light blond hair was cut to his shoulders, as was the fashion at court, and his small, blond mustache was neatly trimmed. His eyes, she noticed, were a cold blue, the color of a winter sky. Although he was only in his middle twenties, the prince gave an impression of an older strength and hardness. His face was etched with lines from the sun, and it made him appear very masculine. Althea could see why so many women thought him fascinating, although she sensed something cold and cruel in him. She could not define what, exactly, it was, but it lurked underneath the handsome face.

"Thank you," interrupted the prince in a low voice when Claude paused for breath. His tone left no doubt that he considered the speech finished.

"It is you who should be thanked, Your Highness, for

honoring my castle," gushed Claude, a little taken aback at the termination of his greeting.

Ignoring him, Philip turned toward Althea and Mathilde. "Introduce me to these fair ladies, my lord count, for their beauty makes me glad that I decided to rest my men at the Castle du Vendome."

"Of course, Your Highness," Claude said quickly. "May I present the Lady Mathilde, wife of my late vassal, Sir Guy du Bonfont. Lady Mathilde has shought shelter here since the death of her husband."

Mathilde gave a deep curtsy, making sure that her breasts were shown to their best advantage. "I am honored, Your Highness."

The prince looked thoughtful for a moment, then broke into a wide grin. "I have heard of you, my Lady Mathilde. It is a shame that widowhood has prevented your appearance at court." He was obviously laughing at Mathilde, but she was so eager to impress him that the irony in his voice was lost on her.

"Ah, Your Highness, nothing would comfort me more than to visit the court of King Philip." She looked up at the prince provocatively.

"And your presence would be a comfort to many, I would think, my lady," said the prince, quite amused. Several of his men chuckled at the innuendo. "Perhaps I could tell my dear cousin how you are languishing from grief in the country."

"Your Highness, if you could but—" Mathilde's words were cut off by Claude, who was visibly annoyed.

"And this is the Lady Althea, who visits us from Wales," Claude said.

The prince turned to Althea. For the first time in her life, she felt what it was like to be undressed by a man's eyes. The prince's smile indicated that he liked what he saw, and when Althea straightened from her curtsy, she felt his eyes boring into her own.

"I have heard of you, also, my Lady Althea," the prince said, then turned to Claude and laughed. "You are a lucky man to have two such magnificent women under your roof."

"Thank you, Your Highness."

The prince and his close companions dismounted. The men-at-arms and the grooms would camp outside the castle, but the boon companions of the prince would be entertained as their station demanded. Servants quickly showed the nobles to their chambers. The prince and his two closest friends would share Claude's chamber. The rest would sleep in the great hall on pallets.

After Prince Philip and his men had refreshed themselves, they joined Claude, Mathilde, and Althea in the great hall, where the afternoon was spent drinking and hearing the news from court. One of the prince's men, Alphonse du Chaulte, was famous for his biting wit, and he regaled them with juicy tidbits of gossip. Philip spoke little, but Althea noted that he was aware of everything that occurred.

Without the concealment of his heavy armor, she could now tell how magnificent his body was. He was slim but very muscular, a fact that was accentuated by the white silk tunic and green leggings that clung to his body because of the damp heat. And though he sat languidly in his chair, Althea sensed that he was a restless man, almost a wild animal that could spring and attack at will. She had seen only one man more handsome than Prince Philip, and that was Guerre. Bitterly, she wondered if he would always cloud her vision when she looked at other men.

She listlessly heard another story about a reckless court lady and her lover. It seemed from the conversation that half the court was cheating on their spouses. As she listened to Alphonse, something told her that she was being watched, and looking up, she met the eyes of Philip. Like a rabbit unable to turn away from the light of the torch, Althea could not take her eyes away from him. When she felt that her face was burning from his stare, he gave her a sardonic smile. It was as if he knew his power over her and enjoyed her embarrassment. Moments later, Philip's jester began to entertain them, and Althea fixedly kept her attention away from the prince. But throughout the long afternoon, Althea was aware when those cold blue eyes would be on her, and a chill would course through her body.

Late in the afternoon, everyone retired to prepare for the evening meal. Althea was pleased to find a hot, perfumed bath awaiting her, and Rachel bustling around her chamber.

"Such excitement," said Rachel, carefully smoothing out the skirt of the gown Althea would wear. "Cook is near frantic. You would not believe the food that is being prepared. And only fifty men will eat inside. The camp cooks are preparing the food for the common soldiers. The castle kitchen is in such a state that I had to leave. Why, it reminds me of when Lady Eleanor was still alive."

Althea gave a little sigh of contentment. "Did she entertain much, Rachel?"

"Oh, yes, my lady. The Lady Eleanor was highborn and had spent a good deal of time at court. There were many visitors when she was alive, and, of course, we went to court often."

"I didn't realize that you've been to court. Tell me about it."

Rachel began to chatter away, happily reminiscing about events long past. She and Althea were both so absorbed that neither heard the opening of the door. It was the shadow that caught Rachel's eye and made her look up. Althea followed her gaze. With shock, she realized she was looking into the cold blue eyes of Prince Philip. He was standing in the doorway, an amused smile on his face.

"Pardon, my lady. I did not mean to disturb your bath. I was seeking my men." He gave a curt bow and nonchalantly closed the door.

For a moment, Althea's eyes were rooted on the door, but Rachel muttered something under her breath, and the sound brought Althea back to reality. She stood up and grabbed the towel Rachel was holding for her.

"The liar. He made no mistake. Damn his arrogance."
Althea rubbed her body furiously. "He sought me out. He
was told where all would lodge!"

Quickly, Althea dried herself and began to dress, cursing Philip, Claude, and anyone possibly accountable for
what had occurred. Rachel wisely said nothing. She helped
Althea don the white silk hose and fine linen shift that
were worn under the main gown, and then stooped to
buckle the fine kid slippers with silver buckles. Althea had
selected a gown of rose-colored silk with gold embroidery
at the neckline and sleeves. The edges of the sleeves were
trimmed in lace the color of ivory. Carefully, the gown was
lowered over Althea's head, and Rachel helped hook up the
bodice. As a final touch, Rachel placed a little cap of rose-
colored satin on Althea's head and secured it with silver
pins. Attached to the cap was an ivory veil of the finest
lace. The veil fell all the way to the floor.

Althea angrily hurried away to the great hall, unaware
that she made a dazzling sight. More than one man
quickly thought of a perfect rose when she walked into the
main hall. The color of the gown was accented by the color
on her cheeks, a color which grew deeper when she found
that she was to sit on the right of Prince Philip. Luckily, a
troubadour was singing the praises of Prince Philip's royal
line during the first course, so she had time to compose
herself.

The soothing sound of the musician's voice calmed her a
little, and she looked around with interest. The servants
were busy carrying out dishes of salmon poached in milk,
mushrooms chilled in wine, small apples baked with baby
quails, and vegetables sautéed in butter and cream. These
dishes were meant to whet the palate for the main courses
to come. When these magnificent dishes began to arrive,
Althea saw how much Claude had spent on this banquet.
As the swan baked with trout, the pheasants stuffed with
sausage, and the rabbits baked with apples and honey began to pass in front of her, she wondered how she would
ever begin to eat all the food that was put on her plate. She

toyed with a piece of pheasant, feeling the eyes of the prince on her. He had not mentioned the incident in her chamber, and she had avoided looking at him. Now that she had calmed down, she thought that perhaps she might have been wrong in assuming that he had come to her chamber on purpose.

"Are you enjoying the entertainment, my lord?" she asked, hoping that the tension that she felt did not show.

"The entertainment holds my interest much less than you do, my lady Althea," Philip said. Althea felt his probing stare and knew that a blush was slowly creeping over her cheeks.

"Such modesty, my lady, is quite a novelty to me," said Philip with a laugh. "One sees it rarely in the women of the court."

"I have never been to court, my lord," said Althea, struggling to maintain her composure. He reminded her of a hunter who was sure he had trapped his prey and was now savoring the kill. With that thought, resentment flared in her. Men! All they thought they had to do was want something, and it was theirs. She was tired of being a pawn for their desires.

"You look annoyed, Lady Althea," Philip remarked. His lips were smiling, but there was ice in his eyes. Althea realized that this man did not like being thwarted and could be very dangerous, but her own temper had been rekindled.

"I hope that I am not displeasing to you," Philip said in a way that indicated that the thought never seriously entered his mind.

"Not at all, my lord," lied Althea, "but you do have a tendency to stare."

Philip looked at her sharply. "The ladies of the court don't object to any admiring glances I cast their way. Am I to believe that you do?"

Althea saw that Claude had noted the look of irritation on Philip's face, and she knew that she would be in serious trouble if he thought that his visitor was displeased with

her. She forced herself to smile. "My lord prince, I don't
have the sophistication and style of the great ladies of the
French court. I have spent my entire life on my father's
land in Wales, and polished visitors were few in that rugged land."

Philip stared at her intently, trying to see if she were
mocking him. "You were not so shy, my lady Althea, when
Sir Guerre du Reims beckoned to you."

Althea turned scarlet from both anger and embarrassment. So everyone knew that she had tried to escape from
Claude by running off with Guerre.

"You certainly did not think such an escapade would
not become the talk of France, did you? Why, it was
a mighty entertaining tidbit for the gossips." When Althea remained speechless, he continued. "But that is in
the past. You are here. Sir Guerre is dead. And I am quite
moved by your beauty." These last words were murmured
softly.

"Thank you, my lord," said Althea, her voice barely a
whisper. She was saved from further comment by the reap-
pearance of the troubadour, who entertained them with a
song that extolled the royal house of France. It was a
lengthy piece, and she relaxed a bit when the prince began
to talk to Mathilde, who was preening like an exotic bird.
Although he did not speak to Althea again that night,
every once in a while she could feel his eyes on her, and she
realized he enjoyed the discomfort that he caused her. She
hoped fervently that she could get through the visit of
Prince Philip without any more problems.

The next few days passed quickly, and Althea had to admit that she was enjoying herself. After months of being
cooped up, her young heart rejoiced in the company and entertainment that was created for the prince. There had
been a hunt every day, and Mathilde and Althea had
accompanied the men. Both were excellent riders, and
Mathilde had spent a great deal of time talking to Philip.
This had been a relief to Althea, who enjoyed the company

of some of his entourage much more than that of the prince. The most wonderful part, though, was the sense of freedom. She could pretend as she rode through the forests and meadows that she was a free woman. She began to laugh a great deal, and her high spirits drew the admiring glances of the men. She felt safe, because Claude was far too busy to bother with her, and Mathilde was monopolizing the attention of Philip. Only occasionally did she feel a thrill of nervous apprehension. These were the times when she would find Philip staring at her, a faint, sardonic smile twisting his face. His eyes would meet hers, and she would squirm under his amused gaze. He still reminded her of the hunter who was sure of his quarry, and who allowed the game to continue for the sheer pleasure of the chase.

One such look had just passed between them. It was the fifth day of his visit, and they were on still another hunt, this time seeking deer. The hunting party, numbering about twenty people this afternoon, had stopped to rest in a small meadow. It was a flawless summer day. A slight breeze kept the temperature from becoming too warm, and she could feel its cooling touch through the apple green silk gown that she wore. The fields were filled with daisies and poppies, and young Sir Leon, a member of Philip's entourage, had picked a bouquet of flowers for her. Sir Leon was very young, and Althea felt safe in flirting with him. Laughingly, she had tied several of the flowers in her horse's harness, and then had leaned over slightly in the saddle so Sir Leon could kiss her hand. It was at that moment that she had noticed Philip watching her. Was it her imagination, or did he look angry? Then Mathilde cantered up to the prince, turning his attention away.

The hunt soon resumed, and the pace was fast, for deer had been sighted. Althea hated the actual kill, but riding exhilarated her. Perhaps it was the joy of being free making her careless or just an unpreventable accident of fate, but suddenly her horse, taking a small jump over a log, stumbled and went down on one leg. The horse regained its balance before Althea could fall off the beast, but she could tell immediately that the horse had gone lame. Tears of disappointment filled her eyes. Now she could not continue. Most of the party had forged ahead, not realizing her accident, but the few men who had seen offered to escort her back to the castle.

She politely declined their offers. "No, don't ruin the day for yourselves. We're not far from the castle, and the horse can walk easily enough. It won't take me long to get back."

After convincing them to continue, she turned the poor mare back in the direction from which they had come. The route through the woods was easy to follow, but she had misjudged the distance. They had covered a lot of ground in a canter, and it would take time to cover it at a slow walk. Nonetheless, Althea's spirits rose, for she loved the woods and the marvelous sense of solitude it gave her. Humming a little tune, she thought fondly of Magara. Wistfully, she thought how much she would like to adopt Magara's existence and live in a little cottage in the woods, far from the conniving and intrigue of a great castle.

So intent was she on her daydream that she didn't hear the sound of hoofbeats until they were quite loud. With a start, she looked over her shoulder just in time to see Philip cantering down the path toward her. A frown crossed her face, and suddenly the forest seemed threatening, a place filled with danger. But it was the animal on horseback that frightened her, not the natural beasts of the woods.

"You have made good time, my lady," said Philip, drawing his horse to a walk next to her.

"You did not have to stop the hunt on my account, my lord," Althea said a trifle coldly.

"I didn't. The others continue, but I could not allow a gentle lady to travel through the forest alone. I have come to accompany you."

"Thank you, my lord," Althea murmured, trying to be gracious. "I do regret, though, that I ruined the day for you."

"Not at all, Althea. I would much prefer spending it alone with you."

Althea could think of no appropriate answer, so they rode along in silence for a few minutes. She took the time to study Philip, and once again decided that he was a fine figure of a man. Today he wore a hunting doublet of maroon velvet with a matching cape that caught the wind as he rode. His blond hair was almost the color of silver in the sunlight, and he rode with a self-assured arrogance that commanded attention. Philip looked every inch the prince that he was.

Then where was the flaw? Althea wondered. She knew there was one, and it ran deep and ugly through his nature. She could see it in his eyes, which were so cold and blue. He was watching her closely, and she nervously searched for a topic of conversation.

With great relief, she thought of something. "You will be quite pleased to reach Flanders and your beautiful bride, I imagine."

Philip's smile twisted down on one side, and he waved his hand as if dismissing the idea. "The Princess Mary is too religious for my taste," he said flatly. "I wouldn't be surprised if I take her to bed and find that she wears a hair shirt under her somber gown."

"That is not the way to discuss your future wife, my lord," said Althea, blushing.

"Just a matter of state. She will give me no problems, I think."

"Perhaps you will grow to love her."

Philip burst into laughter. "She will never make me desire her." He looked intently at Althea. "She does not make my blood run hot at the sight of her. But you do."

"Please, my lord," begged Althea, feeling very uncomfortable. He did not say anything, and they continued to move along the path. In a moment they reached a small clearing, and with a sudden movement, Philip grabbed the reins of Althea's horse and pulled it to a stop.

"What are you doing?" she demanded angrily.

"Stop getting so upset. I merely want to examine your horse's foot, and this is an excellent spot." He got off his stallion and went to Althea's mount. He appeared to be studying the horse's hoof, and Althea felt a pang of regret that she had misjudged him. As he straightened up, he plucked out one of the red poppies that she had entwined in her bridle. Casually, he walked over to the side of her horse, and smiling up at her, he held out the poppy. "I regret that this is not a ruby, Althea, for I would like to give you something costly and rare. But I am limited in what I can present to you in the middle of the forest."

Touched by his words, Althea reached for the flower. He grabbed her so suddenly that she was stunned. With one quick sweep he pulled her off the horse and crushed her in his arms. Before she could let out a cry, he had placed his lips on hers and was bruising her soft lips with his mouth.

"How dare you!" Althea cried when he finally released her lips.

"What I want, I get," he said, smiling down at her. "Admit that you enjoyed it."

"Enjoyed it! I think you deceive yourself!"

"Then perhaps I should try again." He quickly began to kiss her lips and neck, and Althea fought to break away. But he had pinned her arms to her sides, and he was a big man, and strong. Then, suddenly, he loosened his grip for one moment, and she managed to pull one arm free. Throwing her arm back for force, she leveled a heavy slap at the side of his head. With a start, he released her. She knew that the slap had smarted, but the real damage was to his pride. At first his eyes registered shock, but then she saw the surprise turn to fury. With a grunt, he grabbed her arm tightly and dragged her to a patch of grass, shoving her down. She started to rise, but he knelt down and pressed her back onto the grass. Althea read passion mixed with rage in those cold eyes of his, an expression that made panic well up inside of her.

"I would have killed a man for what you did," he whispered hoarsely. "But I have a way to punish you that will be a pleasure to me." With a jerk, he ripped the front of her gown, exposing one rounded breast. Holding her down with his body and one arm, he began to fondle her breast with his other hand.

"I am carrying a child," she pleaded, hoping that would deter him.

"Well, at least it won't be claimed as mine," he answered callously.

"Let me up this minute and I won't tell Claude."

Philip looked down at her and gave an evil grin. "I can't believe that you are that stupid, Althea. Why, Claude would be delighted to hear I got what I wanted. He offered to send you to my room the first night I arrived, but I declined. I wanted to catch you my own way."

Althea stared at him in horror. How right she had been when she thought he looked at her like a hunter assessing his prey. And now she was caught.

"Come now, it's not as if you were a virgin," Philip said. "You liked it well enough with Guerre du Reims."

It was the image of Guerre and the beauty they had shared on that one perfect night that made Althea fight like a lioness. She clawed and bit and twisted with all her strength; but her spirit aroused Philip even more, and with a cry, he pulled at her skirt, pushing up the silk material until her calves and thighs were exposed, and then her most private parts. For one moment, he stood still, looking at her nakedness.

"So beautiful. Like a statue that has come to life," he murmured. Pinning her down with his body, he slowly began to fondle her thighs, and then the warm golden silk between them. Blindly, Althea looked at the trees overhead, trying not to feel his hands as they explored her. And then he was above her, and then entering her. His manhood, swollen by lust, thrust into her like a knife, invading her without love or gentleness. His face loomed over her, and she saw the wild look in his eyes. He cared nothing for her. He was the hunter, and she was the quarry. And he had won. Suddenly, he groaned, and his body trembled as he climaxed; then he fell on her, satisfied and sated.

With a violent push, Althea squirmed out from under him. She was too weak to stand, so she crawled to the little stream nearby. Her reflection in the water scared her. She looked like a wanton, her hair streaming wildly about her, her breasts exposed and swollen. Bitterly, she wondered if she brought these things on herself. Was she tainted by her mother's blood, a whore as the world said? In anguish, she thrust her hand into the water, destroying her reflection. The tears began to fall from her eyes and drop into the swirling water.

CHAPTER THIRTEEN

The pleasant warmth of July had melted into the heat of
August, and Althea, now into her fourth month of pregnancy, felt dispirited and uncomfortable. It wasn't her
size, for she showed only slightly, but she was still
plagued with nausea, which everyone said should have
passed by now. Rachel told her sternly that it was her
melancholy mood that made her physically ill, and
warned that she would harm the babe if she persisted in
brooding over her situation. Althea tried to take the
woman's advice, but her dreams were tormented by
nightmares of Philip, and she got little rest at night.
Exhausted, she spent her days listlessly thinking of
Guerre, which only increased her despondency. Although her waist and breasts grew, she became thinner
of face and ate little. Even Claude was becoming concerned, although Althea herself meant little to him.
It was the hold she held on his position that made him
think of her decline, and finally, in the middle of August, he tried to lighten her heart.

"I have been told that a fair has come to the village not
three miles from here," he said at the morning meal. "Perhaps you would like to take Rachel and attend. The merchants have goods from the East, and the silks they have
for sale are supposed to be quite good. Mathilde and I are
planning to ride over tomorrow."

Althea looked at him with interest. "Would you let me
venture out alone then?"

"Not quite alone," said Claude with a sly smile. "You
must take my two guards, Tom and Rolfe, but I don't think

you'll do anything foolish." He looked at her pointedly, his eyes resting on her belly.

Althea hurried through her meal, and the four left immediately after she was done. All were lighthearted, for it was a beautiful summer day, and the heat had not yet become intense. Even the two guards, Tom and Rolfe, who were usually so bleak and stern, seemed to relax. But none was as happy as Althea. She wanted to sing for joy at her unexpected freedom, and was hard put to keep her horse at the slow trot Claude had ordered. She wanted to spur her horse into a gallop and race through the fields, and for at least a moment, feel that she was as free as the birds flying overhead.

They reached the tiny village of Camprais in about an hour. The town was swollen to three times its size by the merchants who had come to trade, and by the neighboring folk who had come to buy and make merry. The main street was filled with people who were laughing and drinking. Rachel made an acerbic comment about one buxom farm girl who was already quite drunk and was being fondled openly by an equally drunk companion. They were blocking Althea's party, for the street was narrow at this point, and finally Tom leaned down and swatted the amorous lovers with his whip. The man was not so drunk that he did not immediately see the livery of the Count du Vendome, and he stepped back with only a few curse words said under his breath.

Word spread quickly that nobility was visiting the fair, and way was made so that they could pass to the village square. As soon as they reached the main section of the fair, Althea and Rachel dismounted and began to look eagerly at the stalls filled with goods. Tom and Rolfe headed for the wine merchant's stall. They knew that Althea was in safe hands with Rachel, and there was little chance for her to escape. The entire area now knew Althea's story, and no one would dare brook Claude's anger by giving her shelter.

Althea found that most people seemed to be especially

kind to her. When she mentioned this to Rachel, the older woman nodded. "They have no liking for the black-haired bitch. Most of these folk think Mathilde murdered her husband, and her haughty ways have not endeared her to the common people."

Althea frowned at the mention of Mathilde, who was still a great threat to her, but she quickly forgot the other woman in the pleasure of looking at the goods being sold. Claude had given her a few gold coins to spend, and she delighted in examining everything for sale. There were stalls filled with beautiful silks from the East, others with countless ribbons, bolts of velvet, jewelry made from gold and silver, leather goods, skins from North Africa, spices and teas. After a while, they stopped to rest at the stall of the perfume merchant. Althea was blissfully sampling the different scents when Rachel nudged her arm.

"Do you know that man over there—the one whose face is shielded by his cloak?"

Althea looked in the direction in which Rachel pointed. The tall figure turned away and in a second disappeared into the crowd.

"I wonder who he is," Althea said. "What was he doing?"

"He was staring at you with such intensity that he caught my attention," Rachel told her. "He was probably just overwhelmed at your beauty, or perhaps had heard your story and was curious." Noting Althea's flush of embarrassment, the woman smiled. "Come now, you truly are lovely today, and what man wouldn't stare at you?"

Althea smiled. She felt good today, for the first time in weeks. Tossing her bright blue cape over her shoulder, for it had grown hot, she glanced down at the pale yellow tunic that she wore. It was almost exactly the color of her hair, and more than one man that day had called her the golden lady. It was nice to be beautiful. Although she rarely thought that way, today would be different. No brooding! She would revel in the holiday mood of the crowd. On impulse, she purchased a small vial of a musk perfume that had captured her imagination and was pleased to find she still had money left to spend.

"I think, Rachel, that I would like to return to the stall of the silk merchant. With a bit of haggling, I can purchase the pale blue silk that he has."

The other woman nodded happily, and they started back toward the other side of the square. The huge crowd of revelers began to dance, and the circles of dancers pushed Althea and Rachel back against the small church. They watched the crowd, for it was impossible to go through, and suddenly they found themselves encircled by the dancers. The crowd was boisterous, and in seconds Althea lost sight of Rachel and felt herself being swept away by the dancing people. She was not afraid, for the crowd was friendly; but suddenly she felt an arm encircle her waist, and before she could protest, she was being dragged into the church.

Althea looked up at the man in the dark blue cloak, recognizing him as the one pointed out by Rachel. His face was still covered by his cloak, and although she was frightened, she was also angry.

"How dare you touch me like this!" she cried, trying to pull away from the man. He held her around the waist with one iron hand. He did not answer, and she began to struggle. She heard him give a low chuckle, and he shook her gently as a man would shake a disobedient kitten. Then, as she was about to explode in indignation, he allowed the cloak to fall away from his face, and Althea stared up at him, dumbfounded.

"Guerre!" So total was her shock that she could do nothing but utter his name.

"Dead . . . you are supposed to be dead," she finally whispered.

"Do these feel like the lips of a dead man?" he murmured, as he leaned over and took her in his arms. For moments they were locked in an embrace that left Althea breathless with excitement. Her lips eagerly returned his kisses until suddenly she remembered. Revenge. He had used her for revenge. With anger overtaking all other emotions, she thrust herself from his arms.

Startled, he looked down at her. "What is it, my love?"

"You have used me badly, Guerre," Althea accused, tears of rage filling her eyes. "I have learned many things since I was forced to come here. And I know you did not love me. You kidnapped me for revenge, Guerre. Love was never in your heart."

"But I came to love you, Althea, and I love you now!" His words were filled with emotion, and his eyes were gleaming. "That's why I'm here now."

"No, not for love of me," she cried, "but for love of revenge. You still think that you can use me as your tool to avenge your sister! Never. I loved you with all my heart, and I wanted to die when I thought they had killed you. But I won't be used, Guerre, never again."

"Stop it!" He gripped her arm so tightly that she gasped in pain. "Let me explain."

"There is no need to explain," she said hoarsely. "Much as I despise Claude, I would rather live there than with you. With you, the deception was far more cruel."

With a cry, she pulled away from him, and before he could stop her, she raced out the door. He ran into the crowd, frantically looking for her, but she had already disappeared. When he did see her, she was talking to her guards. He wondered if she would give him away; but seeing her hold her stomach, he knew that she was pleading indisposition, and soon they mounted their horses and rode away.

It had never occurred to Guerre that Althea would not come with him. Since that night in May when he had taken her virginity, he had been hopelessly in love with the girl, thoughts of a future together firm in his mind.

Then had come Althea's abduction, and the blow on his head that had left him unconscious for three days. When he awoke, he was in the hut of a tall, thin man wearing a long brown robe. The man had spoken gently to him, telling him not to rise, for he was gravely wounded. The man had fed him a bitter broth, and Guerre had gone to sleep. The next morning he awoke feeling better, although he could not get out of bed. Each attempt had left him dizzy and nauseated.

"Rest and heal yourself, my son," the old man had urged him. "Only then will you be able to pursue your enemies."

Guerre studied the old man carefully. What part had he played in the attack upon Althea and himself?

As if reading his thoughts, the old man smiled. "Fear not. I had no hand in the attack on you. I came upon you in the dawn when I visited the stones. I took you first for dead, for your pulse was so light. It was quite difficult to pick you up and put you over my horse, but I managed."

Guerre looked at the old man. He must have been about sixty, but he reflected a feeling of strength and composure. He was scrupulously clean, and so was the small cottage. Although his clothes were those of a peasant, his manners were of a much higher class. "Are you of the clergy?" Guerre asked at last, satisfied that the man had played no part in the attack on him and Althea.

The man chuckled. "Well, not of the Holy Roman Church." Seeing Guerre's look of puzzlement, and not wanting to say too much, he added quietly, "My name is Dryden, and I am a scholar of the Old Religion. The stones are an old altar." He went on to explain that herbs were his passage into the future. If Guerre was at first wary of this self-proclaimed seer, he gradually learned to care for him a great deal.

After a fortnight's stay, Dryden pronounced Guerre fit to travel. He would have a slight headache at times for months to come, but if he were careful, he could pursue the girl without risk to his health.

Happy to be going, but perplexed at Dryden's knowledge, Guerre asked how he knew about Althea. Dryden looked at him for a long moment, then smiled mischievously. "Part was local gossip. It did not take long to hear about a young girl of noble birth who fled with one man on the eve of her wedding to another. Or to hear about the recapture of the girl. They have sent her to France."

Guerre was consumed with anger and helplessness. "Damn that they caught me unaware. I am to blame for any harm that befalls her. But why didn't you tell me before this?"

"Because you would have tried to leave before you were healed. You are very stubborn, my son. I would not have been able to stop you from leaving, and you would never have reached France alive. It was easier to let you think that she had been taken back to her father."

"How did you know that I thought that?" Guerre was incredulous.

"You talked a good deal in your sleep. You would often plead your case to Sir Richard. It never occurred to you that her betrothed would still want her." As Guerre began to curse his stupidity, Dryden raised his hand for silence. "Wait, there is more. I looked into the fire last night after drinking the herbs that take my mind to many places. I saw your lady. She is in grave danger, but the peril is not immediate. Although she is very unhappy, her real danger will not surface for several months to come. You should leave soon, for it will take you time to reach her."

"I will leave at first light," Guerre said quickly. He forced himself to sleep at dusk so he would be well rested in the morning. When the first traces of light were seen in the sky, Guerre was in the saddle. "Good-bye, my friend. May God keep you," Guerre said to Dryden.

As he leaned over to clasp Dryden's hand in farewell, the old seer spoke. "Beware black. I do not know what that means, but I saw it in the fire last night. It could be a person, or anything under heaven, for the fire often speaks in symbols. Watch for it. It could be the end of you and your beloved."

"Thank you again, Dryden. I owe you much, and I will take heed of your warning." With that, Guerre turned his horse to the east and started the long journey home.

He had traveled hard, across England to the port of

Dover, but his long days in the saddle had been for naught.
No boats were sailing to France. Stories of the plague had
reached Dover only the day before he arrived, and no one
was risking his health by sailing to France until more information could be obtained. It was not until the last day
in June that the captain of the *Mary Joan* decided he
feared his creditors more than the pestilence, and set sail
for Calais with Guerre on board.

Upon reaching France, Guerre had gone to his castle,
where he admonished his men to keep silent about his return. He quickly sent out two spies, a brother and sister, to
go to the villages around Claude's estate to learn what
they could about Althea. It had taken a great deal of self-
restraint for Guerre not to charge the Castle du Vendome
himself, for his nature was one of action. But he knew that
a mistake now could destroy Althea; it was vital that he
exercise caution and restraint. But he had paced the floors
of his keep like a caged beast until the two returned. From
them he learned of Althea's prisoner-type existence, and of
Prince Philip's extended stay at the castle. They also told
him of the fair in Camprais.

He had thought for several days on his next move, and
decided that the fair would be the best opportunity to see
Althea. He would go in disguise and keep horses nearby
for their escape. He planned it all very carefully, right
down to the last detail.

Now, sitting in the Tavern of the Two Ravens in the village of Camprais, he thought bitterly about how badly his
careful plans had gone. He had found Althea, all right, but
he had never considered the caprices of a woman, the
unexplainable whims that could set the best-laid plans to
naught. He silently cursed all daughters of Eve for their il-
logical, stupid behavior. Well, he would return to his own
castle and plan again. The next time she would not escape
him.

Althea paced the floor of her chamber in agitation, her
mind in a turmoil. She had pleaded illness and had been

excused from attending the evening meal. Everyone had believed her, for she certainly looked feverish. Her face was extremely pale except for two red patches, one on each cheek. In fact, she felt feverish, although it was the raging emotions inside her that caused it.

"He's alive," she whispered out loud as she paced back and forth. "Alive!" Part of her was filled with a wild, joyful excitement, but this feeling of elation warred with anger at his betrayal of her. He was alive, but why should she care? she asked herself over and over again. She was nothing but a means to an end for him. Even now, his revenge not complete, he still wanted to abduct her to enrage Claude. He did not love her! He had only made love to her to make the escape easier. Better a willing victim than someone fighting every inch of the way.

A frown creased her brow, and she sat down on the edge of the bed and thought. In all honesty, she had left her father's castle eagerly with him. He had barely spoken to her, yet she had gone with him willingly, unquestioningly. He had been a means to an end for her, also, for he provided an escape from Claude. Neither had spoken of love until that magical night under the stones. Perhaps, perhaps . . . She twisted her hands together in desperation. Perhaps he had fallen in love with her then, and really had meant what he said. If that were the case, then she had made a terrible mistake this afternoon!

Her thoughts were interrupted by the opening of the door. Claude stepped into the room and looked at her with suspicion. "I would have thought you long asleep, Althea," he said in a falsely solicitous voice. She was aware that Claude must never suspect that Guerre was alive, or a countryside search would seek him out, and his death made a certainty.

"I felt too uncomfortable to sleep and have been sitting here saying my prayers." She hoped that he would believe her, but he did not look satisfied.

"I am quite curious about your illness, my dear, for it came upon you so unexpectedly. I spoke to your escorts and to Rachel, and they all said how well you felt. And then, suddenly, you demanded to be returned to the castle. And now you look extremely agitated, as if you had seen a ghost." Claude did not mention that Rachel had told him about the man with the cape.

Claude was a suspicious man by nature—and a clever one. He had often thought that he had no proof Guerre du Reims had actually died, and he had been terribly annoyed when he saw the two jackals who had brought Althea to his castle. As untrustworthy a pair as he had ever seen. He would have been more sure of the dispatch of his rival if it had been done by his own professional men-at-arms, or one of the Parisian assassins that he had employed several times. The wench had gone to the fair in high spirits, and had returned looking distraught. Who, if anyone, had she seen that had upset her so? If it had been Guerre, why had she not tried to escape? He puzzled over these thoughts as he pretended to stir the fire in the hearth. Finally, he decided that to watch and wait would be the best course. And to take precautions that she did not escape.

Feigning concern for her health, he turned back to her. "It worries me when you are ill, Althea. If this is what results when you go out, I must prohibit all riding for a while."

Althea was about to protest, but something stopped her. She nodded her head in agreement, and endured Claude's lingering kiss on her lips. For one moment his hand caressed her breast, and she prayed, "Please, God, not now!" Her prayer was answered, and he straightened up.

"Since I have no wish to catch your affliction, I will depart for a healthier companion. And," he added wickedly, "a more lusty one. Good night, madam."

Althea saw him close the door with relief, and sat back tiredly. She could not have endured his lovemaking tonight. With a shudder she thought how it would have been. Claude would move his fat, bejeweled fingers all over her body, probing in the most intimate of places, trying to get a response from her. And when he failed to arouse her, he would curse and slap her until his desire grew so great that he would mount her in a frenzy and ride her until he was satiated. It was always the same, but tonight it would have been worse, for she would have been thinking of Guerre's lips on hers, and Guerre's body holding her close.

Rachel then entered, carrying a goblet of wine. "It's a sleeping potion, my lady. The count ordered it for you. He said that you could not sleep."

Althea frowned, and the woman laughed, reading her mind. "Have no fear. I prepared it."

Althea sighed with relief. At least she had one friend in the castle. Rachel watched out for her, and Althea felt safer under the kind older woman's care. One never knew if Mathilde would decide to strike, and since Rachel detested Claude's mistress, she was naturally suspicious of her every action. Althea relaxed a little and allowed Rachel to help her disrobe.

Finally, with everything settled for the night, Rachel departed, and Althea leaned back against the silk pillows on her bed. She felt calmer now, for the draught was doing its work. Drowsily, she began to think again of Guerre, of his brooding black eyes . . . of how much she wished he were lying next to her now. . . . of how much she still loved him.

CHAPTER FOURTEEN

Claude and Mathilde were already seated when Althea arrived at the great hall for breakfast the next morning. The girl seemed to be in excellent health, Mathilde thought bitterly. She had been elated when she had heard that Althea was indisposed, and she had prayed for a miscarriage. Now she could hardly hide her disappointment.

"Ah," said Claude with a smile, "I see that you have recovered. She does look well, doesn't she, Mathilde?" Claude knew how this would infuriate the woman.

Mathilde looked at Althea coldly. "Methinks she looks a bit pale, but then she always has a pukey look to her."

Ignoring this barb, Althea took a piece of mutton that a serving girl offered her. "I feel quite well, my lord. It was a brief indisposition."

"Perhaps your next will be longer," Mathilde said acidly.

"Silence, bitch," said Claude, doing the unusual by siding with Althea.

"It was but a side effect of the pregnancy, although you would not know, of course, since you have never carried a babe," Althea could not resist.

Gossip said that Mathilde was unable to bear children. It was an abortion gone wrong, Rachel had told Althea. Mathilde had rid herself of her late husband's child but had almost died in the process. She had called in an old crone who dealt with such things, but the crone had been unclean. That had been five years ago. Since Mathilde would have given her soul to bear Claude's child, Althea's remark was like exposing a raw nerve.

Mathilde jumped up from her seat. Her beautiful face was distorted with venom, and she pointed a threatening finger at Althea. "Beware, my proud lady, for your day will come. You will not carry this child to its full term. I have consulted an old woman, and this child will never cry." Leaving Althea stunned, she fled from the room.

Althea was shaken by the violence in Mathilde's voice, but Claude seemed only amused. "Sometimes I think she is quite mad," he said calmly, taking another helping of fish.

Althea did not answer him. She felt the strangest feeling of foreboding, and she knew that she had baited Mathilde too far. She realized with certainty that the woman would stop at nothing to destroy her.

If Althea had thought that her sudden good health would bring her some freedom, she was sadly mistaken. Before she had known of Guerre's survival, she had been too apathetic to care about venturing out of the castle. In fact, she had gladly spent most of her time in her room, brooding about the past. Claude's restrictions had been an inconvenience, but they had not touched her deeply. Now that she knew Guerre was alive, when everything in her wanted to ride like the wind and search for him, she was trapped in the castle, unable to leave even with Claude's most trusted servants.

She had been afraid to ask him to lift his restrictions for fear of arousing his suspicions. He seemed to be watching her more carefully since the fair. Perhaps one of the guards, or even Rachel, had mentioned the tall man wearing the cloak, who had stared at her. Seething with frustration, she forced herself to appear as if she were calm and happy. It was so difficult to pretend, that she began to spend even more time in her chamber, claiming that she needed the rest because the pregnancy was tiring her.

And then one day a messenger rode into the castle courtyard, and Claude's suspicions were confirmed. Greeting the young squire in the great hall, Claude recognized at once the livery of the house of Reims, and his first emotion was to have the messenger's right hand severed and returned to Guerre. It would be both an insult and a warning. But Claude was practiced in intrigue, and he knew that such a rash act now would forestall a greater revenge later. He forced himself to smile pleasantly and hear the man out. He was pleased that he did, for the message was surprising.

The young squire spoke quickly. He had memorized his speech down to the very last word. "My liege lord, Sir Guerre du Reims, sends greetings to his brother-in-law, the esteemed Count du Vendome. He requests that I ask your pardon for the deeds that he has committed against you. He regrets the trouble that he has caused you, and admits that his actions were of the greatest folly. He only wishes that you will find it in your heart to forgive your poor late wife's brother for the madness that overtook him."

The squire paused for breath. Claude regarded him coldly and said, "Your master must think me a candidate for sainthood if he thinks I am capable of such forgiveness."

The squire, a lad of only sixteen, looked at Claude nervously. "There is more, my lord count."

"Then proceed," Claude snapped.

The squire was withdrawing something from a purse at his waist. "Sir Guerre has sent you this necklace as a token of his good will. It is a very valuable stone, and part of the dowry of his late mother." At this the boy produced a gold necklace with a ruby pendant the size of a small egg. Claude's eyes glittered with greed. He examined the necklace and knew that it was genuine, for Alycia had several times remarked on a fantastic gem that had belonged to her mother. By tradition it was supposed to be given to Guerre's wife when he married, and Claude had regretted that it had not been part of Alycia's dowry.

The messenger cleared his throat, indicating that there

was more to be said. Claude, in a much more pleasant tone than he had previously used, told him to continue.

"Sir Guerre wishes to inform you that he has decided to wed, and asks your forgiveness as your gift to him on his marriage."

Claude was visibly startled. He had not believed a word of Guerre's sudden repentance until this. Perhaps he really had decided to settle down, and wished for peace between them. It was out of character, but men can change. Especially when there was good reason to do so. "Who is the bride, may I be so bold as to ask?"

"Lady Clarissa du Reims, his cousin, my lord."

"Clarissa du Reims! That is ridiculous! She is his first cousin. The Church will never allow the match. Who does he think he is fooling?"

"No one, my lord," the messenger said quickly. He had been warned that this would be Claude's reaction. "They have received a special dispensation from the Church. It was arranged by Lady Clarissa's maternal uncle, who is Cardinal Jean de la Velle. These things can be arranged."

Yes, they could, thought Claude, if the price was right. He considered the situation. Clarissa must be long past marriage age, and he knew that the de la Velles had great wealth. A rich spinster would not be unappealing to Guerre, who had land but no gold. And Guerre du Reims would be an acceptable match for Clarissa, especially since she had proved difficult to wed. He had never met Alycia's first cousin, although they had been close friends. Clarissa had been sent to court when Alycia and Claude had married.

"May I ask, is the Lady Clarissa fair of face?"

"I do not know, my lord. I have not seen her. She was due to arrive on the day I left. They are probably wed by now, for he is much smitten by her."

By her wealth, I warrant, thought Claude, though he smiled. "Tell Sir Guerre that I forgive all that is past. And also tell him that an old acquaintance of his, Lady Althea, will soon deliver me a child."

The squire looked stunned. "I did not know that you had wed, my lord."

"I haven't."

Althea had been correct in thinking that Claude had been watching her more closely of late, but she had suspected only part of the reason. The other part had escaped her. Althea was one of those women who bloomed in pregnancy. Her skin had turned milky and soft, and her hair and eyes had a luster that immediately caught an onlooker's eye. But the most arresting thing about her was her figure. Four months ago she had still been something of a child. Her breasts had been small, her hips those of a young boy. Pregnancy had made her a woman. Her whole body had filled out in soft, womanly curves that were distractingly enticing. Her stomach had only just started to enlarge, and it gave her a sensuous, rather than an awkward, look.

Claude had been watching her with growing lust, and had come to regret his decision to leave her alone while she carried the babe. Willing or unwilling, she would still be an interesting change from Mathilde and the serving girls. He had been especially aroused today at the midday meal. Althea's tunic was getting too small for her, and her growing breasts were straining out of the soft woolen material. He was filled with lust, and he wanted to keep Mathilde in her place; but he also had a third, and most important, reason to visit Althea: he wanted to tell her about Guerre.

Althea had not suspected that he would come to her chamber tonight, and she was surprised when he entered her room. "Welcome, my lord," she murmured politely.

"You look in good spirits, Althea," he said, smiling pleasantly. He was thinking how he could contrive to take Althea without her fighting him. He wanted to savor her body, and then tell her about her old lover.

"I am, my lord." She kept a smile on her face, but she was perplexed at his visit. "I thought at dinner that I felt the baby move, although it is probably too soon for that. I am just overeager, I think." She tried not to cringe as Claude sat down next to her.

He looked at her intently. "I wish, Althea, that you were overeager for me."

Althea stared at him soundlessly, although she felt panic begin to grip her. He couldn't possibly want to make love to her, could he? It had been weeks since he had come to her bed. One close look into his eyes, however, told her what she had dreaded to find. Claude's pale blue eyes were filled with lust. She moved slightly away from him, but he grabbed her hand and brought it to his lips.

"You have no idea how appealing you have become, my dear. Pregnancy suits you admirably. And it makes me desire you with a hunger I can no longer contain."

"I would think that it would make you want to restrain yourself," Althea spat out bitterly. She was no longer afraid. She had endured Claude on too many nights to fear him. Rather, it was repulsion that she felt. She detested his soft, corpulent body, and his fat, greasy, probing fingers. To have to endure him again made her furious.

Claude laughed mirthlessly. "I see that you still do not reciprocate my affection. It matters not, of course, for I will have you with or without your consent." He paused and looked at her intently. "Had Guerre not gotten to you first, perhaps then you would not be such a reluctant lover with me. His method must have been lacking a certain expertise."

At the mention of Guerre's name, and in such an unflattering light, Althea's anger blazed anew. "You can only wish to be as fine a lover as he," Althea said, "a wish that would do you no good."

Fire burned in Claude's eyes, but his voice remained calm when next he spoke. "Then perhaps it will please you to know that Guerre is alive."

Althea stared at him in astonishment. How had he found out about Guerre? Had one of the guards recognized him, or had Rachel? Had he known since the fair and kept silent, or had some other spy just told him?

"Have you nothing to say, or has the shock robbed you of your tongue?"

Pretending total ignorance, Althea spoke slowly, choosing her words with care. "I am amazed. I had thought for sure that he died at the hands of those two monsters that you hired."

"That your dear father hired," Claude corrected. "But no, it seems that the treacherous swine survived. I'm not surprised. The moment I laid eyes on those two imbeciles that brought you here, I began to have doubts about Guerre's death." Claude looked annoyed. Althea seemed genuinely surprised by what he had told her. Perhaps she had not seen Guerre at the fair, and her story about ill health had been true. Well, it really made no difference to him. "Doesn't the news please you?"

"Not really," Althea said. She knew that everything she said would be carefully analyzed by Claude. "He has no part of my heart. He was just a quick fancy, and he served my purpose at the time."

"Then it won't bother you to know that he is to wed." Claude watched her closely, and he smiled as he saw her pale. "That is how I heard of his survival. His messenger arrived this very morning, bringing Guerre's request that we end our feud for he is soon to wed his first cousin, Clarissa du Reims. A rather plain girl, I wager, but she will bring him a very good dowry. They may already have wed, for the messenger said that Guerre was most eager. As a token of his sincerity, he sent me this priceless jewel." Claude reached into his leather pouch and withdrew the ruby pendant.

Althea could only glance at the pendant with feigned interest as anguish ripped through her heart with knife-sharp pain. She wanted to believe that Claude was lying to her, but for once, he seemed to be telling the truth.

Feeling faint, she began to sway slightly, and Claude scooped her up in his arms and set her on the bed. Her thoughts were in such a turmoil that she was caught off guard, and before she could protest, Claude had her pinned down to the bed and was covering her face with kisses. As she felt him press down on her, Althea began to struggle, but it was a futile fight against his massive bulk. In his eagerness, he ripped her gown, exposing her breasts. As he greedily sucked her nipples, Althea squirmed in disgust, but he pinned her arms under her so she could do no more than helplessly twist and turn.

Suddenly, he grabbed her hair in his fist and yanked her face close to his. "Listen to me, Althea, and listen well," he said, his voice as cold and deadly as a steel blade. "From now on, you will do everything I want, because if you refuse, I will sell the brat you carry to the gypsies. I will sell it on the day it is born. Don't think I need this child. You have proved that you are fertile, so it would be easy to beget another, and no one would blame me for rejecting a child that is not mine."

"You wouldn't dare!"

He tightened his hold on her hair, bringing tears of pain to her eyes. "Of course I dare. Who would stop me? Your unfortunate behavior has left you open to suspicion. All would believe that it was Guerre's child, and I will tell them that you confessed as much to me. Women have died for less, and most will think me humane for only selling the bastard child, rather than killing you both." He smiled viciously, showing his yellow teeth. "Guerre will not come to your rescue. A man newly wed will want to put all scandal behind him. He certainly won't claim the babe or cause a fuss."

Althea looked at him in shock and could summon no words to her lips. What he spoke was true. There was no one to help her, or the child that she carried. As she thought of this, something primitive grew in her. At all costs she would protect her unborn child, she vowed. She would do anything to see that Claude would not harm it.

"Now get up. And very, very slowly, strip off your gown." He leaned back on the silk pillows as Althea stood up. "Remember, Althea, you are to do everything I want."

Later, lying on her bed alone, she thought of what Guerre had promised her on that long-ago night in Wales.

He had said that there was more to lovemaking than she
knew, and he would teach her all of it. Bitterly, she
thought how ironic it was that Claude should be the one to
teach her. She wondered which hurt more: the mental anguish of Guerre's betrayal or the bruises on her body from
Claude's beating. She put her hands over her stomach.
What if she lost the baby after all? The thought was too
horrible to contemplate. Tears slid down her cheeks, and
the salt stung the cut on her lip.

She had never imagined that she could feel such despair,
even during the worst times in her life. Or that Claude
would ever use her so vilely. Now that she truly knew
what he was capable of doing to her, she thought seriously
of killing herself. Listlessly, she looked toward the window
facing the courtyard. There was a full moon tonight, and
the chamber was quite light. She reflected on how quick a
leap from one of the castle turrets would be, and how sweet
the oblivion to follow.

She put her hand to her face and gingerly felt the bruise
on her cheek. That was where Claude had hit her first. She
had done what he told her to do. Fearing for the life of the
baby, she would have done much more. When he had told
her to strip, she had done just as he asked, slowly removing her gown and letting it slide to the floor.

"Very good," he had said, as she stood naked before him.
"Now kneel in front of me."

She had obeyed. Looking up into his face, she saw the
evil amusement in his smile. He was really enjoying her
degradation. As she watched, he fumbled with the slit in
his trousers until he was exposed.

"Caress me, you bitch," he ordered.

And Althea had, until he was moaning with pleasure.
She looked up at his face and saw that his eyes were closed.
He was really disgusting, she thought. His greasy hair
curled around his moon-shaped face, and his mustache
still had remnants of dinner attached to it. Little brown
hairs curled wherever his barber had missed with the ra-
zor, and she could see the blackheads and pimples on his

chin all too clearly. It was then that he had opened his eyes and seen the repulsion on her face. It had been too much for him.

With a savage blow to her face, he had sent her sprawling backwards. Before she could rise, he jumped from the bed and began to kick her mercilessly, aiming especially at her swollen belly. She had screamed and tried to shield herself, but it was useless. He began to kick her legs and back, and then had grabbed her by the hair, dragging her across the stone floor until she pleaded for him to stop.

"You dare to mock me, you worthless Welsh bitch!" He aimed a vicious blow at Althea's stomach. "I'll teach you a little respect, you high-and-mighty whore! You dare to look down on me!"

"No, Claude, no!" She was only half-conscious, but she could see that he was removing the leather belt that kept up his linen leggings. With a violent snap of his arm, he brought the belt whipping down across her breasts. She turned over on her stomach so that the belt could only hit her back and buttocks, but the pain became unbearable. As she sank into oblivion, she could hear Claude screaming profanities over her bleeding body.

She did not know how long she had lain on the floor before Rachel entered and cried out, horrified. The woman had half dragged her to bed, and then had carefully washed her with a mixture of water, attar of roses, and an herb that cooled the stinging wounds. Rachel had asked no questions, but had only murmured comforting little sounds. Althea had lain on the bed without uttering a sound until Rachel tried to force some hot wine between her lips. The wine had made her retch violently.

"Please, my lady, think of the child. This retching will surely kill it."

"I can't help it," Althea had whispered.

Rachel had rushed from the room, and returned a while later with an evil-smelling draught of ugly yellow. "Drink this, and you'll sleep."

Althea looked at the medicine with distaste. "No, I'll

drink it later. Leave it." Rachel had protested, but Althea was adamant, and finally the serving woman stoked the fire and withdrew.

That had been over an hour ago, and now Althea considered the brew that the woman had brought to her. Perhaps she would drink it, if it promised oblivion from reality. Forcing herself, she drank it down and concentrated intently on the fire glowing softly to keep her mind off the vile taste. The draught was potent, and in minutes she felt herself begin to relax. Soon she became drowsy and peaceful, and she felt sleep drifting closer. The fire cast shadows against the walls, and these shadows became dancers wearing ugly masks. The dancers came closer and she saw that one was Guerre. He was waving to her. She sighed with pleasure. Her eyes were so heavy, and he was coming closer, closer. She heard the door open, and the draft made the dancers disappear.

She was slipping into a deep sleep when she saw a woman dressed in black. The vision was much clearer than the other figures had been. She looks almost real, Althea thought sleepily. She felt a faint foreboding, and she tried to move, but her limbs were too heavy. A part of her mind recalled that the other figures had been transparent, but that this one was solid. The figure moved closer. She was bent and stooped, but Althea could not see her face because a black veil covered her features. As she came closer, Althea felt that she was being surrounded by a malignant presence. The room seemed to be filled with death and evil, and the shrouded black figure gave off the nauseating stench of decay. Terrified but now totally numb from the draught, Althea could only watch in horror as the form leaned over her bed. And then the drug, which was powerful, overcame her, and she drifted into unconsciousness.

It was the bright sun flooding her chamber that awoke Althea the following day. Groggy at first, remembrance of the night before hit her like a blow, and she let out a groan. Someday, she vowed, she would escape from here, and she would be revenged! She didn't know where she would go, but somewhere there must be a refuge for her and the baby. Tears filled her eyes as she thought of Guerre. She felt betrayed and hurt by his marriage; now he would never help her. That brief, bright hope had been kindled when she had discovered that he was alive. Now that was gone. She had been nothing to him.

She got up slowly, her body aching all over. Her stomach and face were covered with bruises, and welts had risen all over her back and legs. Please, God, she prayed, let the baby be all right. She jumped slightly as the door opened, thinking that it might be Claude. To her relief, it was Rachel.

The old woman looked at her with concern, but Althea smiled, and the woman returned the grin. "I think you are better today, my lady."

"Very sore, and a little light-headed."

"It is the aftereffect of the drug. You'll feel better after you've eaten. Lie back down for a while more, my lady."

Althea lay gratefully back on the pillows and watched as Rachel uncovered a pot she had brought up and poured the steaming contents into a pewter bowl. "What is it?" she asked. "It smells delicious."

"Hot soup," the woman said, setting the bowl in front of Althea. "Beef stock with vegetables."

Althea began to eat it greedily, for she was starving, and Rachel began to bustle around the room, piling up clothes. Althea saw that they were the garments that she had discarded last night, and her cheeks flamed.

Staring at her, Rachel said grimly, "He won't bother you today."

"Why not?" Althea's voice was bitter.

"I told him that you were quite ill, and there was a chance that you could lose the babe. Or perhaps die yourself. Not that there is," she added. The woman held up the tunic for inspection and, deciding that it was soiled, threw it by the door. "Last night I feared that both of you might die," she continued. "When a child goes at this stage, the

mother usually goes with it. But my potion worked quite
well, and you are much improved this morning."

"Yes," said Althea, grateful for both her health and the
lie that kept Claude away.

"In fact, methinks he will give you some peace for a
while, for the other one was in quite a state last night, and
he will have his hands full cajoling her to a good humor
again."

Althea stared at her soup thoughtfully. She was remembering something. Someone in black. She frowned in concentration. "Rachel, did Mathilde wear a black gown last
night?"

Rachel shook her head. "No. She was dressed like a harlot, if you ask me. She changed after the evening meal. She
put on a scarlet tunic that half exposed her breasts, and a
flaming gold underskirt. She was waiting for Claude, and
when he did not appear, she fell into a fit of anger that
robbed her, methinks, of her reason." Rachel gave a
pleased laugh, for she hated Mathilde. "Why, it took her
serving girl a good hour to clean up the broken plates and
goblets."

"I think someone came into my room last night, Rachel.
A woman dressed all in black. She really frightened me."

"It was the drug that I gave you. You dreamt it. It hap-
pens."

"Perhaps," Althea said. "In the daylight I believe that.
But although I did have dreams last night, she was different. She hovered over me until I went to sleep. She was
completely shrouded in black, and the room smelled of
death and decay. And she was solid. The other visions that
I had I could see through."

Rachel pursed her lips in thought. No one had ever
smelled things while under the influence of her sleeping
draught. And it usually brought on pleasant hallucina-
tions, not ones of horror. Well, the girl had been distraught. Perhaps it had affected her differently. Still . . .
there was a lot of evil in this castle. Many had died here,

and the evil continued. There would be a place in hell for his lordship and the black-haired whore, she was sure.

"I will keep my eyes and ears open, my lady, and if I hear of anything, I will let you know."

"Thank you," Althea said gratefully. "And one other thing, Rachel." Althea hesitated. She wanted to know if Rachel had been the one to tell Claude that Guerre was alive, or if the story of his marriage was true. "Did you know, perchance, that Sir Guerre, the Lady Alycia's brother, is alive and plans to wed?" Althea watched Rachel's face closely and saw genuine shock register there. So the woman was innocent, and Guerre really was going to wed!

"Why, thanks be to God for his safety," the old woman said fervently. Then, remembering Althea's condition, she blushed. "I'm sorry, my lady. The news of his marriage must cause you much grief."

"It is nothing," Althea said stiffly. "He was nothing to me, and I wish him well in his new life." She spoke so calmly that if one only heard her voice, he would have believed her. But Rachel was looking at Althea's face as the girl spoke. She saw the sorrow in her eyes, and she knew that the girl still loved Guerre.

CHAPTER FIFTEEN

September turned into October with its frequent dreary, cold rains. Althea shivered and pulled the woolen cloak close around her body. A small fire burned in the hearth, but it did little to dispel the dampness of the stone walls. Althea bent listlessly over her needlework. It was an altar cloth for the chapel. She hated this way of passing time, but there was little else to do. Restlessly, she put aside her needlework, and rose heavily from her chair. Her movements were becoming awkward as she approached her seventh month. She walked over to the window that faced the courtyard and looked out. Although it was overcast and cold, the rain had stopped. The chill wind whipped the cloaks of the sentries as they manned their posts. Althea felt sorry for them. It was more like winter than fall today. She noticed that one guard was chatting with a servant girl, and Althea recognized her as the main serving wench to Mathilde, a pretty girl named Jeanne. Sometimes Jeanne helped Rachel, and Althea heard how hard life was if one served Mathilde.

By the way the girl was talking to the sentry, Althea realized that the two were lovers. Jeanne tilted her head in a flirtatious manner, and the sentry laughed and patted her ample buttocks with affection. How lucky they are, thought Althea. No one cares about Jeanne or whom she loves. She may be a serf and tied to the land, but she has more freedom than do I, a nobleman's daughter.

So intent was Althea on the happy little scene below that she did not immediately notice a figure walking across the courtyard. Only when Jeanne turned to stare did Althea let her gaze wander over to the far side of the yard, and then her heart lurched in her chest. It was an old woman dressed in black, and Althea recognized the figure from her nightmare. She was stooped and bent, and a black veil covered her face, but evil emanated from her like a black mist. She leaned on a crooked stick and seemed to be waiting for someone. Althea stared at her as if hypnotized, and she could not draw her eyes away even when she saw the crone raise her head and look directly up at her. Unable to move, Althea now knew with a sickening terror that she had had a *real* visitor the night she had been given Rachel's drug. Jeanne beckoned with her hand, and the crone hobbled over to her. The two then left the courtyard.

Althea sat down on the bed and tried to think. She had been a prisoner in this castle for almost six months, and she knew almost all the castle servants, at least by sight if not by name. She had never seen this woman except on that one night. Who could she be? She resembled a witch. With a smile, Althea thought of Magara. People had called her a witch, although she had never practiced the black arts. Her kindly aunt bore little resemblance to this grotesque creature.

Althea raised her head with a start as the door to her chamber opened. Rachel entered, and Althea breathed a sigh of relief. "Rachel, I just saw the crone that was in my nightmare. She's real! It wasn't my imagination."

Rachel paused before setting down an urn filled with scented water. She looked at Althea closely. "Where did you see her?"

"In the courtyard. She stood in the corner until Jeanne, the girl who helps you, beckoned to her to follow."

Rachel pursed her lips in disgust. "You had a dream. The woman you saw only resembled the nightmare crone." Rachel's voice was harsh, and Althea heard the note of fear.

Puzzled, but determined to get to the bottom of the mystery, she continued. "No, it was the same woman. I'm sure. Why do you doubt me?"

"How could an old woman get into your chamber? Don't be foolish!"

Startled by the fear in Rachel's eyes, Althea spoke gently. "Rachel, who is the woman? I can see that she frightens you terribly."

The serving woman twisted her apron in her hands and looked nervously at the door. "She frightens more than just me," she muttered.

Althea waited patiently. Finally, almost in a whisper, Rachel spoke. "She's the witch who lives in the woods near the castle. They call her Haggar. She rarely comes out in the light of day, and all decent folk avoid her."

Althea frowned. She was trying to remember something at the edge of her memory. A conversation. What was it?

"She is reputed to have such evil power that all fear her. Even the priest."

"Rachel, Rachel, calm yourself. There are no such things as witches," Althea said.

"Of course there are," Rachel hissed, crossing herself. "How can you doubt when you have seen Haggar?"

This was a good point, and Althea fell silent. Rachel began to look nervously through the cedar chest in the corner. After a moment she pulled out a bright purple tunic that she had let out at the seams to allow for Althea's pregnancy.

"What are you doing? I have already dressed for the day."

Rachel turned slightly. "You are to appear at the midday meal, and this tunic suits you better."

Althea was startled, and fear caught at her throat. She had been escaping most meals by pleading ill health. "Must I?"

"The count has ordered you to attend. He said you were to be brought down in a litter if you could not walk. Something is brewing, I tell you. He was in high spirits this morning when I served at the breakfast meal."

Grimly, Althea allowed Rachel to help her dress; she was grateful for Rachel's selection, and she knew why she had chosen it. Purple made her look sallow, and of all colors, it would make her the least appealing. Also, the cut was large, and the tunic fitted her like a loose sack. All in all, it would make her less desirable than the cream-colored linen gown that she had been wearing.

After Althea had dressed, she sat down and let Rachel comb her hair. With surprise she noticed that Rachel's hands, usually so steady and calm, were shaking. Althea realized that Rachel was still frightened, and her extreme nervousness was puzzling. She remained silent, but in a few moments Rachel put aside the shell comb she had been using and faced Althea.

"My lady, I must tell you something."

"Yes," said Althea quietly, for Rachel just stood there wringing her hands.

The serving woman took a deep breath and continued. "I did not want to alarm you, but now that she has come here, I must speak. They say that Haggar's powers come from the blood of babes. Many young ones have disappeared from the village and the countryside over the last few years, and all feel that it is the doing of Haggar."

Althea felt the baby kick, and her heart jumped in fear. Speechlessly, she looked at Rachel.

"I feel that the hag's presence is connected with you, and you must take care."

Althea heard Rachel's words, but her mind was also recalling a conversation many months ago. With clarity she remembered Mathilde crying out to her in anger, "I have consulted an old woman, and this child will never cry."

"Mathilde," said Althea stonily.

Rachel looked at Althea, and then nodded her head. "It was reported that the witch went to Mathilde days before her husband died, but none could prove murder."

"Thank you for telling me," Althea said. "Now I must decide what to do. Please leave. I'll be down in a moment."

Rachel left, and Althea sat at the small table by the hearth, trying to still the fear in her heart. Mathilde had called in the witch to help destroy her baby. It was clear to her now. Why had the woman hesitated to kill her the night that she lay drugged? That was puzzling. Could it have been mercy? No. Something else. Althea got up and began to pace the floor. She had to escape. But how? She would have to think carefully about this tonight, and make her plans. It had become a matter of life or death, and she had no more time to waste.

The meal was uneventful. Claude was in high spirits; Mathilde, too. Both laughed and joked and ate heartily, ignoring Althea as if she were not there. A month had passed since the night when Claude had used her so brutally, and Althea noticed he had gained more weight, and his face had an unhealthy flush to it. Mathilde, on the other hand, was even more beautiful than usual. She wore a gown of emerald green velvet, and her black hair was worn long and flowing. Althea could clearly smell her heavy musk perfume, and she could see the lip balm that made her lips as red as cherries. Only her eyes remained cold and scheming, and Althea tried not to meet her gaze. When Althea noticed Mathilde regarding her swollen belly with a smile, Althea had to use all her willpower not to run from the room.

When Claude pushed away his last plate, he poured more wine into his goblet, and with a smile, he turned toward Althea. "You look quite sallow, my dear," he said jovially, and Althea blessed Rachel for her wise choice. "Your early months were much more appealing."

At this, Mathilde smiled, and Althea burst out, "It has been a difficult pregnancy, and I have not had an easy time. But I will bear a living child by Christmastide."

She immediately regretted her words as Mathilde gave

her a look of such hatred that Althea felt she had probably increased her desire for vengeance.

Mathilde leaned toward Claude, exposing her huge breasts, and said coldly, "I have consulted a seer who says the child will be born dead."

This was the opportunity that Althea had been waiting for. "A seer! You lie! You mean the witch called Haggar who lives in the woods. I know you have consulted her, and that she has visited the castle."

Mathilde grew pale with shock when she heard Claude's voice, shrill with anger. "What is this? Have you been consorting with that hag, Mathilde?"

"She is not a witch, just an ugly old woman who makes my powders," Mathilde replied defiantly.

Claude's face was red with fury. "Damn you, I warned you before to stay away from her. I don't want that old hag anywhere near here. Buy your damn powders from the merchants!"

Mathilde turned furious eyes on Althea, but her face was calm. She smiled suddenly, an evil, calculating smile. "As you wish, my lord, but I assure you that she is harmless. I find it odd, though, that Althea would fear her. After all, Althea's own mother was burned for witchcraft, and I thought that the black arts were passed down from mother to daughter."

"My mother practiced no witchcraft," Althea retorted.

"The world thought so," said Mathilde, sipping her wine.

Before Althea could answer, Claude pounded the table with his fist, and the jolt was so great that a leg of mutton went flying to the floor. One of his hounds raced for it and carried it into a corner, snapping at the other four dogs who tried to claim it. "Enough!" he shouted. "You women have ruined my meal. I want no more talk of witchcraft, and the woman called Haggar never comes to this castle again." He glared at Mathilde. "Or I will have you whipped in the courtyard with her."

Mathilde frowned petulantly, but her eyes were icy. Althea shuddered. Would Claude's command stop her? She hoped so, and yet, would a woman who had done away with her own husband be so easily swayed? Somehow, Althea doubted it.

"You aren't listening to me, Althea, and I thought this would please you," Claude was saying.

"I'm sorry, my lord," murmured Althea.

"I have decided that we need some amusement before the onset of winter, so I have sent word around that we will be hosting a tournament on Friday next. Not a huge one, but it will still be a good number."

Althea's heart was in her throat, but she forced herself to look calm. Had Guerre and his wife been invited? If so, had they accepted? The questions raced through her mind, but she forced herself to look blankly at Claude.

Guessing her train of thought, Claude smiled. "I have not received word on who will be coming, but Sir Guerre and his new bride were invited. Does that please or grieve you, my lady?"

"Neither, my lord. Sir Guerre arouses no feeling in my heart," Althea lied. She knew that she did not deceive Claude, but she would not give him the satisfaction of showing any emotion. He was staring at her thoughtfully.

His attention was interrupted by Mathilde. "My lord, the day for your tournament is ill-chosen. Have you forgotten that it is All Saints' Day, and a holy day?"

"I did not remember, but if I had, it wouldn't have made any difference," Claude said, irked. "There's no law that says a tournament cannot be held on All Saints' Day!"

"I don't think the Church would approve of levity and amusement on such a holy day."

Claude looked at her as if she had gone mad. "Have you taken leave of your wits, my lady? The Church would never interfere, and besides, when have you taken the holy days so much to heart? Your attendance at Mass is even worse than mine."

Althea was surprised at how distraught Mathilde appeared. If there was anyone less concerned with the teachings of the Church than Mathilde, he would be hard to find. Yet here she was, lips quivering, eyes shining with tears, pleading that the tournament, an event she loved, be canceled for the obscure reason that the Church might not approve.

With another bang of his fist, Claude silenced Mathilde and also set two pewter goblets flying.

"The tournament will be held, even if the pope objects. I expect you both to attend, and to look as lovely as possible. And you, Althea, had better be in good health. I want no excuses!"

With that he strode from the hall, leaving the two women alone. Althea watched him lumber out, but she turned toward Mathilde when she felt the other woman's eyes on her. All traces of pious conscience were gone, and her face was cold and angry. She was looking at Althea speculatively, eyeing her stomach as if calculating something. Althea forced herself not to flinch under her stare and slowly rose from the table. As she walked from the great hall she could feel Mathilde's eyes boring into her back. When she reached the stairwell that led to her tower chamber, she breathed a sigh of relief. But she had taken no more than three steps when she heard the sound of wild laughter. Althea shuddered, knowing that Mathilde was sitting in the great hall alone, laughing like a woman possessed.

The week went by as slowly as if one hundred years had passed. Althea spent the better part of each day pacing in her chamber, thinking and trying to decide what to do. The life of her unborn child depended on her escape. Even though Claude had forbidden the presence of Haggar in the castle, Althea knew that nothing would stop Mathilde in her attempts to destroy the baby. Filled with fear and anxiety, she hatched plan after plan, only to discard them as unfeasible.

She was faced with two problems: where to go, and how to escape from the castle. Carefully she queried Rachel about the convents in the area, pretending that she was interested in someday making a visit to one. She knew that Rachel was her friend, and yet she wasn't sure what the old woman might reveal if questioned by Claude. She was old and not strong, and Althea did not want to endanger her. Her inquiries brought forth the information that the Convent of the Sacred Heart was one day's walk from the castle. Unfortunately, it housed an extreme order of nuns who kept the vow of silence and would be very unlikely to accept fleeing women. More suited to her purpose was the Convent of Saint Agnes, which was two days' ride by horse. The order was known to take in noble ladies who wished to retire from the secular world without taking vows. Unfortunately, payment was expected for this service, and Althea did not have anything of value to give them. The only piece of jewelry she owned was a small silver ring given to her by Magara years ago. She decided that all she could do was plead for mercy and offer to work for her room and food.

After deciding on Saint Agnes as her destination, she had to consider a way of escape. How could she, a woman seven months pregnant, hope to get away from this fortress? Even if she were not carrying a child, it would be next to impossible. Nonetheless, escape was life and she had to find a way. The tournament, which would last three days, seemed like the best time to try to flee. Everyone would be concerned with the tournament, and less attention would be paid to her. With so many strangers here, a disguise would hopefully go unnoticed by the guards. She decided that late in the night of the first day of the tournament, when all were sleeping soundly, she would slip out.

Sitting in her chamber the day before All Saints' Day, Althea reviewed her plans and was satisfied that she

had done all she could. She had borrowed a dark blue
hooded cloak from Rachel on the pretext that hers was
too light for the colder weather. And through different
conversations she had become fairly sure of the route to
Saint Agnes. There were even apples and cheese hidden
in her cedar chest so she would have food for her journey. Now, all she could do was wait until tomorrow
night.

She laughed cynically to herself. Here she was, carefully
planning her escape, and yet part of her wanted to remain.
And for the most stupid of reasons. She wanted to be with
Guerre again. He would be here for all three days, and she
would be gone by the night of the first. The desire to be
with him had tormented her during this past endless week
as much as her fear of Mathilde and Haggar. She had
chided herself time and time again for wanting to see him,
and told herself that he had abandoned her and was now
wed to another woman. Clarissa. The name haunted both
her sleep and her waking hours.

Clarissa. Clarissa. Althea had thought about that
faceless figure as much as she had planned for her escape. Was she beautiful? She must be, for Guerre would
never marry a crone. Althea put her hands in her lap
and let the tears fall unchecked down her face. It was
her fault. She should never have run away from him
that day at the fair. Damn her stupidity! Now she would
never feel his arms around her, nor his tender caressing
hands searching her body in delight. Another woman
would know the feel of his lips and the pressure of his
hard, masculine body thrusting into hers. And in just a
few minutes, Althea would be forced to see them together. It would be unbearable.

It was now midafternoon; soon she would have to go
down to the great hall to help greet the arriving guests.
She was already dressed for the evening banquet. Rachel
had worked all week on her gown, and it was magnificent.
Claude had decreed that she and Mathilde would each
have three new gowns made for the festivities, and this

one was Althea's favorite. It was made of pale ivory silk, embroidered heavily at the square bodice with royal blue and gold thread. The sleeves billowed down to her knees and were trimmed in gold Venetian lace. The waistline was right below her breasts, so the gown helped underplay her pregnancy. Rachel had braided Althea's hair and covered the top of her head with a cap of ivory velvet. Attached to the cap was a veil of gossamer silk that was so light it appeared to float to the floor.

She could delay no longer. For the last hour guests had been arriving. She had heard them riding into the courtyard below, their voices loud with greetings and laughter. If she waited any longer to appear, Claude would be furious. Forcing herself to remain calm, she rose from her chair.

The door clicked open. It was Rachel. "My lady, the count asks that you join him."

"I'm coming. Tell me . . ." Althea hesitated.

Rachel knew what she wanted to hear. "Yes, they have arrived. They were among the first."

So Guerre and Clarissa were here! Althea's heart pounded, but she steadied herself and looked at Rachel. "How do I look?" she asked.

"Lovely, my lady. I have never seen you look so beautiful or so noble."

Althea stared at Rachel searchingly for one moment, as if questioning her words, and then gave her a grim smile. Taking a deep breath, she left the chamber. It took her several minutes to reach the great hall. The castle was large, and the steep stone steps were difficult to undertake with her bulky body. Slowly, she went down the last stairwell, trying to concentrate on the steps lit only by torches that threw off an eerie light. She could hear laughing, boisterous voices coming from the hall. For one second she was tempted to turn back, but she overcame the urge to run. She would not let Guerre know how he had wounded her. He would never guess.

At last she was at the arch leading into the great hall.

For one moment no one noticed her, and she stopped and surveyed the scene. The hall was lit by many torches, and their smoke gave off a haze that made the room look unreal. She guessed that about half of Claude's guests had arrived, and all of them were merrily drinking and visiting. Her eyes searched the room for Guerre. It took only a second to spot him. He was standing by a smaller fireplace and was talking intently to a small brown-haired woman who was looking up at him adoringly. With a stabbing pain in her chest, Althea realized that this must be Clarissa. As she eagerly looked at the two, her view was blocked by Sir Peter Califfe, Claude's closest neighbor, who had joined the couple at the fireplace. His massive bulk blocked all view of Clarissa, and almost all of Guerre. So absorbed was Althea in the scene that she didn't see Claude approaching. She jumped with nerves when he took her by the arm.

"How curious you seem, dear Althea," said Claude with a sly smile. Althea looked at his gross face with annoyance. His eyes were overbright, and his face flushed, and she could see that he had already drunk too much wine.

Althea ignored his words, and he responded by tightening his grip on her arm. She winced in pain, and he smiled. "Come, my dear, and renew an old acquaintance."

Althea felt as if her legs were paralyzed, but Claude began to pull her across the room, and she forced herself to maintain a look of composure. As they drew near Guerre and his wife, Althea felt her heart hammering unbearably in her chest, and her throat felt painfully dry. Frantic, she thought that she would be unable to speak when addressed. Then Guerre, Clarissa, and Sir Peter turned to them. For one second that seemed like a century, Althea felt their eyes raking over her swollen body. It was only inborn courage that made her continue. And pride. She would not run from the man who had betrayed her.

"My dear Guerre, here is your old friend, the Lady Althea," said Claude in a joking manner that completely disregarded the feelings of all present, especially Lady Clarissa. Althea nodded her head coolly, and was hurt to see that Guerre's nod was as cold and impersonal as hers. Lady Clarissa, too, only gave a haughty nod that indicated that she was aware of Althea's story. Sir Peter, on the other hand, bowed as low as his massive bulk would allow and kissed Althea's hand.

"My lady, you are a lovely sight to behold," said the obese baron. Ordinarily, Althea found Sir Peter's effusive comments annoying, but tonight she was grateful for them. Giving him her most enchanting smile, she took his arm and inquired politely of his health.

"Fine, fine. And may I ask how is yours, for your time is close?"

"I have never been in better health, Sir Peter."

"I am pleased to hear you say that," Claude remarked dryly. "I have never seen a woman plead ill health quite so often as you have, dear Althea, and I am glad that you are now quite recovered."

Realizing the trap into which she had fallen, Althea flushed and took a goblet of wine a servant offered her. She took this opportunity to scrutinize Clarissa. She was not the great beauty Althea had expected. Petite and thin, she had light brown hair, and a round face that did not fit the thinness of her body. Her light blue eyes were round, and she had a pug nose, and lips that were pink and heart shaped. Glancing discreetly at Clarissa's body, which was covered by a pale blue velvet tunic and dark blue underskirt, Althea noted that her figure was not well developed. Clarissa was probably a pleasant and dutiful wife, she thought, but hardly an exciting one. As if feeling Althea's stare, Clarissa looked over and her eyes met Althea's. Althea was shocked to see pity in them.

Mathilde then joined the group. Her black hair hung to her waist, and she wore a tunic of purple silk and a black velvet underskirt. Her breasts were molded to the thin silk of the tunic, leaving nothing to the imagination, and her face was flushed with wine. She was obviously drunk.

"I regret my lateness, my lord," she simpered, curtsying to Claude.

"As I do, my lady, for you put your time to ill use. I fear that you have overindulged in your favorite grape." Claude's annoyance was apparent.

Ignoring him, Mathilde turned to Guerre and extended her hand to be kissed. "My dear Guerre," she said with a mocking laugh, "how pleased I am to see you again."

Guerre acknowledged her with a nod of his head, ignoring her offered hand, and Mathilde's face froze at the insult. Claude rushed into the conversation quickly, fearful of what she might say. "Lady Clarissa, I would like you to meet the Lady Mathilde du Bonfont. Mathilde, this is Guerre's new bride."

Both ladies bowed slightly, and Mathilde raked Clarissa up and down with her eyes. "She is but a child," she said in an insulting tone.

"Not at all, Mathilde," said Guerre in a silky tone that spelled danger to all who knew him well. "She is quite of marriageable age, although she may appear young to one of your years."

Guerre's words made Mathilde turn quickly in anger, but Claude again put out a restraining hand, and his fierce pinch made her jump in pain. "Enough of this," he said sternly. "Let us talk of the tournament."

The knights quickly began to discuss the events of tomorrow while the women silently listened. Althea stood stiffly, trying not to stare at Guerre, but her eyes would not obey her will. He had never looked more handsome, and she had never seen him dressed quite so elegantly. Men's styles were now becoming quite outrageous in their gaudiness, especially in France. The long pointed shoes favored by noblemen sometimes had a point almost a foot long, and they were the objects of ridicule by the populace. Sir Peter and Claude were both decked out like rainbows, the first in purple and red, and the second in green and

gold. Both had the exaggerated points on their shoes, and
the popular enormous puffed sleeves that hung almost to
the floor.

Althea thought Guerre's outfit was much nicer, although it was more conservative. His doublet was of
watered silk, and it combined two shades of green, one emerald and one a shade or two lighter. The sleeves were
trimmed in ermine, and he wore black tights that showed
his muscular legs to great advantage. Thankfully, he had
not adopted the fashion of the pointed toe. She had never
seen him dressed as a courtier before this, and she was impressed at how masculine he looked, while Claude and Sir
Peter resembled court jesters.

Althea saw that Lady Clarissa and Mathilde had both
noticed her studying Guerre, but while Clarissa seemed
only thoughtful, Mathilde was openly grinning at her in a
mocking way. Flushing, Althea was glad to see Sybalia,
Sir Peter's wife, coming toward them. Almost as large as
her husband and even more stupid, she was, nonetheless, a
good-hearted soul. She greeted everyone, and then turned
happily to Althea, whom she liked.

"My dear Althea, how pleased I am to see you up. We
had heard word of your ill health," she said.

Althea noticed that Guerre, who stood behind Lady Sybalia, frowned at her words and looked closely at Althea
for the first time that night.

"Thank you for your concern. I now feel quite well."

"That means nothing," burst in Mathilde with a dis-
dainful laugh. "Women do not bear children that breathe
in this castle. Look at your sister, Guerre. I would not celebrate too soon, Althea."

"Enough," cried Claude, furious and worried. He saw
Guerre's hand go instinctively to his dagger, and the expression on the younger man's face was murderous.

Mathilde looked up at him nervously, realizing that
her hatred of Althea had made her reckless. "I'm sorry,
Claude. It was the wine, I fear." She tried to look peni-
tent.

"We cannot tolerate your outbursts any longer, my lady," Claude said coldly. "Please retire to your chamber and recover yourself for tomorrow's festivities."

"But Claude—" Mathilde pleaded.

"Leave!" Claude was furious, all patience gone. His tone left no room for argument. Mathilde quickly curtsied, and then, with one venomous glance at Althea, left the group and retreated to her chamber.

The six of them watched her leave in silence, all lost in their own thoughts. Lady Clarissa looked as if she were trying to fit the pieces of a confusing puzzle, while Sir Peter and his wife looked totally taken aback at the scene. Guerre was white-lipped with rage, and Althea, too, was pale, but from fear. Claude alone was smiling, but it masked the fury that he felt for Mathilde. He had wanted to take Guerre off his guard and make him think that all was forgotten. It was important to disarm him so that someday Claude could have his full revenge. Now that stupid whore was opening old wounds and memories that he wanted forgotten. She would pay for her stupidity!

The awkward silence was broken by the arrival of four more visitors. All were happy to greet them and forget the episode that had just passed. Soon another large group appeared, having ridden together from the south. In the chatter and laughter that followed, Althea forced herself to smile and talk, although she knew that all eyes rested on her stomach for anywhere from a second to a minute, depending on the kindness and the courtesy of the guest. As she moved around the hall, she felt eyes boring into her back, and she knew that Guerre was using this opportunity to scrutinize her.

Damn him! she thought with fury. Let him look as much as he wants. The bastard! Her anger was so great that her face flushed, but this aided her, for several people commented on her bright, glowing cheeks. Finally, Claude gave the signal to be seated, and the guests approached the tables. The high table was set for twenty, and the ones to be seated in the places of honor moved to

the dais. Ordinarily, Althea sat at one end when there
were guests, but Claude grabbed her arm and motioned
for her to sit next to him in the spot where a wife would
sit. This doubled her humiliation, for all knew that she,
along with Mathilde, was his mistress, and now they
would think that she gloried in the role. There was nothing to be done, however, and as she took her seat, she
saw several ladies giggle and give her sly glances.
Throwing back her head with pride, Althea kept her
face expressionless, but she almost lost her composure
when Claude indicated that Guerre was to sit at her left.
Anger with Guerre consumed her as he sat down as if he
never had met her before this night. He chatted quietly
with Clarissa and totally ignored Althea.

Claude was now speaking to the beautiful Countess du
Fornay, Anne du Chelle, on his right. The two were laughing over something, and the whole room seemed filled with
people enjoying themselves. Except for Althea. She felt totally alone and humiliated. If she could have left, she
would have, but Claude would punish her in a way she did
not want to contemplate. Besides, she would not give
Guerre the satisfaction of seeing her leave. He must be
squirming inside, even if he looked composed. Here he
was, sitting at his dead sister's table with a new and obviously innocent wife, while the woman he had abducted
from her marriage bed sat pregnant next to him. It really
was scandalous!

Forcing herself to concentrate on something besides
Guerre, Althea looked around the great hall. Light was
provided by the great fireplace and three smaller ones,
plus innumerable torches on the walls and stone pillars.
Although it was usually cold and dark in the winter, the
hall tonight was ablaze with light, as it would be for the
next three nights to come. Tapestries, usually barely visible at this time of night, were clear to the eye. They pictured scenes from ages long past. One large one depicted
the First Crusade.

Fifty knights had accepted Claude's invitation to

show their skills in the tournament, and forty had brought their ladies. All had also brought their squires and pages and grooms, and the ladies who could had brought their maids. Claude had estimated that the usual inhabitants of the castle, which included fifty men-at-arms and around thirty servants, would now share their quarters with at least three hundred guests. The scene would have been exciting to Althea if circumstances had been different.

Everyone was in a gay mood. Except for the lucky nobles who were invited to live or visit at the royal court, life in most castles was lonely and fairly dull, especially in fall and winter. Travelers were fewer then, and unless a skirmish occurred between two neighbors, there was little to relieve the boredom. The anticipation of the long winter to come was one reason that almost everyone had accepted Claude's invitation. Personally, he was not very well liked, but few could resist the opportunity to visit.

Now all were eagerly awaiting the food and enjoying the hot spiced wine that was on every table. Althea saw the servants begin to enter the hall with their trays held high, and her stomach lurched in nervous response to all the food that she would be expected to try. The most magnificent banquet would be on the last night of the tournament, but Claude had not stinted for the other nights, either. There were ten roast pigs cooked whole with apples in their mouths, and three cows had been butchered for the huge platters of roasted beef. Other platters were loaded down with venison and rabbit. Each table also held a huge platter of fresh river fish decorated with fall fruit. Althea thought that all the food had been served until she saw more servants come out with wooden trays piled high with pastries of chicken and beef, and then more pastries stuffed with pheasant and quail. Claude took a good portion of each dish as it was served, but Althea could only nibble at the food. She noticed that both Guerre and Clarissa also ate sparingly.

At last, after two hours of feasting, the bowls of fruit

and comfits were brought out, and Claude signaled to a
troubadour. The man had been quietly strumming his
lyre throughout the meal. Now he began to sing, and his
beautiful, melodious voice was soothing to the overstuffed listeners. He first sang songs of war and fighting, and the knights, who were all getting drunk,
clapped in appreciation. Nothing appealed more to
these warriors than a good song about their favorite
pastime. After he had sung on this theme for a while, he
changed to a song of love, telling the tale of a maiden
who lived in a castle by the sea and who died of unre-
quited love. Although the tale was trite, the gentle
words and lovely tune touched Althea deeply. The song
reminded her of Wales, and she suddenly yearned for
the wind from the Irish Sea, and the misty woods filled
with the scent of home. Would she ever see Magara
again, or be free to run through the meadows and fields?
Her father's old, dank castle could not compare with the
beautiful castles of France, but she yearned for her na-
tive land. At least there, there were two people who
loved her—Magara and Edwina. Here there was no one.

As the song ended, Althea realized there were tears on
her cheeks, and she hastily dabbed at them. Looking up,
she saw that Guerre was staring at her, and she read concern on his face. Smiling ruefully, she gave a brittle laugh.
"A woman gets a little addled when she is in her seventh
month. 'Tis nothing." Before he could respond, she turned
to Claude, who was staring down the low-cut bodice of
Anne du Chelle's gown. "My lord, I beg your leave to retire."

Her face was so pale that Claude was tempted to let her
go. Besides, he was engrossed with the countess, who had
just informed him that her aging husband was not long for
this world. The countess had imparted this fact with no
visible sign of grief, and Claude was debating on whether a
nice little liaison might be possible. Then he noticed the
tears in Althea's eyes and felt a feeling of satisfaction. He
had arranged the seating of the table to make both Althea

and Guerre squirm, and she was not going to escape so easily.

"Impossible, Althea," he said with a silky smile. "I'm sure you will feel better soon. You cannot possibly abandon our guests."

Realizing how useless it would be to argue, she began to pick up the conversation a little farther down the table. It was the Count du Bargonne who was speaking, and she turned to listen, for the genial, handsome count had made a good impression on her when he had come to visit last month. He was a distant kinsman of Claude's, and his lands were near the Channel. "You can smell the sea from my battlements," he had said on his last visit.

" 'Tis truly a horrible curse," the Count du Bargonne was saying. "The victims suffer terribly, and almost always die."

"What gloomy talk is this?" Claude asked with a laugh.

"I was just telling Lady Sybalia about the curse they call the Black Plague. I was in northern Italy after my last visit here, and the rumors coming out of the south were dreadful to hear."

"I heard something about a plague, but I can't recall what," Claude said thoughtfully.

"It was brought to Italy from the Orient," the count told them. "No one had it in Genoa, but they said that thousands are dying in Naples. It is a grotesque illness, for the victim is inflicted with black boils the size of an egg, or even larger, and the stench from the afflicted is quite insufferable."

"When I was brought to France, there was a ship in the harbor that was carrying the plague. It had a black sail," Althea remarked, remembering the fear that the ship had inspired in everyone.

"Ah, that," said the count, who lived near Calais. "That was a false alarm. The ship carried the pox, and thanks be to God, it was contained."

Claude twisted uneasily in his chair, for he had a great fear of illness, no matter how remote. "Come now, this is no discussion to have on such a festive occasion. Naples is many days' journey from here. Come, troubadour, sing us songs of love and romance!"

All turned their attention to the minstrel except for Guerre. He was recalling the words of warning spoken by Dryden. "Beware black. I do not know what that means, but I saw it in the fire last night. It could be a person, or anything under heaven. . . . Watch for it. It could be the end of you and your beloved."

CHAPTER SIXTEEN

Althea slept little that night, for her mind was tormented by thoughts of Guerre. Even though they had exchanged few words at the banquet, sitting close to him for the evening had reawakened desires that could not be quenched. The long night that followed was one of torment and unfulfilled longing. She had tossed in her bed, thinking of when they had been lovers, and the frustration had been unbearable. She could feel his hands caressing her body, and his lips kissing her nipples, until she thought she would burn with longing. At last, she had risen from her bed and gone to the window, hoping the cold night air would cool her fever.

The cold air made her shiver, but in a perverse way she wanted to suffer, so she continued to look out over the tents that had been erected for all the servants who had come with their lords to the tournament. Although Castle du Vendome was the largest fortress within two days' ride, it still could not house the serving maids, pages, grooms, and squires of all the nobles who had decided to attend the festivities. Tents had been put up for them, and fires burned cheerfully throughout the courtyard and beyond the castle walls.

The cold night air had a calming effect on Althea, and she slowly turned her mind from thoughts of Guerre to plans of her escape. She saw with satisfaction that the tents and people outside the castle would help her greatly tomorrow night. With her disguise, the guards were very unlikely to stop her. They would think that she was just another serving wench. Claude feared no attack with so many knights visiting him, so people were allowed to come and go as they pleased. She smiled to herself. Tomorrow at this time she would be on her way.

She started to turn from the window when her eye caught a movement that stirred an uneasiness in her. She looked closely at the drawbridge, her eyes drawn by a sinister, crablike walk. She strained her eyes to see in the dark, and she felt her heart skip a beat when she recognized the figure. It was the old crone, Haggar. Appalled, Althea watched as the bent and menacing figure moved across the courtyard. Suddenly, as before, the old woman stopped, and then lifted her head slowly, looking directly at the window of Althea's chamber. Althea jumped back fearfully, and when she gained enough courage to peer out again, the hag was gone.

Althea awoke at dawn, and as she prepared to dress for the day, she shuddered at the memory of Haggar. She was leaving none too soon, she told herself. If Mathilde was deliberately disobeying Claude's orders, then she truly was desperate. Even in the light of a new day, Althea could not dispel the feeling of doom that Haggar had left in her wake. She was glad when Rachel entered with hot spiced wine and fresh bread spread generously with honey.

"I thought you might like something warm to start your day, my lady," said the serving woman.

"Thank you. Since it is All Saints' Day, Mass should be quite crowded, and it will be long before we eat."

"Claude left notice that all are to break their fasts as they choose. Men are already beginning to assemble outside to decide who will challenge whom in the lists."

While Althea munched on the delicious bread, Rachel brushed her hair until it shone like silk, and then tied it up in a blue silk ribbon. After she was done eating, Althea put on her gown. It was made of blue velvet, the color of a robin's egg, and the sleeves were trimmed in white fox fur. Her headdress and veil were of the same shade of blue, and she wore a headband of silver filigree. Claude had spared no expense on this occasion, and Althea's heart leaped with pleasure at the feel of the beautiful gown. For a moment she saddened when she thought of the two other gowns that hung in her closet. One was the ivory that she had worn last night, and the other was a gold satin creation that she loved. She would never get a chance to wear them in the convent, she thought miserably, and all that was young and lively in her cried out in anger at her fate. Life certainly was not fair, she thought with disgust.

"You are absolutely lovely," said Rachel, tactfully ignoring the frown on Althea's face. The serving woman adjusted the white scarf with gold trim on Althea's wrist. At a tournament it was tradition for the jousters to wear the scarves of their ladies, and no lady would dream of attending a tourney without a scarf to give to her love. Ruefully, Althea thought of whom she could adorn with her scarf. Certainly not Guerre! The scarf he would wear would be Clarissa's. She turned sadly toward the window and glanced out. Rachel had spoken the truth when she said the men were already gathering and planning the day's events. A scribe was busily writing down the challenges in the jousts, while many knights were already decked in light armor and were warming up in mock duels.

Althea spotted Claude talking to two knights who were involved in some argument, probably over whose prowess in the battle and on the tourney field was greater. They almost came to blows, and Claude was trying to calm them down. Both men towered over Claude, and they were very red in the face. It would serve him right if he got caught in the middle and received a good healthy blow, Althea thought grimly. Then her eyes began to search for Guerre. She knew that she would be late for Mass, but she couldn't tear herself away from the window. Her eyes scanned the milling crowd of knights. And then she saw him, and she almost fainted with shock. He was engaged in conversation with another man, and in one second she recognized him. It was Philip du Bois!

Althea gripped the stone casement until her knuckles

turned white. She could not believe it! Where had he come from? Claude would certainly have mentioned it if he had been expected, for his rank was higher than anyone else's, and the honor to Claude if he attended would have been great. Terrified, her mind flew back to the day in the woods. She still often had nightmares of it, but she had convinced herself that Philip would never return to Vendome, that Mary of Flanders and the promiscuous ladies of the royal court would have driven all thoughts of her from his mind. She had been wrong. He had returned.

She stared at the two men fixedly. Guerre and Philip were of equal height, although Guerre was broader in the shoulders and chest. Both were excellent fighters, renowned for their skills in battle, and the joust that they were evidently planning would certainly be the highlight of the day. As she watched, they turned toward the clerk who was recording the jousting opponents, and she saw their faces. Both looked grim, and it was evident there was no love lost between them. Althea's heart quivered at the sight of Guerre's face. How she longed to be the one to give him her colors today. How she longed to be his wife! As if feeling her gaze on him, he turned for one moment and looked up at her window. Startled, she realized that he saw her, and their eyes locked. It was only for one second, but to Althea it seemed like an eternity. When he turned away, she felt as if the sun had disappeared. The chill deepened when she saw that Philip was also looking up at her, and he was smiling.

At midmorning the ladies trooped over to the viewing pavilion. It was covered with a red silk canopy that billowed gently in the slightest breeze. The ladies were all dressed in their best finery, and from a distance, the viewing pavilion resembled a huge bouquet of flowers. Althea sat in the front row of the viewing box, nervously twisting the white silk scarf. The tournament was about to begin, and all around her women were chattering in excited anticipation. If circumstances were different, she would have been as eager as they, but she was filled only with nervous dread.

Trying to compose herself, Althea looked around at the festivities. Below the viewing box stood the heralds with their trumpets. There were six of them, and they had polished their instruments until they glowed like silver in the late morning sun. To the right and left of the pavilion had been gathered the banners of all the participating knights, and they waved in the breeze, adding even more color to the tournament. Over in a far field, Althea could see the crowd of peasants who had come to watch. To them it was a festival of the best type. Besides the entertainment, Claude had loosened his purse strings and had provided wine and food for the common people. The knights who would joust and fight were in a huge group on the other side of the tourney field, receiving last-minute instructions.

Althea rubbed her hands together to warm them, although it wasn't the cold weather that made her feel like ice. Mathilde was sitting next to her, and the mere presence of the woman filled her with dread!

A movement behind her caught her attention, and she turned to look. Clarissa was sitting directly behind Mathilde. Althea had not seen her enter, and was surprised when the young woman smiled at her in a friendly fashion. Could it be possible that Clarissa did not know about her and Guerre? Althea started to smile in return, but she caught sight of Anne du Chelle, who sat next to Clarissa. The beautiful countess did not try to disguise her contempt for Althea, her smile openly mocking. Althea flushed and turned toward the field.

Then the heralds lined up, and in a moment the trumpets sounded. The tourney was about to begin. Slowly, the knights approached the viewing box; they rode two abreast, with a squire on each side carrying his lord's colors. As the knights approached the box, they would tip their lances, and their squires would tip the colors that they carried. Then the knight on the left would turn to the left, and the one on the right to the right, making two long rows facing each other. When all had come forward, the abbot of Saint Michael's Abbey, who was the younger brother of Sir Peter Califfe, came out onto the field and gave a blessing for a successful day. Behind her, Althea heard Anne du Chelle titter. "The old abbot loves tourneys far more than his abbey. Why, he said the blessing at a good five that I have been to this past year."

"Doesn't his superior protest?" asked another lady.

"Of course not," Anne replied with amusement. "His father paid a fortune for the abbot's chair, and the bishop would turn a blind eye to much. Besides, the bishop is too involved with his mistress."

Several women laughed, but Althea saw that Clarissa was frowning. She realized that Guerre's wife was probably pious, as well as kind, and looking at her small, troubled face, Althea felt inexplicably drawn to her.

The chief herald announced the first contestants. Claude had challenged Sir Peter Califfe, and there were a few snickers. Sir Peter was old and heavy, and he was Claude's vassal. It would be easy to predict the outcome of this joust. Both knights cantered over to the pavilion and saluted the ladies. Sir Peter's wife threw him her scarf, and Claude made an obvious point of smiling at Mathilde, who immediately handed him her scarlet colors.

As the two jousters cantered back to the field, Mathilde turned to Althea with a gloating smile. "Do you plan to give your colors to anyone today, Althea?"

Ignoring her, Althea kept her attention on the field. The joust lasted longer than expected, for Sir Peter, with his years of training for battle, forgot that he was supposed to lose to Claude, and put up quite a resistance. At one point, he almost unseated Claude. Since both men had raised their visors, Althea could see that Claude was red with fury. Evidently Sir Peter realized it, too, for when the two men again clashed in the center of the tourney field, Sir Peter conveniently lost his balance. Again there were titters from the ladies, but they were subdued, for Claude

was their host. Althea saw Mathilde turn beet red when
Anne du Chelle commented that she was glad that neither
of the two knights wore her colors! Mathilde did not dare
retort to the Countess du Fornay, who was a good friend of
the queen's.

The next five jousts were almost as boring as the one between Sir Peter and Claude, but the ladies watched avidly.
Then the chief herald announced Sir Guerre du Reims and
Prince Philip du Bois as the adversaries. A gasp of astonishment broke out in the gallery. Few of them had ever
met Philip, but his reputation as a fighter and lover was
widespread.

"Anne, my dear, the prince must have followed you
here," one lady said to Anne du Chelle in a whisper that
was meant to be heard.

"Nonsense," said Anne loudly. "It is the love of the tourney that drew him." But Althea turned to see that she was
flushed with pleasure, and that she really believed that
Philip had followed her here.

Mathilde had been so busy preparing herself for the
tourney that she, too, had not known of Philip's arrival.
At the announcement, she looked overjoyed. She had
relished the lovemaking of the prince on his first visit,
and she had secretly hoped he would return and take
her to court. But at Anne's words, she frowned and lost
her sense of caution.

"I was not aware that you knew our guest," she said
with irritation.

"Of course you wouldn't, for you do not come to court,
madam," said Anne with a sly smile. "I am a friend of
Mary of Flanders."

"And a better friend of her husband," retorted one of the
ladies whose father was a duke, and who could dare to
tease Anne.

Tossing her head, Anne du Chelle ignored the insult. In
fact, her pride in being a "good friend" of the prince made
her happy that she was being discussed. Since his marriage to Mary, Philip had not kept an "official" mistress

but had spread his favors around the ladies of the court. Anne gloried in the attention she received from him, and she secretly prayed that her husband, the elderly count, would not last too much longer.

The ladies continued their chatter, but Althea's eyes were now glued to Guerre. He looked so strong and handsome in his polished armor. His visor was thrown back, and she could see his hard, strong features. He was speaking to Philip, and both men looked tense. Even from a distance she could sense the hostility between them. After a few minutes, the two men approached the viewing pavilion.

The two knights reached the stand, and Guerre spoke first. "My lady wife, will you favor me with your scarf?" He did not even glance at Althea.

"Of course," said Clarissa, throwing him her yellow silk. Althea forced herself to be calm, but the pain of witnessing this scene was torment for her. She tried to turn her eyes away, but they stayed riveted on Guerre's face, absorbing with agony the smile that he gave to his wife. So intent was she on Guerre she did not notice for a moment that Philip was directly in front of her, smiling down from his great war horse. It was only when Guerre turned toward his rival and her eyes followed that saw him. Flustered, she looked down at her hands.

"My lady Althea," Philip said in a low voice that carried through the silent box of women. "Would you honor me with your scarf, and let me be your champion today?"

Althea heard his words as the memory of his attack on her coursed through her mind. Embarrassment turned suddenly to fury. This man had raped her and abused her with no thought or consideration for her feelings, but now he dared play the courtier, and asked to be her champion! The arrogance of the man! Angrily, Althea looked up at him and said with cool fury, "There are others here who would be more than pleased if you selected them, my lord."

She spoke softly, but everyone heard her words, and the horrified intake of breath sounded like a wind rustling through the pavilion. The insult to the prince was beyond their comprehension. Boldly, Althea looked up at Philip, whose lips had curved from a smile into a snarl of anger. Their eyes locked, and Althea knew that she had made a deadly enemy.

Then, with a quick laugh, Philip reached over and snatched Althea's scarf from her hands. "I told you before, Lady Althea, that I take what I want!" With a kick to his horse's flank, he wheeled his great destrier to the left, waving the scarf in the air. Laughing, he rode out to the field, and Althea glanced at Guerre. His expression was unreadable. For a moment he looked after Philip, and then, with a sudden start, he cantered after him.

The awestruck silence remained for only a moment before the ladies burst into excited whispering. Never had they seen such a thing! Althea's face flushed with anger as she heard their comments. The nerve of the girl, to insult the prince in such a manner! Who was she? Nothing but an insignificant little Welsh whore! Almost every woman in France would give all they owned to be taken by Philip du Bois, and this hussy, swollen with a bastard brat, dared to scorn him!

The comments went on for several minutes until good sense began to prevail and they realized that they could be insulting the prince's future mistress. Who really understood men? Perhaps he would be intrigued by her rejection. Slowly, they started to comment about her bravery and her great spirit. Only Anne du Chelle, Clarissa, and Mathilde were silent. Althea could feel Anne's eyes boring into her back, and she felt terribly uncomfortable. Mathilde was staring at her out of the corner of her eye, and her look of naked hatred made Althea feel even worse. Desperately, she looked at the two knights who were at opposite ends of the field. She prayed silently that Guerre would not be hurt, and that the rest of the day would pass quickly. She could not wait to begin her escape from this place.

At the signal from the herald, the two men spurred their

horses and began to gallop toward each other, their lances
poised for attack. With a clash, they met in the middle of
the field, and the ring of metal slamming into metal
chilled everyone. The previous contests had been tame,
predictable jousts that had stirred little excitement. But
Guerre and Philip were two of the best knights in France,
and were well matched. It would have been an exciting
joust just for that, but all onlookers could sense the rivalry
that existed between the two men. Tension permeated the
air, and everyone watched spellbound as the two cantered
back to strike again. Again they clashed, but neither was
unseated. The force of their blows would have unseated
lesser men, but Philip and Guerre returned to their original starting places, preparing to attack again. For the
third time they spurred their horses forward, and the
horses kicked up clods of earth as they came toward each
other. The two men again joined lances, and this time
there was a resounding crack as Philip's lance broke in
two. The force of the blow almost unseated the prince, but
he quickly regained his position.

Shouts of praise rang out for Guerre, and Althea relaxed
for a moment. Her feelings of relief ended as the squires of
the two combatants rushed forward with their swords.
Guerre dropped his lance and took hold of his new weapon.
The men again cantered toward each other, now preparing
for a different phase of the contest. Philip had lost the battle of the lances, but he was a famous swordsman, and the
fight between the two men was furious. Jousting was
meant to be a sport, and no ill feeling was supposed to be
shown, but no one watching Guerre and Philip could doubt
that the fury between these two men was real.

With horror, Althea saw Guerre almost drop his sword,
and she held her breath till he had once again regained his
balance. Around her all the women were calling out encouragement to Philip. Only she and Clarissa were silent,
each praying for Guerre. The two men were locked in furious combat, and dust kicked up by their horses made it difficult to see clearly. Althea heard Clarissa gasp, and then

saw Guerre almost tumble from his mount. Philip was on
his right, and was leaning back for a killing blow. Then,
suddenly, Guerre reached over his horse's head and hit
Philip in the rib cage. Taken off-balance, Philip tumbled
from his horse. It had been a brilliant maneuver, and the
other knights began to cheer. Guerre had won the joust!
The ladies in the box applauded politely, and Althea could
feel her heart beating wildly. Although she felt exhilarated, she did not show it. This was Clarissa's moment of
glory, not hers.

There were three more jousts after Philip and Guerre's,
but all were boring and pallid by comparison. After the
last one, everyone retired to the castle to prepare for the
evening banquet. Althea managed to avoid Philip by walking back with a group of ladies. Once in her chamber, she
hurriedly washed her face and combed out her hair. There
would be no time for a bath, for she was expected in the
main hall immediately. Quickly she gathered the few articles that she would take with her tonight. In a large
woolen scarf she tied the few coins and trinkets that she
owned, plus her prayer book and cross and the food that
she had hidden away. Grimly she looked at what she
would be taking with her and felt disheartened. She had
nothing of real value to help pay her way into the convent.
Carefully, she put the scarf under the bed, thinking for the
millionth time how difficult escape would be. She didn't
want to speculate on her chances. She had no choice. The
danger here presented by Mathilde, and now by Philip,
was too great. She had to go.

She left her chamber and headed for the stairwell. The
steep steps that led from the tower to the great hall were
getting more and more difficult for her each day. Concentrating on each step, she did not see Philip standing at the
bottom of the stairwell until it was too late. With a start of
fear, she hesitated, debating on whether she should go
back, but he reached out and took her arm.

"Pray be careful, Althea, for if you took a tumble, it

would do you and the child great harm," he said gallantly, but his eyes glittered dangerously.

Seeing that he was leading her toward the main hall, Althea did not resist him, but she whispered sarcastically, "I was not aware that you were concerned with my bodily welfare."

Leering at her, Philip smiled. "Your body is of great concern to me. Although I was tempted to wring your neck this afternoon."

"What did you expect? I wasn't flattered by your attention."

"Most women would be."

"Most women have not been brutally raped by you," Althea snapped, snatching her arm away from his hand.

"I prefer to call it seduction. And you were no virgin," he said silkily. "I think I did you a favor, considering that you only had Claude to enjoy."

"I prefer to call it rape, and I did not want to enjoy either of you," retorted Althea heatedly.

"Only Guerre du Reims has that privilege." Philip's voice was like ice.

Althea looked at him, taken aback for a moment. His pale blue eyes looked slightly wild, and his lips were twisted in a snarl. She knew she was baiting a dangerous animal, but anger made her reckless. "He had that privilege once," she admitted, "but since then I have learned the perfidy of men, and I want none."

"Even if he were free?" Philip demanded, again grabbing her arm and halting her progress.

Althea stared at him. Part of her wanted to answer that if Guerre were free she would move heaven and earth to reach him, but she bit her lip. Her face told her thoughts, however, and Philip gripped her arm even tighter.

"I can see what you would do," he said coldly, "but it doesn't matter. He's already married to that drab little wench, although I can't imagine why. And I want you."

"Well, you will never have me willingly. I despise you.

The very thought of our coupling has given me nightmares since that day."

Taken aback by her vehemence, Philip stared at her wordlessly for a moment. "What you want doesn't matter. I take what I want, and I want you. When the brat is born, I'll be back for you."

Althea looked into his contorted face and prayed that tonight would go well. Only in a convent would she find any safety from her enemies. She felt him release his grip, and she moved her arm away.

"Remember." He said it with a smile. Then he offered her his arm in the formal, courtly manner, and since people were now watching them, she could not refuse. Together they walked across the great hall to the dais.

The banquet that followed passed like a dream for Althea. Rather, half dream and half nightmare. The ladies and their lords were dressed in their finest attire, and the torchlight caught and reflected the beautiful colors of the silks and velvets that the guests wore. Jewels set in gold and silver sparkled everywhere, and the mood of the guests was even brighter than the gems that adorned them. Althea thought that everyone but she was in the gayest of moods, and as laughter filled the air, joking and flirting were the spirit of the night.

Seated between Philip and Claude, Althea chose the latter as the lesser of two evils and tried to talk to him. Unfortunately, to his right was Anne du Chelle, and Claude was overcome by her charms. The lovely countess considered her humiliation of the afternoon only a minor setback in her plans for Philip, and now she sparkled with laughter and charm.

Althea sipped her wine slowly so that her senses would be alert tonight, and looked at Mathilde with amusement. She was the only other person at the banquet who did not look happy. Not as adept as Anne du Chelle in hiding her feelings, Mathilde was obviously annoyed that she did not sit in the place of honor next to Claude, but was put instead between Sir Peter and his brother, the tourney-loving abbot. She kept throwing angry glances at Althea, who was between the two men Mathilde desired most.

Past Mathilde and the abbot sat Guerre and Clarissa, and the pain that ripped through Althea when she saw them quietly talking almost made her ill. He looked so handsome. The red of his velvet doublet set off the darkness of his complexion, and the doublet was opened carelessly at the neck, revealing the dark hair of his muscular chest. He held a pewter goblet in one hand, and had carelessly flung his other arm around the back of Clarissa's chair. As she watched, he leaned over to hear what his wife whispered in his ear.

"I am quite surprised at his taste, aren't you?"

The voice at her left made Althea jump, and with embarrassment she looked into Philip's mocking face. "I was looking at Sir Peter," she lied.

"Of course you were." The sarcasm in Philip's voice made Althea flinch. "I see I caught you at a tender moment. It must be painful to look at a former lover who is so enamored of his wife."

"It is probably difficult for you to comprehend either my emotions or his, since I think you lack almost all feelings yourself!" Althea's voice was cold, but her lips trembled with emotion. She hated to think that her feelings were so easily read.

"You are wrong, my lovely little Welsh lady," said Philip smoothly. "I know one feeling well, and it is called desire." Smiling pointedly at Althea, he reached out and took her hand.

"Let go of me—now," she hissed angrily.

Ignoring her tug away from him, Philip continued gazing at her. "How delighted you will be when I take you from Claude," he whispered.

"You'll never succeed. I will plead to the king, or better yet, to your wife." Althea knew that these were hollow threats, but she could think of nothing else to say. To her surprise, Philip threw back his head and laughed loudly. Many heads turned to look at them, and Althea saw that they were the center of attention. Most smiled pleasantly, assuming that Philip had conquered another heart. But Althea noticed that Anne and Mathilde were glaring at her, and that even Guerre was frowning. For one fleeting instant she thought she saw jealousy on his face, and her spirits surged with joy; but the moment passed as he turned back to his wife.

Wearily, she regarded Philip. "I fail to see your amusement, sir."

"Why, the king would approve my taste and dismiss you as mad for rejecting me. He would probably make me your jailor." Philip smiled at her. "Perhaps that would be a lovely situation. I could lock you up in a tower and keep you all to myself."

Watching his cold eyes light up at the thought, Althea felt a moment of intense unease. If any man would enjoy such a thing, it would be Philip. Hoping to distract him before the idea could root in his mind, Althea asked, "And your wife? I doubt the Princess Mary would approve."

Philip leaned back in his chair and stretched, and once again Althea was reminded of a wild animal—a lion, perhaps—that had staked out its prey and, being well-fed, could afford to bide its time until the kill. He looked at her calmly. "The Princess Mary is grateful that she is married at all, and will do nothing to rock the boat with me. My mistresses keep me from her side—a fact that makes her extremely grateful to them. She would probably be very annoyed with you if you were the reason that I returned to her bed."

"I am surprised, Philip, that she could find your charms not to her liking," Althea said sarcastically.

"My wife is very plain, totally devoted to the good sisters of the convent she has founded at St. Cloud, and is, in short, a total bore. Bedding her was one of the most unpleasant tasks I have ever had, and she, in turn, loathed every minute of it. She thinks I am the devil himself and is quite afraid of me. But not afraid enough to return to Flanders, where her father would beat her to a pulp for ruining an alliance with France."

The poor woman, thought Althea to herself. Mary's plight was even worse than hers, for there was not even a glimmer of hope that she could escape. Life with Philip was probably a living hell.

Althea's thoughts were interrupted by Claude, who leaned over her to address Philip. "I believe that you are being challenged, my lord," he said, pointing to a group of men who were testing their strength by trying to raise several large iron bars. One had just succeeded and was now waving a challenge to Philip. There was no way he could ignore it, so he released Althea's hand and rose.

As Althea watched him go, she decided that now was the time for her to make her escape. The meal itself was over, but the evening's entertainment was just beginning. Everyone was mellow with good food and wine. They would soon forget that she was gone. She had to return to her chamber and get her cloak and the scarf that contained her food and small valuables, and she tried to think of an excuse to leave. Much to her surprise, she received some help from an unexpected source.

Anne du Chelle had been biding her time to bait Althea, and when Philip left the table, she released her claws, unaware of how helpful she was being. Leaning over Claude, she smiled at Althea and purred like a cat. "My dear Althea, how terribly pale you look. It must be your pregnancy that makes you look so ghastly."

Althea's first instinct was to come back with a sharp retort, but she saw the marvelous opportunity that Anne was giving her. "Yes, I'm afraid that the day has been too much for me. I feel very faint."

"Then you should retire," Anne said boldly.

"I would like that, but I am afraid that my lord will object," Althea said, looking pointedly at Claude.

Claude was in a dilemma. He couldn't care less if Althea left or stayed, but he did not want to upset Philip, and he also wanted to please Anne. A quick caress on his thigh made him decide. "Of course you may leave, Althea, if that is what you wish. I am not an ogre, keeping a sick woman here at the table."

"Thank you, my lord. My lady Anne." Althea gave them each a slight bow and left.

As Althea pushed open the door of her chamber, she was surprised to see that the candle by her bed was burning. And the tapestries that she had closed over the windows were now pulled free and were flapping in the wind. A feeling of unease overcame her, and she hesitated in the doorway. Someone had been in her room! She peered cautiously into the chamber, searching for an intruder. Her eyes could make out no one in the dim light, so she stepped forward.

Suddenly, she was pushed forcefully into the room by someone behind her. With a cry she fell on the floor, gasping in pain as her unshielded stomach hit the cold stones. Before she could turn and rise, she heard the door slam shut. Moving her head slowly, the sight she saw sickened her with fear. Above her towered Ruthin, and next to him was Johnny the Mouse. Both were grinning down at her, Ruthin with his simpleton's smile, and Johnny with malicious glee. Doing a little dance, Johnny pranced around her and cackled at her speechless stare.

"So we meet again, sweet lady," he chortled. "I'll wager that you never expected that, did you, miss?" When Althea did not reply, he went on. "The good count thought he could refuse to pay us our just wage for bringing you here. Ha, well, he was wrong!"

"What do you want?" whispered Althea.

"Why, we is just doing our work, my lady," whined Johnny.

"You make no sense! Are you mad? The castle is full of men. You can never take me from here."

"We don't want to take you from here, dear lady."

Before Althea could answer, the door once more swung open, and with horror, she looked up to see Haggar enter her chamber! Numb with terror, she looked at the gnarled, evil form was swathed in black. Even a black veil hid Haggar's face, but her gray, filthy hands were visible. They were covered with running sores, and her twisted fingers ended in nails caked with dirt. She was pointing one of those filth-encrusted fingers at Althea.

"Do as I tell you," the hag said softly.

She nodded to Ruthin, who bent down and swept Althea into his arms. Pleading and kicking brought no help, and in a second Althea was thrown on the bed. She tried to rise, but, impeded by her pregnancy, she could do little against Ruthin and Johnny. While the big man pinned her down, the smaller one tied her arms to the headboard. That accomplished, he moved to the bottom of the bed and grasped her right foot. She tried to kick him, but Ruthin held her leg down, and in a moment both feet were securely tied to the footboard, her legs spread wide. She began to scream, but Johnny gave her a sound smack on the jaw, and for a moment she was stunned into silence. When Haggar moved closer to her, Althea could smell the odor of decaying leaves and death that moved like a cloud with this woman, and her stomach lurched in nausea.

"No one will hear you," came the soft voice from under the black veil. "Everyone is celebrating in the great hall, and the servants are either working or drinking. The timing is perfect!"

"What do you want from me?" Althea managed, tears brimming.

"Revenge on the count," squealed Johnny, prancing around the bed.

"Silence." Haggar turned to Johnny, and though her voice had been only slightly louder, he obeyed her as if she had bellowed a command. "My two assistants here have rather vulgar reasons for aiding in tonight's work. Mainly, the excellent silver that I shall pay them. And, of course, revenge on the count for not paying them their due."

"And these are not your reasons?"

"Oh, I have been paid gold by Mathilde, but it just

worked out well that we could use you tonight. If you had not been available, I would have had to use another."

"Another what?"

"Pregnant woman, of course."

The reply made Althea's heart jump in terror. Rachel's words of warning came back to her. Who was this woman, and what did she want with her and her baby? She had to find out what was planned, even though she dreaded to hear the answer. "I don't understand."

"Do you know what today is?" asked Haggar as she opened a black sack on the floor, and took out different objects and set them on the table.

"It's All Saints' Day."

"That is a fine Christian answer. But it is also a sacred day for my religion, a faith much older than yours."

Althea began to feel sick. When explaining the Old Religion to Althea, Magara had stressed that it did not follow the practices of witches and sorcerers. She had used the harvest festival as an example. The true followers of the Old Religion had seen the harvest festival, which fell on the last day of October, as a time of rejoicing in the fruitfulness of nature. Witches and sorcerers perverted this day, and celebrated it with lechery and death. In their gatherings they usually sacrificed a baby or, better yet, a pregnant woman near her time. With mounting terror, Althea could now understand why they had not killed her immediately. Mathilde wanted her dead, and she had employed Haggar to do the act. And Haggar had selected this night, sacred to her perverted faith, to perform the ceremony. Althea's mind flashed back to the day Claude had announced the tournament. This was the reason that Mathilde had been so upset. She had not wanted the castle filled with people on this evil night.

Frantically, she watched Haggar set out her articles of evil, transforming her cozy chamber into a macabre shrine. Haggar draped large black cloths from her bed to the surrounding walls, creating a partial tent over Althea. Althea's candle had been put out, replaced by six large

black candles that gave off a greenish light. Some miner-
als had been thrown on the small fire in the hearth so that
it crackled and burned in weird hues of yellow and green.
On the table at the end of the bed were instruments of torture and a long black knife. A black chalice sat next to
them. The tapestries were tied back, and the wind made
the black sheets billow and the candles flicker. Through
the window Althea could see the moon, gray clouds racing
across its face.

Realizing that her time was getting short, Althea spoke
desperately to Johnny. "Surely you will die for this, and
then your soul will burn in hell for all eternity. You traffic
with the devil this night. Save me and I will see that you
are amply rewarded. I promise!"

Ruthin shuffled uneasily, and it was obvious that the
weird shadows and the unnatural light in the room were
making him nervous. But Johnny leaned down and put his
rodent face close to Althea. "It makes no difference to me
who pays my wage, my lady. I'll take coin from the devil
himself. And enjoy the work, too. Especially in your case!"

"Enough! It is time for the ceremony to begin," Haggar
ordered. She moved to the foot of the bed, holding the black
chalice high in the air.

"O Lord of Darkness, emperor of the night and ruler of
all creatures of darkness, this sacred night, I, Haggar,
your devoted slave, offer you a double sacrifice. A mother
and babe will be yours as a gift from me. O Prince of Evil,
who rides the wind tonight to receive the gifts of your followers, accept my sacrifice to you."

Haggar lifted the chalice six times into the air, and then
raised it to her lips. At that second the wind roared
through the casement, whipping the black sheets to a
frenzy and making the fire in the hearth leap like dancing
devils. Althea's heart froze in her breast, and even Ruthin
and Johnny cringed back into the shadows. It was as if the
room had been invaded by Satan and his devils.

Haggar went to the hearth and threw a substance on the
fire that made it soar into flames of vivid green, giving off

a putrid, sweet stench that filled the room. Then, slowly, she came up to Althea and lifted her skirt to her waist. With the knife, she tore off Althea's undergarments, leaving her naked. Althea saw Johnny start to move forward, but Haggar ordered him back with an imperious wave of her hand. Very slowly, she began to chant in words that had no meaning to Althea, moving her hips slowly and waving her arms like a snake. Althea watched with unutterable horror as the witch performed her fiendish rites over her body, but when Haggar picked up a pair of tongs from the table and indicated that she would take the baby with them, Althea began to scream and scream.

CHAPTER SEVENTEEN

As if to prove that good must triumph over evil, the door flew open, and Althea, half-blind with tears, thought she had gone mad and was hallucinating. For there in the doorway was Guerre. In one moment, Haggar was thrown in the air like a gnarled branch and fell with a thud onto the table, her clothes catching fire on the candles. Frantically, she beat at the flames, while Guerre took out his sword and strode toward Ruthin and Johnny.

So intent had they been on the ceremony that both men were befuddled by his sudden appearance, and Guerre ran his blade into Ruthin's heart with no resistance from the giant. The huge man died with a look of surprise still on his face, toppling down on Althea, who moaned in agony as his weight hit her. Guerre lifted the corpse off her body as Johnny ran from the room. Althea looked up at Guerre, tears streaming down her face, as he cut the ropes that bound her. His dark face was twisted with rage at what they had done to her, and when he saw the tongs still resting between her legs, he uttered a horrible curse and kicked Haggar the length of the room. Her black form came to rest against the wall like a dead bat.

Having freed her, Guerre gently cradled Althea in his arms, his face twisted with emotion. She wept softly in his arms from both shock and joy that he had saved her.

"My love," he whispered hoarsely, "are you badly hurt?"

"I don't think so," she sobbed. "Oh, Guerre, they planned to take the baby with those tongs and sacrifice us both to the devil."

"Those fiends! Well, the giant is dead, and I will track the rat down till he holds my sword in his stomach, I swear, Althea!"

"I think you stopped them before any damage was done to the baby. She hardly had touched me when you arrived."

"Thank God," said Guerre huskily.

He began to kiss her gently, and Althea sank in pleasure, brushing away the thought of Clarissa. It was enough that he had come for her and saved her from this vile tragedy. Then, suddenly, her peace was shattered by a curse at the door. Lifting their heads, Guerre and Althea saw Mathilde standing in the doorway, her face contorted with rage.

"What is going on here, Sir Guerre?" she demanded. "Why aren't you with your wife?"

Placing Althea back against the bed, Guerre walked slowly toward Mathilde. "It is no concern of yours, my lady, but it is good that I did stray up here, or the Lady Althea would now be dead."

"Be careful, Guerre," Althea warned. "She's the one who hired the witch!"

Mathilde stepped into the room, shock registering on her hate-twisted face when she saw Haggar on the floor. Before she could flee, Guerre brought his fist up and hit Mathilde on the chin. She slumped unconscious to the floor. "She will not sound the alarm for many hours, but we must move quickly," he said to Althea.

"What do you mean?" she asked as he gave her some clothing and wrapped her in a light woolen blanket and lifted her gently into his arms.

"Once again, my lady, I must kidnap you from your chamber," he said with a slight smile. Then sobering, he asked, "You do not protest?"

"Not at all, Guerre," whispered Althea weakly, her heart filled with joy. "But I don't understand."

"I'll explain it all to you at our leisure. Now we must get out of this castle before we're discovered."

Guerre moved quickly down the hall, holding Althea as
if she were a kitten. He slowed his step as they edged down
the narrow stairwell, not daring to move faster and risk a
fall. When they reached the lower floor, they could hear
the sound of laughter coming from the great hall, and
Guerre very gently set Althea down.

"You must walk from here until we reach the horses,"
he whispered. "The part that you must play is that of a
slightly drunken lady being walked in the fresh air by her
friends."

Totally puzzled, Althea nodded, and was even more
amazed to see Clarissa step out of the shadows at that moment and join them. She could not believe it! Guerre was
helping her escape with the aid of his wife! She had suspected that Clarissa was naive, but this was impossible.

"Trust us, Althea," Clarissa said gently. "All will be explained to you." Althea nodded dumbly, and the three
walked across the courtyard, which was filled with servants making merry.

"My lady, is that you?" asked a sentry as the trio started
across the drawbridge.

Paralyzed with fear, Althea looked into the face of a
guard who had frequently smiled at her. For one moment,
they all looked at each other, and then Guerre took the
guard aside and said in a jocular voice, "I am afraid the
Lady Althea partook of too much wine at dinner and is a
bit tipsy. Sir Claude asked that my wife take care of her,
and we thought a little night air would help."

For one minute Althea pretended to bristle at the impli-
cation that she was intoxicated. The guard smiled and
waved them through the gate and onto the drawbridge.
They walked slowly, trying not to look suspicious, although their nerves were taut and their ears strained to
hear if the alarm had been sounded.

Finally they were out of the light of the castle, and they
quickened their pace until they reached a grove of trees.
Althea's eyes had now adjusted to the dark, and she could
see that ten armed men, besides Guerre's page and squire,

were seated on their horses and ready to move. Two other horses were also being held. Clarissa ran to one and quickly mounted, while Guerre placed Althea on the saddle of Le Fer and swung up behind her. In moments they were moving away from the walls of the Castle du Vendome; once out of sight of the sentries, they broke into a gallop and raced through the night.

While close to the castle, Guerre had indicated to Althea to be silent, but now they were a good mile away, and Althea could be still no longer. "Guerre, what does your wife think of this?"

He smiled down at her gently, his rugged face softened by the love in his eyes. "I'm afraid I have no wife. At least, not yet."

"I don't understand."

"I pretended to marry Clarissa so that Claude would allow me to enter his castle. It was a ruse, and it worked. I regret any pain it might have cost you."

Althea looked at him with both joy and disbelief. She could not believe it, and yet she wanted to so desperately. At her stunned silence, he smiled a little sheepishly. "Are you angry with me? It was the only way I could reach you."

"Oh, no, Guerre," she whispered joyfully. "I just can't believe that you're really free. I've longed so for this moment. All through the terrible months that I was a prisoner."

"It tortures me that I can't give you the kiss that you deserve, my lady," he said wryly. "But I would imperil us both if I lost control of this horse."

"There will be time enough, although I do wish it were here," said Althea, smiling a trifle wickedly.

"Don't look at me like that, or I *will* lose control," chided Guerre. She could feel the heat of his body through the light cloak that she wore, and she felt excitement stir in her.

"I fear I'm not in the best condition to finish anything that I might start."

"You'll be delivered of the babe soon."

Althea noticed that he did not say *our* babe. So there was
doubt in his mind, too, about the father of this child that
she carried. They would have to discuss this when there
was peace and quiet.

"Guerre, who is Clarissa?"

He laughed. "My cousin. She's bound for the convent,
but she decided that she wanted one great adventure before she took up her chosen vocation. I fear the convent's
gain will be some man's great loss."

So the nagging thought that Clarissa was too good for
this world had been correct! Althea bit her lip to keep from
giggling.

"What amuses you so, may I ask?" said Guerre, pretending to be stern.

"How did a future nun enjoy sharing your chamber, my
lord?"

"My dear lady, I had the pleasure of sleeping on the floor
next to the hearth. Clarissa is very strong-willed."

"A wise woman," Althea teased.

Guerre's face turned serious. "No woman needed protection from me when you were under the same roof. All I
could think about was you."

They rode hard for several hours, but the horses could
keep the pace for only so long. Finally, Guerre called a
halt, and they stopped to rest. After they dismounted,
Guerre drew Althea away from the others into the shelter
and privacy of a small cluster of trees. Taking her into his
arms, he stared down at her face, which was touched with
moonlight.

"You are so beautiful, Althea," he mused, gently pushing back the hood of her cloak. He took a strand of her hair
and let it slide through his fingers.

"I still can't believe that you came back for me," she
said.

He gave her a wry smile. "I had hoped at times that I
could forget you, but I quickly gave that idea up as futile.
Then I spent all my waking hours—and they were many—in

planning how to capture you back. It took all the wisdom of
my friends to prevent me from riding up to Claude's castle
and taking you on the spot!"

Althea reached out and touched his face gently. "I
thought you had truly given up after my stupid behavior
at the fair. When I was told that you had married, I was
heartbroken."

Tightening his grip on her, he spoke with quiet intensity. "Did you really think that I would wed another? How
little you must think of me to believe that I would give up
so easily."

"I could only believe what I had heard. I was a prisoner.
I had no access to the world."

Guerre's expression became hard, and Althea could see
why men walked carefully around him. "He will pay someday for this. I swear it."

"Do you think they are in close pursuit?"

"I doubt it. Claude has no real claim on you. You were
never betrothed to him, and he has not wed you. There
have been many bad comments made about his behavior.
I assure you that not all French nobles are as insensitive
as Claude."

"He's so sly," she said with a shudder.

"He will wait for his revenge, but this time he will not
succeed. Enough of this talk. We have but little time."
Slowly he lowered his face to Althea's, and her heart beat
wildly as his lips met hers, kissing her hard and long.
Slowly, as if they had eternity, her lips parted, and his
tongue entered her, gently explored the warmth of her
mouth. So long and satisfying was this kiss that Althea
forgot everything but the warmth of his body molded
against hers. Then his lips moved from her mouth to her
neck, and Althea stood on tiptoe to meet him, for he was so
tall that she came only to his shoulder.

"Ah, I wish we had all night, but we must go. I only assume that Claude does not follow, and I can't endanger the
others if I should be wrong."

"We have the rest of our lives to linger together. Just to

be near you is enough,'' whispered Althea, her voice low with passion.

"Then let us go, and we will be at my home all the sooner." He held one arm around her as they returned to the others.

"How far is it to your lands?"

"Two days' slow ride from here. But if we push hard, we should make it by tomorrow in late afternoon."

"I thought we would be here until next week, the way you disappeared," a mocking voice remarked.

"Ah, let me introduce cousin Stephen, Clarissa's brother," laughed Guerre. "He has more courage than brains, and someday he will learn to fear me."

"Never," protested Stephen, stepping closer. "But the prize would make me linger, too. Your lady Althea is the loveliest I have seen since Paris."

Althea smiled at the knight, who looked as if he were about five years younger than Guerre. "You mean I have competition in Paris, my lord?" she asked with a smile.

"Only my beloved Veronique. And now I wonder if her charms equal yours."

"Don't let your 'beloved Veronique' hear you say that, or your head will be on the chopping block, my dear brother." Clarissa was already in the saddle, and Althea could see that she was amused by her brother's antics. Now that Clarissa was not playing the role of wife, she was much more outgoing and witty. Her humor enlivened her face, and Althea could see how this woman might long for some adventure before becoming cloistered. Althea thought that perhaps Clarissa might not be pursuing the right course. The walls of a nunnery might be too confining for someone as brave as she was.

She had little time to speculate on Clarissa, though, for Guerre quickly swung her into the saddle and jumped up behind her, and they were again riding through the night. It was about an hour later that Althea started feeling chilled and nauseated. At first she thought it was fatigue, but when she felt the first pain tear into her body, she realized with horror that she might be going into labor. Frantically, she thought that she was not due for a month, but as her body was torn again and again with agonizing pains, she knew that her time had come. She gritted her teeth when a cramp assailed her, but soon they grew so great that she moaned out loud, and Guerre looked down at her with concern. He saw that her face was white and her lower lip was bleeding.

"Althea, what is it?" he asked anxiously.

She bit her lip as another contraction tore her body apart, and she could not speak. Guerre quickly halted his horse, and the others reined in their mounts. The pain lessened for a moment, and Althea whispered, "I think the baby is coming a little early." Then another contraction ripped through her, and she moaned in pain. Guerre held her close, his face twisted with worry.

Clarissa had quickly surmised what was wrong, and she nudged her horse close to Guerre's. "The Convent of the Sacred Heart is not far from here. Perhaps a half hour's ride if we turn right and follow the river. The sisters have taken the vow of silence, but I think they'll give Althea shelter."

Althea groaned again, and Guerre and the rest quickly turned back toward the river. They reached it in about ten minutes and made a right at the cow path that Clarissa remembered. Althea was only half-conscious by now.

Guerre tried to hide his concern for Althea, but inside he was wracked with fear for her health. Her moans were becoming worse, and he had to support her with his left arm to keep her on the horse, for she had become weak from pain. He would never forgive himself if something happened to her, and he alternated between praying for her safety and cursing wildly at the convent that failed to appear before their eyes. Then, suddenly, he saw a small building lit by the moonlight. All the windows were dark, but Guerre spurred his horse to the front entrance.

Stephen and Clarissa quickly dismounted and pulled the bell at the heavy wooden door. The clang of the bell rang through the silent night as if it would wake the dead, but no one appeared at the door. Guerre boomed out that he would break the door down, and in response to his threat, the door slowly opened. A nun holding a candle in one hand looked out at them with fear on her face.

"We ask aid of your house, dear sister," Clarissa explained. "We have a woman with us who is giving birth and needs shelter."

The nun looked at them dumbly, and her eyes darted to the men of the party with apprehension. Guerre was about ready to leap from his horse and force entrance when a tall woman, garbed in the white robes of a nun, appeared behind her quaking sister. The second woman commanded respect, and the first nun looked at her with open relief, stepping back to let her take charge. The woman, who was the abbess of the convent, listened coldly as Clarissa repeated her tale, and hesitated only for one moment when she finished. Then she beckoned slowly to Guerre with one thin, white hand. Stepping back, she allowed him to carry Althea through the narrow door, with Clarissa following. But when Stephen and the others tried to follow, she put up her hand with such authority that they stopped. It was obvious to all of them that the abbess had relaxed her rules to the limit. The other men would have to remain outside.

Guerre and Althea were led to a tiny, clean cell that contained one bed. The nuns brought water and clean cloths, and made preparations for the birth. Althea was only faintly aware of what was happening. She was consumed with long, searing stabs of sheer agony that felt as if they were cutting her body in two. Her white face and low cries ripped through Guerre worse than any wound that he had received in battle. He was inexperienced in such matters, but something told him that this was not a normal birth, and since a third of all women died in childbed, his fear was intense. It was increased by the knowledge of the things that Althea had endured at the hands of the old crone earlier in the night, and he vowed a terrible revenge on anyone involved if Althea should die.

The hours that passed between then and dawn were a total blur to Althea. Between the agonizing pains that ripped through her, she would sink into oblivion, and dreams would take her away from the small cell where she lay. She saw Mathilde smiling at her with a gleam of triumph in her eyes, and Haggar prancing around the bed, laughing wickedly and waving a knife. A pain shot through her, and she knew that Guerre had been a dream, and that the evil of the night was going to win and take her baby. Then, suddenly, she was in Wales, and she could see a blonde woman dressed in pale green, laughing in a meadow. "Mother," Althea screamed, "help me!" But as the woman started to run forward, she dissolved into flames.

And the flames were now consuming her! She could feel the agony searing through her, and she knew that she would die. Peace returned as she saw Magara by the hearth in her small cottage. Here was help! But Magara never heard her cries, and she continued to stare into the fire, saying that she could see nothing in the flames. Then the most agonizing pain of all ripped through her, and she saw Philip astride her in the woods, forcing his swollen member into her and smiling, smiling as he tore her body to shreds. She could see the light blue sky through the trees of the woods, and then the sky slowly turned a darker blue. It was now the Irish Sea, peaceful for once, caressing the sand along the shore; and with gladness she wandered into the warm water, calling for Guerre. Then there was nothing.

She had been staring at the pale Christ on the crucifix for hours, although she had stopped praying days ago. But it was peaceful to stare at the cross and thereby avoid everyone who came in and out of the tiny cell. She did not want to talk to anyone, although the only two who were allowed to speak were Guerre and Clarissa. The nuns had all taken vows of silence, and they used sign language to communicate with her. Every day one would come and kneel at her bed and pray, and Althea knew that they prayed for her and the baby—or rather, for the soul of the baby. For her son was dead. He had never even given a cry, Guerre had told her sadly. He had been born too soon, and the terrors of the night before his birth had not helped him in his fight for survival. They had buried him in front of the altar, where the good sisters were laid to rest when their time came. Althea never even had time to hold him, for he had been put in his small coffin before she had resumed consciousness.

They had feared for her life, Clarissa had whispered to her. But now she was recovering. She would live. Strangely, she didn't care. The will to live had left her, and all her emotions had dulled. It was only her youth and her healthy body that refused to give in to death. Even Guerre could not make her desire anything but to sit and stare at the tiny cell. It was her whole world, and she wanted nothing but its peace and tranquillity. One cot, one candle, one small stool, and the crucifix hanging on the wall.

How simple life was in this tiny room. No outside world to disrupt and destroy things. The world was a cold and cruel place, and it had cost her child his life. She was tired, and she thought how tempting it would be just to lie here refusing food until death quietly came and took her to join the poor, innocent babe that now slept eternally under the cold stones of this convent.

Guerre came to see her often, at least five times a day, but she often did not hear him when he spoke. She could hear his voice, but she blotted out the words. When he took her into his arms, she lay lifeless, wishing he would go away; and if he held her hand, it was like ice in his.

She could hear him coming down the corridor now. In this place of extreme quiet, his natural masculine movements could be heard clearly, although he tried to move softly. Slowly the door opened, and he entered, his dark face a picture of sadness and anxiety.

"Althea, I must talk to you," he whispered. He knelt on one knee beside the bed and took one of her cold hands in his. "You have lain in this bed nigh on one week, and Clarissa tells me that your bleeding stopped more than four days ago. She thinks you are well enough to travel if we keep a gentle pace."

When Althea did not respond, he continued. "The longer we stay here, the greater chance of Claude and his men finding us. Men stand out conspicuously in a convent, and the peasants have already noted our presence. Soon Claude's spies will locate us."

"Leave then, if you fear for your safety," said Althea coldly.

Anger flared in his face, and he scowled at her. "You know that I am not a coward, and I would face the devil himself for you. But it's foolish to needlessly endanger us all when it is only two days' ride to the shelter of my castle walls."

"I think I will stay here. I do not choose to leave my son," Althea stated calmly, and Guerre gazed at her in astonishment.

"Althea, we will have sons . . . and daughters. Many of them." His voice was pleading, and Althea raised herself on one elbow and looked at him angrily.

"That is exactly it!" she screamed. "We will have sons. But what about the one who is dead! I don't hear you say that your son is dead. You just refer to him as the babe, never as your son! You never believed that he was your child, did you?" Suddenly, all the resentment surfaced, and both Althea and Guerre had to face what was between them.

Guerre looked away, his eyes remembering the tiny little corpse that he had helped to bury. How torn he had been. He had never really known if the child was his or Claude's, and part of him cried for his son, while the other part was glad that his rival's bastard was gone. He had hated himself for it, but he realized that he never thought that Althea had noticed his confusion.

He faced Althea, "I am guilty as you accuse me," he admitted. "I didn't know for sure, and that was worse than knowing. I have not slept well for days with worry about you and guilt over the child. I cannot say 'my child' because I do not know." Althea was crying softly, and he tilted her face up to look at him. "Althea, can you say for sure yourself that the child was mine?"

The angry outburst and the relief of tears had released the pain within her. What he spoke was the truth. She had so wanted the baby to be his that she had started to believe it, and his confusion only added to hers. Now it was out in the open, and she suddenly knew that she could not blame Guerre. He was being honest.

Her crying went on, as if she were shedding all the tears that had built up in her. Guerre put his arms around her, and she sobbed, "My son, my son," over and over again. It did not matter who the father was, nor did it matter that Guerre suffer with her. His presence gave her strength, and she knew that he loved her enough to take her when she was carrying a child that might not have been his.

After her tears were spent, she allowed Guerre to bring her some broth and cold chicken, and then she consumed a goblet of wine. The food and drink lifted her spirits, and she felt remarkably better. Although she was a little shaky, she realized that she was glad to get up and start preparing for the journey to Guerre's home.

CHAPTER EIGHTEEN

They traveled slowly because Althea was still quite weak, but the ride through the French countryside was pleasant for her. Clarissa and the men who accompanied Guerre went out of their way to be pleasant and keep up her spirits. Althea was particularly drawn to Stephen, Clarissa's brother, and to Michael, Guerre's squire. In two more years he would become a knight, but he had such fine gold hair and innocent blue eyes that Althea found it hard to believe he was old enough to fight. He was three years younger than she, but she felt much older, and talked to him like an older sister. It was apparent to all that poor Michael had developed a crush on his master's love, but he took the kidding he received with good humor, and continued to wait on Althea whenever they stopped and rested.

Everyone from Guerre to Michael told her about all the interesting points that they passed, and Althea was interested and impressed. It was November, but the weather was unusually mild, and the sky was blue. The peasants and the small villages through which they traveled looked fairly prosperous, and children waved to them as they rode by. As they got closer to Guerre's lands, she sensed the others getting excited about returning home, and the pace quickened.

At dusk they arrived at an inn that bordered Guerre's lands. It had been a long day for Althea, and she went to her room gratefully. She was pleased to see that the bed was clean and the floor had been freshly swept. She lay down on the bed and watched as Guerre directed the serv-

ing wench to start a good fire, and then ordered mutton
and wine for their dinner.

"You make me too comfortable, my lord," she whispered
lazily, smiling at him.

Putting his hands on his hips, he pretended to glare at
her. "Do not smile at me like that, madam, or you will feel
something more than comfortable."

Arching her eyebrows, Althea gave him a wicked grin.
"I think my virtue is safe with your entire company
nearby. You would not dare anything rash with Clarissa
so close."

"I would not bet on that." He sat down on the edge of the
bed and took Althea's hand in his. "I am an imprudent
man. When I see something I want, I take it, and damn the
consequences." He laughed. "And perhaps an example of
our ardor would change that silly notion Clarissa has of
entering a convent."

"It would probably make her run there as fast as possible," giggled Althea. "She would feel duty-bound to pray
for our souls."

"Well, that's her problem," whispered Guerre as he
leaned over and gently kissed Althea on the lips. "It is not
the Church that keeps me from loving you right now, Althea. I will not touch you until you are well." He began to
stroke her hair, and his black eyes grew even darker as he
gazed at her. With wonder Althea thought how good it was
to have a man who could be so fierce and strong, and yet so
gentle. Slowly, she lifted her hand and caressed the scar on
his cheek.

"Thank you," she whispered at last.

"For what?"

"Thank you for loving me enough to risk your life to
save me."

He slowly touched her lips with his finger, and then his
mouth was on hers, sensuous and demanding. He had removed his armor, and he wore a loose-fitting velvet tunic
the color of amber, and dark brown leggings. The softness
of his clothes could not disguise the hardness of his mus-

cles. She put her hand under his tunic and caressed his chest. He gave a soft moan and abruptly sat up, releasing her.

"What's wrong?" she asked, bewildered.

"I'll forget my good intentions if you continue." He smiled at her. "Let's just sit here for a moment and relax." He took Althea back into his arms, and they sat and gazed contentedly at the fire.

The wonderful peace between them ended when the serving girl entered with a tray of food. Guerre told her to place the tray on the table by the bed, and Althea propped herself up on the pillows. She hadn't realized how famished she was until she smelled the aroma of the seasoned food. Eagerly, she watched Guerre lift the covers, revealing mutton seasoned with garlic and lemons, and hot bread smothered with butter and cheese. There was also a pitcher of steaming hot wine. They both ate with relish, and finally Guerre laughed at her.

"I had no idea you could consume such a quantity of food. I would not have decided to marry you if I had known," he laughed.

Stunned, Althea looked at him over her goblet of wine.

"Why do you look so surprised? I was only joking."

Althea's face fell, and she suddenly wanted to cry. So he didn't want to marry her after all.

"Althea, what's wrong?" demanded Guerre, getting serious.

"Nothing," she whispered, not trusting herself to speak.

"Yes, there is," he said sternly. "Just because I joked about your appetite, you got annoyed . . ." He paused and looked at her quivering lips. Then, suddenly, he realized what was wrong. Pity for her welled in him. She was so young and had been through so much that she did not even trust his teasing. He took her into his arms and held her close. "Althea, I was not joking about marrying you. I would do that if you ate like an elephant."

Unable to say a thing, Althea clung to his strong body, tears of happiness streaming down her face. For the first time since she had left Magara's cabin, she felt that she had come home. Home was in the strong arms of this man, and she didn't want to let go. Understanding her need, he held her close for long moments, until she straightened slightly and smiled at him.

Guerre's expression then changed, and his hands, as if they had a will of their own, moved to her breasts. Slowly he began to fondle them, staring at her intently. Althea felt the heat of his passion, and felt it rising in her, too. She lay back on the bed, the firelight coloring her hair so that it shone like polished gold. Guerre's lips found hers, and they kissed with an intensity that startled them both. Passionately, he pressed his body next to hers, and Althea moaned with pleasure at the feeling of his body.

"Althea, we will be wed as soon as we reach my castle. I promise you." Then he sat back, pushing her slightly away. "I had better leave or my willpower will not last the night." Althea wanted him to stay, but she knew that she was not yet ready for lovemaking. Silently, she nodded to him, and with a chaste kiss, he left the chamber.

Althea sat staring at the fire for a while, feeling herself growing sleepy, but still wanting to be awake to think about Guerre and how pleasant the night had been. If this was how it would be when they were married, she could not wait to take the vows. Her happy thoughts were interrupted by Clarissa, who entered the room she would be sharing with Althea for the night.

A small smile lit up Clarissa's face, but she shook her head in mock anger. "I was ready to enter this room if my cousin did not depart much sooner. Now that he has compromised your reputation, he will have to marry you. That is all there is to it!"

Althea smiled, knowing that the other girl was just teasing her. "I'm afraid my honor was compromised long before this night."

There was just a touch of sadness in Althea's voice, but Clarissa's sharp ears heard it, and she answered quickly. "Don't be silly, Althea. You did not compromise yourself. Claude du Vendome forced you to be his mistress. Guerre—

and everyone else—knows that. Forget the past, and start to live for the future. And Guerre is your future."

"Thank you for being so understanding. And thank you for helping me to escape. You took great risk for me."

"I enjoyed every minute of it," Clarissa told her. "Except when I saw the pain on your face. Then I realized what our deception was costing you."

"It was necessary," said Althea. "But I must admit that I was very jealous of you."

Clarissa laughed and finished undressing. She put on a plain linen sleeping shift and got into bed beside Althea, pulling the fur rug up close to both of them. For almost two hours the two women told each other of their lives. Althea related her childhood in Wales and told Clarissa some of the things that had happened at Claude's castle, though she omitted the most humiliating events. They were still too painful to discuss. And she didn't mention Philip at all.

Clarissa told Althea about her peaceful childhood in her father's castle, and how she and Stephen had loved to visit Guerre and Alycia. "Her death was quite a blow to me. She was like my older sister. It was then that I decided to enter a convent. And it was also because of her death that I was so eager for this escapade. It has helped me feel that she has been avenged."

"That's not a very good reason to cloister yourself for the rest of your life, Clarissa."

"My mother died in childbed, and so did Alycia. I think the fate of women who marry is often very sad. Look at your own mother, Althea. I would prefer to be a nun."

"All that you say is true, but sometimes it's worth the risk. I love Guerre, and life with him will be wonderful. Perhaps you have not yet met a man who is worth the risk."

"Well, I've already made up my mind. Soon I will enter the Convent of Saint Theresa."

"When will that be?"

"I haven't quite decided," answered Clarissa with a yawn.

Settling down for the night, Althea smiled to herself.
Perhaps Clarissa wasn't as committed as she thought she
was.

The next day Althea rose refreshed and eager for the
journey to begin. The faster they reached Guerre's castle,
the sooner they would be married. Fairly dancing with anticipation, Althea had to smile when Clarissa chuckled at
her impatience.

"It's a full day's ride at least, so try to restrain yourself.
After all, Father John can't marry you tonight!"

"I know, I know," said Althea, twirling around in a little
circle. "But perhaps tomorrow."

"My goodness, you Welsh women have no restraint at
all," murmured Clarissa, pretending to scold. "Now if it
were me, I would make my lover wait until he was so frustrated that he would break the door down to reach me."

"I see that you have your strategy all planned," said Althea slyly. "I find it difficult to see how you will put it to
good use with a mother superior hovering near."

Clarissa blushed, and then looked at Althea ruefully.
"Well, I had plenty of time to consider these things before I
decided to become a nun." Ignoring Althea's open grin, she
adjusted her clothes. "Besides, if one grows up in the
French court, one learns these things quite young. The noble ladies of France pride themselves on their ability to se-
duce and hold a man."

Althea had been putting on her cloak, but now she
looked at Clarissa in surprise. "I didn't realize that you
grew up at court."

"Well, not really grew up. My uncle is the Duke du Marton. He arranged that I go to court to assist my aunt, the
Duchess Anne. I was there for two years."

Seeing Althea's puzzled expression, Clarissa continued.
"My grandfather on my father's side was the late Duke du
Marton. He had three sons, and Norman, the eldest, is the
present duke. The second son, John, was Guerre's father,
and the third, André, was father to Stephen and me. He

died about a year ago," Clarissa explained. "He didn't last long after John died. The men in this family marry late, so they were both well along in years."

As the two women walked down to the common hall, Althea asked another question. "The present duke must be quite old then?"

"Yes." Clarissa frowned. "But he lives a soft, corrupt life at court, as does his son, and he may live quite a while longer."

"He has a son?"

"Yes, also named Norman. Although Guerre and his sister and Stephen and I were all close, none of us had much to do with him. He's quite dissolute. He's good friends with Philip du Bois, and the crowd they run with is the worst at court. They were half the reason I decided to enter a convent."

They reached the common room and joined Guerre and Stephen at the table.

"Clarissa, you are always talking," chided her brother. Both he and Guerre rose so the women could slip into the benches at the large table.

"Clarissa has just been telling me about your family," Althea said.

"Good lord, now she will run away again," laughed Stephen, and he frowned in mock dismay.

"Now, now," said Clarissa, breaking off a hunk of fresh brown bread and passing the loaf to Althea. "The only bad part I told her about was dear old Norman."

"That was enough," groaned Guerre.

"I take it that Norman is not too popular," said Althea.

Guerre grunted, and Stephen rose. He took Althea's hand and made a mock bow over it, changing his voice in obvious imitation of Norman. "My lovely lady," he said in a slight falsetto, "I have never seen such loveliness. I think that I will pluck you like a rose in the garden, and cherish you in my chamber."

"Until you fade, and then you will be tossed out with the vase water," added Clarissa.

Sitting down in a huff, Stephen said pettily, "Dear cousin, you have wrecked my lovely seduction."

"I am your sister, and you do it as poorly as Norman," said Clarissa acidly.

"Enough," Guerre said. "We have to suffer Norman's presence once a year, and I do not wish to see him even in a charade."

"He should be arriving soon, too." Stephen's frown was genuine this time.

"Why?" asked Althea.

Guerre looked a little bitter as he spoke. "He is our liege lord, although he rarely knows what is happening on his lands. Actually, his father, our uncle, is our liege lord, but he never leaves the side of his mistress and is well advanced in age, so he forces Norman to call on us each year. Young Norman cannot get out of it, for he will inherit his father's lands. Luckily for us, he hates to leave court and detests us as much as we detest him. So his visits are very brief."

"What made him turn out so badly?"

"His father spoiled him," said Guerre. "He was the only child, and his parents doted on him. They should have sent him away from court; but they didn't, and he fell in with Philip du Bois and the dissipated group that runs with the prince. They will ruin him in the end."

Althea said nothing, and the conversation changed to another subject. But as she ate, she wondered if it was her imagination that made her think that Guerre had looked at her more closely when he talked of Philip, almost as if he were gauging her reaction.

They arrived at the Castle du Reims at dusk, and Althea could make out only the outline of the castle in the fading light. She could tell that it was smaller than Claude's fortress, but it appeared well constructed and in good repair. A sentry saluted them, and they quickly rode over the drawbridge.

"I wish it were lighter so that I could see my new home," Althea said to Guerre.

Tightening his arm around her, Guerre smiled. "You'll have plenty of time to see the place. After all, you'll be spending the rest of your life here. Unless, of course, you have any objections."

"None at all."

They dismounted in the courtyard, and a middle-aged man carrying a torch rushed out to greet them. Bowing low, he said happily, "Welcome back, my lord. We have missed you."

"Thank you, Pierre," said Guerre, smiling at the man. "Pierre, this is Lady Althea, who is to be my bride. Althea, this is my steward, Pierre, who runs the castle—and I think, at times, me."

"I am pleased to meet you, Pierre," smiled Althea. "You must have your hands full if you try to keep Sir Guerre in order."

"Thank you, Lady Althea. At times it is a trying task." The short, chubby man beamed at her, and she decided immediately that she liked him. Guerre had told her that he had come to the castle over thirty years ago, and though he was a servant, they all thought of him as an uncle of sorts. He was totally devoted to Guerre, and the knight trusted Pierre completely.

"Clarissa, show Althea to the main hall. I will be with you shortly," said Guerre.

Pierre, too, stayed in the courtyard, but he spoke to the women as they passed. "The sentry saw you coming, so there is hot wine on the table and the fire is lit."

Althea and Clarissa nodded their thanks and entered the doorway that led to the main hall. Inside, Althea was impressed with the warmth and comfort of the large room. There were two big hearths, one at each end of the room, and in one a fire was burning brightly. Near it were six comfortable chairs and a small table on which rested a decanter of wine. The center of the room held an enormous oak table that could have seated sixty people. Taking a goblet of wine from Clarissa, Althea gratefully sipped the steaming drink and continued to look around the room. A few torches were burning at the other end, and she had enough light to see the tapestries that decorated the walls. As she sat in one of the chairs, she noted the huge bearskin rug at her feet.

"It's a beautiful room," she said at last.

"Yes, it is quite comfortable. When there are more people here, the other fireplace is lit, and it really helps the chill in the air. Right now I am going to move my chair closer to the fire."

Both women settled down by the warm hearth, and Althea realized that she felt at home already. More at home than she had ever felt in her entire life, she thought happily. Although a castle was a fortress, and comfort was not often to be expected, Althea could tell that someone had thought carefully about this room and had tried hard to make it as pleasant as possible. She confided her thoughts to Clarissa, who nodded.

"It was Guerre's mother. She grew up at court, and she was used to pleasant surroundings. I agree that she did a very good job with the place. I love the fur rugs that she had placed here and in the bedchambers. They're so much nicer than rushes on the floor. That's her portrait over to your right. The woman with the ruby necklace."

Althea stood up to look more closely at the painting that she had missed in the poor light. The woman in the picture was about twenty, with long black hair and bright blue eyes. Guerre had evidently inherited his dark coloring from his mother, although his features did not come from her. The woman in the picture was very delicate and small. Althea glanced at another picture next to the portrait and thought for a moment that it was again Guerre's mother, but Clarissa read her thoughts and interrupted.

"That was Alycia. She was almost an exact replica of her mother. Her father had the portrait done several months before she married Claude."

Althea studied the picture carefully, noting the sad look

in Alycia's eyes. With pity, Althea wondered if Alycia had regretted the betrothal to Claude. The sad eyes of the girl already had a haunted look. Had she known what fate had in store for her?

Guerre and Stephen then entered the hall. She saw that Guerre was frowning, and that Stephen, too, looked distressed. Pouring wine for the two men, Althea wondered what could be wrong. Suddenly she had a wild thought, and she turned with fear to Guerre. "Is Claude pursuing us?"

"What?" Guerre looked at her, startled out of his thoughts. Then, realizing that he had frightened her, he continued. "No. I just had disappointing news." At her inquiring glance, he sighed. "The priest who would have married us, Father John, has died. Pierre received word while we were gone. Now we must wait until a new priest arrives."

Althea's face fell with disappointment. She had so hoped that they would marry tomorrow. Sharing her frustration, Guerre guided her gently to her chair, and then rested his hand on her shoulder. "I am as sorry as you are, Althea. But hopefully, the new priest will be here in a matter of days."

Althea smiled at him. "We've waited so long. A few more days won't matter."

"I cannot believe that Father John is dead," said Clarissa with shock. "Why, he wasn't that old. In fact, only about ten years older than you, Guerre."

"Evidently, he died from some sort of plague. I've heard something about it. It's been killing many in the Italian states, and now it has crossed into France."

"The captain of the ship that brought me to France told me about it," said Althea, shocked. "It's a terrible disease. People suffer terribly, and they get horrible black pustules on their bodies. The Count du Bargonne was talking about it at dinner the night before the tournament."

"That is the disease," said Guerre, nodding slowly. "No one knows what causes it. Some think it is caused by rats, although not all sufferers are bitten. If it strikes in one area, it seems that just about everyone gets it. The messenger who brought the news of Father John's death said the entire village next to the one John was visiting died of the curse. There was no one left to bury the dead, and signs have been posted for no one to enter the village. It's a charnel house."

"I don't understand," said Clarissa. "What messenger?"

Guerre turned to his cousin, and in the light of the fire, Althea could see the lines of concern on his face. "Father John asked me over a fortnight ago if he could visit his home village about three days south of here. I granted him permission to go as long as he returned within twenty days. He was in his home when he caught the plague and died. But before he died, he begged a young boy in the village to take his horse and ride here to tell us that he was dying, and to beware the plague. The boy arrived this morning."

"Perhaps it will not come this far north," said Althea hopefully.

"I don't know, Althea. The village that John called home is on a river and has many travelers. The boy was well informed, and he said that the curse was hitting many other areas. He called it the Black Death."

"How horrible," said Althea, shivering. She saw the others were as grave as she was, and even Stephen, usually so exuberant, was frowning. "Where's the boy?"

"Pierre has bedded him down with a family in the village near the castle walls. You did not see the village, Althea, for it is on the other side of the castle. Only ten families live there. The rest of my serfs live scattered over the land. They are an independent folk and like their privacy."

"Like their master," said Althea with a smile.

"Yes. Now their master—and yours—is hungry." Guerre straightened and turned to the large table. Althea saw that while they had been talking, someone had entered and placed food on the table. They all sat down at the end near the fireplace, and Althea looked ravenously at the roasted pheasant and steamed fish with mushroom sauce that were on the table. There was also fresh bread and a large cheese. A young servant girl entered with a steaming bowl of mutton stew for the table.

"We are happy to have you back, Sir Guerre," said the young girl, smiling happily.

"Thank you, Marie. This is the Lady Althea, who will soon be my wife and your new mistress."

Althea smiled as the girl bobbed a clumsy little curtsy, and the girl shyly smiled back. Althea realized that both Pierre and Marie were genuinely glad to have Guerre back. He was evidently a popular master, and Althea felt her pride in him grow. Then she noted his expression and was puzzled. He was staring at his food but not eating anything.

"There must be some logical answer for it. I cannot believe the explanations that people are giving."

"For what?" asked Stephen.

"For the Black Death," said Guerre. "All sorts of rumors are afloat as to its cause. Some say it is witchcraft; others say the Jews are poisoning the wells to kill all the Christians. But that makes no sense, for Jews are dying, too. And others say it is the wrath of God, sent to destroy us for our wickedness. There seems to be no logical explanation. I wish we knew more about how our bodies worked. Perhaps then we would know the cause of this pestilence."

They all discussed the little that they knew, and soon the meal was finished. Settling down in front of the fire, they continued their conversation for a while.

"I think the hour grows late," Clarissa soon said, rising. "And I intend to retire. Will you follow me shortly, Althea?" Her tone left no doubt that she felt some suitable chaperonage should exist.

Before Althea could answer, Guerre spoke, irritation clear in his tone. "Sleep easy, cousin, for Althea will have the chamber next to yours. I only wish a word with her alone before she retires."

Taking the hint, Clarissa and Stephen both bade Althea and Guerre a good night. Alone at last, Althea suddenly felt shy, and she stared into the glowing hearth. The wine and the heat of the fire had warmed her into drowsiness, but part of her was alert and excited.

"Is the fire more fascinating than me, Althea?" asked Guerre softly.

Althea looked up at him quickly. He was standing up, his arms folded, staring at her with an intent expression of desire. "No, I was . . . just confused for one moment."

"Confused?" Guerre arched one black eyebrow, perplexed.

She looked back at the fire. "Flustered would be a better word."

Guerre chuckled. "Over Clarissa and her ill-disguised prudity? Damn, sometimes I really think I can see her as a mother superior."

Althea smiled, and he moved toward her as lithely as a cat. Before she realized what he was doing, he had lifted her from the chair, sat down, and deposited her on his lap as easily as if she had been a kitten. They looked into each other's eyes for one moment, and then his lips eagerly sought hers, and they were lost in each other. Althea felt as if his arms would crush her, but she thought with wonder that it would be heaven to die that way. He drew back, and a little moan of disappointment escaped her. She saw that his black eyes were lit with passion, but there was a small, rueful smile on his lips.

"I think Clarissa was more accurate in her fear than I realized. It is taking all my self-control not to take you here in front of the fire."

"I'm afraid that my resistance would not be enough to restrain you," she grinned.

"Minx," he said with a laugh. Then he turned serious. "You have been through so much, Althea, and I was partly to blame. I want the next time we make love to be in our marriage bed. I think you do, too."

Deeply moved by his kindness, Althea stroked his face

with her hand and looked at him with love. "Thank you. In truth, it *is* what I want. But if you wished it otherwise, I love you too much to say no."

"Thank you for that," said Guerre gently. "With luck, a new priest shall arrive soon. I sent my most trusted messenger to the archbishop and demanded a replacement with the utmost speed. The man was ordered to travel through the night, so he should reach Orleans by tomorrow, midday." He paused, his face turning thoughtful. "Do you remember the night we made love on that plain with the strange stones?"

Althea thought of that magical night, and nodded. "Many times when I was Claude's prisoner I would remember. Sometimes the nights were so long, and I would take out that memory and live it again in my mind. I thought you were dead, but something inside me never let me forget you . . . and that wonderful night."

She spoke so simply from the heart that Guerre was deeply moved. "An old man rescued me and nursed me back to health. His name was Dryden. He was a priest of the Old Religion, although he assured me that he did not practice witchcraft. I am very indebted to him, although at first I thought he was dangerous."

"No, he wouldn't have harmed you. The priests and priestesses once were all over England and Wales. They were finally driven into the mountains. There are only a few of them left, and they aren't as powerful or wise as the ancient ones. Yet they still know much."

"You seem to know a lot about them, Althea. Clarissa would not approve."

Althea looked at Guerre quickly and saw he was teasing her. "My aunt Magara is a priestess of the Old Religion." She looked at him closely to see if he was shocked, but his eyes held only interest, so she continued. "She is a wonderful, kind woman, and she uses her skills only to do good. The village people both love and fear her. I think the love is far greater. Often, she is their only hope. She taught me to value love and life, and to turn from evil. That is what the priests of Mother Church say, too, so I see no problem."

"Neither do I, but many would disagree. Clarissa, for one. She's a good woman, but she has spent too much time at her prayers." He smiled at her kindly. "Was your mother a priestess also?"

Althea flinched as if she had been hit. "No," she answered quietly. Suddenly, she wanted him to know everything, including her mother's story, even if he later rejected her for the truth.

"My mother was burned at the stake for witchcraft."

"I know."

Althea was stunned. It was not something that most people would discuss, and she knew that Claude had tried to keep it from his people. He didn't want them to think he was marrying the daughter of a witch.

Guerre stroked her hair. "Dryden told me." Seeing her surprised look, he told her the story. "I learned to trust him, and finally I confided to him my love for you. He seemed to know so much about everything. He said that your mother had been accused of witchcraft and executed, but that it had been a false charge."

"It was my father's revenge," said Althea slowly. "My mother had taken a lover, and he had discovered it." She paused, staring into the fire. "All my life I have been called the daughter of a witch and a whore. My father hated me. Edwina said that I looked too much like my mother. I think I finally drove him mad."

"It was his own guilt, Althea, that drove him mad. A man does not do that to a woman, even if she has betrayed him."

"Then you do not mind?"

"Althea, I certainly do not condone adultery, but I do think that your father may have given your mother good cause to betray him. Dryden said that he would often beat and abuse her. Many men do not practice the code of chivalry in their own homes, but I think that your father was worse than most."

Althea felt tears come to her eyes. They were tears of joy that he could be so understanding. So many men would have rejected and ridiculed her for her mother's past. Putting her arms around him, she began to cry softly. "I only remember her as if in a dream. Sometimes that dream is a nightmare, and it is always the same. I am hiding under a bed, trying to blot out the light of the flames that comes from the window. The memory still terrifies me. Her only crime was to find love, but I have often felt cursed by her fate."

"That's all behind you now," whispered Guerre. "You're in France, and Wales is very far away."

"I do feel safe here," Althea said softly.

"Well, don't feel too safe, my lady, for your closeness is again making me reconsider my temporary chastity." He kissed her gently on the lips. "I think I better show you to your chamber, or Clarissa will come down to rescue you!"

CHAPTER NINETEEN

The following days were a combination of extreme pleasure and total frustration for Althea. The pleasure came from the closeness to Guerre, and the time they spent together. When he was free of his duties, he showed her the castle and the surrounding countryside, and she was entranced with everything she saw. The castle, although large compared to her father's, was still small when one thought of Vendome. This, however, was not a fault to Althea. It was very well built, and Guerre told her proudly that it had once resisted a siege for three months. Althea could see that it was in an excellent position for defense, having been built on the crest of a hill, and surrounded by a moat. There were four large towers: one to house the men-at-arms; two for storage, which also held the cooking area and the workrooms of the artisans; and the fourth tower for the living quarters of the family. In the center of the castle was a large courtyard, and Althea was pleased to discover a rose garden off to one corner. Guerre saw her studying the plants, and told her about them.

"They were planted by my grandmother. Things were very unsettled then, and my grandfather did not want her to venture beyond the safety of the castle walls. He gave her permission to plant her garden in this odd corner. Pierre takes good care of it now. You'll love it in the spring. Once, when I was a boy and was practicing my fighting skills, my father advanced on me and I retreated until I fell right into the bushes. I had on no armor, so you can imagine the teasing I got when I had to have the thorns removed. It taught me always to cover my retreat!"

They had laughed over that incident, and Guerre showed her the rest of the castle, which housed thirty soldiers and over twenty servants. She admired the upkeep of the place, and was proud that Guerre took such good care of his property. He made it plain to all that she would soon be his wife, and Althea began to take up the duties of the mistress, supervising the cooking and conferring with Pierre about supplies and servants' problems. She enjoyed the work, and she was grateful that Clarissa stepped back and only gave advice when it was asked.

On good days, she and Guerre would ride into the countryside and visit his lands. She found that he rode out frequently and knew all his serfs and freemen by name, and in two weeks they had talked to at least three hundred people. They were all glad to see him, and they felt free to discuss their problems with him. All smiled shyly at Althea, unsure of her, but she tried to put them at ease, and most were more friendly and open by the time they had left.

These tours served two purposes. They kept Guerre abreast of what was happening on his land, and they served as a wonderful escape for both him and Althea. Riding across the land, they could find secluded nooks in which to stop and kiss without the prying eyes of the house servants, and Stephen and Clarissa. Castles were not made for privacy, and they had few moments alone when they were home. But the woods and the meadows were perfect for lovers, and they went out almost every day.

It was this escape from the others that was a mixed blessing. Both were dying from frustration, and the priest had not yet appeared. The days were turning into weeks; now December was here, and Christmastide was fast approaching. The weather was still unusually mild, and they could still reach for each other out of doors; but with each day it was becoming harder and harder to restrain themselves. Sometimes, when Guerre would push her away, he would brood all the way back to the castle, and Althea could feel his frustration and impatience building. He had made a vow not to touch her until they were married, and

she found that he took such things seriously. Not wanting
to tempt him, and yet wild with her own pent-up passions,
Althea felt torn by conflict. Sometimes she longed for
snow, and a respite from their frantic, unfulfilled lovemaking in the woods. Soon, they kept telling each other, the
priest will come.

It was after one such exciting yet frustrating afternoon
that they rode across the fields for home. Dusk was rapidly
approaching, and the night had turned cold, with snow
flurries being whipped by the wind. Althea felt chilled,
and she wrapped her cape tightly around herself. Ahead
they could see lights from the castle, and she thought eagerly of the hot wine and warm fire waiting for them. They
were approaching the castle from the east, a new way for
Althea, and she could see three or four cottages huddled together. Startled, she realized that there was a figure walking toward the cottages, and she was surprised that anyone would be out walking on such a night.

Evidently Guerre had seen the figure too, for he slowed
his horse and changed direction slightly so they would in-
tercept the person. Althea saw it was a woman wrapped in
a long brown cape. As they neared her, the cape fell back,
and Althea saw that the woman was actually a young girl.
She had long black hair, and though she appeared to be a
peasant by her dress, there was something regal about her.
She would have been beautiful if she had not been so thin,
and Althea felt a curious stab of jealousy as she saw the
girl look up at Guerre with an expression both inquiring
and haughty. Althea thought that there was something familiar about the girl, but she couldn't place her, and then
her thoughts were redirected when she noticed that the
girl carried a baby under the cape.

Guerre was frowning, and he looked annoyed. "The
baby will get ill if she stays out in this weather, Theresa."

The girl looked steadily at Guerre. Althea, feeling uncomfortable, wondered if the girl was mute. Then, acting
as if she had decided on something, the girl spoke, her

voice steady. "She is my concern, Guerre, not yours." She never acknowledged Althea with even a glance. With a nod to Guerre, she turned and left them, heading for one of the cottages.

Guerre silently watched after the girl, and Althea sensed that she was more to Guerre than another serf, and the child concerned him deeply. Anger flared in her. He could at least have told her about any illegitimate children he might have fathered. It was common for noblemen to take their pleasure with women of the land, but she was still hurt to the quick, and with an angry kick, she spurred her horse to a gallop and rode with fury toward the castle. In a moment she heard Guerre's horse behind her and his cry to halt, but she ignored him and galloped on. Le Fer was much faster than her mare, and in a second he was next to her and grabbing the reins. Enraged, she tried to hit him, her fury increasing when she saw that he was laughing at her. When he had succeeded in stopping her horse, he was roaring with laughter.

"What a jealous little minx you are!" he cried. "By the Rood, I never dreamed that you would have such a temper!"

"Only when it is justifiably aroused, my lord," she said hotly.

"Is it?" He was suddenly serious, and with a firm grip on her reins, he started toward the castle. She could barely see the expression on his face, but she knew that he was now back to the mood that the girl had brought on him.

"Althea, I may have sowed my seed in some women somewhere, for I have not lived a chaste life. But I kept myself to women who knew what they were doing, and who surrendered to me with pleasure. I have never inflicted myself on an unwilling child who would not be able to say no to me!"

"Perhaps Theresa was willing," Althea said sarcastically.

"She was not willing, and she was not with me." Guerre's tone was harsh.

"I don't understand," said Althea hesitantly. "She didn't speak to you like the other serfs. She spoke to you like an equal."

"She is my sister."

Althea started, shock overwhelming her. Guerre was riding slightly ahead of her, and she could not see his face, but she sensed the tension and outrage in the stiffness of his body.

After a few moments, he began to speak. "She's really my half sister. After my mother died, my father found consolation with one of his servants. She was willing and happy to be his mistress. In time she gave birth to Theresa. My father let the woman stay on in the castle, although she soon grew fat and unappealing. He took good care of them, and he intended that Theresa would one day take over Pierre's job. It is more than most men would do for their bastard offspring."

Althea thought sadly that what he said was true. Unfair, but true. She could tell that there was more to the story, and she waited for Guerre to continue. He had slowed his horse and she could see his face more easily. The strain was clearly visible.

"After my father died, there was trouble on some property that is two days' ride from here, and I left soon after the funeral. While I was gone, my cousin Norman"—Guerre spit out the name like something foul in his mouth—came for his annual visit. He was accompanied by his usual cronies, Philip du Bois and the like. It didn't take them long to spot Theresa."

Althea felt sick. "Didn't he know that Theresa was his first cousin?"

"Of course." Guerre's voice was deadly. "But as he said, such things are not acknowledged when the cousin is only an illegitimate brat."

"Norman sounds like a monster to me!" Althea felt sick, and it wasn't only over Theresa. Any mention of Philip du Bois made her almost physically ill.

Guerre nodded grimly. "I would have killed him if I had

found out when I returned. But when I arrived home, Theresa had disappeared, and I, absorbed in other things, did not notice the absence of a . . ." He stopped, and Althea knew that he had almost said "servant." He looked at her bleakly. "Alycia and I were always separated from her in important things. The difference in our stations was always made very clear. But I was fond of her, and would have taken good care of her."

"Then what is she doing out there in one of those hovels?" Althea knew it was a cruel question, but she could not stop herself from asking.

"I didn't discover what had happened for some weeks. Theresa's mother said that she was feeling poorly and had taken to her chamber. Then one day I saw her in the meadow, and I was horrified by the change in her. She had become gaunt and pale, and when we talked, she finally told me the truth. Later, she discovered that she was with child. It was then that she moved down to a cottage. I've tried to get her to come back, but she refuses. Now she lives down here with her mother and her child, and I see to it that they have food and clothes."

They had reached the castle, and they rode quickly over the drawbridge. Althea could not wait to reach the warm fire, for she needed to dispel the gloom that had descended on her.

The days passed slowly, and soon winter covered the countryside with snow. Guerre and Althea went out only for short rides, and as a result, they had become more tense and irritable with each other. The unnatural strain of abstinence created an atmosphere that sent Althea into tears at a harsh word, and Guerre into a brooding silence that could last for a day. Althea spent hours working on a tapestry for the chapel. She would look up quickly and see Guerre watching her, his dark eyes intense. When she smiled at him, he would turn and leave. Once, after such an incident, she had gone to the window and seen Guerre mount his horse and gallop furiously over the drawbridge,

racing through snow-covered fields until he had disappeared from view. He returned late that night, and Althea
did not ask where he had gone. The tension on his face
showed that he had not spent his desire on some willing
peasant or village whore.

Clarissa and Stephen tried to keep the mood lively, but
they were not very successful. To add to the gloom, the
few messengers who ventured to the castle brought tidings
that depressed everyone even more. The plague had not
yet struck close to them, but the news from other areas
was terrifying. One messenger from the south of France,
who was heading for England, told of entire villages suc-
cumbing to the dread disease. He told them of men sitting
down to eat dinner and, before the last course was served,
falling dead on the floor. The messenger's own sister had
died the day after her wedding, and the groom and over
half the guests had died within a week of her. One good
note was that the plague seemed to be contained around
the area of Marseilles and the French villages bordering
on Italy. Perhaps the outbreak in Father John's village
had been a freak occurrence.

He had another piece of bad news, as well. So great was
the dying in areas infected with the awful disease that the
archbishops were sending all available priests into the
south to perform last rites. The messenger was doubtful
that any would be available to perform Father John's
duties. The gloom that descended on them after his visit
was so great that Clarissa and Althea decided that something must be done to lift their spirits. Christmas was only
a week away, and they decided to decorate the main hall.
After some discussion, Althea realized that customs in
Wales were a little different from those of France, and she
decided to implement some old Welsh traditions as well.

Leaving Clarissa in the main hall, where she was setting up a nativity scene, Althea ordered her horse and set
out for a copse of trees not far from the castle. With relish,
she felt the cold on her face, and she looked with delight on
the fresh snow that had fallen last night. The sun was

shining, and the sky was blue, and she loved being out of the castle for a while.

She rode carefully, for the snow was slippery, and she didn't want her horse to fall. After a few moments she noticed fresh footprints in the snow, coming from the direction of the cottages near the castle wall. It seemed as if they were heading toward the group of trees. For a moment she paused, wondering if she should return to the castle, but then she dismissed the idea as silly. None of the peasants would hurt her, and besides, she was armed. She felt for the silver dagger that she had brought, and, reassured, continued forward to the grove.

As she got closer to the small wood, Althea recognized the person up ahead as Theresa. Not wanting to alarm her, Althea raised her hand and waved, but the small girl in the gray cape continued to stand rigidly, staring at her.

"Good day," Althea said, throwing back her dark blue cloak so the girl could better identify her. "It's Althea." The figure did not respond, and, slightly annoyed, Althea slowed her horse and approached the silent girl slowly. "You have nothing to fear. I just came out to cut greens for Christmastide. It's the custom in my land to decorate the main hall with evergreen boughs." Althea looked down at the pale face and saw that there was no fear in Theresa's eyes. She was regarding Althea with a distant reserve. Knowing her sad history, Althea could see why this child wanted nothing from the people who lived in the castle; but because she herself had suffered so much, she could not turn her back on Theresa. Smiling, she dismounted.

"I see some boughs on that tree that would be perfect over the hearth." Knowing she could not rush this friendship, Althea walked away from the silent girl and began to cut little branches with her dagger. She stole a glance at Theresa, and saw that she had resumed what she had been doing before her own arrival—gathering kindling. Althea moved farther into the wood in search of some berries that could be used as a substitute for mistletoe. Clarissa had told her that the favorite Christmas decoration of the English did not grow here, and Althea wanted to use something in its place. When she finally found some berries, she returned to the entrance of the wood and saw a lone figure far in the distance. Theresa had started the long walk home.

Just thinking about Theresa brought back the awful memories of her own rape at the hands of Philip du Bois. What made it worse was that it was a burden she carried alone. Although Guerre knew what she had suffered at the hands of Claude, he did not know about Philip. The memories of that abuse were so bad that she could not bring herself to discuss them, although she wished that she could confide in Guerre, hoping that talk would exorcise the nightmares that disturbed her sleep and the memories that would suddenly distract her in the bright light of day. She feared Philip du Bois far more than she feared Claude. Claude was basically a coward who would not strike unless he was sure that his prey was helpless. But Philip was a hunter, and the greater the danger, the greater his excitement. Claude was an opportunist who had used her for certain ends. Philip had no purpose other than to satisfy his lust.

As if to match her mood, the sunny day became cloudy and overcast, and she could smell another storm brewing. Her mare whinnied nervously, and the small copse of trees took on a sinister cast. Suddenly she longed for the safety of the castle. She knew that her fears were irrational, but still she felt threatened. Gathering her boughs of evergreen and the red berries, she swung herself onto her horse and started the ride back home. She cursed herself for her silliness, and yet, as she rode back to the castle, she knew that her fears were not groundless. As long as Philip du Bois was alive, she would be in danger. He had singled her out for the chase, and he would not rest until he had captured her. A strong premonition filled her, and no matter how hard she tried to deny it, she knew that it was only a matter of time before he appeared to claim her.

* * *

Back in the castle in Clarissa's lively company, Althea was able to dispel some of her apprehension by decorating the main hall. They worked all afternoon without disturbance, since Guerre and Stephen had gone hawking. With happy abandon they covered the room with greens and ribbons, and Clarissa even wrapped streamers around the columns of the hall. Althea admired the nativity scene that Clarissa had set up in one corner, and she studied the manger very carefully after Clarissa explained that all the figures had been made by Guerre's mother. Clarissa watched with fascination as Althea hung the berries in strategic locations around the room. Her rapt attention showed her approval of the Welsh custom of mistletoe.

"Anyone who stands under the mistletoe can be kissed by anyone else that person chooses," Althea explained. "Of course, this isn't true mistletoe, but it will have to do."

"I imagine that you and Guerre will accidentally come to rest most often under this plant," said Clarissa shrewdly.

"You have a very suspicious nature for a future nun, Clarissa," answered Althea tartly. "Although I think that you would not be angry if some handsome knight caught *you* under the berries."

Althea had expected Clarissa to make some quick retort about the stupidity of men, but to her surprise, Clarissa looked suddenly sad and turned listlessly toward the fireplace. "There will be no handsome knight for me at this table. After all, Guerre is my cousin, and Stephen is my brother. That does present a problem, doesn't it?"

Althea looked down from the stool on which she was precariously balancing. Once again she wondered why Clarissa was planning to become a nun. Although she was deeply religious, she did not seem to have the zeal that was necessary to seclude oneself in a convent.

"Perhaps the Magi of Christmastide will make one appear from out of the blue," Althea teased to lighten the mood. "Do you have a preference for color of hair, or eyes, or the type of build?"

"Oh, let him have dark hair and green eyes, and let him be tall and wide of shoulder," said Clarissa airily. "And let him be rich and at least a count."

"I'll see what I can do," said Althea with a laugh.

It was as if the Magi of Christmastide had heard their wish, for when Guerre and Stephen returned at dusk with the birds that they had caught, they brought along a guest. Sir Guy Melville was English, but his mother had been French, and he was on his way to visit with her family, who lived near Paris. But if the Magi had produced a knight for Clarissa, they had provided one who was the exact opposite of her description. Sir Guy was poor and, as the third son of an English knight, he was landless. He made his money by traveling from one tournament to another, competing for prizes. He was short, red of hair, brown-eyed, and slightly plump. But his face radiated kindness and mirth, and all were glad to have him as a guest. As he recounted his adventures, Clarissa's eyes began to sparkle at his humor, and Althea thought that perhaps there was indeed such a thing as Magi. It was one of the most lighthearted meals that they had had in a long time, and they all retired to the fire with hot wine and ale to continue listening to Sir Guy's tales. He was quick to notice the berries, and knew at once that Althea had been trying to duplicate mistletoe. With a laugh, he warned the ladies that they had better be on their guard, but Althea saw that he looked at Clarissa as he spoke. The heavy mood that had been on Guerre for days lifted, and he, too, joined the merriment, while Stephen picked up the lute and sang a plaintive lament to his Veronique in Paris.

"I don't think that this fair Veronique truly exists," said Althea with a laugh, after he had finished a haunting ballad. "If she is so fair and full of charm, then how can you keep yourself from her?"

Stephen looked rather sheepish, and Clarissa bubbled with laughter. Althea noted again that Clarissa seemed unusually lively tonight. "She does exist, and all the traits that he gives her are true," said Clarissa, with a grin at her brother. "Unfortunately, there is one stumbling block."

"She is already wed," said Sir Guy, sadly shaking his head.

"No," said Clarissa, her eyes twinkling.

"Tell us," begged Althea.

"It is her age," said Stephen with a sigh.

"She is an old crone," said Guy eagerly.

"No," snapped Stephen with irritation. "She is not too old but, alas, far too young."

"Veronique will not see her thirteenth birthday until this spring," Clarissa explained.

"So that is the problem," said Guerre with a laugh. "I have often wondered why you stayed here or at your own estates when you could be in Paris with your Veronique. Now I understand. It is not a jealous husband or lover that keeps you away, but a careful father."

Stephen hung his head, trying to take the situation in good humor, but still obviously embarrassed. "I spoke to her father, but he refused to consider a betrothal until the girl is at least fourteen."

"A smart move," said Althea. "By the way, does the girl know of your undying love?"

Clarissa burst into laughter. "I should think so. She and my brother carried on quite a flirtation until her father, the Marquis du Gascone, found them in the garden."

"Certainly you did not compromise the poor child?" said Guerre, half laughing, half serious.

"Of course not," said Stephen hotly. "We were just kissing, and I immediately asked her father for permission to marry her, but he refused."

"If anyone was compromised, it was Stephen," Clarissa teased. "Or perhaps I should say seduced. The Lady Veronique, although only twelve, is quite a temptress."

"My lady Clarissa, from the way you talk, I believe that all the stories of the French court that I have heard must be true," Sir Guy said.

"It depends on what you have heard, my lord," said Clarissa, and once again Althea was surprised at her flirtatious manner.

"I have heard that the ladies of the French court are the most beautiful in the world, and their skill in matters of love is matched by none." Althea looked keenly at Sir Guy Melville. He might be short, a little plump, plain of face, and the impoverished third son, but his words were those of a polished courtier. Althea saw that Clarissa's face flushed with pleasure at his words.

For a moment the group was silent, and then Stephen rose and stretched. "I think that I am exhausted. Guerre gave me a hard day in the saddle."

Sir Guy and Clarissa also rose, but Guerre remained seated, and Althea followed his example. Sir Guy was sleeping with Stephen, so there was no need for her to show him to his chamber. The three left, and Althea took a sip of her hot wine and pushed her chair closer to the fire.

"I think your cousin may not make it to the convent after all," said Althea with a grin. She looked down at Guerre, who had seated himself at her feet. They were both relaxed—a mood that eluded them more often than not lately—and she wanted it to continue.

He looked up at her lazily, and she felt her heart stir. He was on his side, propped up on one elbow. He had changed for dinner tonight, and the dark green tunic and green hose showed off his muscular frame to its best advantage. Her eyes drifted to his thighs, where the muscles bulged through the sheer material. Fascinated, she could not draw her eyes away.

"Althea, are you listening to me, or just scrutinizing my body?" His voice was languorous.

She hesitated, then answered honestly, her face turning pink. "I'm afraid it was the latter. You look uncommonly good tonight, my lord."

"And I don't always?" he asked with a pretense of bad humor.

"You always look good, Guerre, but tonight you seem so relaxed and happy, and . . ."

"And I haven't looked like that in a long time." He finished the sentence for her. His gaze on her was steady. "You know the reason why, Althea. It hasn't been for lack of love, but rather, from too much."

"I know." She said the words so simply that Guerre felt touched by her honesty. Looking up at her, he felt too moved to speak. The fire and the wine had colored her cheeks a warm rose, and her eyes were like a set of turquoise stones. Her long blonde hair was lit by the fire to a pale gold, and the velvet dress that she wore, the color of cream, looked soft and inviting to his touch. It molded to her round breasts, larger since the birth of the baby, and yet still high and virginal. Desire grew in him toward an inexorable conclusion.

They looked at each other wordlessly for a moment, their eyes speaking for them. Guerre reached out for her, and she rose and sat down beside him. Hungrily, his lips sought hers, and the shock of their touching was like lightning coursing through both of them. The fire seared their souls, and they melted into each other. As he kissed her lips and face, Althea could feel the glow of the fire, and the intensity of his desire warmed and engulfed her. His lips sought her throat, and as his fingers loosened the ties of her bodice, his lips followed quickly, burning her skin with the heat of their touch. Then his lips found her nipples, and she groaned as his tongue played and teased first one, and then the other, until they stood upright with desire.

"Althea, Althea, I swore I would wait, but I cannot!" His voice was hoarse with passion, and she could hear the plea in it. She knew that he was pleading with himself more than with her. And then, as his arms tightened around her and his lips feverishly sought hers, she knew that he could no longer pull back. The knowledge that she was at the mercy of a man aroused to the breaking point made her own desire soar with excitement.

With quick movements, they both removed their cloth-

ing until they were naked for each other. With a desperate
moan, he joined her on the rug and began to stroke and caress her until she thought she would die from the fire burning in her flesh. Her body pushed upward, higher and
higher, searching for fulfillment. And then, just when she
thought she was going to scream with desire, he thrust
into her. At first he moved slowly, but as his pace increased, she felt the passion that he had aroused in her
grow again, and she wrapped her legs around his waist,
lost to everything but his body moving within hers, faster
and faster. Together they rose with every thrust to a
greater and greater sensation, until at last they soared
into ecstasy.

Later, as they lay under the fur blankets in Althea's
chamber, Guerre held her in his arms. Althea half slept,
satiated with pleasure but fighting the oblivion of total
sleep. She was so happy that she wanted to remain awake
to experience the contentment that she felt. Guerre, too,
was still awake. His hands were caressing her gently.
Passion had been spent for the moment, but they both
wanted the joy of physical contact to remain.

"This is the right thing to do," Althea whispered to him
in the dark. She saw his face turn toward her, and she
kissed his forehead. "It was wrong for us to hold back our
love. It is as essential to us as breathing. When the priest
finally comes, he will confirm a fact that has been true
since that night in Wales. I became joined to you then."

Guerre's answer was to take her in his arms and kiss her
with tenderness and love. As they lay there in the dark,
Althea and Guerre forgot the world in their rediscovery of
each other.

It did not take the other occupants of the castle long to
discover the new situation between Guerre and Althea. Sir
Guy, of course, had only arrived yesterday, and he did not
realize that their failure to appear at the first meal of the
day was out of the norm; but Clarissa and Stephen quickly
understood. Stephen could not have cared less. He knew

that they would soon wed, and he had long doubted the wisdom of their restraint. He was relieved that his cousin would now be in a better humor.

Clarissa, however, was rather grave when Althea and Guerre finally came down for the midday meal. Althea could see that though the girl did not condemn them, her moral values were being strained to the limit. It was to everyone's relief that Sir Guy took a hand in entertaining Clarissa, turning her mind from Althea and Guerre. Guy also accepted Guerre's invitation to spend the holidays with them, and the week leading up to Christmas was one of merriment and happiness for all.

CHAPTER TWENTY

Christmas Day dawned sunny and cold, and it was the best day of the holiday season, although there was no priest to hold the Mass. Clarissa conducted a short prayer service in the chapel, and then they broke their fast with a delicious Christmas ham, fresh bread with butter, eggs whipped in cream and chives and cooked over a low heat, and selected cheeses. After they ate, Althea and Guerre went out into the courtyard and distributed Christmas bread to all the serfs and freemen who came to the castle. It was a tradition that any who worked the land for the du Reims family could come to the castle on Christmas Day and receive a share of the honey nut bread, which was usually blessed by the priest. But even without the holy blessing, Althea was surprised at the number who came to the castle. Christmas greetings were called out, and Althea was the subject of much attention. She heard several men comment on her beauty, and she was pleased that she had taken pains with her hair and dress. The red velvet ribbons she had braided into her hair fell down over the dark green velvet cloak that she wore. The cloak had been a Christmas present from Guerre, and it was lined with fox fur. He had given it to her this morning before they had left their chamber, and she adored it.

Althea took advantage of a lull in the arrival of the peasants and watched Guerre as he talked to several men she did not remember meeting on their tours. A smile crossed her lips as she looked at him. She was so proud of him. The scarlet tunic that she had carefully embroidered for his Christmas gift was visible under the fur cape he wore, and his black hose and shoes were quiet but elegant. He looked every inch the noble lord. Feeling her gaze upon him, he turned slightly and nodded to her, startling Althea by his rather serious expression. She glanced at the two men he was with and saw that they, too, looked troubled.

Before she could join them, another group arrived at the drawbridge and crossed into the courtyard, and Althea again had to distribute the Christmas bread. By the time she was free again, the men were gone. When she and Guerre walked back into the castle, she saw that he still seemed preoccupied. She had to check on the dinner, but she made a mental note to ask him what concerned him at the first available opportunity.

Inside the main hall, the servants were setting up the room for the Christmas feast. Both fireplaces had fires blazing in them, and Althea gladly sat down in front of one and took a glass of wine from Clarissa, who had been supervising the preparations inside the castle. A small table had been set up in front of the south fireplace, and it was set for Guerre, Althea, Clarissa, Stephen, and Guy. The large table in the center of the room was for the men-at-arms and the servants. Today the inhabitants of entire castle would take their meal together.

Guerre's castle and staff were not large, and the festivities that would be found in a greater keep would not go on here. There were no troubadours, mummers, or jesters to entertain them, but it was still a time of celebration. In the next hour, before the meal was served, Althea and Guerre talked and laughed with the men who defended the castle, and with the servants who tended to all their needs. Hot wine and ale flowed freely, and once Althea explained the idea behind the mistletoe, more than one man caught his favorite wench under the berries.

Dinner was delicious, and Althea told the others that French food was far better than Welsh or English fare. Sir Guy agreed, and Guerre called to the cook and told her of their compliments. The fat woman blushed with pride, and she doubled her supervision of the courses as they were served. They feasted on venison cooked in wine, and hare stuffed with apples. Then came fish in a jelly sauce, followed by pheasant and duck. After that came pastries stuffed with lamb and vegetables, and the meal ended with a custard made of eggs and milk and honey.

"I don't think I will eat again for days," said Sir Guy as they enjoyed the custard. His naturally red face was now scarlet from the food and wine.

Althea looked around the room. Everyone was relaxed, and the merriment was increasing. A young boy was playing the flute, and the soldiers were singing along to his tune. In one corner a rather plump kitchen wench was doing a little dance. The dogs that always slept and ate in the hall moved over in fear of being stepped upon. Althea was so involved in watching the revelry that she did not at first hear the conversation at the table. But finally Guerre's voice caught her attention.

"We will miss you, but I understand that you must see to your lands."

"Is someone leaving?" Althea asked.

"Tomorrow we must return home," Clarissa explained. "We've been away far too long, and Stephen is right in feeling that we should see to our lands."

"We will miss you terribly," said Althea sadly. They had all spent so many happy hours together.

"We're not that far away, and we'll be returning for your wedding," Stephen said. He made it sound as if that event was in the near future, and Althea and Guerre smiled at him.

"How long will it take us to reach your lands?" asked Sir Guy, and Althea realized that he was going with them. She shot a quick glance at Clarissa and saw that she was blushing furiously.

Catching the look, Sir Guy said easily, "Stephen and Clarissa have been kind enough to invite me to their keep, since it is on the way to my mother's people. I have trespassed on your hospitality long enough, my lady Althea."

"Not at all, Sir Guy," said Althea with a sincere smile.

"We enjoyed your company immensely. But I understand why you would want to continue your journey." Her words were innocent, but the smile that she gave Clarissa made the poor girl blush even more.

"Well, I, too, am sorry to see you all go," said Guerre with a frown, "but I have received word today that makes me think perhaps you leave none too soon."

"Is there trouble?" Stephen asked, suddenly alert.

Everyone looked at Guerre, who was pouring himself more wine. His face looked concerned. "I did not want to tell you today and worry you on such a holiday, but since you are leaving tomorrow, I fear I must. Two of my serfs, who live half a day's ride from here, said that there has been an outbreak of illness in their village." He looked at Althea, then at Stephen. "I fear, from their description, that it's the plague."

He spoke calmly, but Althea could see the tension on his face. "Is there any chance they could be mistaken?" she asked.

"Little," he said soberly. "They said that five have died already, and those afflicted were covered with black boils that oozed a foul pus." Turning to Stephen, he said, "This village is south of here, in the direction of your lands. Since this curse is moving north, I think you must prepare yourself to find it on your lands, Stephen."

Guerre's cousin, usually so lighthearted, now looked grave and thoughtful. "Perhaps you should remain here, Clarissa?"

"No," said his sister sharply. "You will need me if the plague has struck. Besides, these things are in God's hands. I wouldn't be any safer here."

"That's not true, Clarissa," said Guerre, but he did not try to argue with his cousin. He knew that she intended to go, and nothing would stop her. "I think that I'll ride out with you tomorrow and visit this village. I'll get a better understanding of what is happening."

"I'll come, too," Althea said quickly.

"I would prefer that you did not," said Guerre. "I'll be

riding hard and long, and I plan to take only four or five men with me." Seeing her disappointment, he smiled. "Besides, I want you to remain in charge here. Word has spread among the servants about this curse, and if we all take off, they might think that we are fleeing."

Althea nodded. She wasn't fooled by his excuse, but she decided to give in gracefully. She would slow them down, and she knew that Guerre wanted to make good time. She signaled for more wine, and they all began to talk of happier things. The fires blazed, and the merriment continued, but Althea knew that the dark curse that was descending on them was in the back of everyone's mind.

Guerre was unusually quiet that night in their chamber. He sat in front of the fire, looking into the flames with a preoccupied expression on his face. He had removed his dress clothes and was simply clad in a long woolen robe.

Althea finished untying the red ribbons that she had braided through her hair, and stepped out of her crimson gown. Carefully, she placed it in a cedar chest at the foot of the bed. She thought with appreciation of the clothes that Guerre had ordered made for her since they had arrived here. She had been amazed when Clarissa had shown her the bolts of material that were stored in the sewing room. Alycia had been fond of clothes; she had ordered many bolts of silks and velvets, and they had been left here when she married Claude. The cook's daughter was an excellent seamstress, and Guerre told Althea to have anything she desired made.

Now she stepped into a robe of pale yellow velvet trimmed with white fur and walked over to the fireplace. "Are you still worried about the illness that has struck?" she asked Guerre.

He looked up and smiled. "I'm sorry to ignore you, Althea. You looked beautiful today, but even lovelier now in that robe you wear."

"Thank you. In fact, I was thinking the exact same thing

about you." She sat down on the bearskin rug. "But you didn't answer my question."

"I was hoping that you wouldn't notice."

"Aha, your compliments were merely flattery to distract me." Althea gave him a mock frown.

"I meant to distract you, but I also meant every word."

"Well, perhaps I might forgive you since it is Christmas, but you must pay a price for my forgiveness."

"And what is that, may I ask?" whispered Guerre in her ear.

Her body tingled at his touch. "I think a kiss would be sufficient penance for a first offense."

With one quick movement, his lips met hers. Althea could feel the muscles of his thighs through her thin robe, and she felt passion begin to grow in them both. After a moment, he got up and carried her to the bed that they now shared. He removed his robe and looked down at her, a small smile on his lips. She returned his gaze, and then let her eyes travel down his body, caressing with a glance his broad muscular chest, the flat stomach, and then the dark triangle where his thighs met and where his manhood left no suspicion of his state. She reached out and gently ran her finger down one of his taut, lean thighs. She could feel him quiver slightly under her light touch.

"It is not right that I should stand here dressed like the day I was born, and you are still clad in that robe." His voice was light, but Althea could hear the undercurrent of tension, and she shivered with anticipation.

Then, as quick as a panther, he knelt beside her and pulled her robe apart. With one long, lingering look, his eyes encompassed all of her, and then his lips found her nipples. As his tongue teased them with flickering little licks, Althea leaned back on the velvet pillows and blissfully forgot everything but sensation. As he traced a languorous line down from her breasts to her stomach with his mouth, she writhed with desire. She reached to pull him up to her, but he gently brushed her hands away and continued his slow descent down her body. She felt herself dissolving into an ecstasy that she had never imagined. She felt that she could not endure the passion that was rising in her, and she cried out to him to stop; but his tongue continued to caress her until suddenly she felt an explosion so sweet and yet so overwhelming that she cried out in joy as her body contracted again and again with unbelievable intensity. And then he was quickly guiding his manhood into her, and with quick, urgent thrusts, he again aroused the passions that were still hot. Reveling in the physical joy of their coupling, Althea looked up at his face, now straining with desire, and her fingers raked his back as he grasped her in a shuddering spasm that filled her with the heat of his passion.

Their return to reality was slow and gentle. Lying in each other's arms, they began to talk languidly about the events of the day. Both were contented and satiated, but too wide awake to sleep. Guerre's mind had turned to the problems of tomorrow, and he told Althea some of the things that she had to do in his absence.

"I only plan to be gone for five nights at the most, and Pierre will help you with most things. I foresee nothing that should be a problem. If there should be any trouble among the peasants, the type of thing that I would judge, tell them to return in a week. If it should be something of a violent nature, have the captain of the guards throw the culprits in the dungeon."

"That seems rather heartlesss. Perhaps the man could be innocent."

"Innocent or guilty, a week in the dungeon will not hurt him," said Guerre gruffly. "I can't let everyone be endangered if there is some question of guilt. But I hardly think that you will have any such problem."

"They all seem like such good folk. I really enjoyed giving out the Christmas bread today." Althea took a sip of the wine that was on the small carved oak table next to the bed. "I meant to ask you before, Guerre, but where were Theresa and her mother? I did not see them today."

Guerre looked grave. "I don't think they want any part of this castle. The memories are too painful."

Althea stared at the fire, her mind recalling Philip du Bois. Her heart went out to the poor girl, and tears of anger at the humiliation that they had both suffered filled her eyes.

Guerre noticed the tears. Gently, he took her hand and kissed it. "You're so softhearted, Althea. Perhaps Theresa will get over it with time."

"You never get over something like that. It haunts you till the day you die," she said bitterly.

"Someday Claude will pay for what he has done," said Guerre with controlled rage. "I will thrust my sword into his overripe belly with a relish that few men could equal."

She nodded, but it was an absent motion, and Guerre bit his lip thoughtfully. "Althea, may I ask you something?"

She looked at him and nodded. Something in his tone made her uneasy.

"What is Philip du Bois to you?" Now that he had asked, Guerre was tense with apprehension. He had noticed the attention that Philip had shown Althea at the tournament, and he had been enraged. And then the night that she had given birth to the little boy that died, she had screamed out Philip's name in her delirium. He had been on the point of asking many times, but now the question in his mind had become words that would have to be answered.

It was the moment of truth for Althea. She had longed to tell Guerre about Philip's ravishment, but something had always held her back. Now she looked at him steadily. The time for secrets was gone.

"He used me as Norman used Theresa." Although her voice was expressionless, her eyes bored into his with desperate anxiety.

She had expected anger on his part, directed toward Philip and Claude. Even fury would have been no surprise. But she could never have anticipated the blind rage that came over him, and it was directed at her! Guerre drew away from her as if she were made of hot coals. Somehow, despite the sick fear in her heart, she managed to tell him the entire story. When she finished, he grabbed her shoulders and began to shake her as if she were a limp doll.

"Why did you never tell me this before? Why did you keep this to yourself?" he said furiously, still gripping her shoulders.

"Guerre, stop! You're hurting me!" she cried. He released her with a push that sent her sprawling back on the bed. She glared at him. "Why are you angry with me? I was his victim! I fought him, but it did no good!"

"You're lying," he said viciously, half-crazed with jealousy. "I saw you at the tournament giving him your colors, and then walking with him around the castle. You encouraged him!"

Althea was stunned by his reaction. "He attacked me before the time of the tournament. It was when he visited Claude in the summer. My horse went lame on a hunt, and I was returning to the castle when he overtook me. Claude did nothing. In fact, he was pleased. Then Philip left for Flanders. The next time I saw him was at the tournament."

"And you were overjoyed," Guerre spat out bitterly.

"I was frightened to death, and I did not give him my colors. He grabbed them from me, and you saw it happen. Your accusations are unfair and untrue!"

"Unfair and untrue," he mimicked her cruelly, getting up and putting on his robe. "It is you who have been unjust to me. Coupling with that whoremonger and never telling me! Perhaps it was *his* brat that you carried!"

The cruelness of his words hit Althea like a physical blow. She sat upright on the bed and looked at him coldly, her eyes bright with anger. "I was already pregnant when he took me. I told him, too, thinking that he would stop, but it only urged him on. I was his prey, and he was too much the hunter to let go."

The cold dignity in her voice quieted, but didn't extinguish, Guerre's rage. Turning to her with one hand on the door latch, he said, "Then you still have to narrow the father down to two." And with that, he left the chamber.

Althea stared at the door in shock. Men! The complete stupidity of the lot! She would never have imagined that he would react in such a jealous and cruel manner! He had accepted the fact that Claude had used her shamefully, and did not hold her accountable. Yet he was enraged at her because Philip had used her in the same vile way. As she sat on the bed, which now felt large and lonely, her anger slowly turned to sorrow, and tears filled her eyes and rolled down her cheeks. She felt hurt and abused. Guerre now hated her and thought her a whore. Perhaps this was the end. Her thoughts grew more and more depressed as the night lengthened into the early hours of the morning. She wanted to search for him, but her pride would not let her. And over and over, she asked herself why. Why had he reacted so violently over Philip? The question haunted her through the night till dawn touched the sky.

She did not know that Guerre was asking himself the same question. He, too, spent the night in mental agony, torn by conflicting emotions. He had left the chamber and gone down to the main hall, where a bright fire still burned in the hearth. Christmas decorations were everywhere, increasing his depression. He found a large decanter of wine and seated himself in front of the fire.

The part of his mind that was still rational told him that the blind fury he felt toward Althea was silly and unfair, but the powerful emotions that had him in their grip pushed logic away. He had always hated Philip du Bois and his cronies. When Guerre had gone to court, or when Philip visited the castle with Norman, the two men had always been polite on the surface, but the enmity between them was great. Perhaps it was competition. Both were the same age, and both were excellent in the craft of warfare. And both had been the favorites of the ladies of the French court. In some cases this would have created a great friendship, but with Philip and Guerre it had bred a deadly hatred. Guerre had always felt that there was something evil behind the prince's smooth facade, and rumors and stories had proven this to be true. Philip, in turn, had sensed the contempt the Baron du Reims had felt for him, and the warrior in him had waited to find the soft spot in the armor of his foe.

The soft spot had been Althea. Tales of the beautiful Welsh girl kidnapped by Guerre du Reims from the bed of Claude du Vendome had titillated the French court. It was the stuff of which troubadours sang. And Philip, hearing that the girl was recaptured and living with Claude, had ventured out to taste the fruit that Guerre had tried to seize.

Guerre poured himself more wine, emptying the large decanter. The warrior in him told him to stop drinking, that his head should be clear for tomorrow. But the man in him cried out for oblivion from the thoughts that were tormenting him, and he drank deeply from his goblet. He could accept Althea with Claude, and even pity her for the experience.

Philip du Bois was a different story. All the competition and dislike that had festered between the two men for years prevented him from being rational about Philip and Althea. He could not bear to think of her body under Philip's probing hands, her soft, long legs open to his rival's pleasure. The image sent him into such a fury that he hurled the goblet across the stone floor, where it clattered with an echoing crash through the empty hall. Totally drunk, he staggered to the large table that had seated the servants and men-at-arms, and searched for another pitcher of wine. The flagons that proved empty he threw aside in rage, as if he were attempting to throw aside the terrible picture of Althea with Philip. Finally, he found a pitcher that was half-full, and he seated himself at the table and continued to drink.

Philip du Bois still would not leave his mind. The man was a roué; his escapades with women were well known. The mistress who had been found dead at the bottom of the staircase was only one such story. The scullery maids of the royal palace had whispered of orgies that had taken place in his chambers, and about the pretty ones of their group who had been forced to attend. Some were never seen again, and rumor had it that Philip had sold them to the whorehouses of Paris to keep them silent. The peasants on his estates were helpless when he went foraging for pleasure in their hovels, and Norman had once bragged about Philip's killing the one serf who had tried to prevent the prince from raping his wife. Norman and Philip had trussed the man up and forced him to watch as first Philip, and then Norman, had raped the woman. Then they had killed the man for his impudence in protesting their attack.

But Philip was at his best with the ladies of the court. He prided himself on his taste and high standards of beauty, and when he set out to charm, there were few women who resisted him. His poor wife, Mary of Flanders, loathed him, it was said, and prayed that she would soon become pregnant so that her duty to him would be done. The women that he seduced rarely saw the cruel streak in him until he grew tired of them or was angered in some way. Then the handsome prince turned into the monster that he truly was.

If sophisticated women of the court fell for his seduction, then why wouldn't Althea, an innocent girl? She said that she had been raped, but Guerre could not believe it. He knew well her passionate nature, and he knew about Philip's legendary charm. Hadn't the truth been that she had fallen for that, and then felt betrayed when Philip left? That would explain her silence about the rape—since it hadn't been rape at all.

Guerre looked into the goblet of wine, seeing in the depths the picture that his imagination conjured. He saw it all so clearly, and his face grew dark. Philip had seduced Althea. The rape in the woods had really been a scene of passion and excitement. And Althea had treasured it enough to keep silent, except when she was in the delirium of childbirth. Then her lover's name had come to her lips. Yes, he saw it all clearly. Guerre put his head down on the table and fell into a drunken stupor. But if anyone had been in the dark hall and had looked at him closely, they would have seen the tears that were on his ravaged face.

CHAPTER TWENTY-ONE

He had been gone for fourteen days, Althea calculated. She gazed out from the south tower window onto the snow-covered countryside and felt as bleak as the day. It was overcast, and snow was falling lightly. Everything she saw was gray, and she, herself, was dressed in a dark woolen gown that matched the mood of the day. Her eyes searched the horizon, but there was nothing out there. Sadly, she turned from the tower window.

She thought back to the day of departure. She had barely slept the night before, and had risen early with the first light of dawn. Going down to the main hall, she had found the servants cleaning up the mess of the previous day. A girl told her that Guerre, Stephen, and Guy had already eaten and were out in the blacksmith's shop, looking at Sir Guy's horse. Then Clarissa had come down, sharp eyes taking in Althea's haggard look immediately, and she asked bluntly if something was wrong. Althea shrugged it off. She was just upset at being separated from Guerre.

"My goodness, Althea, it is only for a few days! What if he went on a crusade? Why, you would die before he left!"

"Who is going on a crusade?" asked a male voice, and the two women turned to see Guy, with Stephen right behind. The men sat down, their faces red from the outdoors.

"Althea is grieving over Guerre's leaving for a few days. She looks terrible," said Clarissa.

Stephen chuckled. "You should see Guerre! His face is like death, and his mood is gruesome. I fear he will not make a pleasant riding companion this day."

"Such agonies lovers feel when they separate, even for a moment," said Guy in a falsetto, imitating some of the troubadours who affected a high-pitched voice. Their bantering continued until Guerre appeared in the entrance to the hall. Clad in full armor, his face like a thundercloud, Althea could see why he terrified his opponents in battle. The armor made him appear even larger than he was, and his face when angry was like a warrior carved in stone. And with a heart to match, Althea added to herself.

"It's time to go," he said brusquely. "The horses are saddled and waiting."

His voice was so curt and cold that they all looked at him in shock. This was not the genial host who had entertained them with kindness and courtesy, or the lover who had been eager to please his future wife. Clarissa looked quickly from Guerre to Althea, seeing with different eyes the sad, pale face and the thunderous one, and realizing that it was a lovers' quarrel rather than sorrow over parting that had changed these two. Stephen and Guy sensed it, too, and they quickly stood up. Both bowed over Althea's hand and thanked her for her hospitality, and then Stephen kissed her on both cheeks.

"He can be a bear when his temper is up. It will soon pass," he whispered to Althea. His warm smile made her feel better, and they walked out to the courtyard together. But Guerre's impatience was so great that no one tarried in leave-taking. Clarissa and Althea embraced, and Clarissa, too, murmured words of encouragement.

"He will return in a better mood. He has had his way for too long, and it has spoiled him," she said with a laugh. Since Clarissa had no idea what the quarrel was about, Althea felt great doubts about her judgment of the situation, but she nodded in agreement.

She watched Guerre mount and move around the courtyard, trying to control the great beast who, sensing his master's tension, was straining at the bit.

Please smile at me at least, Althea begged him silently. Now that it is time to go, please forget this silly argument and forgive me. Her eyes gazed at him with desperation, but she could tell from his dark expression that there was no forgiveness in his heart. His only recognition of her presence was a cold salute with his sword as he was about to depart. Then he wheeled his horse toward the gate and, without a backward glance, cantered across the draw-bridge, the others following.

Althea felt cold, but it was not the winter wind that chilled her to the depths of her soul. She knew that Guerre was deeply angry with her, and this was not a light lovers' quarrel that he would soon regret. Unfair though it was, he felt that she had betrayed him, and until they could talk and she could explain more clearly, the anger and hurt would remain with him.

As the days went by, her feeling of melancholy increased, and with it came a dreadful fear that she and Guerre would never again be together . . . never to talk . . . never to love again. She tried to keep busy, but there was little to do in the dead of winter. The servants worked well under Pierre's supervision, and she did not want to interfere. She tried to do some needlework, but she would pick up her tapestry and work for only a few moments before her thoughts would turn to Guerre, and then the needlework would fall to her lap and she would stare unseeing into the flames.

Now she left the tower where she had been watching for Guerre, and went into the main hall. She had had enough of this castle! she decided. She would go for a ride. She gave orders to a servant to have her mare saddled, then she ran up the stone staircase to her chamber. She dressed quickly, putting on leather boots, her black wool riding dress, and the green velvet cape lined in fox fur that Guerre had given her for Christmas. Glad to be doing something active for a change, she pranced down the stairs and out into the courtyard. A groom was holding her horse, and the sentry on duty was talking to him.

"I will call for an escort, my lady," the sentry said.

"No need, Jacques," said Althea quickly. She wanted to

be alone, but she could see that the guard felt that she should not venture out by herself. She gave him a brilliant smile. "I won't be going far. I plan to ride near the castle." The guard looked dubious, but there was little that he could do. Althea was in charge of the castle in Guerre's absence.

Althea rode hard for several minutes, enjoying the brisk winter air, the fresh smell of the snow. The light snow that had been falling earlier had become heavier, and although it was almost noon, the sky was the color of slate, and she could tell that night would fall early today. She stopped her horse and looked at the high, gray walls of the castle, feeling a strong urge to stay out as long as possible regardless of the weather.

Ahead she could see the small copse of trees where she had gathered berries for Christmas, and she urged her horse across the field. They reached the woods, and Althea slowed the mare to a walk. Everything was so quiet and peaceful under its blanket of snow. She sat on her horse for a few moments, a lonely feeling of peace descending on her. Soon, though, she began to feel cold, and when her horse began to stamp and shiver, she reluctantly turned the horse toward home.

As they returned across the meadow, Althea realized that the storm was getting worse, but the mare was fairly surefooted, and she decided to ride toward the little gathering of cottages near the shelter of the castle walls. A restlessness in her made her want to delay returning to the castle, where nothing awaited her but needlework and loneliness.

As she rode along she noticed that there was a group of people gathered a little distance from the cottages. Puzzled that a group of people would be standing outside on such a day, she decided to ride closer. She felt no fear on Guerre's lands. These were the same people to whom she had given Christmas bread only a fortnight ago. She was still too far away to distinguish faces, but she could tell that they were moving slowly away from their homes, and they projected an air of sadness.

Since they were walking away from her, and the snow muffled the hoofbeats of her horse, she could observe without their noticing her. As she drew closer, she could see that the men in front were carrying something, and after a few moments, she realized that it was a coffin. She drew her horse to a halt, not wanting to intrude on their grief; but one of the group, a young boy, turned and saw her, and the sad little procession stopped. Realizing that they were not going to move until she approached them, she spurred her horse forward.

"Do not get too close, my lady," called a man, waving his arms to stop her. She halted her horse about fifty feet away, puzzled.

"I'm sorry that someone has died," she said sincerely. She looked over the crowd and saw that their faces held not only sorrow but fear.

"And she goes to her grave without the blessing of Mother Church. Unshriven. No last rites," a woman screamed. "Doomed to hell, like the rest of us!"

Althea heard the hysteria in the woman's voice and realized that this was no ordinary funeral. Although the absence of a priest was terrible, something else was wrong. Althea moved her horse closer, ignoring the man who kept telling her to stay back. Her eyes moved over the crowd, searching, and at last she saw her. Theresa was at the front of the group of mourners, holding her baby, and Althea could see the tears rolling down her face.

"Who has died?" Althea asked softly.

"My mother," the girl answered. Dressed in a black, ragged cape, she looked both very young and very old.

"And she's not the first!" cried the same woman from the crowd. She was middle-aged, and her face was white with fear.

"Tell me what's happening," Althea insisted.

The peasants hesitated for a moment; but they had spent their lives trusting the judgment of the nobility, and though Althea was a woman, she was part of that class. It was her responsibility to protect and take care of them. An older man, short and gnarled from years of hard work, motioned for the men who held the coffin to lay it down, and the group relaxed for a moment. The old man walked up to Althea and cleared his throat. Althea could tell that he was nervous about approaching her, so she smiled encouragingly and nodded for him to begin.

"She is the third to die, my lady," he said.

"The third?" Althea repeated, still not quite comprehending.

"Yes, the third in as many days."

"And what is the cause of these three deaths?"

"We don't know," the man said, his voice breaking with fear. He looked up at Althea with tear-filled eyes. "First it was my brother, Jean, who took sick. He fell ill and began to vomit black blood. In hours there were black boils under his arms and he was in agony. It was horrible to behold. He never lived to see the dawn of the next day. Then Charles, Jean's neighbor, noticed that his son was ill, and the boy died even faster than Jean."

"It is true, my lady," said a bent old woman who stepped out from the crowd. Her face was ravaged with grief. "I am his grandmother, and none of the herbs that I knew could save him." Her shoulders began to heave with sobs, and another woman came forward and led her back into the crowd.

"And last night it was Marie who came down with this curse. Theresa nursed her through the night, but she died before the dawn," the old man finished.

Althea looked out over the sad and frightened little group, sorrow for them welling within her. The curse from the south had finally reached them. What could she tell them? Would the news that the disease was traveling all over France frighten them more? Should she just tell them to pray for deliverance? How she wished that Guerre were here! Her eyes sought out Theresa's. The hostility that was usually in the girl's eyes was gone; there was nothing but grief in them now. How insignificant everything seems in the face of death, Althea thought bitterly.

"I have heard of this disease," she finally said. "A traveler from the south told us about it, but my ignorance of its cause is as great as your own. I know how much you suffer, knowing that your loved ones are going to their graves without the last rites, but perhaps God will make a special dispensation for their souls since no priest is here. As soon as the new one arrives, I assure you that he will say all the necessary prayers over their graves."

She dismounted while the crowd murmured their thanks, and she announced, "I am coming with you." Her voice left no room for argument.

The men picked up the coffin and the crowd moved over the snow to the secluded graveyard. Althea could see two crosses over two fresh mounds of dirt that the new snow had not entirely covered. Next to them was a gaping hole in the ground awaiting Marie, once a mistress to a nobleman. Althea heard a man thank God that the winter had been warm and that the ground was not frozen. Since there was no priest, the service was short. The women mumbled some prayers, and Althea stood at the back of the group, not wanting to intrude on their grief. She and Guerre might have the power of life and death over these people, but she was still an outsider here. In the face of their common sorrow and fear, they had forgotten her. Althea looked at Theresa's bowed head and was moved to tears. The daughters of the late Baron du Reims were not a lucky lot: Alycia dead in childbirth, the victim of a cruel husband; and Theresa, the bastard, holding the child of her rape as they buried her mother in an unshriven grave.

As the group finally turned and began to go back to their huts, Althea waited for Theresa and called gently to the girl as she passed. "Theresa, I want you to know that there is always a home for you and your child in the castle. If you ever change your mind, please come to me."

Theresa looked at Althea for a long moment with old

eyes set in a young woman's face. Althea remembered with shock that Theresa was only fifteen.

"If you will have me, I will return with you now," the girl said with steady dignity.

"Of course," said Althea with surprise. She had expected a curt refusal.

Reading her thoughts, the girl gave a half smile. "It will be much safer for my baby in the castle. More will die of this curse before it runs its course, and there is no escape from illness in the crowded huts of the poor."

Althea nodded. They walked back to the small group of huts, but Theresa did not stop.

"Don't you want to get your things?" Althea asked.

"There is the smell of death in there," Theresa said. "I want nothing from that spot."

The two women then traveled back to the castle. Althea wanted Theresa to ride behind her, but the girl refused. Carrying her baby, the small figure draped in black trudged beside Althea. Looking down at her, Althea thought it could have been herself, escaping from Claude. She vowed that she would try to make life better for Theresa and her child.

CHAPTER TWENTY-TWO

The days that followed became an unending blur to Althea. The cold, damp grayness of despair and fear was echoed in the weather that buffeted the castle for days on end. In the beginning of February, Althea realized that the sun had not shone for a fortnight. The wind howled outside the castle walls, seeping in through the cracks and moving the tapestries with a chill hand that made Althea huddle next to the fire in the hearth for a comfort that lasted only until one stepped a few feet away from the flames. Once in a while she would brave the wind and the cold and climb to the high tower to search the horizon for Guerre, but the grayness made it difficult to see.

At night she would lie huddled under the heavy skins of fur that covered her bed, and she would think of Guerre; and although her body was warm, her heart and spirit were like ice. No word had come from him, and she would toss and turn through the night, wondering if it was anger that kept him away, or if some disaster had overtaken him, and he now lay injured or dead. Illness was rampant in the land, and the one traveler who had made it to the castle, a merchant, told of the spreading plague and the hysterical fear that surrounded it.

The merchant had been a kindly man, and Althea let him use the stables for the night and gave him food for his journey when he left the next day. She had been sick at heart when her guards, out for a routine patrol two days later, returned with the news that the merchant's body had been found by the side of the road. The black pustules on his face were evidence of the way he had died. The thought of the man dying alone on an empty road, unprotected from the rain and cold and without any human comfort, filled Althea with grief and fear for Guerre's safety.

That night she paced the floor of her chamber, agonizing over Guerre. Where could he be? Did he, like the merchant, lie dead on the side of some road, the cold keeping his body from decay? Was he already buried, perhaps by people who had died soon after, and so no message could be sent to her? Or was he right now lying in the arms of some wench or noblewoman, warming his body, while his heart still remained cold toward her? Althea knew that Guerre was not a man to forgive quickly. His hate, once aroused, could burn in fury until he had taken his revenge.

As these thoughts tormented her, Althea thought of Magara. For the first time in her life, she wished that she had inherited her aunt's powers. If only she could look into the flames and with the second sight allow her mind to travel to Guerre! If only she could see if he were sick or well, alone or in the company of another. If only she could just answer her own questions and put her mind to rest. So deep in thought was she that she didn't hear the door open, and she was unaware that Theresa had entered the room until the younger girl coughed slightly. Whirling around, Althea was relieved to see Theresa.

"I didn't mean to disturb you, but you didn't answer my knock," the girl explained. "I thought the news of the merchant's death might have disturbed you. I wanted to see if you were all right."

"It did disturb me, both for the poor man and for . . . other reasons." She hesitated, not knowing how much Theresa knew or had guessed about her relationship with Guerre. Their meals were usually spent in silence, unless the baby, Michelle, did something they could comment upon. Althea, lost in her own problems, had made a few vain attempts to start conversation with Theresa, then had given up, and the two lived in almost total silence. It had not been uncomfortable, though. Now, satisfied that all was well, and unwilling to intrude, Theresa turned to leave.

"No, wait," said Althea quickly, putting out a hand to restrain her. She could not bear the thought of returning to her tormented visions. "Won't you stay and have a glass of wine with me?" Althea knew there was pleading in her voice, but she didn't care, and she felt relief swell in her when Theresa paused and, without saying a word, nodded assent. She walked over to the hearth and sank down on the fur rug, and Althea poured two goblets of wine and joined her. As she handed Theresa her goblet, she noted with a stab of pain how much the girl resembled Guerre. It was the coloring and the shape of the eyes. Althea pulled her blue woolen robe around her and settled down on the fur rug.

"I have never thanked you for your kindness in allowing my child and me to come to the castle," said Theresa quietly, taking a sip of wine.

"It was nothing," said Althea. "I enjoy having you here. It's very lonely without . . ."

Theresa looked up as Althea paused, then nodded. "Don't worry. He will return."

Althea flushed. She hadn't realized that she was so transparent in her emotions. "I hope so. I expected him back within a few days of his departure, and that was over a month ago."

"He needs time to understand what ails him." At Althea's curious look, she smiled slightly. "Pierre is an old friend. He told me that Guerre left in a rage that was pure du Reims. I don't know what caused the quarrel, but all the du Reims men need time to cool their heels when their anger is aroused. My father treated his wife very badly when they quarreled. Once he left her for a year, and only returned after visiting the Holy Land."

For one moment, Althea thought that Theresa was talking about her own mother, but at the look of confusion on her face, Theresa smiled again. There was just the barest trace of bitterness in her voice when she answered. "Not

my mother, his mistress, but his wife. The du Reims
women were a frail lot. The old countess was very beautiful, but she died young, and Alycia took after her. She
didn't have the strength to fight Claude, and he killed
her."

At the mention of Claude, Althea shuddered. The reaction was not lost on Theresa, and she put out a sympathetic hand. "I'm sorry. I know about that, too, and I
should not have spoken. But you have a strength that Alycia never had. You would have survived. I can feel it.
You're a lot like me. It will take much to kill us."

Althea felt her eyes fill with tears at the girl's words.
There was something that drew them together—the closeness in their ages, perhaps, and the way they had both suffered. Suddenly, all the years of sorrow and pain and
loneliness welled up in Althea, and she found herself telling this girl with the long black hair and dark eyes about
her life: the years in Wales with her father and stepmother; Magara and the sanctuary of the forest; her escape
with Guerre; the nightmare of Claude and Mathilde; the
terrors of Haggar; and, finally, the loss of the baby. Theresa listened intently, showing emotion only when Althea
told her about Philip du Bois and the rape in the woods. At
that, the younger girl's face hardened with hatred and anger.

"Someday they will all pay for what they have done, Althea," Theresa said with fury, and Althea could see the du
Reims temper in her.

"I hope so," said Althea with a little sob. "I still feel
hunted by Philip."

"I know him well. It could have been him that raped me,
but Norman, my own cousin, was the one." Seeing Althea's look, she nodded fiercely. "Oh, you don't know the
story?"

"Guerre told me that you had been raped, but I assumed
it was one of Norman's cronies, not himself."

Theresa nodded her head. "I was serving them the evening meal that night. My mother was helping me. As the night wore on, they drank more and more, and as their drunkenness increased, so did the lewd remarks. My mother realized what was happening and ordered me to stay in the kitchen. But Philip du Bois had set his eyes on me, and he saw her game. He told Norman, who became enraged at my mother, and he hit her until she was unconscious. Then they called for me. I was hiding in the wine cellar, but they found me, and I was dragged to the main hall. They decided that whoever won the toss of the dice would have me. It was Norman who won, and not Philip."

"Why didn't you stay in the castle when Guerre returned?" Althea asked softly.

"I knew that I was not meant for the castle," Theresa answered. "I had been raised here, and Alycia and Guerre and I had played together when we were very young. It didn't matter then, but as we grew older, I could see the differences. They were nobles being groomed for a different life. I was a bastard, and I would go another way. I could accept that. My father had planned for me to become the housekeeper of this place and someday take Pierre's job. I wanted that. I could use the lessons that I had learned. Did you know I can read and write, and also do sums?"

Althea was surprised. The fact that she could do the same shocked some people, although it was much more common for nobles to read and write in France than it was in the remote corners of Wales.

"Yes," continued the girl. "I was well trained and knew my place. If not happy, I was content. Especially after I saw the horrible match that was made for poor Alycia. I could see the benefits in my life that the others would not have. At least no one would force me into an advantageous marriage with a man I despised." Here she grinned ruefully. "No, instead I was raped by my own cousin, bore his bastard daughter, and no one would avenge me because it was his right to take me!"

Althea shuddered. "I hope I never meet him."

"Of course you will. He's Guerre's overlord. And someday he will be the duke. You will have to be civil to him."

"Not if I can help it," said Althea with determination. "But why did you leave?"

Theresa looked down at her wine goblet. "Because I was humiliated," she answered softly. "After Norman, I was nothing. I was raped the way any other serf could be. I was no different than the people in the village. I wanted to leave the place that reminded me of my humiliation and agony. I wanted no help from any of them. I spurned Guerre and Stephen and Clarissa. Their offers of help came from a class that I despised."

"Have you now changed your mind?"

"Not really. I know that Guerre would do anything to help me, but he is still part of the nobility. I am here because of my daughter. I will swallow my pride for my child." With a quick movement, she rose. "I did not mean you when I spoke of those I hated. I'm grateful to you, and . . . I trust you."

"Thank you, Theresa," said Althea softly, watching her move toward the door. "I want you to remember that this is your home. I show you no charity by asking you to stay."

The girl nodded and, with a small smile, left. Althea sat staring into the flames until the late hours of the night, thinking about all she had heard. For the first time in her life since knowing Magara, she felt that she had a friend.

As the days wore on, Althea and Theresa became closer. Theresa had almost taken on the role of companion. She cared for Althea's clothes, after noting that needlework was not one of Althea's strong points, and she also began to help with the household accounts.

Althea saw how capable and well trained the girl was, and she secretly decided that she would try to convince Theresa to take up the role that she had been trained to perform—that of head housekeeper. Pierre was getting old, and the winter had been hard on him. The pains in his joints were getting bad, and he was half crippled. He could use an assistant, and eventually a replacement. And he adored Theresa, whom he looked upon as a favorite niece. Althea said nothing of her secret plotting, however. She knew the scars were still too raw for Theresa.

One day as they were sitting in front of the hearth chatting, Pierre hobbled in to see Althea. "Excuse me, my lady, but the sentry sees a group of horsemen approaching. They're about a half mile down the road, and moving slowly. Perhaps twelve men."

Althea leaped to her feet, splashing her wine. "Guerre must be returning, Theresa!" She could barely contain her excitement. "My cloak, quickly. Oh, I am not dressed. If only I had known!"

All her words came tumbling out in a rush. Then, frantic with impatience, she ran out of the main hall and up the stone stairs that led to the battlements. The wind whipped at her face and body, but she barely noticed. Far in the distance, she could see the horsemen, but they were too distant to make out individually. Theresa joined her, handing her a cloak, but Althea did not even acknowledge her presence. Guerre! Guerre had come back to her!

"I took leave to send out a horseman to check the men, my lady."

Althea had not heard the captain of the guards approach. Taking her eyes off the small cavalcade, she saw a lone horseman galloping away from the castle. He moved much faster than the larger group and was soon upon them. Althea saw them all stop, and then after a moment, her guard began the gallop back to the castle. Glowing with anticipation, Althea was surprised to see the strained look on Theresa's face and the frightened way she clasped her child. She looked poised for flight. The captain also looked worried.

Tension was in his voice when he spoke. "I gave the sentry a red scarf to hide beneath his armor. If he thinks the group is hostile, he will wave it when he reaches the large oak, and we will prepare to raise the drawbridge."

Althea could not bear the thought that this might not be

Guerre, and her heart stopped in anticipation as the horseman galloped toward the oak tree. All of them strained to
see if the red scarf appeared, and when the horseman
galloped past without waving the warning signal, they
breathed with relief. As the horseman approached the castle and reined in his horse, they leaned over the battlements to catch his words.

At first Althea could not believe what she heard. The
wind must have garbled his words. It could not be! But the
little gasp of horror from Theresa told her that she had indeed heard correctly.

Again the messenger repeated his news. "His Grace,
Count Norman du Reims, son of the Duke du Marton, ap-
proaches the castle of his kinsman, Sir Guerre du Reims,
and requests shelter." It was politely worded, but it was a
command.

Although she was numb with disappointment and fear,
Althea thought immediately of Theresa. "Theresa, can
you make it to the village?" she asked with urgency.

"It's too far," said the captain. "There's a secret passage
below the main hall that leads to a room that has no windows. I'll show you. No one knows it exists except Sir
Guerre and myself."

"I know of it. I'll go there now." Quickly, Theresa turned
with the baby clutched to her breast and ran down the
ramparts to the stairway that led to the floor below the
main hall.

"I'll send food to you," Althea called lamely, feeling
helpless.

The sight of the frightened girl, and the thought of all
that she had suffered at the hands of the man now approaching, made Althea furious. Fear and disappointment
vanished, replaced by rage. Turning to the captain, she
told him to tell the visitors that she would receive them in
the great hall. Hurrying to her chamber, she decided on
her course of action. Norman would find no weepy mistress
cowering in the corner. She was the daughter of nobles,
and she would greet this man as the noblewoman that she

was. He would find only cold dignity in her. Then another thought struck her. If he believed that she was already married to Guerre, she would be even safer. The wife of his cousin was more important than a mistress.

Quickly, she took off her gown. Opening her chest, she pulled through the clothes neatly folded there until she found a golden wool gown trimmed in brown fur. She put it on, and then tucked her hair under a headdress of dark brown with a gold veil attached. Ordinarily, she rarely wore the formal headdresses that were the fashion at court, but this one gave her height and dignity, and that was the look that she strove to achieve.

When she reached the main hall, it was still empty. Then she heard voices in the courtyard, and she realized that they would soon enter. She went to the hearth, posing herself for the greatest effect. But when they entered, she thought her heart would stop beating. For behind the tall, thin, effeminate man with the hawk nose stood Philip du Bois.

They looked at each other for only a moment, but to Althea it seemed like a lifetime. Slowly, she stepped forward, nodding her head in cold greeting. She felt frantic with fear, but she was determined to play the part that she had decided to follow. "My lords, I welcome you to my husband's fief and regret to inform you that he is not here at the moment." There, get that out of the way, she thought.

Althea watched their expressions closely. Norman looked surprised, but Philip seemed angry. And he smiled as if suddenly finding her words pleasing.

"Did he really marry you?" Norman asked. His high effeminate voice grated on Althea's nerves, as did the insulting tone he used.

Holding her temper in check, Althea nodded. "Didn't you receive word? He planned to inform your father. Of course, he left so soon after our wedding that he perhaps lacked time." She coolly pointed toward the chairs in front of the hearth. "Won't you please sit down, my lords. You must be weary after your trip. Have some hot wine."

Calmly, she began to pour wine into some goblets. She must appear as if nothing were amiss and she had no call to be alarmed. A noblewoman would not fear attack from her husband's kinsman and overlord. Her ploy seemed to be working, for both men seemed nonplussed for the moment, and then took the chairs that she offered them. As she served the wine, she studied Norman and was disgusted with what she saw. A weak chin and watery green eyes showed a man dissipated by a life of excess. A mole on his left cheek had a long hair growing out of it, but otherwise his face was hairless. He looked like a mockery of puberty, when a boy's voice has started to change and the feminine has not completely left his appearance. He looked nothing like Guerre and Stephen.

Norman glanced at Philip as if waiting for instructions. Althea did not miss the slight nod that Philip gave to his friend. Norman smiled at her, revealing long yellow teeth. "Perhaps you are wondering why we have arrived so suddenly, dear cousin?" The words were formal, but Althea heard the mockery in them.

"The question did occur to me," murmured Althea, "but it is not unusual for an overlord to visit his kinsman." Keep the right tone, she told herself.

"Of course. And it is my job to see that you are protected."

"Protected?"

"Of course. You come under my care. I am responsible for you. Both as your kinsman and as your overlord."

"But only if something has happened to Guerre." She spoke the words softly, apprehension growing. What he said was true. If a knight died, it was the responsibility of his overlord to care for his widow and children. But Guerre could not be dead! He couldn't be! She refused to believe it. Her mind went numb with pain, and she felt the room begin to spin. But before she could sink into the peace of oblivion, she felt a slap across her face, and with shock she realized that Norman had hit her.

"I think you had better repeat what you said before,"

she heard Philip say languidly, and she forced herself to look at Norman.

"Stupid wench, you should have listened the first time," he muttered, but he obeyed Philip. "I said that your husband is a traitor!" He glared at Althea. "You are not a widow yet, but you soon will be, and I am now responsible for you." With that he poured himself more wine and leaned back in his chair.

"I don't understand. My husband has always been loyal to you," she said with a calmness she did not feel.

"Loyal, bah. He has always hated my guts. He and that other traitor, Stephen."

"You will have to be more clear, my lord," said Althea, irritation creeping into her voice. Part of her was relieved that Guerre was still alive, and it gave her courage.

Norman leaned over and snapped his fingers in her face. "I don't have to be anything I don't choose," he said pettily, but a frown from Philip made him sit back and continue. "It was brought to my attention that my cousin Stephen was disloyal to my father and to me. And though I was shocked and saddened, I was forced to send out men to take back the fiefdom that he has so blackened with his disloyalty!"

"I find it hard to believe that Stephen could be a traitor any more than Guerre," said Althea heatedly. The way the man spoke made it obvious that he was spouting a practiced lie.

"What you believe is totally irrelevant," snapped Norman. "It was made clear to me by people I trust that Stephen openly mocked me and my father, and made it plain that he would side with another lord if I were challenged for the dukedom."

"My lord," said Althea politely, trying to calm troubled waters, "I think that he was unwise to say anything that might upset you, but he has no treason in his heart."

"Bah, I have taken their insults all these years. I am well rid of Stephen and Guerre. I want my own people in these fiefs."

It was then that Althea saw their plan. The charge of treason was simply an excuse to rid those two strongholds of two men that Norman obviously hated. The fact that they were his kinsmen—or that they were innocent—was immaterial. She had to find out what had happened to Guerre. "How did my husband become involved in all this? When he left here he was going to investigate reports of the plague."

"He was at Stephen's castle when my men arrived. When the captain of the guard read the arrest order for Stephen, your husband helped that traitor fight off my men and seal up the castle. Of course I sent other men immediately, but now we have to lay siege, and that is such a bore in the dead of winter."

Althea could not prevent a feeling of joy from rushing through her. The reason Guerre had not come home was that he was locked up in Stephen's castle! Wonderful! She knew that this was a terrible situation, but she still felt like dancing. At least he was alive!

"My men—" Norman began, then corrected himself and glanced at Philip. "*Our* men—for Philip has been good enough to lend me his troops—will complete the siege, since we have rather pressing matters to attend to at court." He gave Althea a wolfish grin. "But then His Highness, with his usual concern for the fair and helpless, remembered you. Philip thought you might be safer in Paris." He watched Althea carefully, enjoying his power over the beautiful young woman. "After all," he continued slowly, "you will soon be a bereaved and helpless widow and will need all the comfort and protection you can find."

His tone was so degrading that Althea sprang to her feet. "I don't think that you or all your men are capable of killing Guerre. He will survive, and until that time I will remain here. I need no protection, especially from the likes of you!" Fury had brought color to her cheeks, and her blue eyes flashed with emotion. She now looked dangerous and wild, and this appealed hugely to Philip. With one swift motion, he was on his feet and had grabbed her, pinning her arms to her sides.

"Let me go!" she screamed, rage giving her strength and courage. For one second, he loosened his grip, and Althea seized the chance. Before Philip knew what was happening, she reached out and clawed his face, drawing blood from the left temple to his chin.

Philip was momentarily stunned, then total anger filled him, combined with a burning lust. He vowed to break her spirit. Swiftly, he gave her a slap across the face that sent her reeling to the floor.

"You will pack a few things at once. Just what you'll need for a two-day journey. In Paris I'll see to your wardrobe. We're leaving as soon as your horse is saddled." Philip stared down at her imperiously, his cold eyes raking over every contour of her body.

Althea knew that her situation was hopeless. All the men here would obey Norman, for he was their overlord, and they were sworn to follow him; and he would do anything Philip wished. No one would come to her aid. She would have to go with them.

CHAPTER TWENTY-THREE

Althea's first sight of Paris was in late afternoon. It had been dreary and overcast all day, but as they approached the city, the sun came out. The late-afternoon rays gilded the gables and spires of the buildings, and Althea gasped in awe at the size and magnificence of the city. In her entire life she had never been anywhere that had a population greater than one thousand; Paris, she had been told, had one hundred times that amount. As they rode down the narrow streets filled with people, she would have loved to slow her horse and look closely at all there was to see, but Philip and Norman and their troop of men increased their pace and galloped down the narrow streets, heedless of the poor people who scurried like rats to get out of their way. Althea heard more than one curse muttered at their group, and her heart ached when Norman slashed his riding whip at an old man who was slow to clear their path.

As they rode deeper into the city, the odor of human refuse and garbage became stronger, and Althea felt nauseated as the stench became overpowering. The streets were filthy, and several times she felt her horse slip as he galloped through the slop that had been tossed from the windows above them. When they came into a little square, their way was blocked and they had to stop at the end of the street. Puzzled, Althea wondered what was causing the delay, for Philip and Norman brooked no interference from anyone. She could see several wagons ahead, but she could not see their contents. Then the troops began to edge into the square, and with a shock that sent cold shivers down her spine, Althea looked into one of the four wagons that had come to a stop. Inside, piled one on top of the other, were bodies: men, women, children, grotesquely twisted and covered with flies, their faces black and putrid. The stench was sickening, and the scene so horrible that Althea reeled in her saddle, coming close to a faint. She felt a hard pull on her reins as the captain of their troop pulled her horse forward. She could see Norman and Philip galloping across the square, fleeing the macabre scene.

"Spur your horse, my lady," said the captain.

She needed no further prodding, and her horse, scenting death and terrified in the natural way of animals, lunged forward. "My God, what is it?" cried Althea as they rode through the silent square.

"The plague has started again," cried the captain. "Those are the death carts that pick up the victims."

Unable to stop herself, Althea turned her head once more and now saw that people were scurrying like rats out of the old buildings in the square, throwing loved ones into the carts, and then, without a backward look at the body of a husband, child, or wife, fleeing back into the hovels in which they lived.

They must have been close to the palace, for the horses, sensing safety and home, now took their own lead and raced down one narrow street after another. Still sickened by the sight in the square, Althea hung on to her mount and raced behind the captain until they caught up with Philip and Norman. Althea was so busy trying to keep her seat and not fall into the sewage that made the street glisten with slime that she did not at first notice the huge, dark stone building that loomed ahead. It was only when she heard a cry from a sentry that she looked up and saw the royal palace of the French king. She had only a moment to take in its size and splendor before they rode through an arched entrance into a small courtyard. She guessed that this was one of the back entrances to the Louvre, and she was correct. Before she could absorb where she was, she was being bustled up a dark stone staircase that seemed to go on forever. It was lit by torches, but the change from the bright sunlight outside made it seem like a tomb, and she felt her heart sink as they climbed up the stairs.

The stairwell opened into a long corridor that was dark and elegant. She could see lavish tapestries and paintings on the walls, and once they passed two women in elegant dresses and long veils who were obviously ladies of the court. They called out eager greetings to Norman and Philip and stared with amusement at Althea. Dressed in a simple red woolen gown covered by a plain brown riding cloak, she seemed nothing more lofty than a merchant's wife or daughter who had become the temporary plaything of two noblemen and was being hurried into the palace for a bit of amorous sport. So common was this that the court women only looked at her for a moment, and then passed on. Althea felt herself flush under their scrutiny, but before she could snap a retort, she was hustled through a door into a large chamber that made her stop cold in astonishment.

It was unlike any room she had ever seen. Used to the life of a castle, Althea had never seen the inside of a royal palace, and although Philip was only a second cousin of King Philip, this apartment was lavish. Tapestries woven in gold and silver covered the walls, depicting Philip at his favorite pastimes: hunting and seduction. Two marble fireplaces, one on each side of the room, had fires burning in them, and the floor was covered with woven rugs from the East. An enormous bed, canopied in gold and red velvet, seemed to take up most of the room.

"Perhaps you will find court life more to your liking than you anticipated," said Philip with a slow smile. There was a hint of disappointment in his voice. He wanted the pleasure of breaking this spirited filly, and he hoped that the magnificence of the court would not make her give in quickly like all the others he had brought or dragged here. He was not disappointed for long. Recovering herself, Althea remembered where she was, and all her loathing and anger at Philip and Norman rushed to the surface once again.

"It is unfortunate that the men who occupy these rooms do not match the grandeur of their surroundings," she said tartly.

Philip stared at her, pleased that she would once again be good game, and then he nodded to Norman, who reached out and pulled a long velvet cord. Althea had already noticed on the two-day ride that Norman was Philip's lackey. Guerre's cousin was a spineless, dissolute creature who was easily dominated by his clever and cruel companions. Totally without morals, he never gave it a thought that he had helped kidnap the woman he thought was his cousin's wife so that she could be used by his friend. Looking at him now, she thought that she could gladly stick a dagger in his spineless back.

A servant then entered, a withered and ugly hunchback who bowed like a dog in front of Philip. "Welcome, Your Grace. Welcome. It is good to see you again. And you, too, my lord Norman."

Totally ignoring him, Philip turned and poured a glass of wine from a decanter on a small side table. "Charles, this lady will be my guest for some time, and we must find accommodations for her." He paused and smiled at Althea, and she saw the glitter of sadistic amusement in the look. "She is soon to become a widow, and will therefore need solitude. I think, perhaps, that she would enjoy one of the tower rooms."

A slow smirk crossed the servant's face, and Althea realized that Charles was considerably like his master. "I think I know just the spot, my lord. It will be out of the path of all traffic, and perfect for a grieving widow. You may recall it. It was used once before in a similar circumstance."

"Perfect." Philip now seemed impatient. With a wave of his hand, he dismissed them. "Take her there now. And make sure that she is undisturbed."

As Althea followed Charles out of the chamber, she

heard Norman break into peals of laughter, and her courage began to falter. Could they be sending her to the dungeon? she wondered in horror. They turned down one dark
corridor of the palace to another, and then they began to
climb steep stone steps. Finally, they reached a landing
and entered a small, dark hall. A large wooden door was at
one end, and Charles removed a heavy metal key from
around his waist and unlocked the door. With a creak, it
pushed open, and the servant waved Althea to enter. She
heard the grate of the key in the lock and knew that once
again in her life she was a prisoner.

Taking a deep breath, she looked around the tiny room
and realized it must have once been a storage closet. It was
so small that it contained only a bed with a low table next
to it. A rag rug was on the floor, and the ceiling sloped so
steeply over the bed that she had to hunch down, short as
she was, to lie down. She did so now, and was happy to see
that the window next to the bed had no bars on it. Peering
out, she could see why. She was evidently in a garret room
in the top of the Louvre. Her room faced a square that bordered one side of the palace, and she was so high that the
people below looked like miniatures. A leap from this window was certain death.

Sighing, she leaned back on the bed and stared at the
ceiling. She was definitely trapped. Philip could come here
anytime he chose, and no one would know. And if they did
know, who would care? Even if by some miracle Guerre escaped and came looking for her, he would never find her in
this out-of-the-way spot. He could spend days in the palace
of King Philip VI of France and never find the stairwell
that led to this lonely garret. Feeling tears come to her
eyes, Althea forced herself to think practically. Somehow,
she would be strong, and somehow, she would escape. First
she had to learn what was planned for her. She had a fairly
good idea, but Philip's behavior had been puzzling, and she
felt that he had more in mind than seduction.

A slight noise caused her to sit up. She thought she
heard a voice, and her heart began to pound. Was it Philip,

coming to torment her? She heard the sound again. It was more than one voice. The key turned in the lock and she braced herself.

At first the sudden light blinded her, and she shaded her eyes. Then she saw with surprise that the person holding the candle was a woman, and behind her stood the servant Charles. For a moment the two women stared, assessing the other. Althea saw a girl of about her own age and build, but with black hair carefully wound with pearls. She used a good deal of face paint, and her lips were unnaturally red. She was dressed in a gown of scarlet velvet that was cut so low that her breasts were almost exposed to the nipple, and the sleeves were the extreme in fashion, for they came almost to the floor. She held a candle with her left hand, and Althea could see the jewels flash on her fingers.

Althea assumed her to be one of the glittering creatures of the court, a lady of the nobility, but when the woman spoke, her heavy accent and poor grammar quickly told another tale.

"So this is the baggage that those two asses have returned with this time." The girl handed the candle to Charles and moved closer, putting her hands on her hips and staring at Althea, taking in every detail. "Well, you look clean, but very messy. Your hair is terrible. You look as if you've just been tumbled in a haystack and are not yet over the flush of pleasure. Except for your expression, that is."

Althea bridled at her words, and her answer was sharp. "It is a little difficult to be neat when one is pitched into a dark room without a mirror, comb, or water in which to wash!"

"Aha, so there is fire under that little blonde head," said the girl with a laugh as she sat down on the bed. "Well, you mustn't expect too much until his high horse meets with his wife, although I wager the old girl would prefer him here than with her."

Seeing Althea's puzzled look, she added, "Princess

Mary, his wife, I'm talking about. He must do the formalities and dine with her this night. And my Norman with his father."

This was obviously Norman's mistress, for she certainly wasn't his wife. And she foolishly thought that she was pining away for Philip. The thought made Althea cringe.

"Well, I hope that he becomes enamored with his wife and forgets all about me," Althea could not resist saying.

The girl looked at Althea sharply, and her worldly eyes became knowing. "Little chance of that." Nodding to Charles, she commanded him to leave. "Go fetch some food and wine for this poor girl, and some sweets for me. And bring back some candles and water, too. The rest can wait till morning." She spoke curtly, like one unaccustomed to giving orders but enjoying the new power. Charles looked angry, but he left. The key turning the lock proved that the girl's authority went only so far.

"Well, now, it seems we will be company until the ugly little monster returns. I hate that twisted monkey. But forget that. My name is Anna, and I am the countess of something, or soon will be."

Althea tried unsuccessfully to repress a grin, but the girl saw it and took it in good humor. "Well, I'm not used to these fine titles yet. Anyway, Norman says he will soon have the king make me a countess, and then I'll learn the proper way to call myself." Scrutinizing Althea, she said, "You must be one of them, by the way you talk and hold yourself. I've been studying them. Trying to learn and all. But you aren't French, that I can tell."

Althea felt sorry for the girl. For all her worldliness, she naively believed Norman's lies that he could have her made a countess, and it seemed so important to her. Speaking kindly, she answered, "I'm Welsh. My husband . . ." she hesitated over the lie, "is the Baron du Reims, so that makes me a baroness. My father was also a nobleman."

"Is a baroness less than a countess?"

"Usually." Althea repressed her smile this time. The girl seemed extremely pleased.

"So Norman locked up your husband. The ass. Well, there isn't much he won't do for the prince." She seemed disgruntled at the thought. Tossing her head, she looked at Althea out of the corner of her eye. "And you don't seem too happy about it all. I don't have to be real smart to know that they must think you'll try to escape."

Tears welled up in Althea's eyes. This girl, ignorant and vulgar though she was, was not hostile to her, and having a sympathetic face near made her defenses come close to crumbling. Shaking her head, she tried to speak. "I hate them. They dragged me here."

"Now, now," soothed Anna, putting a gaudily jeweled hand on Althea's arm. "It could be worse than to be wanted by a great lord. And life here is very exciting." Althea realized that Anna's comprehension was going to be limited. Obviously a child of the streets, she thought her values were those of all women and that Althea's lot was not bad. To have the prince himself was a thing many court ladies fought over.

Soon Charles returned with food and wine. After setting the tray on the table, Anna told him to leave and to return in a half hour. Althea ravenously fell on the cold chicken, cheese, and bread that was under the napkin, and listened raptly as Anna talked. It appeared that the girl was quite lonely. Norman had found her in a whorehouse in Paris that catered to the merchant class. She had only been in service for a few months when Norman took a liking to her and brought her to court. Here, although she had fine jewels and a good apartment, she did not attend court functions and was an outcast with the other ladies.

Underneath the apparent frivolity of her appearance, she had a fairly sharp mind and knew a great deal about what went on in the palace. One item in particular was especially useful for Althea to know. The reason for her garret room was not only to keep her from escaping, but to hide her from the Duke du Marton. Guerre's uncle would not have looked kindly on this escapade, and though Norman might convince his father of Guerre's and Stephen's perfidy, it would be hard to explain Althea's presence in Philip's garret closet. And the old Duke had the ear of the king. The King of France had already given Philip word to be more diplomatic in his relations with his wife, Mary of Flanders, and to curtail the cruelty he was becoming too well known for. To rape a peasant girl was one thing; to kidnap the wife of a noble and keep her prisoner in the royal palace was another. Althea did not let on to Anna how useful this piece of information could be to her.

Althea also learned that the queen of France, Jeanne de Bourgogne, was an intelligent but dangerous woman who showed no mercy to her enemies. She had a bad leg, and was called "the lame queen" behind her back. She had great influence over the king, who was said to be a little fearful of her, and, much more important, she disliked Philip du Bois. Althea's heart soared with joy at this information. Perhaps here would be a source of aid. She forced herself to look calm, for she suspected strongly that whatever Anna thought was quickly changed to words, and that she would chatter like this with anyone, including Norman.

The girl was now happily recounting how the wife of the dauphin, the future Queen of France, Bonne du Luxembourg, had once nodded to her when passing in a hall. "She's very beautiful and gracious. She even knows who I am, but she still nodded to me. Perhaps someday she will wish me good day." Anna sighed with happiness at the thought of such an honor. "She's not like the other ladies of the court, who are all cats. They have had as many lovers as I have had, but they think they're queens by the airs they give themselves. Especially that high-class whore, Anne du Chelle."

Althea started at the name and her memory lurched backward in time, remembering the beautiful blonde woman with cold green eyes and sensuous lips, dressed in the highest fashion. So she was here. "I believe I've met her," said Althea cautiously.

"Did you like her? I detest her. She shares Philip's bed,

yet dares to call me 'the little whore from the waterfront.'
Anna's frown suddenly turned to a smile. "Ah, but won't it
be a bug in her ass when she discovers that you're here.
She thinks she's so secure in her position as Philip's mistress that he will never stray again. Except, of course, for
the girls they drag in from the street. This will lower the
countess a peg or two."

"But no one is to know that I am here," Althea said, hoping that Anna would tell Anne du Chelle about her. If the
duchess knew and told a friend in anger, how long would it
take for the rest of the court to find out? That might be her
salvation!

But Anna just groaned in frustration. "True. And Norman said he would beat me with his whip if I told anyone.
He only told me by accident, and then he swore me to se-
crecy. In fact, he doesn't even know that I'm here, although Charles will be sure to tell him."

"Won't you get into trouble?" asked Althea with genuine concern. She could imagine Philip's rage.

"Norman will give me a swat or two." The girl shrugged
that off. "Norman needs me. I'm the only woman who can
do what he needs to be a man. He has a problem, you
know." She glanced at Althea and giggled. "Well, now you
know. He usually likes the company of young boys, but
once in a while he'll take a woman. I know tricks that
arouse him, and it makes him feel good to keep a mistress.
And it makes his father, the duke, very happy."

Anna recounted all this as if she were discussing the
weather, and Althea felt herself begin to blush. She had
heard of men who favored boys, but she had never met one.
And those who had told her of such things had always ex-
pressed their contempt. They had called it sodomy. She
tried to hide her expression of disgust, but Anna saw it.

"Well, it worked in my favor," the girl said with a re-
signed shrug. "If he had been totally male, he would have
married long ago. This way I make out pretty well—and
without too much work, I may add."

Althea only nodded. She heard a sound, and listened intently. Someone was coming up the stairwell. Anna had heard it, too, but she did not seem concerned. Her expression changed to alarm when Philip entered the room.

His size filled the tiny garret room, and even though he stood there silently, he seemed to dominate them. Anna started to rise, but he grabbed her arm and yanked her to her feet with a violence that made the girl scream. "Get out of here, you meddling bitch," he hissed in a deadly whisper. "If you breathe one word of this, I'll personally put the poison in your wine!"

The courage and bravado that she had displayed before vanished like a mist, and the girl fled from the room without a backward glance. Without taking his eyes from Althea, he slammed the door shut. A sinister smile hovered on his lips. "I intended that I would be your only visitor, my sweet. Norman's little drab won't trouble you again." He sat at the foot of the bed, in the spot where Anna had sat.

Althea was also on the bed, her back against the wall, her knees pulled up to her chest. She wished she were in a more dignified position, but it was now impossible to move since there was no more room. She tried to meet his eyes with courage, but her heart was beating so rapidly that she was sure he could hear it. She loathed this man with all the hatred she was capable of feeling. To be trapped so closely to him made her skin crawl. She knew without a doubt that he was the one who had engineered the plan to have Norman attack Stephen's castle. He had known that Guerre would go to his defense, and then be trapped by the siege. He had planned the whole thing carefully so that he could capture her, and he had succeeded. She felt the deadly intensity of his passion as if it were smothering her.

Then, something reckless and rebellious leaped in her chest. She wasn't a cowering Anna who took the bones that life threw to her and was grateful. She had pride, and this man was trying to break her. Well, his task would not be an easy one, she silently vowed. "And how is your good wife, my lord?" She forced herself to meet his eyes as she spoke, and was disappointed to see that there was cold amusement in them.

"She is quite well, though still not with child."

"Perhaps if you spent more time in your marital bed, what you desire would be accomplished."

"I've sired enough bastards to know the fault is not with me. The woman should have been a nun. She wasn't built for the breeding of princes." He fingered the dagger in his hand and grinned. "Perhaps pregnancy is contagious, though, and she will conceive tonight."

He stretched his legs and placed one hand on her knee. "We dined with a couple that should be expecting their first heir in several months. I say 'should' because the lady's word is often in question. This may have been a ploy to bring the man to the altar."

Althea was puzzled at the turn of the conversation. Philip had never seemed interested or concerned with others before this, and he had never been prone to idle chatter. She sensed that he was leading to something, but she didn't know what.

His hand went higher on her thigh. "Oh, but of course, you've been quite out of the way on Guerre's estate. You haven't heard the news. Claude du Vendome married the Lady Mathilde, and his heir will be born here at court."

Althea was stunned by this information. Claude and Mathilde here at the palace! Now there were two more deadly enemies she had to contend with.

"I hope that look of shock doesn't mean you're jealous," Philip said smoothly. "I didn't think that fat old pig really caught your fancy."

"Of course not," snapped Althea, struggling to regain her composure. "I didn't think that she was allowed at court. And I had also heard rumors that she could never conceive."

"I arranged their entry to court. As for her pregnancy, her stomach is slightly rounded, but she doesn't look very pregnant to me. I think a miscarriage of convenience will occur shortly." He shrugged with amusement. "But her timing was perfect. To finally breed a child for Claude, just when he had been humiliated by you for the second time. It helped his pride considerably to wed her. Your timing, on the other hand, is really poor for a man's ego, my sweet. To run away from your nuptial bed, and then to escape on the night of a tournament when all his friends were there to share his shame. Really quite unforgivable." But there was no sympathy in his smile.

"I care nothing for his pride or his shame," Althea said. "He is a gross, miserable man, and I despise him. He got what he deserved."

"I agree." Philip's voice turned low and seductive. "You are far too wild and beautiful for that oaf. He would never appreciate you except as a vessel for his lust."

"And isn't that what I am to you?" she retorted.

"I, my sweet Althea, appreciate you as the hunter appreciates the beauty of the deer, or the grace of the gazelle. You were not easy to catch, and I vow you will not be easy to tame, but it will be fascinating to try."

Althea looked at him sharply. His pale blue eyes were glittering, and his hand was now pressing hard into the flesh of her thigh. She could feel his fingers above the soft wool, and with each stroke, his hand moved upward. Her eyes darted to the door.

"There is a guard out there who would not hesitate to run you through." Philip spoke with the calmness of power.

The expression of cold lust on his face made Althea furious. She was a new game for him. A woman, instead of a horse, that he would break and tame. Fury grew in her breast, and she pushed his hand away. As fast as the lightning that streaked the sky, he grabbed her hands and threw himself on top of her.

"You bitch!" he whispered in her hair. "You can't fight, you little fool. You're mine, and surrender will be far more pleasurable than struggle."

His words only inflamed her more, giving her strength to free her hands. The only thought in her mind was to stop him. He would not violate her a second time! She scratched at him like a madwoman, but that did not stop him from ripping her gown from her shoulders and down the front until her breasts were exposed. Suddenly, she felt a blow to her face that made her head reel in pain. Stunned, she opened her eyes and was shocked to see that Philip's face, only inches from hers, was streaked with blood. She had clawed at him in fury, and had instinctively gone for his face. Now he was looking down at her with a viciousness in his eyes that made her heart almost stop with fear. All lust was gone; only the hunter, tired of the attack, hungry for the capture, remained. He hesitated for only a second, and then he began to slap her across the face with a vengeance. She could feel the blows and see his face, but then he began to blur, and finally she slipped into unconsciousness.

CHAPTER TWENTY-FOUR

She awoke slowly, and her mind was confused. She had never been here before. Her eyes, aching with some strange pain, tried to focus but everything was blurred. She realized the bed was far too large and soft to be the one in the garret. And the room had a sweet scent to it, almost as if perfumed incense was burning somewhere. She thought she saw a figure at the far end of the room. Her lids fluttered with the effort to see.

"I think she's waking." Althea heard the soft voice and then movement toward the bed. She shut her eyes, too terrified to see who her jailor might be. It was only when she felt a cool hand against her forehead that she dared to open them, and she saw with surprise that a lady was looking down at her with concern.

"Where am I?" asked Althea. Her voice sounded tiny to her ears, and it was difficult to speak.

"You're safe and in good care," the woman said reassuringly. "We did not think you would live at first, but you have grown stronger every day."

"Every day?"

"You've been unconscious for three days," the woman told her. "Rest now. I assure you that all is well."

Althea didn't know until later that she slipped into a deep sleep that lasted for almost another day. When she awoke again, her eyesight was normal, and she was hungry. Curious, she looked around the room. She was amazed at the luxury of her surroundings. She was lying on a large bed with red silk pillows and soft wool blankets. The room was huge, with a large stone fireplace at one end where a

fire burned brightly. There were large windows on one side
of the room, and they went from the floor to the ceiling
with red velvet drapes on each side. There were fur rugs on
the floor, and beautiful tapestries on the walls. On the
table next to the bed, a silver candelabra sat, and next to it
a silver bowl filled with water. She moved her legs and
arms slowly, and was happy to find that though she was
sore, the pain had decreased considerably.

The door opened to an old woman, plump and dressed in
servant's garb, who busied herself at the fire without even
glancing at Althea. A moment later the door opened again,
and a small young woman entered. She said something to
the servant, and then walked toward the bed. Her eyes met
Althea's and she smiled.

"Look, Joanna, the patient is doing much better. She is
awake."

Althea tried to smile as the lady put a hand on her brow,
feeling for a fever. "I feel quite well now. But where am I?"

"You are in the palace of the king of France," the woman said, but when she saw the fear in Althea's eyes, she
added quickly, "Don't worry. You are safe. No one will
harm you again."

Althea instinctively believed her, and settled more com-
fortably into the pillows. "I can't begin to thank you for all
that you have done for me, but may I burden you with
some questions?"

The woman settled into a high-backed chair near the bed
and nodded. "I am sure that you have many questions, and
I have some of my own. Feel free to begin."

"First of all, who are you, and how did you find me?"

The woman seemed to choose her words càrefully. Althea saw that she was plain in the usual sense, but there
was a kindness about her that made her seem pretty. One
could forget the double chin and overplump cheeks when
one looked at the tender mouth and the sincerity in the
clear gray eyes. She now seemed torn between honesty and
the desire to soften her words.

Finally, she looked straight at Althea and spoke. "My name is Mary du Bois, and I am the wife of Philip du Bois."

Althea regarded her in horror. She could not believe that Philip had forced his wife to care for her. The humiliation for this princess must be beyond imagination. As if reading her mind, Mary gave a slight smile.

"It is not as you think. He did not bid me take care of you. In fact, quite the reverse." Seeing the bewildered look on Althea's face, she settled back into her chair. "Perhaps I should explain more clearly. When Philip returned to his apartments, I was there waiting for him to discuss a point about my dowry. He hadn't expected to see me, so he hadn't bothered to clean up his face, which was covered with blood." She smiled at Althea, as if the thought pleased her. "Anyway, he tried to tell me that he had been in a fight with another lord, but I am not a fool. At first I thought that he and Anne du Chelle had quarreled. She is his mistress, you know." The girl said it in such a matter-of-fact tone that Althea could only nod dumbly in response.

"He was in a terrible temper, and I left quickly," Mary went on. "I was suspicious and curious. It did not fit Anne du Chelle's personality to maul a man she desperately wanted, so I sent out a few servants to make inquiries." Here she paused and smiled again. "I don't know what you may have heard, but I am not as stupid as most people think. I have my ways of finding out what occurs in this court."

"I have never heard a thing that was bad about Your Highness," said Althea quickly.

"Then you have not been long at court. My husband makes great sport of me." She waved away Althea's protest. "Don't try to be kind. He is a monster, and I know full well how cruel he can be. But to continue. My faithful Antoine found out about a girl brought to the garret room in the north end of the palace, and that she had been visited by Anna, the mistress of Norman du Reims. I had Anna brought to my room, and when she arrived, I also had a surprise visit from the queen. The girl may have tried to lie to me, but she was terrified of Queen Jeanne, and she told the truth. She did not know that you had been beaten, but when I put two and two together, I realized that you were either dead or close to it. With the queen's permission, I had you moved to this room which is in my suite."

"My lady, you have put yourself in grave danger for me. I cannot begin to thank you for your charity." Tears began to flow from Althea's eyes.

"I know that you came here under duress, and that you were Philip's victim. It has given me great pleasure to thwart him. He won't dare to touch you now. The whole court knows about this escapade. Both he and Norman have been asked to leave, and are now far away. Hopefully, for a long time." She gave a little grimace of disgust.

"Then I can return to Guerre's, my husband's, castle?"

"I'm afraid not. Not until the question of your husband's treason to his overlord has been cleared up. They explained the reason for your capture to the king by saying that they had only planned for your protection, and that you went mad and attacked Philip. No one believes that part, but the Duke du Marton has asked for a special detachment of soldiers to ride to Stephen's castle to investigate the charges. Until then, you are to remain here as a ward of the old duke."

Althea tried not to show her disappointment. It would be only a matter of time before she was free. "I owe you a great deal, my lady. Many women would not have been so kind or understanding."

"Perhaps we can become friends. A German princess is not really popular in the French court. They think me gauche and unappealing."

"You are neither. You are a wonderful, kind woman who deserves everyone's respect," said Althea hotly, rising quickly to her defense.

"Thank you. And now you must rest, for you are still pale. Joanna will stay in the room, and if you want anything, she will get it for you. I will return later."

* * *

Althea had many visitors. She had become a curiosity at the court, a fixture in the scandal that everyone was discussing, and as many people as could came to Mary's apartments to see the girl who had been abducted by Philip and Norman. The men were instantly taken with her appearance. She had lost weight, but the new thinness accented her cheekbones, and her eyes were even more pronounced. Sitting in the high bed, dressed in a blue silk robe trimmed with white fox, and her long blonde hair cascading around her, she looked like the helpless victim that every man longed to rescue.

The women, on the other hand, spoke to her kindly enough, but Althea could see their sly titters to each other, and their frank appraisal of her looks. They shrewdly studied her, knowing that she would be competition if she stayed at court. The big topic was the blondeness of her hair, since it was not a color that was common in France, and there was much speculation about it. One enterprising court lady, believing that it would become the fashion, had her chemist make up a mixture that would bleach the hair, and then used the compound on her own raven locks. The mixture turned her hair a shade of violet, and the lady had to hide her head beneath a wig. Althea and Mary laughed over that like two schoolgirls, especially since the lady had once been the favorite of Philip du Bois.

One afternoon, almost a week after first finding herself at court, Althea was sitting in front of the fireplace in Mary's chamber when there was an imperious knock on the door, and then it quickly swung open to admit two ladies. Joanna and Mary, who were both in the room, immediately fell into deep curtsies, and Althea followed their example, although she was puzzled as to the identity of the women. One was old, with a slight limp, and sharp, darting black eyes; the other was small, blonde and very pretty. The woman with the limp walked over to Althea. "You may rise, Mary, and present this lady to me," said the old woman in a harsh, masculine voice.

Mary placed a hand on Althea's shoulder as if to steady her. "Your Majesty, this is Althea du Reims, wife of Sir Guerre du Reims. Althea, this is Her Majesty, Queen Jeanne of France, and with her, the Princess Bonne, who is the wife of the dauphin, and who is also a cousin of mine."

Althea hoped the queen did not see her nervousness. She rose when the queen indicated, but she was at a loss for words. After a moment, it appeared that she did not need any. The queen seated herself on a chair, but did not indicate that the others could be seated. Bonne, with the regal grace that would be required in a future queen of France, drifted over to the window, but Althea and Mary stood before the queen.

"I suppose it would be silly of me to ask how you like life at court, when you have been kidnapped, beaten, and abused by one of our shining princes," said the queen, her dark eyes watching Althea closely. "You are a pretty thing, so it is no wonder they fight over you. Don't blush, girl. All here know how you jilted Claude du Vendome, not once, but twice." She laughed suddenly, a harsh, barking sound. "Even if you are a silly twit of a girl, you picked good men to insult. I couldn't have chosen better myself. The chief glutton and the chief lecher of this fair land, both brought to shame by you."

Althea had heard that the king and most of the court were afraid of Queen Jeanne, and now she could see why. She seemed unusually intelligent and strong, but she also looked as if she could be a dangerous enemy. Althea realized quickly that it was not sympathy for her, but an intense dislike of her husband's cousin, that made her pleased with events. She was delighted that Philip had been banished from court.

The queen and the beautiful Bonne left almost as quickly as they had arrived. Breathing a sigh of relief, Mary sat down on a chair. "Thank God she likes you."

"I didn't get that impression, Your Highness," said Althea, also sitting down.

"I told you to call me Mary when we are alone. Yes, she

did like you. At least, as far as she is capable of liking people. You helped serve a purpose, so she is pleased. Her Majesty either takes a strong dislike to people, or she is neutral about them. She strongly loves no one except the king
and her sons."

"The wife of the dauphin is quite beautiful," said Althea.

"She is a kinswoman of mine. Her mother and mine
were first cousins.".

"Then you do have other friends at court," said Althea
kindly.

"Not really. Bonne is one of those beautiful women who
are remote from the cares of the world. She and I have
never been close. But Bonne is adored by the people, for
she is so different from the queen."

They spent the rest of the afternoon in pleasant discussion. Mary, through her network of spies, knew a great
deal about the happenings at court, and with girlish relish,
she and Althea gossiped until it was time for Mary to prepare for a banquet given by the ambassador from Venice.

Mary had been correct in her assumption that Queen
Jeanne liked Althea. Two days later, a tailor and his assistant arrived, and much to Althea's delight, she discovered
that she was to be outfitted with several new gowns suitable for court life.

"I must go and thank the queen," said Althea with joy,
as Mary came into the room. "Look at the gowns I have
chosen." Around her lay bolts of silks and velvets, samples
of mink and ermine and fox. Threads of gold, silver, and
other hues were on a table, while samples of lace were
spread on the bed.

"Better to thank the Duke du Marton. This will come
out of his purse," said Mary with a laugh. "The queen is
not overly fond of the old reprobate, and she found a way to
hit him in his money purse. I was there when she told the
king that it was shameful that the duke had not purchased
clothes for his ward. The king said he would look into it,

and here we are!" Mary waved her hand in delight and smiled at the tailor, who was busily taking measurements with his ruler.

"I wonder if I'll meet him," said Althea. "I think he's the only man at court who hasn't visited me."

"He's quite disgruntled at the turn of events. He hates to have his life disturbed in any way. I think Norman inherited his indolence from his father. His late mother was more ambitious and lively."

"Late mother?" Althea did not know that the Duchess du Marton had died. Clarissa had not known either, and she had been her lady-in-waiting.

"Yes. I guess none of you could have known. They wouldn't have bothered to send special word. She died of the plague last fall. She was one of the first victims. Twenty-two people died in this palace, but she and four others were the only nobles. The rest were servants."

Althea sat quietly for a moment. She was thinking how close the disease had come to them. A cold chill went up and down her spine.

"Come now," laughed Mary, "don't look so glum. You didn't even know the woman, did you?"

"It was the thought of the plague," said Althea quietly. "It seems so sinister."

"Well, don't think about it. Besides, the worst is over. It spent itself last fall, and is now dying out. Come on, show me the colors you've selected."

Althea nodded and returned to the little tailor, who had been waiting patiently. She realized that Mary, secure in the royal palace of the king of France, did not know about the death carts that made their macabre rounds in the streets of Paris.

CHAPTER TWENTY-FIVE

For Althea the days that followed were ones of great excitement and of great anxiety. The excitement came from her introduction to court life. Having grown up in her father's isolated castle, she had never even hoped of going to the court of the English king. Few noblewomen from Wales traveled that far unless their father or husband was an important knight of the realm. Althea's father was only a minor knight, and the most that she had ever dreamed of was a visit to the great castle at Cardiff, where the Duke of Cardiff held a sumptuous court of his own. Her father and Maura had once traveled there, and the tales they had told had inflamed the imagination of the young girl who only knew the life of the castle and the surrounding woods. But anything that she had heard of Cardiff paled to insignificance when she saw the Louvre.

The castles of Europe, both great and small, were primarily fortresses. The first and overriding concern in their construction was the idea of defense; comfort was a second thought. In France Althea saw that the nobles were trying to introduce some aspects of comfort and luxury into their castles. But even the fortresses at Vendome and du Reims could not touch the Louvre. It was a palace built for a king, and comfort and beauty were the guiding lights in its construction. Althea would wander through the huge state rooms and halls, taking in all the beautiful tapestries on the walls, the carpets from Byzantium, the marble columns, the velvets and silks that draped the windows, and she would shake her head in wonder.

She and Mary spent the late winter afternoons strolling

in the gardens, and the head gardener told them how forty
gardeners toiled in the spring and summer, growing all
manner of flowers and shrubs. At first Althea did not believe that the statues sitting in the middle of now empty
fountains could really blow water out of the trumpets they
carried, but Mary called in the man in charge of the fountains, and he carefully explained how this was accomplished. After showing Althea the pipes that led to the
statues, she finally believed him and was filled with anticipation of the day that the fountains would be on again, in
the beginning of April.

Court life itself intrigued her, primarily because it was
so novel to her. She suspected that it would soon grow dull
and boring, and that she would begin to long for the simple
life of the country, but for now she would observe and enjoy
all that she saw. She tried to be inconspicuous, for she felt
naive and countryish around the sophisticated members of
the greatest court in Europe. Since Mary was also shy, the
two would usually stay in the background and watch all
that passed with eager young eyes.

And there was a great deal to see. There were dinners
and balls, receptions, and small soirees. Mary was invited
because of her position, and Althea because she was still a
novelty. Many nobles frequently entertained in their own
rooms, so when no state functions were planned, Althea
and Mary would often spend the evening in the apartment
of some noble, listening to musicians playing the latest
songs, or watching the antics of a jester. The Countess de
la Lambe had recently purchased a strange animal called
a monkey that she dressed in a tunic and little cap with
bells. Niko the Monkey soon became the most popular
member of court, and all wanted an invitation to the countess's dinners. The only person who detested the monkey
was the queen, and since she rarely attended anything
other than necessary court functions, Niko was usually
present at any informal gathering.

Althea soon learned that beneath the glitter of court life
lay a sordid and cruel side. Adultery was rampant, and the

chief topic of conversation was the love affairs of the courtiers. Althea had been shocked to discover that the king
kept a mistress at the Louvre, and that all knew of her existence. Mary told her that Queen Jeanne tolerated her because she was as stupid and lazy as she was beautiful. She
made no effort to involve herself in intrigue, so she was
harmless. One of her more intelligent and ambitious pre-
decessors had not been so lucky. She had died mysteriously
after eating some cakes that the queen's lady-in-waiting
had sent to her. There was no proof that the queen was involved, but there was much speculation.

Althea shuddered at the story, and spent the rest of the
day slightly depressed. It had rained for two days, and the
chill, damp weather made it uncomfortable to walk outdoors. Althea felt caged in, and she was also worried about
Guerre. The king's emissary had left two weeks past to investigate the situation at Stephen's castle, and as yet
there was no word. When she was alone she was tormented
by fears for Guerre's safety. And then she would wonder if
he had yet decided to forgive her. Perhaps he would think
that she had gone with Philip du Bois willingly, and would
be further outraged.

She walked over to one of the windows that overlooked a
formal garden. The garden was bleak. No sign of life
stirred yet, for it was still too cold for the flowers to come
out. The rain fell on the gray statues, and the dark would
come early on such a grim day. Althea thought how closely
the weather matched her mood. The newness of court life
was wearing thin. She had only one friend here, and dear
though Mary had become to her, Althea was homesick, although she was not sure for what. Was it for Wales, and a
life long gone? Or was it for Guerre's castle? As she
watched the rain fall, she realized that it was not a place
that she yearned for, but a man. For her, sanctuary and
safety were with Guerre. Wherever he was, that was home
for her. Slowly, the tears that filled her eyes rolled down
her cheeks, as if the bleakness of the day had joined with
her. She wondered if she would ever know peace and love

again. She had had it only short a time in her life, but it had become precious to her. Now she doubted if she would ever recapture it.

She was in this mood when Mary entered her chamber. Sensing her friend's depression, Mary quickly called for wine and ordered her servant, Joanna, to stir the fire in the hearth.

"Is it not enough that the day is bad, without you giving in to grief also?" chided Mary, kindness taking the edge out of her words.

Althea tried to smile. "I was thinking of Guerre, and if we would ever be together again."

Mary looked at her friend wistfully. "At least you have hope," she said with a sad sigh. "For you there is the possibility that all will turn out well. For me, there is nothing. I detest my husband, and wish that he would never return. But of course, he will."

Althea was consumed with guilt. She knew that Mary's life was far worse than hers. The princess was bound to that sadistic lecher who would never give her a day's happiness. And there was little chance that she would ever have a child, for she and Philip had long since stopped the pretense of living together. Seeing that her mood had spread to Mary, Althea tried to think of something to cheer them both.

"Just yesterday, Mary, you told me to live for the day, and find happiness in each hour. Now we have both spurned your good advice and are sitting here feeling sorry for ourselves. Come, let us dress for the reception for the Princess Bonne."

Mary smiled. "Your moods certainly change quickly. But you're right. My cousin's birthday fete should be fun. It is to be held in the Grand Salon, and the dauphin has ordered the room filled with roses. The gardeners have been coaxing the buds in the greenhouses for days."

Althea and Mary spoke for a few minutes more about what they would wear, and then the princess left for her own chamber to dress. Althea bathed, and then Sybil, her

maid, brushed her hair until it gleamed. Finally, the maid
helped Althea into a lovely velvet gown the color of lemon,
with long sleeves embroidered with white roses. She arranged the high pointed headdress so that the attached
yellow silk veil fell in beautiful folds to Althea's knees. At
last, satisfied with her work, Sybil stepped back and let Althea look into the polished silver mirror that was against
the wall.

"They say that you are the loveliest lady at court," said
the maid in awe.

Althea did not answer. She was staring at her reflection
in the mirror. She realized for the first time how much she
had changed in appearance from the day she had first met
Guerre. Then she had been dressed almost as a peasant,
and her body had still been that of a child. A woman stood
revealed now, taller and thinner, yet curving deliciously.
Her breasts had grown during her pregnancy, and they
had retained their new roundness. They swelled through
the velvet material to tantalize any man who would see
her. She saw something else in the mirror that was not
truly physical, but yet it changed her appearance drasti-
cally. She had lost the timidity of youth. Her bearing had a
grace and sophistication that it had lacked a year ago.
With pride, she decided that she liked the woman she had
become.

A knock came at the door, and Mary entered. After the
two girls complimented each other on their clothes and appearance, they left arm in arm for the Grand Salon. From
all accounts it was to be a great soiree.

They were not disappointed. Even without decoration,
the Grand Salon was a magnificent room. Its large windows, now covered with long red velvet drapes, faced onto
the gardens of the Louvre. The walls were filled with tapestries, and the remaining space was painted the color of
gold. The mosaic floor was considered one of the best in
Europe, and the gardeners of the palace had worked over-
time to fill the room with roses, the favorite flower of the

Princess Bonne. Even the floor had been scattered with rose petals.

Mary and Althea joined a group of young nobles, and even though their wit was often sharp, Althea was enjoying herself. The combined effects of the wine, the scent of roses, and the laughter of the guests were making her head reel with pleasure. The food, like the wine, was plentiful and delicious. There were oysters filled with small bits of cheese, snails sautéed in garlic and butter, the honey-glazed wings of chickens, little fish marinated in wine and honey, and many other treats to tempt the palate. Althea chose a small honey cake and ate it as she surveyed the growing crowd of revelers.

She was just finishing her cake when she felt her heart stop, and the food stuck in her throat as if she would choke. She could not believe her eyes. Not twenty feet away from her were her two old enemies, Claude and Mathilde! They were talking to Anne du Chelle, and all three were so deep in conversation that they had not seen her. Edging away, Althea tried to hide behind a large urn that had been filled with roses. Satisfied that she was not obvious, she stared at them in horror. She'd heard that they had come to court, but later she had learned that they had left and had supposedly returned to their estate. The court rumor was that the countess had become ill, and the count feared for her and the babe.

Now Althea could see that Mathilde was not pregnant. The purple that she wore clung to her body, revealing curves, not pregnancy. So, the whole thing had been a hoax, thought Althea. Somehow Mathilde had convinced Claude she was pregnant, and then had conveniently constructed a miscarriage. Althea thought for a moment, and then remembered that Magara had told her of certain herbs that would swell the belly, appearing as if the woman were pregnant. And the miscarriage? Again the action of certain herbs, if one were skilled enough to know what to take.

Althea almost felt faint as her memory rushed back to

the time when this woman conspired to take her life and
that of her child. The heavy scent of roses suddenly felt
overpowering, and she felt her head swim. The terror of
that night when she had struggled for her life came back to
her in detail. Hoping she would not faint, she walked toward the entrance to the salon, but she realized with growing terror that Mathilde and Claude had spotted her.
Althea had only one goal in mind, and that was to reach
the safety of her room. She was so lost in her own thoughts
that she did not notice that the laughter of the crowd had
died down, and that many people were whispering together in little groups. It was only when she felt a hand on
her shoulder, and she turned to see Mary's anxious face,
that she realized the mood of the revelers had changed.

"It's terrible, but don't be too upset," said Mary, her own
face white.

Althea looked at Mary in bewilderment. How could she
know that Claude and Mathilde were so dangerous to her?
"How did you know?"

"I heard it in the crowd. It's dreadful, but God will protect us."

Althea was totally confused. "Mary, what are you talking about?"

Mary stared at Althea, suddenly realizing that the news
that had ruined the soiree had not reached Althea. "It is
the Countess de la Lambe. She is close to death!"

"What!" whispered Althea, truly shocked. She had liked
the vivacious young countess and her playful monkey.

"Yes," said Mary quietly. "She has the plague!"

Those words were to be heard many times in the next
month. With the warmer weather of spring arousing the
disease from its winter dormancy, Paris was once again
caught in the macabre clutches of a monster that no one
understood. Outside the palace, in the poor districts of the
city, the death carts were out in force, wending their way
through the filthy streets, picking up the bodies of the
poor. The gongs that announced their arrival carried

through the night to the Louvre, heightening the fear. Hundreds were being thrown into mass graves, for too many people had died to be buried individually. Rumors went about that whole families had died in a night and no one was left to throw the bodies in the carts. The neighbors, who could smell the rot of death, hid in their own homes and left the bodies to decay.

The plague had no respect for class or position. With horror, the court of King Philip watched as one by one the privileged fell ill with the curse, dying in agony. The fact that no one understood it added to the rising hysteria. A victim could be healthy and sound in the morning, and covered with the dreadful black pustules by afternoon. Some would cough up black vomit, while others would bleed from the nose and mouth. Slowly, their faces and bodies would begin to swell and darken, and then death would quickly follow.

The Countess de la Lambe had been the first to die at court in this second outbreak. Her manservant died only an hour after his mistress. The Duke du Chatel, who had been having a liaison with the countess, was dead two days later. By the end of the week, three countesses, four counts, three knights, one duchess, and one prince were added to the grim list. No one was counting the number of deaths among the servants. If one rang for one's maid and she did not appear after several hours, one assumed that she had died in the night or had fled the palace.

Although most people stayed locked in their rooms in terror, some sought companionship. They gathered together in frightened little circles to discuss the pestilence. Gone were the pleasant chats about love affairs, clothes, and jewels. Now they discussed who had died, who was ill, who looked feverish and therefore was suspect. Invariably, the question always came back to *why*. Why were they falling ill? What caused the disease?

Today, two weeks after the death of the Countess de la Lambe, Althea sat with Mary in the east garden of the Louvre. They were joined by several other nobles who also sought the peace of the garden where the first flower buds were beginning to appear.

"It is truly a curse of some sort," said one young woman, whose sister had died during a stay in Italy. "It is afflicting all Christians. My sister's husband said that there is no Christian country that has been spared!"

Althea was silent. Her thoughts were in Wales. Had it reached her homeland? The only ones that she cared about there were Magara and Edwina. And what of Guerre? It had been a month since the king's troops had left, and they still had received no word. Was the siege continuing, or had all died, the ones who defended the castle along with their enemies who were attacking it?

"I think we must trust in God," said Mary softly. "He will spare those whom He chooses."

"Well, He did not choose to spare the life of the Duke du Marton. He died last night." This came from a white-faced young fop who had traveled with Norman and Philip's group.

Althea jerked up her head in shock. So, now Norman was the Duke du Marton. She felt as if she had been dealt a terrible blow. Now Norman would hold considerably more power. Although the old duke had been totally disinterested in her, and had never bothered to see her, Althea still saw in him some form of protection. Turning toward Mary, Althea saw that she was pale and upset.

The two women rose and began to walk together through the garden. When they were out of earshot of the others, Mary spoke. "Both Philip and Norman will be returning soon. The king has probably sent word. And there'll be no more talk of banishment. There are too many other problems. I heard earlier that the Princess Bonne felt feverish this morning. Perhaps the Death Angel has touched her, too."

Althea looked at Mary in despair. She was right. No one would worry about Philip and Norman now. In a court ravaged by true horror, the activities of two nobles would not raise any talk.

The next day the Princess Bonne died of the Black Death, and the court went into deep mourning. She was buried the day following, and it was right after the funeral that Norman and Philip returned. Althea and Mary, both gowned in black, were sitting in Mary's chamber when they arrived. Covered with grime from their travels, the two men nonetheless managed to swagger into the room.

"Your Highness," said Mary coldly as she bowed to her husband.

"My dear wife," said Philip, equally cold. He then turned toward Althea, and gave her a tight smile. "Lady Althea, you look well."

Althea just stared at him. She did not trust herself to say anything. Unlike Norman, who was fidgeting and looking around as if he expected the skeletal hand of the Black Death to touch his shoulder, Philip seemed as in control as ever.

"Aren't you going to greet the new duke, and now your overlord, my lady?" Philip asked Althea with obvious relish.

Althea bowed toward Norman. Although this was the correct gesture, she did it with such slowness that it was really an insult. Norman flushed with anger.

"Your behavior, Lady Althea, is almost as boorish as that of your husband," he said with irritation.

But Althea heard nothing but the present tense. Then Guerre was still alive! The deadly siege machine and the more deadly plague had not yet touched him. She felt a smile cross her face.

"Perhaps that is why he married me, Your Grace," said Althea tartly.

Norman glared at her. "They can't hold out much longer. My captain of arms has assured me that they will take the castle by the end of the week. I would keep the black dress that you now wear close at hand. It will serve you well as widow's weeds."

Althea stared back at him defiantly. "We will see if your

prediction comes true. My husband and his cousin are two
of the best knights in France."

Norman looked as if he would hit her. "If you weren't
under the protection of that lame bitch, I'd run a dagger
through your heart."

Althea and Mary looked at each other in surprise. Althea did not know that she was under the queen's protection. At least not now, with Norman the new duke. But
Philip and Norman must still think so, and that would
give her time. She rose to curtsy, and with a mocking
smile, bid them good-bye and left for her own chambers.
She felt Philip's eyes boring into her back as she walked
across the room. She remembered that Magara had once
told her about a wounded wolf that the hunters had let
escape. Having felt the pain, he became more wily, and
stalked his prey with an evil subtlety that made more victims fall into his snare. Althea closed the door behind her
and thought that Philip was now like that wounded wolf.
He had been hurt, and now he would stalk her with even
greater stealth.

The following days were very busy for Althea. She and
Mary had been given the honor of being ladies-in-waiting
to the queen. One of the queen's ladies had died of the
plague and two had succumbed to nerves, so the queen had
to add to her retinue. Ordinarily, Althea would have soon
grown bored with this type of life, for her duties consisted
mainly of doing needlework in the queen's chambers while
waiting for a summons to perform some type of task, like
dressing the queen or pouring wine. But Queen Jeanne
had a nimble mind and loved to talk, so the conversations
were usually interesting. And Althea felt safe in the
queen's chambers. Neither Philip and Norman nor Claude
and Mathilde would dare harm a lady-in-waiting to the
queen. Althea volunteered for extra duty, and the queen,
who despised stupidity and quickly realized that Althea
had both intelligence and wit, was glad to have the girl in
her entourage.

She also appreciated Althea's skill with drugs. The queen had been born with an affliction that had caused her to become lame in her right leg. The deformity had grown more painful as she grew older, and now she was in constant pain. Many close to her realized that her terrible temper and waspish comments to others were often rooted in her infirmity. Althea tried to recall what Magara had used for those with chronic pain, and after a while she had called in a local apothecary. Combining different spices and herbs, and a few seeds of the poppy, she mixed the ingredients with honey and heated it over a low fire until they all had blended together. Finally, she tasted the substance herself, and recognizing the distinctive taste of Magara's medicine for pain, she offered it to the queen.

At first skeptical, the queen finally took it after a particularly bad day, and was amazed to find that a great deal of her discomfort disappeared. Much more relaxed than usual, the queen had thanked Althea profusely, and had been much kinder to all of those around her. Althea was then told to prepare more of the mixture, and anything else that could be of help. A small closet was set aside for her work, and Althea enjoyed the hours that she spent there, remembering the things that Magara had painstakingly taught her. If only she had had word from Guerre, she could have been quite content for the time being. She had dared to ask the queen for news of him, but the queen only knew that no word had yet arrived.

"Communications have all but broken down from this curse," the queen had said, her pity for the girl showing in her eyes. The Black Death had been taking so many lives that the king could not possibly send more soldiers to investigate the situation. "The troops are needed here in Paris to keep order. The people have become so unhinged with fear that there is frequently trouble in the streets. They are constantly finding scapegoats for their fears. I heard yesterday that they stoned a poor old woman who they thought was a witch. Fools!"

Althea had returned to her little closet where she

worked on her medicines, but the feeling of peace that she usually experienced there was gone. She felt slightly sick at the thought of the crowds, maddened by fear, taking the life of an old woman. The thought of an innocent person being executed as a witch brought back terrible memories of her childhood. Once again she could imagine her mother and the witchcraft charges that had brought her to the flaming stake. Trying to keep her mind off the horrible thoughts that passed through her head, she went to work with a vengeance on a medicine for the old Countess of Neims, another lady-in-waiting, who suffered from the gout. This would be a tricky prescription, and Althea lost herself in experimentation.

So engrossed was she in her work that she did not hear the knock at the door. Finally, the maid who had been sent to summon her opened the door and looked rather fearfully into the dark chamber that was lit only by the fire in the corner. Althea had been slowly stirring a brew over the flames, concentrating on keeping the heat just right.

"My lady," the girl said timidly, "the queen has asked for you."

Althea looked up and nodded. "I will be right there," she said, carefully removing the small pot from the fire.

When Althea entered the royal chambers, she found the queen in bed, although it was only early evening. Althea approached the great canopied bed and curtsied. She quickly noticed that the queen was flushed and had a feverish look in her eyes. "Your Majesty," she said, as she rose from her curtsy.

"I think I have taken a chill," said the queen. "I have a slight fever, and my stomach is unsettled. Can you prepare a brew to help relieve the fever?"

"I will try, Your Majesty," said Althea, truly concerned. The queen's voice, usually so strong, was weak and hoarse. Althea quickly left the room, and as she walked out, she beckoned to Mary, who was in attendance that night.

"How long has she been ill?" Althea asked. "I left her at noon, and she was in the best of health."

"I came on duty in the middle of the afternoon, and we were embroidering a tapestry for the Cathedral of Notre Dame. She was fine at first, but suddenly she became quiet. After a while, she said that she felt ill and wanted to go to bed." Mary's face was pale with worry.

"It's too sudden to be an ordinary chill," said Althea. "I pray it is not the plague. Has anyone looked for the black pustule under the arm?"

Mary shook her head. "No one has dared suggest it. She has not even let us inform the king that she is unwell."

"The king must be told immediately in case it is the plague." Althea spoke emphatically. "Go tell him, and ask that the royal physicians be sent for the queen."

"She will be very angry if it is nothing," said Mary, unsure of what to do.

"I will take the blame for calling the king," said Althea. "But now I must go get something to relieve her fever. I will see you shortly."

Althea hurried into her chamber and found a drug that was used to ease the pain of fevers, and one to settle the stomach. She had already prepared a supply, so she was back in the queen's chamber within minutes. But even in the short time that she had been gone, the queen's condition had deteriorated considerably. Althea was shocked to see that she was moaning in pain, almost unconscious. Worried ladies-in-waiting gathered around the bed, their faces twisted with shock and fear.

Althea put down her medicines and quickly went to the queen's side. Just as she approached, the queen began to writhe in a spasm of agony, and as her body jerked back and forth uncontrollably, she began to vomit. All watched in horror as a black, vile-smelling substance was ejected from the queen's mouth. That was a sign! The queen was a victim of the dreaded plague. The Black Death had struck at the heart of France!

Althea held the queen's head as she vomited, and after the attack had passed, she carefully sponged the queen's face, then began to clean up the horrible mess on the bed.

The stench was almost unbearable. As she was working, the king and several other nobles entered the chamber, and they could see immediately what was wrong with the queen. White as a sheet, the king approached the bed. There had been little love between King Philip and his queen, but they had been married for many years, and he had grown to respect her intelligence and her strength. He had always leaned on her in times of crisis, and he could not believe that she was now dying. And there seemed to be little question of her impending death. When the skeletal hand of the plague reached out and claimed a victim, it was rarely denied. Almost all who caught the plague succumbed to the insidious disease.

The king said nothing as the royal physicians arrived and quickly began examining the queen. Althea could hear the indrawn gasps of horror as the doctors removed the queen's robe and the ugly black pustules on her body were revealed. Covering her again, they whispered to the king that the priests should be called, and Mary was sent to summon help to the royal chamber.

It was then a matter of waiting. The queen was now unconscious, though low moans escaped her parched lips. Occasionally she would vomit. Only Althea had the nerve to clean her off and sponge her burning body. The room was filled with candles, as if the people at the death watch could ward away the evil with the light. The priests began to chant the last rites, and the queen, rousing for a moment as if she knew the end was near, managed to confess to the one priest who moved close enough to hear her confession.

In fact, it was only that one priest and Althea who had the nerve to come close to the queen. Fear filled the room so strongly that Althea felt she could smell it. It was the odor of terrified animals who wished to flee danger. Ordinarily, if a queen of France lay dying, the room would be packed with courtiers, but now there were only the priests, the doctors, the king, the ladies-in-waiting, and two men who served the king. Even the king hung back from the bed, and though he forced himself to stay in the room, he had sent orders that the Dauphin, his heir, was not to enter the chamber.

The death watch lasted well into the night, and Althea felt herself becoming limp with fatigue. She said a silent prayer for the end to come soon, for the queen was suffering the pains of hell. Finally, about three in the morning, the queen jerked her body in one final spasm, and her face contorted in agony. She gave one last moan, and then fell back dead. The king began to sob, and was quickly hurried away by his gentlemen, who were only too eager to quit the chamber of death. The physicians left, too, as did the ladies-in-waiting who could slip away. Only the old Countess du Neims, who had been a friend of the queen's for years, and Mary stayed with Althea and the priest who had heard the queen's confession. Mary and the countess began to select clothes for the queen's burial, and Althea began to wash the body, which was still contorted in its death throes.

"You show much courage, my lady," said the young priest softly. "Not many would touch the body of one who has died of the plague. Not even the body of the queen."

"She was very good to me," Althea said simply.

"Do you not fear death?" he asked gently.

"I could ask you the same question, father," said Althea. "I saw that you were the only one who would come close enough to hear her confession."

The priest nodded. "I have faith in God," he said slowly. "If He chooses to take me, then I will go. It is His will, not mine, that will save me."

Althea nodded and continued her work. The prayers of the priest comforted her and began to soothe her troubled spirit. She was just finishing her task with a grateful sigh when the door burst open, and six of the king's guards rushed into the room. The captain looked quickly at the bed and stopped. It was apparent that he was frightened, but he forced himself to speak sternly.

"Is Althea, wife of Guerre du Reims, in this chamber?"

Althea stepped forward. His next words hit her with a
force that almost made her faint.

"We are here to seize you for the practice of sorcery, and
for the murder of the queen."

CHAPTER TWENTY-SIX

Althea had been sitting in the tiny cell for almost an hour, and she still did not entirely grasp why she had been imprisoned. Her eyes were starting to become accustomed to the darkness, and she could just make out the perimeters of the cell. It contained only a cot, and a tiny window with bars. It was a moonless night, and rain fell heavily. Water was coming into the cell from the window. Her feet were soaking wet, and her teeth were chattering, but she didn't know whether it was from fear or from the cold.

Witchcraft! Murder! How could they? It was insane! But with a sick feeling in her stomach, she knew that everyone was half-mad with terror. They would use any scapegoat that was provided. So she had been provided. And she knew by whom.

When the guards had led Althea down the long hall that led out of the queen's apartment, she had seen the looks of horror and curiosity that had passed across the nobles' faces as she walked by them. But then she had seen a small group that was laughing, and she had turned and looked right into the eyes of Philip. The smile of victory was on his face, and Althea had been horrified to realize that this was his revenge. Claude and Mathilde were in league with him, for they were standing close by. All her enemies had joined, at last, to destroy her.

The stake. The picture had been hovering like a monster in a dark corner of her mind, but she had been forcing it back with all the strength that she possessed. Somewhere in the far reaches of her memory she saw a woman weeping in a cell, a woman condemned to die. "Take care of my child," she heard. Another woman, another time, but they were both to share the same fate. And they were mother and daughter. Althea began to weep. There had been no escape for Rosemund, and there would be none for her. Philip would have his revenge, and no one would stop him, for he had harnessed the king's fear and would use it for his own advantage.

She huddled on the cot till dawn slowly lit up her cell. She saw how filthy it was, but she was grateful that it was on the ground floor. If she had been in the true dungeon, she would have no light at all. Daylight also revealed the mildew on the walls and the lice on the cot. She sprang up and began to pace the room. She stopped when she heard a sound at the door, and then a key scraped the lock. She couldn't believe it when Mary entered, her face swollen with tears and grief.

"Oh, Althea, how could they do such a thing?" sobbed the poor princess, throwing her arms around her friend.

"I don't know, Mary," cried Althea. "What is going to happen to me?"

Mary brought out a parcel from under her cloak. "Here is some food. I couldn't carry too much, and there is little time. I bribed the guard, but he would only give me a few moments with you, so listen well. This is all Philip's doing. He is in league with Claude du Vendome and his wife. Mathilde accused you of witchcraft, and Philip took the tale to the king, who is full of grief over the death of his wife."

"I thought it was them," said Althea bitterly. "I saw their faces when I was led out of the queen's chamber."

"Ordinarily, the king would have scoffed at such a story, for all knew how fond you were of the late queen. But he is maddened by fear and grief, and he took heed of Philip's tale. The queen is to be buried late today, and your trial is to be tomorrow."

"So soon!" said Althea, her heart sinking.

"Yes," said Mary grimly. "But I have bright news, too.

Norman is sick with the pestilence, and it looks like he will not live."

"I know it is unchristian of me to say such a thing, but I am glad," said Althea fiercely.

"But don't you see the other good thing about it?"

"What do you mean?"

"Guerre is next in line for the dukedom if Norman should die, and everyone thinks he will. The siege will have to be lifted immediately."

Althea stared at Mary speechlessly. The thought had not even entered her mind. Of course. Norman was now duke, but he had no children or younger brothers. So the dukedom of Marton would go to the next in line, Guerre. "My God," she whispered.

Mary gently shook Althea. "Listen, there is little time. I hear the guard approaching. I discovered all this during the night. At first light I sent my most trusted messenger to Stephen's castle with the news, though Philip has no idea that I did so. I sent the message with my own sealed crest, so it will have more weight with the captain in charge of the siege. I also sent word that Guerre is to come at once to Paris, for you are in great distress. Ordinarily, it takes two days to reach Stephen's lands, but I told my man to ride hard, and there would be a reward for him if he arrived early tomorrow. Of course, it may take days to get Guerre here, but who knows?"

"I will never be able to repay you, Mary," said Althea simply. She would have said more, but the door flew open and the guard beckoned to Mary, who quickly left.

Althea then gingerly sat down on the cot, and thought. At first she had been elated, but now she realized that Guerre would have little chance of helping her. Her trial was to be tomorrow, and she doubted if it would last more than one day. Even if the messenger arrived at Stephen's early tomorrow, it would take at least a day to get the siege affairs cleared up. Then at least a day and a half before Guerre reached Paris. By that time she would be tried, found guilty, and executed. She had little hope about the outcome of her trial.

Althea spent the rest of the day in a slight daze, sleeping on and off and thinking back on the past. When night came she could hear the scurrying rats, so she paced the floor, too afraid to sleep on the cot. It was only when exhaustion overcame her that she rested. The next day dawned wet and rainy, and she tried to clean herself up for the trial. She used the small bowl of drinking water to wash her face and hands, and she ran her fingers through her hair in a vain attempt to neaten it. With a rueful sigh, she looked down at her crumpled, soiled black silk mourning gown. It was beyond repair. She knew that she would look terribly disheveled, and that would add credulity to the charges against her.

At midmorning her guard brought her a hunk of bread and some more water, and told her she would not be summoned until after the noon hour. Althea forced herself to eat the stale, moldy bread, knowing that she had to keep up her strength. The food Mary had brought was long gone. Trying to keep her mind blank, she waited out the long hours until they came for her. Soon enough, she heard the footsteps of marching men. They were her guards sent to bring her to trial.

Althea felt panic rising in her as she was led to the salon in the west wing where the trial was to take place. Knowing that panic would be her deadliest enemy, she tried to destroy it by concentrating on little details so her mind would remain clear. There were ten guards, a huge number, sent to escort her. They walked out of the dungeon of the palace and into the fresh air. The quickest way to the west wing was through the gardens, and Althea saw that the day was overcast and a light rain fell. A few spring flowers were out, and she looked at them with longing. She would never be free to pick flowers again.

They entered a small corridor that led to the grand salon. The doors were open, and Althea shuddered at the huge crowd that had gathered to watch her ordeal. She could see all the courtiers, dressed in their finest, eager to observe the spectacle that would make them forget the plague for a short while. Then the sentry motioned for them to enter, and as they entered, a hush overcame the spectators. She was led to stand in front of a table where three cardinals of the Church sat in full clerical garb. The one to the right was very fat, and the one in the middle had a mole on his chin. The one on the left, younger than the others, smiled at Althea reassuringly. He was the only one who did.

The cardinal with the mole on his chin cleared his throat to speak, and the large room became even more quiet as everyone strained to hear. "Althea du Reims," he said solemnly, "you have been accused of the heinous crime of sorcery, and of endangering the life of our beloved late queen, Jeanne de Bourgogne, by practicing said sorcery. You have been charged with hastening her death by giving her poisonous liquids that weakened and sickened the queen, so that she could not fight off the malignancy of the plague, and thus succumbed to its grievous attack. Do you plead guilty, or not?"

"Not guilty, Your Grace," said Althea, her voice clear and steady. "I am innocent."

"Then be seated in that chair, and bear witness to those who would accuse and defend you." The cardinal pointed to a high-backed wooden chair that faced the crowd of spectators, and Althea gratefully sat down. Her knees felt like jelly.

The cardinal who had read the charges now briefly explained the process of the trial, and Althea listened closely. He and his two colleagues would be the judges of the case, since sorcery was a crime against the Church. They had called for witnesses to testify for and against the charge. After all were done with their testimonies, Althea would be given a chance to defend herself, and then the cardinals would reach a verdict.

The priest who was acting as clerk for the trial called for

the first witness—the queen's personal maid, Katherine. Althea glanced at the crowd and was surprised to see that neither the king nor the dauphin was attending the trial. She could see Mary, who gave her a brave smile, and one or two others who wished her well, but the rest were just there for the excitement. She felt her heart beat faster when she caught sight of a group by the windows. Sitting close together were Mathilde, Claude, Philip, and Anne du Chelle.

Katherine's testimony was brief. Asked if she had ever seen Althea perform an act of sorcery, the woman almost cried from nerves. "I don't know if it was sorcery, Your Grace, but she spent many hours in her small closet preparing brews for the queen. No one was allowed to enter, or to taste any of the things she prepared."

"Did these brews affect Her Majesty?" asked one of the cardinals.

"Oh, yes. They would make her drowsy, and relieve the pain she suffered from her bad leg. The queen wanted the potions."

The crowd murmured at this statement, and the fat cardinal with the double chin pounded his gavel. He dismissed Katherine and called two more maids, who gave identical testimonies. Althea felt a little hope, for the maids had not said anything that actually confirmed her guilt. She could sense some doubt building in the eyes of her judges, and this doubt seemed to grow as the crowd heard the testimony of the respected Countess du Neims, the queen's old friend and lady-in-waiting.

"This girl practiced no sorcery," said the countess. "She was skilled in the mixing of herbs and spices to relieve the suffering of others. That is all. She practiced no witchcraft on the queen. If she had, wouldn't I, the beloved friend of my late mistress, have sounded the alarm?" The crowd roared at her words, and Althea smiled at the good woman.

But her heart sank with the next witness: Claude du Vendome. He walked slowly to the witness chair, and she was frightened when she saw the smile on his face. He was going to get his revenge on her.

"Claude du Vendome, this court of Holy Mother Church seeks to find cause for the charge of sorcery leveled against the accused. Have you known this woman long?"

The crowd tittered at the question, remembering Claude's unfortunate dealings with Althea. He flushed at their laughter, and Althea knew that he would be even more determined to seek vengeance on her. "I have known her for several years, Honorable Cardinals," he said slowly. "I traveled to Wales to wed with her." Again the crowd burst into laughter.

"Enough," shouted the fat cardinal, but it took several moments for the crowd to obey. "Continue. Why did you level the charge of witchcraft?"

"It is an evil that runs in her family. It afflicts the women of her blood. I discovered this terrible curse after I went to Wales, or I would never have agreed to the match. Her aunt still lives in the woods of that country, practicing the black arts."

"And her mother, what of her?" asked the young cardinal.

"Her mother," said Claude slowly, watching Althea's stricken face, "was executed for witchcraft when this sorceress was but three years old."

At his words the silence of the spectators broke into a roar for blood, and Althea knew that the mood of the crowd had changed against her. Once again Rosemund's curse had come down to harm her.

Claude stepped down from the witness chair while the judges tried to quiet the crowd, and Althea watched in dismay as her old enemy, Mathilde, was called to the front. She knew that nothing would stop Mathilde now. Here is the real witch, she wanted to scream. Mathilde was wearing a gown of black silk and a long black veil that covered her head and reached down to her knees. This modest attire was so unlike her usual taste in clothes that Althea knew instinctively that someone had coached her in her dress.

"Mathilde, wife and countess of Claude du Vendome, do you charge this woman, Althea du Reims, with sorcery?"

"Yes, Lord Cardinal." Mathilde's voice was subdued. She had also been coached in her way of speech, Althea realized. "When my poor husband took her into his castle to shelter her, she practiced sorcery, plotting the deaths of ourselves and our loved ones."

"Explain yourself," commanded the cardinal with the mole on his chin. "You must be specific."

"Yes, I will be. She practiced awful rites in her room on the nights of the full moon, and conspired with the devil to rid herself of the child she carried. She did this on the night of All Saints' Day, which falls on a sacred day for witches. My poor mother tried to stop her, and this sorceress and her demons killed her."

Something flashed across Althea's memory, and it was Rachel's voice. She had been telling Althea about Mathilde's childhood, about her mother. She was supposed to have died, but when Rachel and Claude's first wife had gone to the funeral, the body had already been buried. Oh, but it hadn't! Haggar was Mathilde's mother! And Guerre had killed her with his blow to her head on the night of All Saints' Day. Althea could no longer contain herself.

"My lords, please listen to me," she cried out. "The charges this woman levels at me are the crimes she herself has committed. Her mother was the infamous witch, Haggar, who lived in the woods near the Castle du Vendome. All there know of her. She assisted this woman in the killing of her first husband!"

"That's a lie!" Mathilde screamed, jumping to her feet, all instructions to be decorous completely forgotten in her rage.

"No, 'tis true! This woman rid herself of her first husband's child, and practiced the black arts at the Castle du Vendome. She conspired with her mother, the true witch, to murder me and my unborn babe on the night of All

Saints' Day. Guerre du Reims rescued me, and killed the witch, Haggar!"

With a deep cry of animal fury, Mathilde leaped for Althea's throat, her hands outstretched like the talons of a bird. But as she lunged for her prey, the long black veil waved across the candle resting by the witness chair. It took only a second for the gossamer to burst into flames. With a scream of terror, Mathilde became a human torch in less than a minute. Cries of agony almost inhuman in their sound came from her as she ran frantically around the room, but her movements only fanned the fire. Althea watched in horror as several guards tried to catch her, but she ran from the room and out into the garden. Her clothes were totally consumed in flames, and she finally fell dead on the ground, the fire still leaping from her body. So quickly had this all happened that the crowd stood in silent horror, unable to grasp what they had seen. It took several minutes before they came out of their shock and began to talk in excited voices. Claude du Vendome collapsed in shock, his face pale; others were already commenting, however, that he had not tried to save his wife, but had shied away from her like the rest.

The cardinals called for a day's recess. Althea had been granted a respite from her ordeal, but as she left the salon under guard, all she was aware of was the smell of burnt flesh.

Althea thought that it was still early evening, although she really couldn't compute time in her tiny cell after the sun went down. She guessed that had been about three hours ago. She tried to force herself to eat the cold chicken that Mary had brought her. The princess had been allowed to stay for only a few minutes, but she had used that time to tell Althea that feeling was running high in her favor. Mathilde's ghastly death had been seen by many as a sign from God of her guilt. Mary told her that an acquittal of the charges against her would probably be granted tomorrow.

Althea set aside the food, far too nervous to eat. She paced the floor, hoping desperately that Mary was right. She didn't want to die in the flames like Mathilde. That had been a horrible sight to see, and one that she would never forget. She turned slightly, her body alert to any sense of danger. She thought that she had heard something. Yes, there it was again. It was footsteps, and now the sound of the key in the lock. She gasped as she saw who entered.

"Well, my little sorceress, it looks like you may yet try to escape the trap." Philip du Bois filled the doorway of her cell.

"What do you want?" Althea asked, her throat suddenly gone dry.

"I just want to make sure that you are properly punished for your crimes."

"What crimes? You know that I'm innocent of any wrongdoing."

"You humiliated me. You made me the laughingstock of this court." Philip's eyes were glistening dangerously. "That is a crime that you will pay for dearly."

"You're mad!" whispered Althea.

"Not mad, my dear, just seeking vengeance for a wrong. No one ridicules me!" Philip edged closer to her. "We thought we had you. I was sure that I was going to have the delight of seeing you executed for your crimes. Then that whore of Vendome's had to forget everything I told her and attack you. She deserved to go up in flames, the miserable bitch. They say that you will be pardoned tomorrow, and that your husband, the duke, will soon claim you."

Althea gasped. "So Norman is dead? And Guerre is coming here?"

"Yes, Norman is dead," snarled Philip, "and Guerre is already here. He's with the king right now, pleading your cause. Evidently so many of Norman's soldiers died of the plague that the siege was abandoned a week ago. And my dear wife's messenger intercepted Guerre about twenty miles from Paris, telling him to rush to your aid." Philip's grin held only evil. "But that bastard won't have you. If I can't have you, no one else shall. And you *must* pay for your crimes!"

"I don't understand you," said Althea, trying to take a step away from him but stopped by the wall.

Philip began to walk toward her slowly, his lips drawn back in a snarl that revealed his teeth. Althea knew that she had lost the battle. He was going to kill her. She opened her mouth to scream, but he sprang in attack, his hands gripping her throat, cutting off all sound, all air. She clawed frantically at his hands, but he was too strong. She began to grow faint as her lungs felt like bursting. She was dying. She knew it. And he was smiling at her as he killed her. Then darkness descended, smothering her. . . .

They held the funeral the next day. Almost the entire court attended. Even the king came, dressed in deep mourning. Mary, Princess of Flanders, was the chief mourner, and was dressed in black from head to toe. No one could see her face, which was a good thing. Mary's smile could not have been considered appropriate. As she followed her husband's casket to the family crypt outside of Paris, the young princess felt free at last.

When the mourners reached the site of the burial, they knelt to pray, but Mary gave prayers of thanksgiving that Althea had been saved, rather than prayers for her dead husband's soul. She would leave him to God. She smiled again under the heavy veil, thinking of the intervention of the saints in saving Althea. It had to be their intervention that had helped her friend, for if she and Guerre had reached the tiny cell a minute later, they would never have been able to revive her. Philip had been so intent on the kill that he hadn't heard them until it was too late. He uttered only a guttural moan of fury before Guerre's sword pierced him through the heart.

They had carried Althea back to Mary's apartment, and for an hour they gave her sweet wine to help her throat, and applied cold compresses to her bruised skin. Guerre had held her close the whole time, whispering words of love. Althea's eyes, unbelieving at first, had never left his face.

The king's pardon came with first light. And soon after. Althea and Guerre left, finally, for home.

CHAPTER TWENTY-SEVEN

CHÂTEAU MARTON, DECEMBER, 1351

Althea looked up from the letter and frowned. The courier had brought it from Wales an hour ago and she had retired to her chamber to read it. Absently, she now set it down, lost in thought. She put one hand to her stomach, now heavy with child. Perhaps, when her reply reached Wales, this little one she carried would already be born.

The door opened, and a servant entered. "My lady, do you want me to light the tapers?"

"Yes, Lucille, and please bring one close to me so that I can read this letter again." She settled back against the pillows on the chaise and picked up the parchment.

12 November 1351

Dearest Althea,

I hope this letter finds you and Guerre well and in good spirits. And I hope that your little son, Guibert, is also in the best of health. I am afraid that I have sad tidings for you, though I do not expect your grief to be great. Your father, Sir Richard, died from a fall last week. As you know, he had been confined to the tower room at Grydwyn for several years, but he finally escaped his keepers, and leaped from the tower to his death. He was totally mad, and had twice before tried to kill himself. This time he succeeded. We buried him next to Lady Maura. I will oversee the castle until you

appoint a caretaker. I don't want the position. I long
for my cottage in the woods.

The messenger waits, so I must end here. May you
be delivered of a healthy child in your next childbed.

Love,
Magara

Althea gazed at the fire crackling in the hearth. She had
not loved her father, but it was a terrible way for him to
die. And there had been so many deaths in the last three
years. The plague had finally abated, but it had taken a
horrible toll. Her stepmother had died of the curse when it
swept through Wales in 1349, but it was here in France
that it had touched Althea and Guerre most deeply.
Claude du Vendome had died of it at his own banquet
table. Pierre, their old steward, had succumbed to it, and
Veronique, Stephen's betrothed, had been only fourteen
when the plague claimed her. Stephen had grown less gay,
and now ran his estates and lost himself in work.

Althea sighed as she thought over the last three years,
but then she chided herself. There had been much good,
also. Clarissa had married Sir Guy, and they now lived
near Paris. His mother's family had been so devastated by
the plague that the head of the family begged him to take
over one of the estates left vacant by death. Theresa had
been given Guerre's old estate, for now they had to live at
the seat of his duchy, the Château du Marton. The gift of
the estate had transformed Theresa, bringing to the surface her intelligence and organizational abilities. It had
also made her an eligible heiress, but she still had not wed,
and Guerre had not forced her. Mary of Flanders had returned to her homeland, and once again had married one
of her father's choices. But she had demanded a say in this
marriage, and it was very successful. She was the mother
of twin boys, and she wrote to Althea frequently.

But best of all was *her* life, she thought with a smile on
her lips. She had at last found peace and happiness. Well,
perhaps not peace. Not with a husband like Guerre and a

little boy like Guibert. And another one soon to join them. She smiled to herself.

"You look lovely when you smile," said a voice from the shadows.

"Guerre. I didn't hear you come in," said Althea, reaching out for him.

"I didn't want to disturb you. I like to look at you when you're thinking of something pleasant. What was it?" He put his arms around her, and she could feel the strength of him through his velvet tunic.

"I was thinking of how happy I am, and how much I love you."

He smiled at her, and his lips gently caressed her hair.

"As I love you, Althea. As I love you."

Dear Reader:

If you enjoyed this book, and would like information about future books by this author and other Avon authors, we would be delighted to put you on the mailing list for our ROMANCE NEWSLETTER.

Simply *print* your name and address and send to Avon Books, Room 1210, 1790 Broadway, N.Y., N.Y. 10019.

We hope to bring you many hours of pleasurable reading!

Sara Reynolds, Editor
Romance Newsletter

Book orders and checks should *only* be sent to Avon Books, Dept. BP Box 767, Rte 2, Dresden, TN 38225. Include 50¢ per copy for postage and handling; allow 6-8 weeks for delivery.